It begins cynically enough. A bored writer, churning out frivolous books for a quick buck, pays for a beautiful girl to be his companion for a week in Ibiza. And at first, she appalls him. Like other girls of her sort, she doesn't know how to behave, and while he is proud to be seen with her for her beauty, he despises her for her intellect. She's there to be used. And she, he has been warned, will use him mercilessly.

But that isn't quite how things turn out. For when he's with her in the nightclubs and bars of Ibiza, when she's high and outrageous, she acts on him like the most powerful drug. And as the game-playing, the ritual jealousies, the dishonesties, continue, an addiction begins to take hold of him. Only with Melissa, his Princess, can he be truly alive. What began as a seven night stand, becomes an obsessive, painful affair, recalled by him as he writes the account of events that would destroy her. Like any addict, there are no lengths he will not go to to satisfy his craving: the betrayal of a fifteen-year-old relationship; the squandering of his savings; the buying of cocaine to keep her in the happy state that is so necessary to him. But what was a beautiful dream in Ibiza, turns into ugly reality in London, as Melissa is drawn into a squalid society scandal, and as her addiction takes a vicious and disastrous turn.

In his bestselling *The English Way of Doing Things* William Donaldson hilariously chronicles the manners and mores of a seamy world of pimps, prostitutes and drug-pushers. *Is This Allowed?* is a powerful vision of the dark side of that world, where the rich and privileged rub shoulders with the demi-monde, where the search for kicks is a full-time occupation. It is a novel of addiction and obsession, and of manipulation and betrayal. It is both satire and tragedy, told with brutal honesty and sharp wit.

IS THIS ALLOWED?

William Donaldson

Macdonald

A *Macdonald* Book

Copyright © William Donaldson 1987

First published in Great Britain in 1987
by Macdonald & Co (Publishers) Ltd
London & Sydney

British Library Cataloguing in Publication Data

Donaldson, William
  Is this allowed?
  I. Title
  823'.914[F]   PR6054.04/

ISBN 0-356-12293-X

Photoset in North Wales by
Derek Doyle & Associates, Mold Clwyd.
Printed in Great Britain by
Redwood Burn Ltd, Trowbridge.
Bound at the Dorstel Press

Macdonald & Co (Publishers) Ltd
Greater London House
Hampstead Road
London NW1 7QX

A BPCC plc Company

*

I remember summer holidays in Broadstairs, the Grand Hotel and little pier, and fishing with my father. And I remember Canterbury Week and the old oak inside the field of play, and Todd and Fagg and Leslie Ames, and somewhere or other the Cathedral, I wouldn't be surprised. And I remember the visiting Australians of '48, tanned and muscled (but gentlemen in those days) and the men of Kent, arthritic, rationed, knobbly-kneed – except the amateurs who'd been to Charterhouse, not least the captain B.H. 'Bunny' Valentine, whom my mother admired for his well-cut flannels (later she preferred Budge Patty and his tailored shorts). And I remember Lindwall coming on to bowl and old Todd wisely taking guard beside the square-leg umpire. With his first delivery Lindwall hit him on the toe. 'Out!' cried Todd, and off he limped to safety, even though a no-ball had been called. That's good, I thought, that makes sense – giving yourself out off a no-ball – but my mother, who unaccountably liked David Niven and who, at the outbreak of war in '39, had driven south from Scotland to be bombed, looked personally betrayed.

And we had been bombed. The Luftwaffe, aiming at London, I suppose, dropped the lot on Sunningdale, missing our house by fifty yards. Assuming the invasion had come at last, Saunders, our chauffeur for twenty years, seized one of my father's shotguns and, placing himself four-square outside the dug-out door, said: 'The Germans will get at you and the children over my dead body, ma'am.' After the war Saunders voted socialist, whereupon my mother sacked him on the spot for ingratitude to Churchill, David Niven, B.H. 'Bunny' Valentine and so forth. Then it was Winchester and 'Manners Makyth Man', which is such a silly slogan, after all, I think. You start by being polite, which is pretending to be kind. It pays so well that it becomes second nature and the artificiality no longer matters. My mother hadn't been very polite to

Saunders, but my manners have always been impeccable.

'Hullo. God what a flight! I'm whacked actually.'

Go off and come on again. You're not being funny enough. You're not being pretty enough. No one will think I'm lucky to be fucking you.

'Sorry.'

That wasn't very polite, perhaps, but she could try harder to be pleasing, to be a credit to me. While she's back in the wings, I pace Ibiza Airport's glossy new arrival hall, reflecting. They're so graceless these girls you can book by the week, who are women for a living – they take it all for granted. You offer them seven days in the sun, cock a sympathetic ear, teach, explain, crank down the vocabulary a gear or two, give them a chance to meet a gent, and yet they behave as if they're doing *you* a favour. Who do they normally meet, these silly girls who've been to Bogota and back? Men in hotel suites. Money men with soft white hands and hairy backs. I've few illusions, but I am a little different. For one thing I have a saving sense of humour. It's not every day that one of these performing girls steps off an aeroplane with her Louis Vuitton douche-gel holder to meet a man who, because of his saving sense of humour, has been invited by a respected house to write his memoirs.

I continue to pace, from time to time entering enlarged thoughts in my writer's notebook. I become indignant – justifiably, in my opinion – turn over past ingratitudes. Silly Serena, who was playing this part last year, sat on the beach and talked about her husband, a quantity surveyor with unnaturally large feet, I've always thought, who, wishing he'd been a pop musician, once sang 'Tie A Yellow Ribbon' in the Lone Star hamburger restaurant to a roomful of startled tourists. And yet I treated her with respect, read a poem – obviously copied from an anthology – which she said she'd written. Many would have sneered. I didn't. Politely aware of her need to be taken seriously, I read it with care, nodded, offered constructive criticism. You show real ability, I said. I'm impressed. Well done. Keep it up. Take your clothes off and stand over there by the sink.

That wasn't very polite either, I suppose, but for the most

part that's how Wykehamists speak to women. When I was thirteen I persuaded my parents to take me to see the *Folies Bergère*, then visiting London. I was enthralled. I understood at once that these tall silent women pacing the stage with fruit on their heads — so different to anything one saw in Sunningdale — were the obviously desirable representatives of their sex since men would pay to see them without their clothes. There was no one in Sunningdale you'd pay to see without their clothes. I smuggled the souvenir programme back to Winchester and gazed at it in private, from then on confusing sex with vaguely illicit displays of nudity for cash down — a confusion very much reinforced when the souvenir programme was confiscated by my housemaster and I was thrashed for immorality. And yet I used to kick a QC up the arse until he blubbed, without so much as a 'Hold hard there! You can't do that!' He wasn't a QC then, of course, he's a QC now, and since he mainly prosecutes it serves him right that I should be candid enough to say that his name is Hislop and that I used to kick him up the arse until he blubbed — without a reprimand. I blame my parents, and then Winchester. That's by the way, however.

I stroll disdainfully among the packaged holiday wallies — the polite, good-looking Germans, and the disgusting British, dressed for Southend, comically misshapen, false teeth clacking like castanets, scared and aggressive, the young already looking around for someone to hit, and the old fools who've brought their own breakfast products and will overdo it on the first day, sunbathing in their satin corsets and getting scorched behind the knees. (I have with my own eyes seen on a beach reserved for Germans a sordid British granny waddle into the sea with her dress tucked into her pink ballooning knickers.) At least we won't see them again. The British are no longer allowed in Ibiza Town, but are kept in San Antonio behind barbed wire. I get by in Ibiza Town by pretending to be German. It's an odd language, German. You don't have to be Peter Ustinov to talk gibberish which sounds like German — even to Germans. I have before now dined with Germans without their tumbling me. *Flöken schlick fahrten flurtz*, I say, and they nod earnestly and answer.

7

Is it worth it, this annual airlift, this ferrying in of a performer with a screw loose? For one week I want not to be out of it and envious, to have at my side an admirable girl with courage enough for us both. No harm in that, surely? No one can get hurt, least of all me. Just a small act of defiance against not being welcome where the music is, against fifty-one weeks of bitter continuous dreaming and a nasty future. And yet I feel a shaft of guilt. I was here in Departures only yesterday with Alison, packing her off after the ten days I'd allowed her over Easter. All day she'd behaved quite badly, becoming silent on the beach, glancing at her watch from time to time, like someone going back to school. She'd grown smaller before my eyes. This is the worst bit, she'd said, I hate this bit, how much longer have we got? That was very thoughtless of her. She knows I can't work with her around, that I have to come out here to work, that I can't concentrate in London. Apart from my memoirs, I'm behind with the Christmas toilet books (books in which one makes jokes about imaginary social groups, books with inferior cartoons). I have to write six toilet books for Christmas.

'Hi!'

Not yet, I'm reflecting here.

'Oh bollocks!'

You have to know when to pack it in, of course. I don't want to get like the old fool who buckets around Ibiza Town with his personal drum-sticks. He takes his drum-sticks everywhere and beats abstractedly on table-tops, accompanying the music in his head. He's black, so nobody minds too much. It helps to be black. If you're black you can wear a hat, relax and turn the wrist, stay alive longer without embarrassing yourself and others. Otherwise you've got to pack it in before even the kindest girl will tell you that you've had it. In wars, they say, soldiers fight on with the backs of their heads blown off. They're perfectly all right until someone says: 'Hey, you haven't got a back to your head.' Then they keel over. I don't want that to happen to me. I don't want some bought girl to look at me and say: 'Hey, the back of your head's come off. You've had it, believe me.'

Perhaps the girl now waiting in the wings will be the one to

8

tell me that I've had it. She's ruthless enough from all accounts. She has no idea, for instance, how much her presence here would hurt Alison, and if she did, she wouldn't give a stuff. I feel quite sad. I hum a tune – 'Can I Forget You?' – a Thirties tune, usually crooned. I've been humming this tune in luxuriously sad moments since 1953. During National Service in the Navy I wore a sailor suit and stood on guard duty outside Victoria Barracks, Portsmouth, in the middle of the night holding a rifle with no bullets in it, humming 'Can I Forget You?' I wonder why? A received sadness, perhaps, inherited from my father, a disappointed man who sat at the piano in Sunningdale on thin summer evenings singing Scottish songs. 'Tonight there are four Marys, tomorrow there'll be but three. There's Mary Beaton and Mary Seaton and Mary Carmichael and me.' A strange song to sing in Sunningdale while my mother played tennis in the softening light with her friends the Pinkneys – Daph and Gee. My father worked in Glasgow, so he didn't really want to live in Sunningdale. My mother had ruled that he should live in Sunningdale, which she judged, mysteriously, to be less common than Glasgow. It killed him in no time, of course, commuting between Sunningdale and Glasgow. Is this one for the memoirs? Should I tell everyone that my mother made my father live in Sunningdale? It might be significant, or seem so. My mother was an exceptionally strong-willed woman. When I was called up for National Service by the Navy I didn't want to go at once because I had just begun to do the season. My mother rang up the Lords of the Admiralty and told them they couldn't have me yet. Their Lordships knew they'd met their match and said I could pitch up when it suited. (Alison, quite the opposite of pushy in the normal run of things, is equally formidable on my behalf. She'd ring up their Lordships to tell them that they couldn't have me yet.)

My father was a most unhappy man. All his life he wanted a boat. It was quite possibly the only thing he did want. On summer holidays in Broadstairs he'd go into Ramsgate every day to gaze at the boats for sale. There was one which he particularly wanted. Every day he used to go and look at it. I asked him why he didn't buy it. It seemed simple enough to me.

9

If you want something, you buy it – no problem. He smiled sadly. It was too expensive, he said. It cost £9,500. He shook his head and walked away. Later, when I was at Cambridge, he bought me a green sports car and threw money at me so that I could start literary magazines and be sponged off by Indian poets. We used to drink his gin, the poets and I, and laugh at him because he didn't understand. He's dead as mutton now and he could have bought anything he wanted. He could have bought a hundred boats. When he died (burst liver) he left a million, enabling me to put on musicals, meet satirists and wear a silly overcoat.

I begin to wish I hadn't hired the girl still waiting in the wings. It will be a week of talking about astrology and reincarnation, of 'beam me up Scotty!' and 'pardon my French', of ordering in English and sending things back and dour, resentful sex. That's the silliest thing about booking these girls who'll fly anywhere at a moment's notice: they don't like sex, or, to be more precise, they don't like sex with the old optimist at the business end of the flight. I blame Tiffs the Tizer girl, ex-*Sun* Page 3 etc, when Page 3 girls weren't by necessity freaks. You probably know her, still as pretty as a picture, still doing bits and pieces here and there, still wheeled on in gossip columns for old time's sake – bitten by a camel on location, taken up photography, embraced celibacy, gone mad, that sort of thing. Awash with indignant, undirected lust, I'd rung her one meaningless afternoon in London, just in case. She was writing her memoirs for the *News Of The World*, she said, and she read me an excerpt involving Anthea Redfern, if I heard her right. My brain boiled in my head, melted down, came out of my ears. I said something distasteful, to be regretted. She laughed, not unkindly. 'You're obviously in a bad way,' she said. 'You'd better see Melissa.' She sounded like a doctor filling a prescription. 'If you think I'm good,' she said, 'wait till you see Melissa, she's beautiful. She looks like Catherine Deneuve.' Then she warned me. 'For God's sake be careful. She's as hard as nails and drives a Porsche. She's got it made. She's quite unscrupulous. She'll use you if she can.' (She's sweet, Tiffs, but not very perceptive. I'm not a turkey in town for the day, to be skinned by a tart in a Porsche. If anyone's got it made it's me.) That had been six months ago and now Melissa's waiting in the wings.

I continue to pace, trying to remember what she's like. I met her twice, I think, after Tiffs introduced us. I know she wasn't beautiful, and she no more looked like Catherine Deneuve than I do. She must have been all right, though. If she hadn't been more or less all right I wouldn't have asked her to Ibiza. She'd been quite classy, I think, but whether going up or coming down I couldn't tell. It *is* hard to tell with these performing girls, they hide their origins quite expertly. On the one hand she could have been someone's daughter off the rails, on the other a resourceful girl from Stratford-atte-Bow. She hadn't been trying very hard, I do remember that – a minimum of make-up, hair not recently attended to, scuffed boots and jeans – all of which suggested confidence, or apathy. I think she quite amused me, though, and she had a quality – a kind of relaxed assurance in the way she came on stage – which seemed to be a guarantee that she was expert where it mattered, that in spite of the scuffed and casual clothes everything was lovely underneath. Her body was a delight, in fact, satiny, unflagging, softly inflated everywhere – the sort of body which looks at its best on a beach, which should be sold in beach shops with other inflatable things. Tiffs had said she'd got it made, but I didn't think she'd got it made at all. She was rather pale and easily startled, running around to not much purpose, eager and regretful, with huge hurt eyes. I thought she was adrift and a little bit afraid, but I'd been pleased about the eyes. There's nothing less boring than a woman with hurt eyes, she'll do anything just in case, she'll believe what you tell her just in case it might be true. It was probably the hurt eyes that had made me ask her to Ibiza. Ibiza's just the place for women with hurt eyes, who want to think there's still a chance. After a month in Ibiza everyone's got hurt eyes, of course. Visitors, who don't get off in time, acquire the blank look of people who imagine you can do what you like and get away with it. That's not on. You have to have the will of a criminal to get away with that. These bozoes aren't criminals, merely fantasists, sitting on bar-stools silly with drugs or wandering round in exclusive, self-regarding groups with the bewildered look of out-patients on the

11

Minnesota method, afraid to go home and put the light out. With Melissa I can join them, with her they'll let me in. That's why she's here.

'Hi! It's your baby! Am I tanned? How tanned? What's not tanned about me?'

That's better – she's regressed, she's building up the part from the right direction. The suggestion of emotional immaturity is very clever. Childish women are much the most fun – not that children are any fun, of course.

'Hey, this is Jack the Actor, by the way. He knows thingummy and so forth naturally enough. Darling, he tried to eat me in the toilet! Is that gross or what? Why shouldn't I say toilet? Are you a Sloane or something? I'll do my seagull impression. Does that sound like a Sloane? Is that good or what?'

It's not bad, actually, but she hasn't got her wardrobe right. She's not wearing her legs. She should know that with girls like her half of it's in the legs. The key to the character's in the legs. The legs should be all over the place – long and brown and irresponsible. Shall I send her off again to change? No, she's trying hard, she's doing better, and what was that about Jack the Actor? That was promising. A foxy-looking forty-year-old in jeans, he now pats his carefully tousled hair, crinkles his eyes menacingly behind unnecessary shades and bids her a supporting actor's *au revoir*, exiting backwards. I hope he exits on his arse. He doesn't. He reverses suavely between the other passengers and their piles of luggage.

'Bye Jack!'

Now she'll say: 'If you can't be good be careful!' She doesn't. That's unusual. Jack the Actor clearly found her attractive, which is most encouraging. She's no use to me unless she's attractive to other members of the cast. The character I'm playing needs an accessory who obviously earns a living from her looks. She has to impress for both of us. 'We all started modelling on the same day,' Tiffs had said, 'me and Melissa and Lindy Benson. I thought Melissa was the best.' She's very generous, Tiffs. I look at Melissa, assess her. Yes, she could have been a model – just – she could have been a Tiffs or Lindy, but had probably found that she could get what she wanted anyway

12

by reassuring silly men – and now regrets it. She probably keeps an old portfolio of dated model shots, consulting it from time to time, wondering what went wrong. I could tell her, and no doubt will. She's looking very pretty actually and fairly mad. I don't remember her like this at all. She's flushed and excited, bouncing up and down like a pink squash ball. She isn't beautiful, but she is pretty, with shining, excited eyes – not hurt at all – and she seems to be on the edge of some enormous joke. She keeps laughing – not nervous laughter, but deep, serious laughter, like someone who's seen a fat woman sit on a chair which isn't there. I hope she doesn't see her role as comic. Wasn't it Scott Fitzgerald who said: 'There's undoubtedly something funny about not being a lady, or rather about being a gold-digger. A gold-digger should laugh a lot.' I don't agree at all. There could only be one thing worse than a tart with a heart and that would be a tart who laughed a lot. She's as high as a kite, of course, and mad enough to have brought it with her. Before setting off she probably swallowed a balloon of coke with a street value of £100,000 and now it's burst inside her. I do hope not. Someone might think she'd brought it in for me. I'd better check on this.

Are you straight?

'Slightly. God I'm randy actually. Let's do it here. Why *not*? I *want* to! Who cares about these silly people? I bet they're Germans. Of *course* I'm high. I've been fucking flying, haven't I? I hate flying. Where am I anyway?'

Ibiza.

'Horrors! Where's that? Let's fuck, why won't you?'

Here, in Arrivals, she pouts and pulls her trousers down, waggles her bottom like a stripper. This is unusual, I must say, I've never seen this before. Is it too much one-day cricket, so to speak, too many foreign girls now playing London, keen to make a killing and beetle back to Dusseldorf in time for dinner? Have English performers, as a consequence, forgotten how to pace an innings? I'm quite diverted, touched actually, but I scowl indulgently, like a silly father on the beach whose little girl is cutely driving others mad.

'If you won't do it here I'll fly straight back to London. I will, I will. I've got £500 and my return ticket. I always carry

£500 in case there's violence. Here, darling, do you like my little pink boots? I got them in Harlow New Town. Do I delight you?'

She does a little dance, pirouetting on one pink boot and tapping the ground with the other as she revolves.

'You're not *watching*! I'm dancing and you're not watching. *Watch* me!'

In fact I'm glancing casually to left and right to see whether she's being admired, whether others envy me. She is and they do. You couldn't take her everywhere, of course, but she is the sweetest thing in Arrivals by a long chalk. You could take her to more or less the same places, I'd say, as you could take Silly Serena or Stella the Stylist or any of the other desperate girls who've played this part before. You couldn't take her to tea with my sister Bobo, obviously, or to weddings in Hampshire, or to dinner with men who live in Regent's Park and have French wives, but you could take her to a Blues Brothers party given by South London intellectuals. Intellectuals would understand. They'd smile behind her back (not unkindly) and make entries in their writers' notebooks in an amused spidery hand. It must be awful to be the sort of person who couldn't be taken everywhere. No wonder they become quite rude, criticising your taste in sounds and trousers as if these things mattered. I could be taken anywhere, in spite of my sounds and trousers, and they naturally resent it. I'm still amusing value after dark; I roll joints with aplomb and put the music up, move easily in my mind into that possible world where everyone's brave and can dance and play the saxophone, where it's always after six o'clock and the people who want to get you into trouble have all gone home for the day. They only exist in the mind, of course, this possible world and the girl who could take you there – a tanned, courageous, dancing girl – which isn't to say they don't exist at all. (I rely here on the ontology of Popper.) The world of the imagination has existence, if not of the same sort as that of the 'real world' – the world of the woman you live with, of dry cleaning and money off, of *DIY* and final demands and guttering and veins. You couldn't park them in your garage, of course, this possible world and the perfect girl, but they do exist, if only in Popper's World 2. They

14

do have an objective truth, but – like the truth itself – we can never be sure we've found them. Optimists must just keep searching, trying to get closer; in the case of the perfect girl, trying to get the casting right. (This may be more or less correct. Generally speaking I know enough Popper to get by at lunchtime, to get past business girls in wine bars.) This year have I got the casting right, or more nearly right than usual? I was never much good at casting in the old days. My casting was a bit slap-dash then; I usually cast with the tour in mind when someone with talent might have brought us into London. I couldn't see it mattered, still can't.

Has Melissa got talent, will she do? Had I been born yesterday I might now imagine that she's pleased to be here, that she isn't acting. Normally they arrive, these performing girls, with a sullen, resentful look, with a wariness in their calculating eyes, as if fearing the worst, fearing – like real actresses – that they'll make prats of themselves and not get paid. You can't blame them, I suppose. You'd be wary if you'd made a fool of yourself for three hours on stage every night for a week and at the end of it not got paid. I once left Moira Lister in Liverpool without her train fare back to London, and she's still going on about it twenty years later, the mad old bag. But Melissa doesn't seem wary at all, she seems happy, glad to be here. It's all a bit confusing, but she'll amuse me for a week. With her I'll qualify – once she's got her wardrobe right – with her I'll get through doors, past burly touts keeping out the old, the fat, the badly dressed. I'll give her lessons in manners, and young people will want to sell us drugs.

✳

'I was telling them today how I embarrassed you at the airport.'

You didn't embarrass me. You embarrass me now. You look disgusting.

'I'll cry if you talk to me like this. I cry every day in here.'

I'm not surprised. Come home.

'I can't. Not yet. You don't understand how ill I am. I've got to be cured.'

Of what? Your stupidity? Your vanity? Your childishness?

'Yes, of all that I hope. They say I've got to grow up.'

Give up, they mean. Mumble prayers and never dance again. I hate these cunts.

'Don't swear!'

Jesus Christ, Princess, have these cunts told you not to swear?

'Yes. And point. We can't point. It's aggressive.'

Mad fucks. Why don't they have proper names? Des. Jeff. Liz. Chris. Mel. Christ, do they call you Mel? Isn't there anyone here with a proper name? Who's that imbecile over there? What's his problem? What's he on?

'That's Steve. He's my counsellor.'

Why don't his legs work? Is he drunk?

'He had polio.'

Stupid cunt.

'Please don't talk to me like this. He's helping me. They all are. I'm getting better. I haven't wanted to use for weeks now.'

Oh well done! What about drugs?

'Why are you so bitter? I don't think I've used you since I've been in here.'

You must be kicking yourself.

'Please don't be so bitter. What news of the book? I'm relying on the book.'

She thinks I'm writing a book about her, and in a way I am. I might get some of my money back – sell the more lurid bits to

16

the News Of The World, *perhaps. Her story's crappy enough, God knows, with most of the right ingredients: drugs, tarts, Tories, orgies, toy-town junkies, a Mickey Mouse bust, a comic Marquis, a Greek dwarf, a flash detective sergeant in the Drugs squad, a black man who carried the gear in his pork-pie hat, and a blonde divorcee called Melissa. I could get mileage out of that, surely, I could poke fun at that lot. The black man was Mr Big, in fact, but the police didn't know that, they didn't even know he existed, the silly sods — they were too busy trying to get their names in the papers by capturing the comic Marquis. When the bust took place, the flash detective sergeant went to pick up the Greek dwarf, thinking he was Mr Big, and sent two uniformed wallies to pull the comic Marquis, who was camping in the basement of a men's wear shop in the Edgeware Road. As the two uniformed wallies were leading the comic Marquis out of the shop — eyes bulging with coke and terror — the real Mr Big came in to buy a pair of trousers. Seeing his friend the comic Marquis handcuffed between two wallies, he made a run for it, and his pork-pie hat fell off. Inside were several ounces of the best cocaine. The uniformed wallies telephoned the flash detective sergeant who was on the other side of London arresting the Greek dwarf. We've got a black man here, they said, with several ounces of cocaine in his pork-pie hat. What shall we do? Ask him his name, you dozey prats, said the flash detective sergeant, and find out where he lives. This they did, later escorting him to a flat in Maida Vale where they found two loaded revolvers under the bed and enough cocaine to fill a dustbin-liner. So, the flash detective sergeant had a result, and Mr Big went into the frame with the Greek dwarf, the comic Marquis and the blonde divorcee — just because his pork-pie hat fell off. I could make money out of that lot.*

I've started it.

'That's good. You won't use any of the private things I've told you?'

Of course not.

I will, but she'll never read it. And if she does, she'll never understand.

'Promise?'

Promise.

'*I'm trusting you.*'

I thought you never trusted anyone.

'*I'm learning to. What are you calling me?*'

Mandy the Model, perhaps, something like that.

'*Mandy the Model? That's gross. I definitely don't like that.*'

I'll change it.

'*Can't I be something important — like a researcher? Model sounds like a tart.*'

No one will think you're a tart. You're quite sweet, actually. You say things like: 'If you can't stand the heat, get out of the oven'. Things like that.

'*I wouldn't say that!*'

Your type would.

'*What do you mean — type? I'm no more of a type than you are.*'

You are actually.

'*Hm. It definitely is fiction?*'

Might need counsel's opinion on that. Fact, probably.

'*Why fact? If it was fiction we could tell the truth.*'

In fiction you have to tell the truth. What would count as a lying fiction?

'*Hey — I painted a wall this week! I got paid £4!*'

What the fuck's the point of that?

18

∗

'Where are we going?'

I'm in two minds. I'd planned a series of previews, so to speak, in front of the less demanding, a kind of out-of-London try-out, a tour of the less fashionable bars to give her a feel of the part before exposing her to judgement. Ponce Corner – the Bar Zoo, the Bar Chic, the Bar Tango and the Tierra – where the island's self-appointed hot-shots (pimps, dealers, naked negroes) pose with insolent self-regard, where they make you feel like a bumpkin unless you're dressed like a girl or in a body-stocking, would be for later in the run. At Ponce Corner I might be greeted with affection by Baby Boo the snake-thin Inca. I might be kissed by Baby Boo. She'd think more of me were I to be kissed in public by a snake-thin Inca, she'd be impressed. Before introducing her to the aristocracy, however, I have to be certain that she's up to it, that she isn't going to let me down – hence the previews. But she hasn't got her wardrobe right; she should be wearing her legs, even for the previews. I can't take her on tour without her legs. A pity – I used to enjoy the tour in the old days, it was the best part. Ducking and diving out of town, fiddling with the nuts and bolts in Brighton and Bath, tinkering, conferring, changing the ending, firing the director in Bristol, the leading man in Hull, jacking it in in Oxford. I always fired the leading man – and the director, I don't know why. Had to blame someone, I suppose. But I'm the director, this time, I can't fire myself, so it's either back to the flat to work on the script, or to dinner at a restaurant off the beaten track. I don't want her to be seen yet by anyone who matters. We're out now, so it might as well be dinner. After dinner I'll rehearse her back at the flat, and then, if I judge her up to it, I'll take her out on tour.

I pick up her luggage with cautious vigour – cautious because Stella the Stylist, who doubled this part in '84 with Silly Serena, was hospitalised for a week due to my picking up

19

her luggage with too boastful a display of manliness ('*I'd* better take that,' she'd said). I lifted it too suddenly and with it I lifted Stella the Stylist, who was standing on a trailing strap. She shot six feet into the air in her smart high heels and landed on her arse. The week was a write-off, which was annoying for me, and for her too in a way, I suppose. I couldn't sit on fashionable beaches with a fat stylist in a cast, so I walked her round Ibiza Town while she got crosser and crosser. God what a fuss — you'd have thought no one had ever broken a leg before. So — I pick up Melissa's luggage carefully and head towards the car.

'Here, this car is gross. I've got a Porsche. No I haven't. I've got a Granada. Where are we going?'

To dinner.

'I don't want dinner. I don't like dinner. I want to fuck.'

Why does she keep saying this? It's almost as if she means it. She's either very good at this, or very bad. Could she be such a natural hustler that she actually enjoys it? It's not a formally contradictory proposition, after all — 'This hustler enjoys hustling'. It is possible, albeit logically possible only. I'll hang on to my hat and heed Tiffs' warning: 'Do be careful, she's as hard as nails, she'll use you if she can.'

Later.

'Oh phooey. Why later? Why not now? I want to *now*.'

This is Barbarian rugby in the mud, running the ball in the wrong weather — which is always dangerous. Someone can get hurt or end up looking silly — in this case her — dancing boastfully over the line without the ball while a prop forward built like a Polish sausage waddles it in at the other end. I'll have to slow her down, bewilder her with money and stun her natural flair with racontage. Over dinner I'll tell her who I am.

'You mustn't get old and boring. You only live once, you know.'

Now she'll say: 'This isn't a rehearsal for something else, you know.' That's the most arduous aspect of the week — the predictability.

'Okay, we'll go to dinner. But I'm really pissed off you won't fuck me now. I'm not at all pleased actually. I want you to know that.'

I'm beginning to wonder whether she'll take direction. Silly

Serena couldn't take direction. She sat around on the beach with her great buttery thighs, looking lewd but stupid. A solid degree of stupidity's just the job, of course, but it must be enthusiastic stupidity. Silly Serena simply didn't know what she was doing. You could see it in her eyes. Back at the flat I have stacks of photographs of her, bald naked with bewildered eyes. At the appropriate moment I'll show the photographs to Melissa. I've got photographs of all the mad girls who've played this part before, like a fisherman's trophies back at the flat, like mounted trout with dead eyes. Melissa will be impressed. If you think I'm old and unattractive you're plainly wrong. Here's my life – look at her and at her and at her. On the spur of the moment I change my mind. We'll forget dinner and go to the flat. I'll make her change her wardrobe, persuade her to put some more stuff up her nose, perhaps (whatever it is she's smuggled in), and then, if I judge her up to it, I'll take her out on tour.

'Here – this is okay.'

The flat has scored more points than my car.

'It's not very feminine though. I'll improve it. I'll change the curtains – and those cushion covers are dire.'

I'm a little cross on Alison's behalf. Alison spent the two weeks I'd allowed her here last year indoors sewing curtains and cushion covers instead of sitting in the sun. She'd been so proud of the results. When she'd finished she walked round the flat with a happy expression looking at her handiwork. 'It's our first real home, isn't it?' she said. 'I mean the first we've really done together?' She'd wanted to stay on longer to enjoy it for a while and I'd had trouble getting rid of her before Silly Serena dropped out of the sky with her creamy legs and dead resentful eyes. I feel a little guilty now, and get a flash of Alison's little hands sewing endlessly, a happy smile on her face. Melissa has no idea how much she's hurting Alison. It's bad enough her being here without criticising her behind her back. Even having made allowance for their lack of background, I find the insensitivity of these international airport girls really awful sometimes.

'Hey – you've got a phone. Can I make a call?'

That's right, be on the phone for half an hour. Silly Serena used to ring Central Casting every day and she hadn't worked for six years, hadn't so much as carried a tray in an episode of *The Professionals*. Now she straps Arabs to whipping-stools and leaves them trussed and baffled while she rings her agent.

'I want to ring Mummy. She worries. "Hullo, Mummy." Here, darling, where did you say we are? Oh yes. "I'm in Ibiza, Mummy. Yes. Yes. Of course. Love you and miss you. Bye." She'd really like you, my mother. She'd think you were from the top shelf. Well, she lives in Essex, right? I send her money, of course. The trouble is I don't like money at the moment. She thinks I'm a courier. Ha!'

What if she knew what you really are?

'She'd think it was better than marrying Americans. I've been a worry to my mother, I've exasperated her, let's face it. She used to chase me with a leather belt. I was fifteen, okay, and she used to chase me with a leather belt! Gross, eh? I'd run to my father for protection. I could twist my father round my little finger. I'd wear short skirts that showed my knickers and I'd run to him and sit on his knee. My father was a highly intellectual man. He played chess against the world champion. He was a grandmaster. No he wasn't. He was a brick-layer. But he read books and never saw anyone. He never allowed anyone into the house. He was a recluse, I guess. Plus he had lots of pens. My mother said the other day: "Your father really liked pens. Every Christmas I gave him a pen. He never used them, of course." Funny, eh? Actually, he wasn't really my father. I don't know who my real father was. He was my step-father. I'd better unpack.'

She starts to unpack, opening cases on the spot, throwing clothes all over the place. They're nice clothes, as far as I can judge, quite expensive, perhaps, suitable and casually revealing.

'Mess? What mess? That's because I haven't hung everything up yet. I'll hang my clothes up eventually, but it's a bad sign when I do. I only hang my clothes up when I'm leaving. It makes it easier to pack if everything's hung up. It's a bad sign when I hang my clothes up, I can tell you. It means I'm leaving. If we have a row you'll find me hanging up my clothes. Does that make sense?'

22

Perfect sense.

'Let's not have a row.'

She's kneeling on the floor, looking up at me with a butter-wouldn't-melt expression. Her eyes are huge and innocent. She could fool a lot of people, but she couldn't fool me. She reminds me of Dawn Upstairs's psychopathic daughter, Ursula. One night when Ursula was about six, I was left in charge of her while Dawn went out. She sat on the sofa looking like a little angel, and then she stuck her thumb in my eye. In my shock I nearly killed her, took her by the ankles and was about to swing her hard against the wall. Someone will come close to killing Melissa one day. That's the most dangerous thing about these girls: they make you behave so badly. Melissa won't stick her thumb in my eye, of course. She'll pout and pirouette and reach for my nest-egg. I have a feeling that she doesn't know the rules.

'This is Ted, by the way. I hope you're into baby bears. I take him with me everywhere. Be careful what you say to Ted because he tells me everything. If you don't fuck me soon Ted will be ever so cross. He'll think you don't like me. I'm going to take my clothes off. Why not? I want to. Have you got a camera? You can photograph me. I used to be a model, you know. Did I tell you? Tiffs and I and my best friend Lindy all started modelling on the same day. Tiffs wanted to be an actress and I wanted to be a model, but Tiffs made it as a model and I did better as an actress. No I didn't. I hardly did a thing. A couple of confession films. Tiffs has just sold her story to the *News Of The World*, you know. Is that gross or what? She's going to tell the whole world that when she was sixteen some fat comedian asked her into his dressing-room and said: "You be nice to me and I'll be nice to you." Then he pulled her knickers down and wanked all over her. Ha? Funny, eh? Put her off sex for life. Wasn't that atrocious, though? Wasn't that a dreadful thing to say?'

You be nice to me and I'll be nice to you? Quite appalling.

'*No*, not that. She asked for that, the silly bimbo. I mean saying who it was, *naming* the poor man. That's gross. One should never do that.'

Who was it?

'Jimmy Bruce. The funny thing is that the next man she met did exactly the same thing. He pulled her knickers down and wanked all over her! She kept meeting these fat men who said 'You be nice to me and I'll be nice to you' and then they'd pull her knickers down and wank all over her. Until she was twenty-three she thought that was all men did. No wonder she's cuckoo. Hey – one time I went in for a bottom of the year contest with Tiffs and I won! She's got a great arse and I won! I was Bottom of the Year in *Penthouse*. No I wasn't – it was *Mayfair*. Well, *Knave*, actually. I'm finding it difficult to lie to you. That's a bad sign. But I was Bottom of the Year and Tiffs came second! How about that? I've got the photographs at home. When we get back to London I'll show them to you.'

That's odd. They don't usually talk about the future, the future's not part of the arrangement. She must realise, surely, that in London I won't need to use her, that in London I'm fixed up.

'Here – what are these photographs, who are they of?'

She's found the mounted trout at last, she'll be intrigued. She's leafing through them, frowning, pouting, pretending to be put out – she's much better at the small touches than anyone who's played this part before. If she particularly admires Silly Serena – which she will – I'll say that she's the person I live with in London. When she gets to Alison I'll say that she's just someone I know on a casual basis. She'll be impressed, she'll know there's more to me than meets the eye.

'You're not very confident, are you?'

I could be rude, I could say: you little cunt, how dare you? Or I could be generous. I could take her hand and look at her earnestly and say: you'll make me confident. It's my instinct to be generous. That's the difference between us, I suppose. I know how to behave, she doesn't. She, in her fear, will take preemptive revenge on those who've never done her harm, mistaking generosity for weakness – which she thinks she'll catch. I decide to play for time, while my temper settles.

What makes you say that?

'I don't know. Having all these photographs, I suppose. It's gross keeping them all like this. By the time I leave you'll tear them up. You won't need them anymore.'

She's crackers.

'You won't, I promise you. Anyway – I don't like photographs unless they're of me. Who's this? I don't like her. She looks really hard Ah – she's better. She's sweet. She looks really nice.'

She must be looking at Silly Serena. I say it's Alison, that I live with her in London. Then I get up and look over her shoulder. It's Alison she's looking at, and it was Silly Serena she hadn't rated. Well I never.

'Are you married or what? I don't care. Does she telephone you? Why does she have to telephone you? I don't want her to telephone you. Not while I'm here. That's not fair. It's thoughtless. Oh dear, why am I always the other woman? Do I look like another woman?'

She does, actually. I'm beginning to think I've never met anyone who looks more like another woman (or who can act it better), who appears more abundantly in possession of another woman's attributes. She can act the very essence of another woman. It's impossible to imagine her eating an apple in bed, or wearing rubber washing-up gloves, or watching *EastEnders* with her stomach hanging over her tights, or getting old, or ever being there when you were frightened and cold and needed her. She is another woman to perfection: surprising and petulant, demanding and inappropriate, with none of the moral woman's instinct to be kind.

'Come to bed. Why won't you?'

She really is crackers. It's far too soon – can't she see that? Once over, there'd be nothing more to do, nothing more to say. The satisfaction of mere lust should be theatrical – deeply imagined, with a whip-cord narrative line, and carefully rehearsed. It should be discussible afterwards, like a great production. Without production values lust is pancake-thin and amateurish. She's far too high, she's laughing too much to play her part correctly. The celebration of mere lust should be solemn and ritualistic. It's far too fragile a fiction to withstand laughter.

Not yet.

'Photograph me, then.'

That's okay, that's not a bad idea. I'll need some

photographs, need a small collection for the wallet, to be produced with a flourish back in London. She quickly takes her clothes off – far too quickly – and poses happily here and there, laughing and confident, seeming to enjoy it. It's not in the least erotic, of course – she's being far too jolly, almost Australian in her out-door ease, her lack of shame – but I had almost forgotten how sweet she looks like this: velvety, brown and softly rounded. Tomorrow I'll be envied on the beach. I take mainly polaroids, but she insists on some proper ones, taken with the time control, of us together. She is clever. They don't usually want to use the time-control. No one has previously wanted one of us together – or pretended to. She keeps asking me how she compares with Tiffs, daring me, with a simulated pout or two, to place Tiffs first. I tell her that she's better, a hundred times better.

'Have you fucked Tiffs? Nor have I. No, I *wouldn't* want to. That's gross. I'm not a lesbian, I'm sure I'm not a lesbian. I expect you're disappointed. Men seem to like that. My husband liked that. When we lived in New York he was always trying to set it up. One night we went out in the car to pull a hooker. We drove up and down until we saw this terrific-looking black girl. My husband wound the window down and beckoned her over. They fixed a price and then he said it was for me. She was appalled! She looked me up and down and said: "*Uurrgh!*" '

Christ she's confident. Perhaps Tiffs was right, perhaps she has got it made. She can stand in front of me with nothing on and tell such a story against herself quite innocently. She's so in credit she reckons she can afford this small extravagance against herself, knowing I won't go off her.

How did you feel?

'I felt damn silly actually.'

Why did you agree to do it?

She frowns, she seems baffled by the question – or the need to ask it.

'Because he wanted me to, of course. I wanted to please him. Mind you, if I had he'd have killed me more than likely. He was always killing people. He was very possessive. He broke Andy the Barman's arm and I hadn't been with him for *years*. I'd do it for you if you wanted me to. Let's go to bed.'

26

It's still too soon. She may never look this good again, or be so high. I want others to see her like this, I want others to envy me. I tell her to get dressed, that we're going out. She looks startled, but recovers quickly.

'Okay. But I'm quite hungry now. Can we eat?'

I thought you weren't into eating?

'I've changed my mind. But it must be Indian or Chinese. I only eat Indian or Chinese at the moment.'

That's all right. There's an Indo-Chinese restaurant near the flat. I'll take her there, and after that I'll take her out on tour.

'Give me a minute.'

She disappears into the bedroom, and I think she'll take forever, but she emerges moments later looking crisp and adorable in a little white skirt and little white boots to match. She's the best I've had, I think. She's frightened and brave, her conversation is extraordinarily interesting to a man of my age, and sometimes I think she's as pretty as anything I've ever seen. I can have some fun with her, I think, bounce her into experiences that she may be too silly to see she'd really like.

*

'What time is it now?'

Six-thirty.

'Christ where is he? What time did you phone?'

About six.

'He should be here. I know he isn't coming. Phone again.'

I can't phone again. He'll be here. Take it easy, Princess.

'I'm not your fucking Princess. My name's Melissa.'

Sorry. Try to relax.

'Relax. How can I relax? You don't know what it's like. Phone someone else. Phone Stella.'

He'll be here. He's never let us down. Are you hungry? Shall I get you a Chinese take away? You like Chinese.

'Oooh you like Chinese, Princess, you know you like Chinese! Do you have to speak to me as if I'm a fucking child?'

Sorry. Do you want a drink? Shall I get you a drink?

'No I don't want a drink. What's the use of a fucking drink? What have we got?'

Some white wine. I think there's some white wine in the fridge.

'Okay, I'll have some of that. That'll be better than nothing.'

Or I could go out. I could go and get you something else.

'Christ, I said that would be all right. I said I'd have what we've got.'

Sorry.

'For God's sake stop saying you're sorry. Do you have to apologise for everything?'

I'll get it.

'Why are you staring at me? Stop staring at me.'

Don't you feel close at all?

'I don't feel anything.'

Do you want to talk?

'What about?'

The book.

28

'No. Why should I want to talk about the book? I don't want to talk about anything. I don't want to think.'

Okay.

'I need help. You said you'd look after me.'

I will.

'When? When will you get me help? Proper help?'

Soon. As soon as we've finished the book.

'Christ I feel dreadful. Where is he? I know he isn't coming. Is it cold? Are you cold?'

Not really.

'I'm cold. Why's this flat so cold? Why's this flat so fucking cold? Phone someone else.'

He'll be here. He's never let us down.

*

I wasn't always like this.

'Nor was I.'

Never mind that. I remember summer holidays in Broadstairs, and the Grand Hotel and little pier, and fishing with my father. And I remember Canterbury Week and the old oak inside the field of play and Todd and Fagg and Leslie Ames, and Doug Wright grazing in the deep. Ames didn't keep wicket any more, of course, they parked him in the slips. He couldn't bend over after the war. If he'd bent over he couldn't have straightened up again. He'd have crouched for life. And I remember Lindwall coming on to bowl. Those were the days. It all made sense then.

'Will this take long? I'm 32. I've got decisions to make.'

I'm telling you my memoirs here. I've been commissioned to write my memoirs by a respected house. I've decided to tell it all to you. Set up tension, do you see, odd conjunctions, significant contrasts – 'A rose, a toad, a thingummy and a whatsit', you take the point? – a person like me telling it to a person like you. Interesting, eh? The past and the present side by side? From Winchester to this?

It's not such a bad idea, I think. It dropped into my head fully formed, even as we ordered. She's why I did it, after all, splashed money around, put on musicals, wore a coat – all to impress silly girls like her. I'll be telling her my life-story anyway – a habit of mine these days – so this way I'll kill two birds with one stone. She might even be deductible.

'What's Winchester? What's wrong with this? Are you ashamed of me?'

Not necessarily, hardly at all in fact. Bit of a comedown, though. Started normally enough. Sunningdale. Broadstairs. Canterbury Week. Oak trees. Todd and Fagg and Leslie Ames. Then where was I? Hobnobbing with Australians, opening model agencies and giving my money to girls like you.

30

Uncentred, do you see? When my son phones I say: tell him I've moved. Not on, really, keeping one step ahead of your son. They don't teach you that at Winchester.

'I've got a son.'

I hope she doesn't mention him again. She certainly shouldn't have a son.

'It's okay. I never see him.'

Thank God for that.

'They're a worry, children. My best friend Sarah's got a daughter who's a thief. She's twelve years old and a thief, okay? She steals everything right under your nose. She's called Vanessa. One time my best friend Clare asked Sarah and Vanessa to Hurlingham for the day. Pimms and croquet, isn't it?'

I wouldn't know.

'She's a bit flash, my best friend Clare. Everything by Cartier. Cartier watch, Cartier cigarette case, Cartier lighter, Cartier knickers, you know the type. Anyway, by the end of the day Vanessa had got the lot! Watch, lighter, cigarette case, knickers – everything. My best friend Sarah was *stripped*, I tell you. She didn't like to say anything, of course. She's a bit cuckoo, Clare. If Sarah had said anything Clare would have burnt her house down. Something daft like that.'

I'm trying to tell you my memoirs here.

'Are you a writer, then? I've never heard of you. Are you any good?

I could say yes, I could say no. Either way she wouldn't know the difference. I decide to say no, realizing my mistake even as I say it. She looks disgusted.

'Good gracious. That's an odd thing to do badly. Must be embarrassing. Like a fat man flirting.'

Nevertheless that's what I do.

(Or what I should be doing. I'm in a spot of bother, as it happens, a consequence of being sued for breach of copyright by a man called Schultz. The costs are huge and mounting daily. I've signed contracts for twelve toilet books as a precaution against losing the court case, which I will according to my lawyer, Mr Wiseman. Twelve toilet books already in the pipe-line, and two more at least, I hope, if I can do business

31

with Mark Staughton, who's coming out here at the end of the week. Staughton – ex-OUP, now on his own (backed by a crooner, I rather think), is keen to get into toilet books to subsidise his poetry list. There's something fishy about Staughton – a married man in a corduroy suit, he could sing in a choir, if you ask me, or take his holidays in Wales. I'll have to get rid of Melissa before Mark Staughton comes. If she's still here, he'll think I'm on drugs. (She's still as high as a kite, here at the Indo-Chinese restaurant. She *must* have smuggled it in.) She'd get bored, sulk, career into conversations from the wrong direction like a lorry full of fruit in a silly chase film. We'd be talking some literary matter through, Staughton and I, legs stretched, and she'd suddenly say: 'Do you think my bottom's too fat?' I'll have to get rid of her before Staughton arrives.)

I used to kick a QC up the arse.

'Golly. Are you gay or what?'

Almost certainly not. And no thanks to Winchester. At Winchester homosexuality was greatly encouraged. We used to bathe in the nude in Gunner's Hole, a disgusting stretch of river cordoned off. It was like bathing in bronchial phlegm. In my day the whole school was in love with Johnnie Patterson. He won't mind my saying this. He's a sheep farmer in New Zealand now. When he appeared at Gunner's Hole the word went round in a flash. Cricket matches were abandoned, the chapel emptied, visiting parents were left wandering up side-streets on their own – the whole school descended on Gunner's Hole, masters included. They all pitched up, breathing asthmatically on their rickety bikes – 'Sponge' Walker, Head of History, 'Oily' Mallett, 'Botty' Firth – the school chaplain – Hardisty, who unstrapped his artificial leg and hopped about bare-arsed on one, and 'Hearty' Hodges, the PT master, who wore a dress and jogged up and down on the spot. All as mad as hatters, do you see? They'd stand at the edge of Gunner's Hole with their reedy shanks and ghostly pubic bushes squinting with lust at Johnnie Patterson posing on the high-board.

'This curry's gross. I'm bored. Why won't you fuck me out of doors? Would that be exciting at all? Let's go to the beach and fuck.'

I tell her that it's far too soon, that I'm a Wykehamist, that Wykehamists have it in the head, and then I give her the stuff about visiting the *Folies Bergère* at thirteen and from then on seeing women as performers only. I only like women who earn a living from their looks, I say, qualified women who can take their clothes off without embarrassing themselves and others. Dancers. Showgirls. Strippers. Models with mad heads swinging down cat-walks. Women on display, tamed but defiant, with a prowling, predatory quality in the eyes and the legs.

It's in the eyes and the legs. I blame my parents. That's why you're here.

'I know! I'll pay you! I'd like that, I think. I've never paid a man. I bet I wouldn't have to pay Jack the Actor. What if I went to the beach with Jack the Actor? Would you get the hump? Would that be exciting at all? Oh God you're boring. You're no fun.'

Now she'll say: 'This isn't a rehearsal for something else, you know.'

'I met this guy the other day, okay. He was from the old days, right? The Sixties, I guess.'

Oh dear – now she's going to criticise the Sixties, a decade for which girls like her should thank their lucky stars. Where would they be, girls like her, if it weren't for old optimists left over from the Sixties? And shall I explain that for young people every decade's the Sixties, that for my boy Charlie it's the Sixties now – except that it isn't, because the silly prat's goofed and is living in a squat in God knows where? I can't be bothered; she wouldn't understand.

'He wears a uniform, and carries a gun, this guy I met the other day. I'm quite turned on by guns and uniforms, I think you should know that. He's a mercenary. No he isn't. He works for Plessey. Anyway, he's left his wife and lives alone in a one-room flat in SW6 surrounded by Co-op carrier-bags. A carrier-bag here, a carrier-bag there. He hasn't had the heart to unpack, I guess. Of course he's got a trust fund that enables him to see girls and that.'

What is she talking about?

What are you talking about?

33

'I thought it was rather sad. I thought it might happen to you. I thought you might end up in SW6 with all your possessions in a carrier-bag. I don't think you're very happy. Sorry.'

Suddenly I feel a little tired. If there's anything more enervating than an ignorant stranger making a preemptive snap-judgement about one's state of mind I don't know what it is. Unhappy is the last thing I am. I collapse inside and smile sardonically, suggesting that she's missed a few layers of irony in the way I present myself – which she has.

'Laura's paid a man. She's my best friend. She does the shopping and bosses me around. I don't do the shopping, by the way.'

That's a relief. I can't imagine her doing the shopping.

'I don't buy cling-wrap. I've definitely never bought cling-wrap.'

What's cling-wrap?

'It's for preserving food, I think. I very rarely preserve food. I think you should know that too.'

Thank God. It's bad enough her having a son. I couldn't stand it if she bought cling-wrap and preserved food.

'Laura buys the cling-wrap and tells me what to do. She's one of *them*.'

Who's them?

'Oh – mothers, friends, *men*. They boss you around, tell you what to do. Just because they do the shopping. *You'll* be one of them. You'll spoil me and then you'll tell me what to do, what to wear, what to think. You'll believe you have the right. It's a kind of deal. I'll look nice and you'll tell me what to think.'

Is that the deal you have with Laura?

'Sort of.'

I bet she's plain.

'*Plain*? That's not a word one hears a lot these days. My best friend Laura *plain*? How dare you!'

Sorry.

'Rough, that's what she is. She doesn't really like me, my best friend Laura. Women don't like me very much. Why's that, do you think?'

34

She's touched on something I understand.

Because you're too unsuspicious. At a party I bet you'd please every man in the room quite mercilessly, you'd make a promise of a sort to every one of them. Women don't like that. You remind me of my ex-wife, Mrs Mouse.

'My husband used to call me Mrs Mouse! He was Mafia.'

Of course. Women didn't care for Mrs Mouse. They resented her expertise at play, her ability to make silly men happy, so they looked after her and betrayed her behind her back. As you say, it's a kind of deal. 'You look pretty and take risks and I'll walk slyly behind you and raise an eyebrow and pick up the left-overs', that's what the plain ones are thinking.

'I think I'll go to the loo.'

Look, I'm telling you about Mrs Mouse. Spontaneity and negligence, that was her thing. No code, only instincts, and sudden passions suddenly over. Everything on the spur of the moment – sleep, food, friendship – everything suddenly or not at all. She'd disappear for weeks on end and then pop up with useless spontaneous presents – sausages, alarm clocks, the wrong cigars, clothes that didn't fit. All her compassion was directed towards strangers with nosebleeds and animals in distress. At close quarters she was unforgiving, absolutely lethal.

'I don't want to talk about this, okay?'

Of course she doesn't. I'm telling her about herself. She won't tell *me* I'm unhappy and get away with it.

Ten years ago I ran a glass-bottom boat out here, I can't remember why. On the last day of the season Mrs Mouse took off with Birmingham Paul. Up and away just like that. I wasn't worried. I settled in for the winter with Mr Gabriel, the Yugoslav housepainter. We did okay. He cooked, I advised, told him what it was all about. Got him reading *Dance To The Music Of Time*, as I recall. He rather liked it, as it happens, but that's by the way. We were doing all right, then Mrs Mouse dropped out of the sky with all these useless presents. Paints for Mr Gabriel, sausages for me. She stood in the passage and sobbed: 'I want a friend. I want a friend.' What did she expect? I bet you make a big thing of Christmas. Get sentimental, put up decorations, become regretful, buy useless presents for all your best friends – those who are still talking to you. Nasty all the year round and then make a big thing of Christmas. You're definitely a Mrs Mouse.

She looks at me with dumb defiance, an expression Mrs Mouse had worn a hundred times when cornered.

'Who *called* her Mrs Mouse? *You* did. How did you expect her to be? I *am* going to the loo.'

I've brought her down, and now she's off to take a hit of whatever it is she's smuggled in. That's good. It seems I can control her by telling her about herself. If I tell her about herself she has to take something to get her courage back. Coke probably. That's okay. With her courage up she'll be more fun. She'll need courage enough for both of us when I take her on tour, when I take her to where the music is.

She's back in a minute with shining eyes and her head held high. Whatever she took it certainly worked. She looks years younger and ten times prettier. I hope she smuggled in enough to last the week.

'I know what I'll do. I'll draw you a picture of the Princess of Wales. That will cheer you up.'

She scribbles briefly on a napkin, then hands me the result. It's startlingly pornographic, and quite accomplished.

'Is that good or what? I went to art school. I could have been an artist. Don't laugh. You should know better than to laugh at me. You think I'm stupid, but I'm not. I left school at sixteen. I didn't have a proper education.'

You shouldn't tell everyone. They'd never guess.

I say it a little more coldly than I'd meant to, but I'm still slightly upset by her suggestion that I might be unhappy like the man from Plessey adrift with his carrier-bags in SW6. She looks confused, draws back, covers up behind a phony smile. At Winchester there'd been a custom called a 'bross blow' whereby a senior boy, imagining himself to have been cheeked by a smaller boy, could line him up against a wall and pot him in the stomach. Accomplished thugs could knock you senseless with a bross blow. Our housemaster, entering hall for evening prayers, had to pick his way carefully between the bodies of small unconscious boys. He never said a word. There was one difficult little boy, who'd never go down from a bross blow, who'd never show that he was hurt. He'd bite his lip and wear a goofy grin, but he wouldn't go down. All that accumulated hurt must have really fucked him up. He's probably on drugs now, or wearing a dressing-gown and slippers in the garden of a clinic. Melissa reminds me of that difficult little boy. She's hurt, but she won't go down. I feel a little kick of pleasure. She'll watch her tongue in future. She may be pretty, but I can spit.

And her drawing has given me a good idea. I've been wondering what to call her, how to refer to her in public without either of us losing dignity. Potentially, let's face it, we look a trifle silly – I'm too old, she's too blonde. It's not altogether her fault, she's lovely, actually, on her own no problem, but in context, lined up with me, she might look a little too like one of those ladies who came out of the woodwork in mail-order underwear to contest the will of the late Dick Emery. It's important, it seems to me, that we laugh at ourselves before others do. I'll call her my Princess. That's got the right ring to it. It's what an old-time Hollywood tycoon would have called his latest chorus-girl. People will pick up on the irony of 'my Princess'. We're not real, do you see, it's all a bit of a joke. We've spotted the joke ourselves. I fold up the pornographic likeness of the Princess of Wales and put it in my pocket.

I'll keep this forever, but *you're* my Princess.

She thinks about it for a bit, and then smiles happily. She's missed the irony, I think; she's missed the joke. That's good. I wouldn't want to hurt her again so soon; it's not time yet for another bross blow. That's the difference between us; she'll hurt me – not seriously, of course, merely confusing me for a moment, unaccustomed as I am to bad manners, by her sudden, uneducated candour – but I'll be careful of her feelings all the time.

'I like that. I want to be your Princess. I definitely want to be your Princess. This restaurant's dire. Let's go home.'

Soon. First we're going for a little walk.

*

'Look at my eyes, how are my eyes?'
Amazing.
'Wow. That worked. You?'
I'm okay. I'm high just watching you. Can you talk?'
'Almost. Christ — what was that?'
What was what?
'That noise.'
My glasses fell off. Sorry. Haven't you had enough? There'll
be nothing for tomorrow.
'Just one more — please. Then you can hide it. Hide it
somewhere I can't find it.'
That's what you always say. And you always find it.
'We do get very cunning! I warned you about that.'
I love you being cunning.
'This time I mean it. Just one more and then I'll tell you
everything.'
Really everything?
'I promise.'
Okay.
'Hold it for me, will you? That's right, a little higher, hold
the flame a little higher. That's it ... God this is really good —
the best we've had.'
I told you he'd come. My friend Martin's never let us down.
'That's true. Oh wow ... did I ever tell you ...'
What?
'Um?'
You said — did I ever tell you? Tell me what?
'I don't know. It's gone. Probably not important.
Blow-back?'
I'm okay. You're my high. I get high just looking at you. You
look so beautiful.
'God I love it when you say that. Am I still your Princess,
then?'

38

You'll always be my Princess.
'Forever and ever?'
Forever and ever.
'If you abandoned me now I don't know what I'd do.'
I'll never abandon you. How could you think I would?
'I don't know. I still get scared. It was a nightmare, you know.'
Don't think about it. It's over now. I'll look after you. I'll always look after you.
'One more? Can I have just one more? Please.'
It's nearly all gone – you've nearly finished it. There'll be nothing for tomorrow.
'We can call Martin again. Please.'
We can't call him every day. Do you know how much money we've spent this week?
'Don't talk about money. Money's not important.'
That's true. Okay, one more. Shall I hold it?
'Yeah ... that's it ... oh Christ ...'
Careful.
'Sorry ... I shouldn't do it standing up. Right – where have you got to, then?'
Got to? Got to with what?
'The book! Golly, you really are high. You're as high as me.'
I told you I was. I remember when it first happened. It was your first trip to Ibiza. We were sitting outside the Tierra and I got high just talking to you.
'I told you that could happen. I warned you.'
It was frightening.
'You should have said something. You should have told me. I'd have explained.'
I thought I was imagining it. I didn't understand.
'Now do you believe Dr Lefever?'
I don't know. It doesn't seem possible really. What's the matter?
'I shouldn't have thought about him.'
Who?
'Lefever. I ought to see him again. When can I see him again?'
Soon. As soon as we've finished the book.

39

'Ibiza was so lovely. I wish we were there now. Will we ever go back, do you think?'

Of course we will. I've been thinking about that black girl.

'What black girl? I don't remember a black girl.'

The black girl you and your husband tried to pick up in New York. The one who took one look at you and said: Uurrgh! I loved that. That was beautiful.

'Christ! You're not going to put that in the book, are you? That would kill my mother.'

Of course I'm not. It's just that I've been trying to get everything clear in my mind. Then I'll scramble it up. Nothing will emerge that anyone could recognise. I've been trying to describe you.

'That must be hard. Hey – if it was a film you wouldn't have to! Why can't it be a film? I want it to be a film. I could play me! I've always wanted to be in a blue film.'

It's a book. Your book.

'Okay. Which bits can I do, then?'

The good bits. The bits for the News Of The World.

'Now? Can I start now? I've been thinking about it. It's all coming back. Drugs, orgies, God knows what with people who should have known better, nice girls from the Thai Embassy tied to beds with Old Harrovian ties ...'

Not yet. It's too soon for all that. I've got to establish you first, make you seem charming before you take your clothes off ...

'... and ugly people start to fuck me. Horrors! Uuurrgh! Hey – I know what it was!'

What?

'What I was going to tell you. It was about Sophie. Mr G was always trying to get us at it. Me and Sophie. When she was still with Alexander.'

Did you?

'No.'

Oh.

'I was keen. But not with him. With you. Oh God – why didn't you come round, smash the door down and drag me out of there? That's what I wanted you to do.'

No you didn't.

'That's true. Can I drop names yet? God what a ropey crowd they were. Hey, darling – do you think you can grow to look like the people you fuck?'

Probably not.

'Thank God for that. Can I be on the cover, then? Here – if it comes out before the trial, will that be attempt of court, or is that laughing? Write that in your notebook!'

'I already have. Why am I in inverted commas? You're not in inverted commas.'

It's sort of disrespectful, I hope – a way of roping you off, of turning you into a 'character', I think. It's a literary device. You wouldn't understand.

'Fuck you – I'm real! I'm not a character. You should treat people with more respect. Do you think you're inventing me or something?'

I'm not inventing you. You invented yourself – years ago. Something happens to people like you at an early age which means you're going to be 'women' rather than yourselves. 'Identity is a role we impersonate'. Sartre.

'You're cuckoo.'

We leave the restaurant, set off across the Vara de Rey, past the Montesol and Mar y Sol, where the 'B' team losers pose – dealers, 'models', dodgers, whatnots – hoping to impress the tourists with their comic clothes and piebald hairstyles. My Princess is bouncing along, marching innocently towards the music in her little boots, knowing she'll be welcome. I drop behind, assessing the effect she has on others. Heads turn as she passes, people have a second look. That's good. The bogglers get blasé out here; there are so many good-looking girls walking their legs that people hardly notice another pair, however sweet. It's not like the King's Road, where turkey-necked old frauds from the Sixties still rock carefully forward on their toes, eyeing the girls in their summer dresses. Perhaps she's cheating – like Judy Garland in *Easter Parade*, pulling grotesque faces to get attention. I catch up with her to check – no, she's doing it straight.

I drop behind again, move more easily myself, with nonchalance, with pride. If only they could see me now: Simey, who was out here in February in a white suit and earphones and lectured me on how to pull the girls – 'Bear down on them, Will, let me feel the breath on the back of their necks, grip them suddenly' (not such good advice, I think) – and Ben, who was here last year and was quite unkind. 'Peel off, grandpa,' he said whenever a pair of secretaries, often Swedish, came in view. I was chagrined, but I didn't show it, I peeled off immediately, didn't want to spoil his chances. In the end I was peeling off on my own, just in case, dummying myself round corners with not a secretary in sight, Swedish or otherwise, once nearly dummied myself onto the Barcelona ferry pulling out. Ben never got anything as good as I've got now.

Suddenly she notices that I'm not with her. She looks round, comes back and takes my arm. She's doing everything right at the moment, the first who has. She makes me feel oddly unafraid, I bounce a little too, move with greater confidence below the waist. We join the enemy – the happy crush of young people pulled by the weight of music in the distance, pushing, laughing, celebrating this once-off, unexclusive triumph – being young – hurrying towards the wall of sound coming from the Bar Zoo as if afraid they may grow old before they get there. We leave them here and head towards Ponce Corner, where, dazed with flirty self-regard, the island's hotshots lounge outside the Bar Chic and the Bar Tango, where everyone under eighty deals in drugs, not least Tanit, the heavy centre of the in-set, a massively composed half-naked negro, who came out of the sea ten years ago proclaiming himself to be the island God of Ibiza. In spite of his divine powers Tanit the island God carries cocaine in his *cache-sexe* in case chemistry's required. With him as usual is his pal El Pimpo, an enormous Italian with a tiny head no bigger than a lemon. Tanit and El Pimpo never go to bed, but spend their nights gazing into one another's eyes, as if the other is a mirror reflecting the only company worth keeping. With them is their exotic retinue of twerps.

My Princess can see no reason not to join them, but I explain that that's not on, that that would be like stumbling stupidly into the action from the audience. These are professionals, I say, paid to sit on beaches and take their G-strings into Ku. Their lives are a small, continuous floorshow, starring themselves; they do everything with the self-adoring concentration of a girl putting on her make-up, including putting on their make-up, I imagine. Look at Tanit, the island God, look how he moves: all his movements are elaborately slow and are completed, like a dancer miming. Even the simple business of stirring an ostentatious cup of cocoa (bought for him at the cafe opposite by the Bar Chic's owner, a Barcelona gangster) becomes an elaborate mime. He does everything as if expecting applause, as if there's an audience, which there always is.

He's fascinating, Princess.

'He's stoned, darling, that's what he is, stoned out of his head.'

That's one way of looking at it, I suppose. He certainly

doesn't say a lot, having lost the power of speech some years ago, unless on coke, in which circumstance, so the rumour goes, he can form whole sentences, often to do with Mrs Thatcher and Her Majesty the Queen, who is shortly to abdicate, he says, and settle out here with him, the two of them planning to open 'Tanit's', the most stylish brothel in the Balearics.

We sit down respectfully outside the cafe opposite, among the audience, and order drinks. Suddenly my Princess howls like a wolf – whoa! whoa! whoa! – and then – catastrophe – screams at Tanit and his retinue in a high-pitched, comic Brooklyn shriek.

'Hey you arseholes! Where you from anyway?'

Mother of God, if the ground could open up and swallow me. Tanit the Island God has never been spoken to like this, indeed he's never been spoken to at all by anyone outside his circle. Not since my friend Craig Brown, dressed in a green suit, button-holed the Queen at a Buckingham Palace garden party, padded round after her when she tried to break away, gripped her by the elbow and told jokes involving a knowledge of Kafka has such a *faux-pas* been committed.

Tanit, the Island God, looks up, looks in our direction, smiles with sleepy recognition – though recognition of what I'm not quite sure.

'Hey – I'm from everywhere.'

'Will you suck on that! I'm from there too! What fucking street you live on?'

She's screaming, people are laughing, I don't know why – embarrassment, I suppose.

'I live on Utopia Boulevard.'

'No shit! That's my street too! What fucking number?'

'Hey – number one!'

'You putting me on? *I* live at number one!'

Tanit the Island God eases himself smoothly off his bar-stool, pads silently towards us, stares at Melissa with sleepy, unbewildered interest.

'Do you want to dance?'

She smiles sweetly, then looks down, shyly, playing a different part. She is clever.

'You'll have to ask my Prince.'

Tanit turns to me.

'May I dance with your Princess?'

Jesus I've been coming to Ibiza for at least ten years and I've never been spoken to by Tanit the Island God in his *cache-sexe*; I've never imagined it possible. It is, perhaps, the social summit of my life. I consider past triumphs – lunch with Princess Margaret at the Bishop of Southwark's Tooting Palace, when he told a dirty joke and laughed so much himself that he fell off his chair; the Duchess of Argyle's coming out dance for her daughter the Duchess of Rutland, where I waltzed with the Lord Great Chamberlain's daughter; a wife-swapping party in SW10, organised by Victor Lownes, where men who looked as though they cleaned their cars on Sundays fucked middle-aged women in Harrods coats – no, there has been nothing to compare with this.

Of course.

My Princess gets up, does a dozen accomplished little steps – brown legs, white boots – and then leaves Tanit with a smile, promising to dance with him again tomorrow. Who was it who said that people are either drains or radiators? (There could be a toilet book here, I think. One for Staughton, perhaps.) My Princess is a radiator; she leaves people feeling better, feeling warm and hopeful. She's high, of course – and working. I'm in danger of forgetting this. *I mustn't forget she's only acting.*

We walk on, round the corner to the Tierra, where normally I'd not be welcome, where, on my own, Toni, the owner – a swarthy boy in leather from the mainland – would greet me with a sullen lack of interest. Now he sees my Princess, does a Spanish double-take – more insultingly startled than an English one – and gives us a big hullo. We perch outside on stools, Toni brings us drinks, she flirts a bit, arranges her legs. Toni sways inside his leather knickers, adjusts what's underneath – his brains I wouldn't wonder. I sway a bit myself, say hey! hey! hey! – not too loudly.

'Good, eh?'

I nod. I do feel good, I feel warm and encouraged – and yet I've taken nothing. Suddenly I want to speak to her directly, simply, not to the part she's playing. I want to tell her that she's lovely, that I'm proud of her. Luckily something stops me

45

just in time, some sense of anticipated rejection, some foreknowledge of an icy moment when I'll know she's a stranger, and always was.

'May I ask you something? Promise not to laugh?'

I do want to laugh, she looks so serious – and I am a little high, on what, I can't imagine.

'Why do men ask me to take my clothes off? They definitely don't ask other people, I've noticed that. My husband's friends were always asking me to take my clothes off. No one asked *their* wives to take their clothes off. Once in New York my husband and a business associate were discussing something quite important. I was in the kitchen. "Hey, Melissa," the friend called out. "Come in here and take your clothes off. I want to see you with nothing on." I don't think he should have said that, do you? I don't think it's very nice. It doesn't show respect. Should men speak to me like that?'

Has Toni turned the music up? It's in my head, pounding in my brain; and my brain itself is badly out of shape, sliding around fatuously in my head like a balloon full of warm water. I consider my friends' wives with difficulty, ponder which of them I'd ask to take their clothes off. None of them, that's the fact of the matter. She's right, it doesn't show respect. But it is a kind of compliment, it means that men aren't frightened of her, they sense she wouldn't snub them, leave them feeling nude and silly. She's a radiator. I decide to tell her this.

It's because they think you're a tart.

Why did I say that? I can hardly remember what her question was, or how long ago she asked it. I do feel very odd. I can't work out how long we've been here. Minutes? Hours?

'Hey, that's not very nice! That's definition of character. I'll take you through the courts!'

How long have we been here?

'We've just arrived. Are you okay?'

I'm not sure. I feel light-headed and reckless. Is she feeding helium into my brain through an invisible nose-pipe? She's staring at me, her eyes are enormous and unnaturally bright, and I have a feeling that everything's gone dark around her, that her eyes are glowing brilliantly in a black sky. Has Toni laced the drinks? I haven't felt like this since Mrs Mouse and I

46

dined with her Harley Street gynaecologist and he laced the drinks with mescalin. And now I get a sudden rush, a pounding in the ears that lasts for about ten seconds. She's smiling at me, as if she understands, as if she can see into my brain. I look away. This uneducated girl from Harlow New Town can see into my brain.

'This is the best, right?'

Did she say that? I can't speak. My mouth's gone dry and now my eyes are playing tricks: her face is out of focus, swimming away into the distance – and now it's clear again, leaning into me, and her eyes are huge and innocently wicked. Who is she? I don't know her at all, and yet I have a sense of continuity, whether backwards or forwards, I can't quite tell – backwards, I think – like *déjà vu*, like stumbling on something familiar in an impossible setting. I think she knows this too.

'This is what I do best. I give a man everything he's ever wanted and then a light goes out.'

What do I want?

'Only what isn't allowed.'

Is this allowed?

'Of course not.'

That's all right, then. What else do I want?

'Could be me.'

What! *Just* you?

(That's not possible. That's never happened. Except in my mind, of course. Except in day-dreams about a nicer life. In real life, as time goes by, one necessarily wants people less, not more. And the solemnity of this heavy-bottomed thought makes me want to laugh.)

'Not the real me, of course. Just the part you want me to play. You may create a monster. You might have to kill me!'

What's real?

(Now I'm prompting her with the attractive, lop-sided concern of a mellifluous Irishman on a middle-brow arts show. This strikes me as so richly comic that I do start to laugh.)

'London. The horrors in the night. Mothers wondering what you do. People crying on their own.'

Are you playing a part now?

'A bit. I'm figuring you out. I'm getting there. You like silly

47

show-offs, right? So that's what I'm doing. The *Folies Bergère*. Professional bodies. Tall girls with long legs prowling round stages. Safe. Silent. Caged. I got all that. You thought I wasn't listening, but I was.'

I think I have a point to make – an objection, perhaps – but I can't remember what it is. Yes I can, I've got it now – or have I registered it already? I'll say it again anyway, just in case. My voice doesn't seem to be my own; it comes from a long way off, echoing in my head.

Caged? I didn't say anything about caged.

No sooner have I said it than I can't remember if I have. If I did, it was a long time ago, so I say it again anyway.

I didn't say anything about caged. Am I repeating myself?

This strikes me as extraordinarily comic, and I start to laugh again, quite uncontrollably now. This must be how she felt when she arrived earlier at the airport. The real world – all of it – has sat on a chair which isn't there, and it's looking awfully silly.

'A bit. Okay – not caged. But prowling and silent. Perfect. Not *real*. Don't worry, I can do all that. That's easy. I'll make your fantasy come true, but you won't thank me for it. There'll be nothing more to dream about. You may go mad!'

I think I may be mad already. I think I've been offered a reprieve of some sort and I don't know if I'm horrified or happy. I think this peculiar person could rekindle my pride, or something, could take me to the very edge and laugh and leave me there.

'Are you sure you're okay?'

I think so.

I'm not okay. I've been where I've never been before – into that possible world where it's always after six o'clock, where the music's in your head and nothing matters. I felt unconquerable for a moment – and I imagined it was real. I've got to come down, return to the real world of dry-cleaning and money-off, of fear and rate demands and veins, I've got to get out of here. I stand up as briskly as I dare and make my way unsteadily towards the gents – light-headed, paranoid. Are people staring, can they tell? I go inside and lock the door, sit down, breathe deeply with my head between my knees. This is ridiculous. I've had the horrors before – that panic when you go too high – but only when I've taken drugs. Get a grip on reality, that's the thing, think hard of all the worst things in the world: of Christian murderers marching to slack drums, of Gilbert and Sullivan and Somerset, of English pubs and dinner party conversations, of the *Daily Telegraph* and toilet books, of church bells and crabs and Maureen Lipman, of 'The Price Is Right' and mad women singing hyms, of Alison and good intentions. It works: gradually I breathe more easily. I stand up, stare at my face in the cracked mirror. I look okay, more or less, I'm all right now. Jesus, what was that then? Even on drugs I've never been as high as that, I've never been up there before. I won't go there again. Ten seconds of happiness – of power, of courage, but it wasn't worth it. It would be okay if you could live at that level always – but that wouldn't be allowed. There are shore patrols with night-sticks to stop people living at that level all the time. I know, I was in the Navy, did my turn at shore patrol. Into a pub in white gaiters, brandishing night-sticks: you're happy – whack! Alison must have been in the Navy, must have done shore patrol. I take a last deep breath and leave the gents, walk casually towards our table.

'What happened?'

Nothing. I'm fine.

I'm a little depressed, in fact, but that's because I've come down too fast. It's like being woken too suddenly from a dream in which I'd been with someone who could alter everything – and now I feel defrauded. I look at my Princess with something like distaste. I'd been deluded for a moment, imagined an end to acting and pretence and it had been her fault, I think. Could she be utterly corrupt? No, that's unfair – I did it on my own, cooked up that silly fantasy myself. I'm okay now. I can handle it, whatever it was, and I can handle her – but she won't take me there again.

'Let's go home.'

I explain that we're waiting for Baby Boo, the snake-thin Inca. I feel I haven't shown you to very good advantage yet – I was *gauche* and out of it with Tanit the Island God, heavy and head-on. Were I to be greeted with affection by Baby Boo the snake-thin Inca she'd see I could come in at an angle, be light on my feet and easy.

49

'Why? Why should I want to meet Baby Boo? It's you I've come to see.'

I frown. She's come to see whoever I say she's come to see. I'm back in control – for a moment I'd forgotten why she's here.

'*Please*. Please let's go home.'

She means it, I think. She's come down too. She seems to have shrunk; her face is smaller and older, and the light in her eyes has gone out. I relent, but grudgingly. Back at the flat, perhaps, I'll be able to make her play her part correctly again, persuade her to take another hit of whatever it is that gives her courage. We walk home in silence, confused, embarrassed, as if something's been mistimed, as if we'd tried to hit a six but instead had fallen over, sitting down with a bump, hitting the stumps and losing our hats.

Back at the flat I do my best; I turn the lights down, put the music on (Bruce Springsteen – 'I'm on Fire'), pull my stomach in and roll the left hip fractionally, like Barry John wrong-footing a foaming Irish forward, and, in time with Bruce, point a languid index-finger in the air. But she's lost interest, she wants to go straight to bed, seems, obscurely, to be blaming *me* for something. All I need now is for Alison to phone – and she does, miraculously on cue as usual.

'I've been phoning all evening. Where were you?'

Out.

'What?'

I said I was out.

'Where?'

Jesus. Having dinner with Amberson the mad American.

'What? I still can't hear you. You sound odd. Why are you talking oddly? You sound cross.'

I'm not cross. I said I was having dinner with Galbraith the mad Australian.

'You don't like him.'

Christ, I know I don't like him but I was having dinner with him nonetheless. Is that okay? All right for cling-wrap, are we?

'What?'

Doesn't matter. How are the cats?

'*I* want a cat. Why can't *we* have a cat?'

50

I shush my Princess, wag my head towards the bedroom. She leaves, pouting deceitfully, simulating crossness.

I manage to get Alison off the line at last, but only after she's told me about her new carpet that isn't meant to show the dirt but does. And that the central heating isn't working and that it might be *cheaper in the long run* to get a new system. And that the VAT man called. So I snarled at her a bit, and now I feel bad, she's made me feel a little guilty. I go into the bedroom, where my Princess is pretending to be asleep. That's absurd — but if it's how she wants it, that's okay with me. I turn the light out and get into bed, at a distance, with my back towards her. After a while she moves across.

'I'm sorry. I didn't like her phoning. I know that's unreasonable, but I didn't like it. I'll get it right tomorrow, I promise. I know this isn't how you want it, but tomorrow I'll be disgraceful. I'll dance on tables for you, anything you want. Do you like sleepy sex? Have you ever taken ludes? They're the greatest, I tell you. In Florida I was at this party, okay? There were drugs everywhere. Servants were handing them round on silver trays — pot, coke, ludes, anything you wanted. You just dipped in, helped yourself. Mark — that's my husband — was making out as usual, and I was bored, so I went into a bedroom with this girl, just to get away from it all, just to talk. We were sitting on the bed chatting and then this enormous man came in. He was a footballer, quite a famous one, with the Miami Dolphins. He was immense, the biggest man I'd ever seen. He had to come through the door sideways. We talked and talked. After a while he asked me if I'd like a pill. I know now that it was a lude, okay? After a while, I don't know how long, I began to feel drowsy, I wasn't asleep, but I couldn't move. It wasn't scary, it was nice, like when you come round after an operation and you feel very happy, but not in control. Like taking a mandy, but much stronger, much nicer. Then I felt myself being undressed. I couldn't move, I could hardly keep my eyes open, and I didn't know who was in the room, whether the other girl had left or what. I didn't know who had undressed me. I didn't care. I wasn't even bothered about my husband Mark, where he was, whether he might come in. Someone was kissing me all over. My breasts, my tummy, my thighs, between

51

my legs. It was the most fantastic sensation ever. I didn't care who was doing it, I didn't care who came in, I didn't care about anything just so long as whoever it was didn't stop. I was lying there in ecstasy with my eyes closed and I said: 'Is that you, Mark? It *was* him, it had been him all the time. Wasn't that awful? He beat me up, of course. I've still got the scar. He was always beating me up. He beat me up on our wedding day. He was a bit cuckoo, I think. You could be violent. You'll hit me one day. You'll see.'

I'm astonished. One thing I'm not is violent – except once with Mrs Mouse in self-defence. She hit me from behind with a salad bowl after I'd found her in bed with Fat Antoinette.

I'm not violent.

'Yes you are. I saw it in the restaurant when I said I hadn't had a proper education and you said I shouldn't tell everyone, they'd never guess. That was violent. You went quite cold. Really – you'll beat me up one day, I promise you. I know this isn't how you want it, but it is my first night. Perhaps tomorrow we'll get some ludes. I haven't done too badly, have I?'

On the whole she's done quite well. She's quite amusing, perceptive, even, from time to time, in a blundering, purely fortuitous way, of course. I've had glimpses, I think, of the real her, or the real her on drugs – which, to avoid philosophical tangles, we'll say is the same thing – and this is most unusual. She does have a slight tendency to over-act – pretending to mind Alison's phone call was seriously over-doing it – but this is because she's a cat. Cats act so badly you can't believe they think they'll get away with it. They couldn't act worse if they'd been to RADA. I must watch out. Cats are criminals and hypocrites. You can't win with cats. They have the total confidence that comes from not caring. No wonder I can't impress her with my anecdotes. You can't impress cats. You can talk to them, pull funny faces, but they just stare at you with horrified contempt. They know that they're attractive and that in the short run that's all that counts. I tell her that she's done quite well.

Were you acting?

'No more than you when you write, I don't suppose. It's what I do, okay? Just a way of getting attention, right?'

That's quite kind, kinder than Silly Serena would have been.

Silly Serena would have responded with some stupefying crudity: 'You want a pat on the head? Sit under a cow'. Something gross like that.

'Did I give you my morning order? Tea with lots of sugar. Four lumps in mine and two in Ted's. Sleep well, darling.'

I'd prefer her not to call me 'darling'. It makes me think she's going to take me to the cleaners.

I wake up early, feeling cheerful. I still have my self-respect, which is most unusual in these circumstances. Normally it would be over by now; there'd be six more days to go with nothing more to say, nothing more to do but count the cost. I'd glare at the strange, deceitful body in the bed, blame it for my diminished feeling, for this unnecessary lesson in the fact that you can't buy reassurance. But I don't feel like this about my Princess. She's fast asleep, clutching Ted, one little bunched fist beside her head. She looks about six years old, vulnerable and trusting. I feel a little rush of something like affection.

I dress quietly, pick up the polaroids, glance at them briefly, feel a little kick of something like desire – this is unusual too – and bounce across the Vara de Rey for breakfast at the Montesol. Here I'm joined by Mr Gabriel, the Yugoslav housepainter, still out here after fifteen years, the silly sod, still doing his best. I tell myself that I mustn't boast, that I must on no account flash the polaroids. I feel, most unusually, that that would be a betrayal of some sort. I feel oddly protective towards that sleeping body in the bed.

God what a night! I'm exhausted. Here, look at these. Mad little thing. Mafia.

Mr Gabriel glances briefly at the photographs, and pulls a disapproving face. Poor Alison, he says. Then he calls me a silly old fool. That's quite unnecessary. I don't need that. He resents me, of course, he's resented me for fifteen years – ever since I helped him to survive that dreadful winter out here, when Mrs Mouse dropped out of the sky with paints for him and sausages for me. People like him, people with no background, always resent it if you try to help them; they never forgive you. Indeed, in their uncivilised way, they think less of you. It's a moral

53

coarseness for which you can't really blame them, I suppose. My Princess would be like this. She'd never forgive me were I to help her, help her to make something tolerable of her life. I must remember this.

The telephone's ringing when I get back to the flat. It's Mr Wiseman, my solicitor, and he's got a Monday morning bombshell. The court case with Schultz, the fool who's suing me for breach of copyright, has suddenly been put down for hearing next week! Mr Wiseman says that I must return immediately to London for discussion with counsel. This is utterly fantastic. Nothing happens for a year – at mountainous expense – and suddenly we're given a week's notice to appear in court. At this point I would once have made a facetious joke as follows: faced with a serious decision, with having to choose, for instance, between a course of action profoundly affecting my whole life – between signing an important contract, say, and dallying with a tart in the sun – I'd make the right decision. I'd continue to dally in the sun. I don't make jokes like that any more. I've learnt my craft. Besides, this is a serious situation, far too serious for jokes. I tell Mr Wiseman that I will of course do the right thing. He sounds relieved. Stuff the court case, I say; I'm staying on in Ibiza, and he must get the hearing postponed. Mr Wiseman continues to speak in a level, legal tone, but I can tell he thinks I'm crackers. It would be very difficult, he says, to get the case postponed, if not impossible. Perhaps, he suggests, I haven't grasped the seriousness of the matter. I have a vice-like grasp of it, I say, but I'm not coming back to London yet, and that's that. He must say that I am in the south Atlantic, or dead, or up a mountain. Those are my instructions. That would be impossible, he says. He must settle then, I say, give Schultz anything he wants, and more. Mr Wiseman, with the pained forebearance of someone addressing the village idiot, points out that it is I who have refused to settle from the start, against his, and everyone else's, best advice. That's right, I say. But the situation has now changed. Either he must get the hearing postponed, or he must settle on any terms he can. He says he'll try.

The conversation has woken up my Princess. She calls out from the bedroom and I go in to see her. She smiles happily and

54

reaches up with her little arms. Then, acting as badly as a cat, she pouts and buries her head in the pillow, clutching Ted.

'Who was that on the phone? I hope it wasn't *her*. Ted says it was *her*.'

I explain that it was my lawyer in London. I tell her about the case, emphasise its seriousness.

They want me back in London immediately. But I put it off for you, Princess. I said stuff it. I said I wouldn't come back, that I'd rather stay out here with you.

She doesn't seem to take this in. She doesn't seem impressed that I have just put her before my credibility as a writer, that I'd rather be dubbed a breacher of another man's copyright than cut short my time with her. She frowns and looks away. I realise I've made a serious mistake. I've loaded her with a responsibility she doesn't want. This is playtime merely.

'Is it a nice day? Why aren't we on the beach? Where's my tea?'

I make her her tea, and bring a cup for Ted as well. This small touch delights her. She squirms with happiness. It was no great accomplishment on my part, really, but I feel oddly pleased.

Which beach shall we go to, then? Family or fashionable, secluded or fun? Salinas, which is Ponce Corner by the sea, or Cala Boix, where nice people take their children?

'Where do you go with *her*?'

Family, usually. Cala Boix.

'I want to go there. Cala Boix.'

I'm not having that. I won't be unfaithful to Alison in the matter of beaches. We'll go to Salinas, I say.

She's up and ready in no time, which again is most unusual. As a rule they take forever, potter, complain – why can't they sleep a little longer, what's the rush? – try things on, insist on shopping for a new bikini, for more menacing shades. They always want more menacing shades.

We drive to Salinas, where normally I'd feel out of it and old, but with her I fit in, I'm welcome even at the Malibu, the fashionable beach bar where the in-set lounge from lunchtime onwards having posed the night away at Ku. I spread her on the beach, stake her out and, from the safety of the Malibu, monitor her impact, measure the credit that accrues to me for being with her, see whether the predators prowl and sniff. They do – copper-toned men in leather thongs stroll boastfully back and forth in front of her, pause, take a look, pose and flex invitingly – but she shows no interest. Indeed she doesn't seem to be enjoying their attentions; she keeps looking up towards the Malibu, beckoning me to join her. Eventually she's had enough; she comes running up the beach towards me. She's bored, she says, she wants to play dolphins. Will I play dolphins with her? She has decided, she says, to chuck it all up and open a dolphin farm in Florida.

'You'd be welcome. You can come too.'

She's really behaving very badly, as if I'd taken her to a family beach. Next she'll want to hire a rubber duck, or – which would be as bad – a pedalo. On Salinas one simply doesn't play with pedaloes. Worst of all, when Tanit the Island God arrives at the Malibu as fresh as paint to take his morning breakfast – boiled eggs and soldiers, each cooked for precisely three minutes and forty-two seconds, and opened up with the rapt deliberation of a man defusing a bomb – she ignores him. When he calls out to her, reminds her of their date to dance again tonight, she shows no interest. And when he offers to buy her one of those revealing new bikini bottoms at the Malibu's boutique – in two separate parts, each no bigger than a tangerine segment – she's quite off-hand. Instead, to my horror and confusion, she asks him to play dolphins with her – and he agrees! When she at last returns, laughing and happy, I rebuke her, point out that no one has ever played dolphins on Salinas before, least of all with Tanit the Island God.

'Oh phooey. Let's go for a walk.'

She's entirely different to how she was last night; you'd think we were together, not as part of a deal, but because we knew and liked each other. I'll have to put a stop to this. She's quiet and thoughtful as we walk along the beach, she takes my arm. From time to time she stops to collect things – quite unremarkable pebbles for the most part. Mrs Mouse used to do this. It's some desire, I think, to carry the present forward in the jumble of their lives. Mrs Mouse brought back from our honeymoon a collection of shells and stuff which she meant to

56

do things with – though God knows what. I found them years later in a tin, years after we'd separated, and I thought it awfully sad.

When we come to an empty part of the beach, my Princess asks me to take some photographs. She arranges herself in sort of model poses. She's quite good, actually, and we laugh a lot.

'When we get back to London I think I'll have some pictures taken, get a proper set of photographs together, get some work, perhaps.'

Why do they never realise when it's too late? Why do they think a new set of photographs will make everything all right? She's turned out to be no cleverer than the others, and I find I'm quite relieved. I'd had a confusing feeling that she might be, that she had some sense of irony about herself – there'd been small signs – but she hasn't; she's still nailed to a fantasy of being under thirty, when everything's still possible, when you can still be welcome merely for your looks. She's okay for the moment, she's still got another five years, I'd say, before an ambitious man would have to trade her up, before that awful moment when she'll know she's had it, that she can't necessarily get her revenge on those better educated than herself by using or rejecting them. Her deluded state is good for me. She'll be more fun if she's still got hopes. You can take advantage of people who've still got hopes, promise them things, make them think it can all still happen. She thinks she can still be a model. Girls who think they can still be models will do almost anything, they'll do things which will give them the horrors in the morning.

We sit down and talk. I tell her that if she still wants to be a model I can help her. It's a world I know a bit about, I say, I used to be an agent, I'm not unknown among the right people, I'm on wine bar terms with the deputy editor of *Ritz*. I tell her about my time as a model agent.

Male models are twice as difficult as girls, you know. They're far more vain.

'Really? How extraordinary.'

Yes. And not true either. It's the sort of thing one says, I don't know why.

I tell her that she's got it, that she can still make it to the top.

She listens seriously, gazes up at me with enormous, trusting eyes. You can say what you like to these girls – however sharp, they lose their marbles all at once if you tell them that they've got it, that they can still make it to the top. I'm not being unkind – merely polite. And we're on a footing now – now that I've discovered that she's as deceived as all the others. I might even want to see her again in London. You can have fun in London with girls who still want to be models. You can, for instance, pull the Pratt The Playwright trick. It's a bit naughty, I suppose, but I doubt if anyone gets really hurt – except, on one occasion, Pratt himself, I'm glad to say. He's a disgusting old fool, who has recently added 'professional photographer' to his repertoire of bullshit occupations. The caper goes like this: you take some deluded, unsuspecting girl round to his agent's revolting flat – black leather furniture, a poker den, signed photographs of Michael Caine – having told her that Pratt, with his connections, can really help her, get her an Equity card, perhaps. With the help of Martinique The Mad Make-up Artist – as black as your hat with a laugh like a drain – Pratt The Playwright then takes lewd photographs of the silly girl, as often as not pinned to the bed by this mad black girl pretending to be a make-up artist. As a rule there's no film in the camera: an added detail which has always puzzled me. Is Pratt The Playwright merely mean, or is he sick? Does he get some extra, perverted kick out of this silly girl with high hopes *thinking* she's being photographed? What a truly disgusting old man he is. Silly Serena fell for the Pratt The Playwright caper. I took her over to his agent's nasty flat and she absent-mindedly heaved around on the bed under Martinique The Mad Make-up Artist while Pratt The Playwright took photographs with no film in the camera. He got his come-uppance once, I'm glad to say. He'd met this funny little dancer who was desperate for an Equity card. He said he could help her, but she must be nice to important people. He asked me round, introduced us, said I was a bigwig. After an awkward drink or two, he suggested that she and I should go up to the bedroom. She was quite sweet, but I was baffled, couldn't understand his game. We sat on the bed and I took it upon myself to warn her against him. He was a ghastly old fool, I said, and she should

58

have nothing to do with him. He was a pervert and a bull-shitter, I said, a real sicko. I gave her my telephone number. Trust me, I said. The next day she rang me up and told me what had happened later. Pratt The Playwright had had a tape-recorder under the bed. After I'd left he poured himself a whisky, put Frank Sinatra on the sound-system, I don't doubt, took his trousers off, sat back and played the tape. This will be good, he thought. But instead of grunts and groans and the sound of ancient heavings – listening to these must be another perverted kick of his, I take it – all he got was his friend calling him a sicko. He's never said anything to me, so I imagine the dirty old weirdo liked it.

'This is really nice. Today will be one of those days we'll look back on and think, that was a happy day.'

She's inspects the pebbles she's collected with a wistful smile, and hands one to me.

'Will you keep this to remind you? Will you keep it forever?'

She's looking lovely, the soft, satiny planes of her delinquent body – the colour of the palest *cafe con leche* – straining against her tiny bikini in vivid pink. My stomach tightens. When I get back to London I'll pull the Pratt The Playwright caper on her, have Martinique The Mad Make-up Artist fall on top of her. I might even pay for there to be a film in the camera. A photograph of my Princess under Martinique The Mad Make-up Artist would be one for the wallet and no mistake. I mention the black girl in New York, the one she and her husband tried to pick up.

'Please don't talk about that. Don't spoil everything.'

You didn't mind talking about it last night.

'I was high.'

What on?

'I had a little coke. It's gone now.'

That's a bummer, but I could get her some more. We're in the right place. Everyone on Salinas sells coke, even the ten-year-old boy who takes the money for the mattresses, and his mother, and his grand-mother. I have a feeling that she's only fun on coke, and – though I got the horrors at the time – I have a slight, restless craving for that strange rush I got at the Tierra, which I connect, in some odd way, with *her* being high.

59

We could buy some here.

'I don't need that. I'm fine, honest. I'm really happy. Is that okay? Don't you expect me to be happy?'

Not necessarily. I expect her to be with me. Something's going wrong here; we're pulling in opposite directions. She seems to have forgotten why she's here; she's fallen completely out of character. I'll have to pedal faster or we'll start to go round and round in circles like Alison and I did when, just two days ago, on her last day on the beach, she made me take her out on a fucking pedalo. I'd been mortified, and this had made her laugh so much she couldn't pedal. Round and round we'd gone in circles just like sodding tourists. This is fucking silly, I'd said, and I'd abandoned her, hopping off and making for the shore. And then she'd nearly cried, of course, gone on about it being our last day. I'll have to get my Princess some coke before tonight. If she doesn't do something disgraceful soon she'll start to bore me.

*

Tell me more about your husband.

'What about him? I'll need another if we're going to talk about my husband.'

How many have you got left?

'Two, I'd say. Plus what's in the pipe. Can I have one now?'

If you tell me about your husband.

'Okay. Just a minute. How are my eyes now?'

Huge. Astonishing.

'Right. What do you want to know?'

He got into trouble in Bogota. You told me some story about flying out to him with money.

'Christ – I don't want to think about that. That'll bring me right down. You're not going to use that, are you? You can't use that.'

I'm not going to. It's just background for me. So I can understand you better.

'Promise? Promise you won't use it?'

Promise.

'Okay. We were living in Florida. One day he told me about some big drug deal in Bogota. He said he could get in on it for £10,000. It would set us up for life, he said. I had this nest-egg, which I hadn't told him about. He'd taken everything else. I gave it to him, every penny, all the money I had in the world.'

Were you happy about that?

'Of course I was. I loved him. He flew off to Bogota, saying he'd be back in a day or two. I didn't hear a thing for weeks. I went out of my mind with worry. I had no money, no friends. It was a nightmare. Then suddenly I heard from him. He rang up and said he was in some rat-infested Columbian jail. He needed another £10,000 to bribe his way out, he said. He said I had to get it, it didn't matter how. He said that if I loved him I'd go on the streets to get it.'

That's nice. What did you think of that?

61

'I believed him. I even went down to the red-light district, worked out how much I could make. I decided it would take too long. Then I had a brain-wave. My husband had this business associate who'd always fancied me, okay? I went to see him and fucked him in his office. It was gross. But I was sort of triumphant. Then I said I needed £10,000 urgently. He gave it to me, of course.'

Why?

'He knew it was blackmail. He knew that if he didn't give it to me I'd tell my husband that he'd fucked me. He was terrified of my husband. He knew my husband would kill him. He gave me the money and I flew to Bogota. I was so happy on the plane. I'd never been so happy in my life. I thought, this is perfect – if I get him out of prison I'll never be unhappy again. It was a Sunday ...'

What's the matter?

'Can I have another? I really need another.'

Soon. Why Sunday? Did that make a difference?

'It made it better. Sundays were special. We used to make a thing of Sundays. He was nice to me on Sundays. We used to stay at home, cook a joint – like proper people, like a family. I'd really liked Sundays, and I'd thought there weren't going to be any more. Is that silly?'

No. It's sweet.

'God I was happy on the aeroplane. When we got to Bogota I went to the prison and said who I was, why I was there. They smiled and took me to see the Governor. He smiled too. This is going to be all right, I thought. The Governor took me to what were his private quarters, I suppose. A sort of apartment next to the prison. He took me into a bedroom. God, I thought, what's this? Then I saw my husband. He was in bed with this dreadful woman. He asked me for the money and I gave it to him ...'

What then?

'Can I have another? Please.'

Not yet. What happened then?

'He spat at me. He called me a whore and spat at me. I started to cry and the woman laughed. I was crying and she laughed at me. I just stood there saying: what shall I do, what shall I do? They were all laughing, and my husband said he didn't care — just so long as I got out of his sight.'

I'd like to kill him.

'He's not worth it, believe me. You won't use it, will you? Promise me you won't use it in the book?'

I promise.

(I will, of course. Honesty is everything, even when it hurts, and this little story perfectly illustrates, I think, the queasy combination of sentimentality and viciousness that is the very essence of girls like her.)

'Please can I have it now? Can I have the last one now?'

Of course.

'Let's stay in tonight. Let's play house. I could cook us something. Would that be good?'

I can think of nothing worse. She's not a cook. If I wanted a cook, I'd hire a man, they're always better. I'd hire Baby Boo, the snake-thin Inca. His spare-ribs are renowned throughout the Balearics.

'We could watch TV. Do you have TV? Can't we hire one? We could hire a video. I'd cook and then we'd watch a film on video. I only like black and white films by the way.'

I'm not surprised. She'd like *The Maltese Falcon* and *Casablanca* and God knows what with 'Betty' Bacall. Why do uneducated girls share this disgusting taste with *cineastes*?

'Did you see *Saturday Night And Sunday Morning*? That was a classic when it came out. Please let's stay in.'

I'll put a stop to this at once. She did well last night, she didn't let me down on tour, but I won't stay in. I'll let her off the full tour, leave out the short skirt and little boots; I'll let her wear a dress tonight and I'll take her somewhere proper. I'll take her to dinner in Santa Eulalia, which is less louche than Ibiza Town, less louche than Brighton, come to that. It's about as louche as Eastbourne, inhabited for the most part by elderly English arseholes who once acted or drew pictures but now drink gin and tonic in Sandy's Bar and wear blue blazers and lie to one another. In Santa Eulalia they have restaurants with waiters pretending to be French, balancing plates, producing filth from under wraps like conjurors and, with a silly flourish, suddenly setting fire to peculiar messes on silver dishes. She'll like all that. I understand women. Go to some trouble, take them to a disgusting restaurant, spend money on them – that's what reassures them. They don't really like all that crap, of course, any more than men do; they think they like it because it's all so obviously awful – it's the effort, they like, and the expense. I discovered this when I was restaurant critic on the

Tatler. Anyone would eat with me. Baroness Andrea von Stumm would have eaten with me had she been guaranteed that the meal would be disgusting enough. I never mentioned the restaurants during my stint, of course; I reviewed books instead. The restaurants all withdrew their advertising, but Tina was very loyal, or so I thought. This is hilarious, she'd say, thank you so much – but she hadn't read it. Shall I tell my Princess this? No, I can't be bothered. She won't have heard of Tina Brown and I'm sick of my anecdotes hitting fog.

I tell her instead that I'm going to take her out to dinner at a smart restaurant in Santa Eulalia. I was right – the suggestion goes down really well. She disappears for an hour at least and then emerges looking lovely in a dress that could have come from Harvey Nichols, and with an entirely new head to go with it. I hardly recognise her. Looking like this you could take her almost anywhere, alas – which is what I do. I take her to Sa Punta, which is quite the foulest, most expensive restaurant on the island – and she adores it. I can tell she adores it by the way she sits bolt upright throughout the meal with an air of studied concentration as if on second serve, talking of matters that might even bore the Yorks. Nor do I let her down. I won't discuss light opera or interior design or house prices in the south east, but I am gallant. I pay attention, order wine, refer to nothing that might be of interest to an educated person. Just this once I'll let her get away with it; for one night I'll let her think that she could live like this forever, that she's a serious person with a past to be proud of. Tomorrow I'll get her drugs.

Afterwards she's sweetly grateful; she's in a peculiar dreamy mood, relaxed and massaged from having all that money spent on her. I park the car in the little square behind the flat, but she doesn't want to get out; she wants to sit in the car and talk, gaze at the moon and whatnot in the sky.

'Thank you. That was nice. That's what I like, you know.'

It isn't really what she likes, and if it is – well, it's far too late, thank God. She missed that particular bus ten years ago at least. By tomorrow she'll have forgotten all about it. She was just playing a part to go with the Harvey Nichols dress. Women have no substance, they behave according to the way they're dressed. I once took Dawn Upstairs to dinner with the Tynans.

They were all there: Martin Amis, Angela Huth, Jonathan Miller, Claire Tomalin, the Mortimers etc. Dawn Upstairs had overdressed and, as a consequence, she quite forgot why she was there – to tell these serious people what it's like to be a tart. She behaved most oddly, told Martin Amis that his journalism lacked the moral dimension of his fiction, and then criticised his fiction too, told him that he intruded into his own prose, that his syntax was so dazzling that it interfered with the narrative line, not that there was one. I was immensely embarrassed, of course, and her *gaffe* was made no better by the fact that the table politely argued her accusations for an hour, the matter being settled finally by five votes to three in Dawn Upstairs's favour, Amis and myself abstaining.

'I'm not permissive, you know. There've only been five – apart from the ones who don't count, of course. There was my first husband, and my male model – he was gay – and Andy the barman, and my millionaire, and my second husband. My first husband was a villain too. I met him when I was fifteen. I was still at school. He made me pregnant, so we got married. We lived with his parents. Then I had a daughter. She died when she was four months old. My husband was in prison. They let him out for the funeral. After the service he raped me. I had a nervous breakdown. I was on pills for months. That's how it all started.'

Some nightmare seems to be returning; she's staring out of the car window, looking forlorn and troubled. I don't know why she's telling me this, but I feel quite tender. I take her hand.

Don't be unhappy, Princess. Trust me.

'I can't. You're a writer.'

She gives a little shudder of fear, as if writers have some mysterious power to hurt. Being illiterate, she probably imagines all manner of terrible betrayals taking place between the covers of a book.

What's wrong with that?

'Writers can *murder*. You could kill me off – and no one would ever know. You could write a book and say that I was dead. I could run around saying, no – look, I'm alive, I'm okay, that's not what happened at all. But I couldn't tell everyone.

Eventually it might be the only thing people knew about me. It's spooky, I tell you.'

I'd never do that. Why would I want to kill you off?

'Revenge.'

For what?

'Making your dream come true.'

She is weird, she's the spooky one, if you ask me. Presumptuous too – though I'm too polite to tell her this, of course.

Why are you so sure you'll do that?

'I can tell. You're bored. You've been bored ever since you saw those women prowling round a stage with fruit on their heads. It's all you're interested in, but I don't think it's ever worked. If you find someone who makes it work, you'll be hooked, I tell you.'

She's crackers.

'I had this friend in America, okay? She was a junkie, basing coke. I'll tell you what that is when I know you better. She was out of her head. She never went to bed – not to sleep, at least. She'd stay up for days at a time and then fall into a sort of coma. That's how you can tell if someone's free-basing. They fall into these very deep sleeps that can last for forty-eight hours or more – plus they lose a lot of weight. It makes you very randy too – you'll fuck anyone.'

We'll have to free-base, that's for sure. I'll let her finish her story and then I'll ask her where we can free-base – whatever that is.

'She knew she was very sick, that she had to go into a clinic. Her boyfriend was a writer. He encouraged her to free-base, even though he knew how ill she was.'

What a shit.

'Yeah really. He supplied her with coke and got her to tell him her story. She'd had quite a life, fucked a lot of well-known people – all the Kennedys, Martin Luther King, Sam Giancana, the Shah of Iran – the usual crowd. "Trust me", her boyfriend said, "the book will save you. Tell me your story and then I'll put you in a clinic.' He gave her more and more drugs, until she'd told him everything. She believed him. She was really excited. She thought the book was going to be hers, that he was just ghosting it for her, that people would think she was a writer. She thought it would justify everything, give her some sort of identity at last. Ha! She'd never read a book in her life and she thought she was going to be a writer! Gross, eh?'

I've come across this sort of thing before; I've met these mad girls who think that if they reveal enough about their messy, fucked-up lives people will be interested. They imagine that a kind of nervous candour – which is more like flashing, really – is all that's needed. I bridle on behalf of serious writers everywhere.

'She trusted him completely. She was so excited. She got herself together, bought new clothes, had her teeth capped. She thought she was going to be on television! Then the book came out. He'd turned her into a clown. She didn't realise this until she was interviewed on a radio show. She hadn't even read the book. Half-way through the interview she suddenly realised that she was being treated as a freak. Everyone was laughing at her. Her boyfriend made a lot of money.'

What happened to her?

'She went a bit mad. It was his revenge, I guess.'

Revenge for what?

'It was the only way he could get power over her – by betraying her. She'd given him a hard time. You can't control junkies. They don't care, they have no feelings. They can become a drug themselves. They have a lot of courage, and you can catch this courage off them, kind of use it yourself. When they get high, you can get high too, get the same rush – the same feeling of power and courage. It sounds silly, but it's true – I know. You can get very hung up on a junkie, let me tell you. They can become the drug of your choice – and the joke is, junkies can be cured but the people who get hooked on them can't.'

This is gibberish, of course, but something like it must have happened to her, I think; she must be talking about her experience with her second husband. She's probably still in love with him and this explanation comforts her.

'So that's what he did. He got his revenge by controlling her on paper. He killed her off, wrote a book saying she was dead. In fact she got herself into a clinic. They cured her – after a fashion. Now she's a vegetable, more or less. Never put me in a clinic. They play with your brain, I tell you. That's the end. You lose everything. I'd like to trust you, I really would, but you're educated like him. Promise me you'll never put me in a clinic – or say that I'm dead.'

What is she talking about? What's brought this on, what's troubled her so profoundly? She is weird. I decide she needs reassurance, a show of affection even. I'll say something simple, without a spin on it, like a real person talking to another real person. I take her hand, look at her earnestly.

Trust me, Princess. I'll look after you.

She smiles. I've said the right thing. She looks very beautiful and sad. This won't do at all. Tomorrow I'll have to get her drugs.

'Don't fall in love with me. I'll be your Princess for as long as you want, but don't fall in love with me.'

Well really! I want to laugh. The effrontery of these imitation women, the sheer fucking confidence, bucketing round the world warning their betters not to fall in love with them! How can they think that that's what they're for? People must have done, I suppose – but who? Barmen, criminals, stuntmen – not serious people. How, anyway, could you fall in love with someone you'd already had – well, not 'had' exactly, more 'been to' like a fashionable restaurant? And would the owner of a restaurant, after a few visits, come to your table and warn you off, tell you that you were becoming emotionally involved? I should say: why? What's wrong with you? You're not so bad. I would, but I'm speechless. I stare at her aghast. My mouth hangs open, I dare say.

'Now you're furious! The cheek of the little tart, you're thinking. It's just that I don't want to hurt you. I never want to hurt you, I do know that.'

That's rather sweet of her, if a trifle patronising. As it happens I don't mind being hurt at all, though she's crackers to think she ever could. Being hurt gives you a pleasant, mournful glow, as I recall, causing you to listen to the words of pop songs and eat in self-service restaurants on your own, humming sadly to yourself. It's hard to remember the symptoms exactly because I haven't been hurt since 1963 when Jacqui the Dancer went off suddenly with a musical comedy tenor. It lasted for about three days, I think – the mournful feeling, that is. I don't know how long the liason with the tenor lasted. She ended up with Oliver Reed, I do know that. Funny sort of life. Anyway, it was very pleasant, that mournful feeling, and I'd been in love with Jacqui the Dancer, for heaven's sake, left my wife on her uppers, abandoned my boy, moved into the Basil Street Hotel, where they have a bible by the bedside. I've never been in love since, and certainly have no plans in that direction. I love Alison. Love's the thing – everything understood, everything forgiven. Alison and I have no reason to do one another harm.

'I wasn't always like this. My husband made me like this. He was an animal. I don't want to talk about it, okay?'

Okay.

'All right, I'll tell you. He was charming. He could have charmed anyone. He could have charmed you, I tell you. I met him in Florida. He was a villain – drugs mainly. It was exciting, I liked the excitement. He carried a gun. He was very violent, I suppose. I'm turned on by power. I think you should know that.'

I imagined she might be. They have such terrible taste, these girls – psychopaths in Cecil Gee suits, that's what they like. How can I compete with that? I feel a little tired, but I must try to impress her. I rehearse power stories in my mind while she babbles on about her husband. Would she believe I knew the Krays? I met them once. I was in Mr Verdi's Grey Topper night club, having a drink with Birmingham Paul and his bodyguard, Winston, who carried a gun and spoke in a sinister bronchial whisper, the result of a gangland wound across his wind-pipe. Suddenly a fight broke out on the dance-floor. It seemed to be in slow-motion, as in a comic western. Large men in suits a size too small fisted pillars, sailed headfirst into pyramids of bottles, Mr Verdi appealed for order, had his hat knocked off, the band went on playing. It was some time before I realised it was real. Winston tipped us off. 'It's the twins,' he croaked, 'we'd better get out.' I called for the bill, paid with Barclaycard, made for the exit. Then I realised that I'd left my Barclaycard behind. I was nothing without my Barclaycard. I had plans to mount a musical with my Barclaycard, starring Warren Mitchell as the

Pope, I think. There was nothing for it but to go back to our table, even though I'd be duffed up, and maybe killed. I threaded my way back through the scrum. Ronnie was sitting at our table, holding my Barclaycard. That's mine I said. An odd thing to do, but such was the need for credit when mounting musicals. Ronnie handed it to me, smiling like a lizard. The next day the smallest woman I'd ever seen outside a circus tent pitched up at my office and repossessed it on behalf of Barclays. She had a mad look in her eyes. Barclays know what they're doing. Violence is in the eyes, in the head. This mad little woman wasn't leaving without my Barclaycard. This anecdote is a little thin, I realise, and I'll have to convey power by other means – the power of the intellect, perhaps. I raise a scornful eyebrow, look superior, mysteriously powerful in the moonlight.

My Princess doesn't seem to notice. She's telling some long and complicated story about her husband being arrested in Bogota or some such place and her taking him money and people spitting at her and about how these events were made much worse for some obscure reason by the fact that they all took place on a Sunday, but I'm not really listening because I'm trying to think of something I wanted to say when she first mentioned the rackety life she'd led with her dreadful husband. Something due to Neitzsche, I rather fancy, but the bloody thing won't come to mind.

'I was distraught. I was crying, and they were all laughing at me – my husband and his awful tart and the prison governor. My husband told me to get out. I flew back to Florida. I had nothing now. Nothing at all. At last I scraped together enough money to get back to England. I arrived in London with just ten pounds. I was so ashamed, I didn't ring anyone. Everyone had warned me against him. One evening I tried to kill myself. It was a Sunday. I was wandering down the street in a daze and I saw this lorry coming. I stepped off the pavement, but someone pulled me back. The shock made me pull myself together. But I've become very hard. I'll never be hurt again, that's for sure. I still don't like Sundays, though. I was all right yesterday because I was with you, but normally I don't like Sundays. Apart from that I'm pretty tough.'

She doesn't look very tough. She's hunched up, clasping her

little hands, her huge eyes aghast with remembered hurt. I must tell her a story to cheer her up, one involving my own participation in the exciting world of drugs, perhaps, one that will impress her as well as cheer her up. My own life hasn't been entirely hum-drum, after all – I've done this and that. Which anecdote shall it be, then? How the Police Commissioner's son-in-law and I became dealers in cannabis, buying Spade Bill's business when he went to Morocco to discover who he really was? How we paid him £200 for the goodwill, for a list of his clients and suppliers, how we took it in turns to ring them up – pop stars, lawyers, the drama critic of a national newspaper, a lecturer at the London School of Economics etc – and say, in our educated, fluting voices: 'Hullo there! I'm your new dealer.' They all had the horrors, of course, banged the phone down, swallowed their brains. I gave up at that point, but Richard persevered, became quite big in the Mayfair area. He even continued to deal when he married the Police Commissioner's daughter – as good a cover as any, I suppose. Or shall it be the Major's abortive drug-run to Stockholm? That's the one which will impress my Princess, that's the one I'll tell her.

Here's one. After *Both The Ladies And The Gentlemen* came out – that's a book I wrote – I got a letter from some fellow claiming to be an Old Wykehamist too and a friend, what's more, of my sister Bobo. He was a recently retired Guards Officer, he said, married to a Berkshire JP, and now he'd like to be a ponce like me. Could I help? I met him for lunch, but I had to tell him that there was no hope. He was too fat, I said, and too stupid. What about drugs, he asked, couldn't he store them in his locker at the Guards Club? I introduced him to Baby Boo the snake-thin Inca, who happened to be putting the finishing touches to some daft scheme to smuggle drugs from India to Sweden via London. He needed a respectable-looking type to get on the plane at Heathrow and carry the drugs through Swedish customs. After the introduction I thought no more about the matter, and was quite surprised a week or so later when my front-door came down in the middle of *The Streets of San Francisco* and the flat was full of Customs officers and members of the Serious Crime Squad. The caper had gone

72

fatuously wrong, of course. The police and customs had been on to it from the start, watching the progress of the drugs all the way from Delhi to London. They arrested Baby Boo and staked out Heathrow to see who met the plane from Delhi. When the Major pitched up at Heathrow, where he was meant to rendezvous with Baby Boo and collect his ticket to Stockholm, he was momentarily confounded by the latter's absence. Being an army officer, however, he decided to use his initiative. He went to the BA counter and had it announced all over the airport that a Major Scott-Dobbs was expecting to meet Mr Baby Boo the snake-thin Inca at the ticket counter. Announced his involvement over the PA system, do you see? Good, eh? The police can't believe their luck. They think they've got the lot now, but when they arrest the Major he puts his hands up and says that *I'm* Mr Big! Hence the bust at my place, synchronised, I may say, with one at the Major's house in Ascot, where his wife, the JP, who is watching Panorama at the time, has a cardiac arrest as her door comes down and shortly thereafter kicks the bucket. In the course of the search at my flat the police come across a scraping of cannabis. I'm arrested and as I'm being led away in handcuffs my first wife suddenly arrives – a formidable Sloane lady, built like a side of beef, tweeds, a parade-ground voice, silly name – Priscilla, or something of the sort – you know the type. 'I've come to see you about Charlie,' she bellows. Charlie's my son. 'I'm a little worried about him.' The police, thinking she might be another conspirator, pick her up, lift her clean off the ground – pearls, tweeds, sensible shoes – and toss her into the bedroom, where she falls off the bed, legs in the air. 'He needs a father's influence,' she shouts. 'Damn me I'm on my back here.' 'No doubt he does,' I say, 'but as you can see I'm being arrested. Can this wait till I get back?' 'All right,' she says, 'but don't be long. I haven't got all night.' There was the usual stuff down at the station – finger-prints, bail, mug-shots etc – and when I get back a couple of hours later my first wife's still there, shouting at a rather shaken Alison. 'Ah, there you are,' she says. 'Now, about Charlie. He definitely needs a father's influence. I've decided that he should come and live with you.' I got fined thirty quid and the Major got three years.

I pause. My Princess will be impressed.

'Hey! Would that make a great scene in a film or what?'

What? Me and the Major?

'Who?'

The Major.

'The Major? I've certainly never heard of him. No. Me flying to Bogota with the money and being so excited and my husband calling me a whore and spitting at me and that awful woman laughing. Oh God it was dreadful.'

The greatest argument for existence is to live in danger.

'Sorry?'

Neitzsche. I meant to say it earlier when you were telling me about your life with your husband, but I couldn't remember it. You *must* learn to love again – it's all there is. Trust me.

'Never say that. I feel quite safe with you, actually, but never say trust me.'

What we have here is a subjective morality, a sociopath's inability to imagine behaviour better than their own. She can't trust because she isn't trustworthy, and she assumes, in her moral ignorance, that this failing applies to everyone. In a relationship she'd display the random cruelty of a child dropping its best friend just for the hell of it. I know, because I was like this once. I had a best friend at Winchester called Andrew Gourlay. He had a round face and curly red hair. I suddenly thought it would be amusing to drop him. I rather enjoyed it. He was utterly bewildered, begged me to be friends still. That did revolt me. I've grown morally since then, of course, but I guess she hasn't. She'd hop off half-way through, deliver a king-punch for no apparent reason, leaving you ga-ga, reaching for your brain forever. There might be a short, inadequate letter. 'You don't *own* me and you never did.' Something gross like that. I've had enough, I'm tired and I want to go to bed, but she still wants to talk. I'll have to get her some coke or the week will be a write-off.

'The last man to say trust me gave me two hours notice to leave his flat. It was my millionaire. Because he'd said trust me I gave him everything. I didn't like him at all at first – that's the funny part. I thought he was gross. I was a bunny. He used to come to the club every night and offer me the world. I didn't want to know. In the end I had to leave the club – it was too embarrassing. But he followed me everywhere, offering me God knows what. This went on for weeks. He wasn't threatening or anything, so in the end I gave in slightly. I agreed to go to Greece with him for a week, but only if my best friend Candy came too as a sort of chaperone. It was okay, all very proper, and then one night I thought, what the hell, why not? Candy was out with a motor mechanic – she was always picking up motor mechanics, you know the type – and I was alone in our room at the hotel, feeling rather bored. Suddenly I thought it might be quite a turn-on to give myself to someone who wanted me so much. I decided to go to his room and sort of sacrifice myself to him. I dressed myself up in Candy's clothes ...'

Why?

'She's a stripper and she had all the gear with her – stockings, suspender-belt, all that kit. I crept along to his room and I was pretty excited now, I can tell you. He'd longed for me for months, okay, and now I was going to give myself to him. Not bad, eh? That can be quite a turn-on, I can tell you. I opened his door and stood there for a moment in the moonlight. I was looking really good, okay? Well, he sat up in bed, my millionaire, and put the light on. God Almighty – he's only in bed with my best friend Candy! He's as confused as hell, of course, but ...'

Aren't you?

'What?'

Embarrassed.

'Me? No. Why should I be embarrassed? I'm looking really good. *He's* embarrassed, as he bloody well should be, but Candy doesn't turn a hair, the little tart, she asks me to join in!'

Did you?

'Not likely!'

That's a bummer. She'd have joined in quick enough, from all she says, if they'd been free-basing, her millionaire and her best friend Candy. Tomorrow I'll have to find out more about this free-basing.

'I got rid of Candy – no problem – and stretched out on the bed next to my millionaire. I'm looking great, right? Well – he couldn't do it! He couldn't do it at all! Funny, eh? That was a challenge, I can tell you. For two months he couldn't do it. We tried and tried all over the world – in hotel rooms, in his Lear jet – but nothing.'

Why?

'He was too in love with me, wasn't he? By the time he *could* do it I was in love with him, of course. He was married. He installed me in his company flat in London and promised to leave his wife. Trust me, he said. I waited and waited. Then his wife found out about us. My best friend Candy tipped her off, I think. She tried to kill herself.'

Your best friend Candy?

'*No*. My millionaire's wife. He blamed me, of course. His secretary rang up and told me to get out of the flat within twenty-four hours. I'll never be hurt again, or listen to anyone who says trust me. I'd rather hurt someone than be hurt myself.'

Of course she would. If she's ever frightened someone half to death she won't have noticed, and if she has noticed she won't have given a stuff. And yet she's had a rough ride, the poor little thing – if she's to be believed, which she probably isn't. Raped by her first husband at her daughter's funeral, kicked out of a company flat by a money man with a Lear jet and manicured finger-nails, I wouldn't wonder, spat at by her second husband and dumped, once he'd got her money, in favour of a Columbian doxy with hairy legs, no doubt, and armpits like a jungle swamp, but with another nest-egg to be filched. God knows what her gay model and Andy the Barman did.

'Anyway, I have this problem. I don't like people I have good sex with. Love's with, sex is against – the two don't seem to go together. I can only do it with someone who frightens me a little. If I like someone I want to cuddle them. They're never the same people, the ones I want to fuck and the ones I want to cuddle. After a good fuck I want to turn away. I guess I'm like a man in that respect.'

I could say: no, not *all* men, merely the monkeys *you* like – but I can't be bothered. Her best chance of a relationship is with her teddy bear.

'I only want to sleep with people I love. But I don't want to

76

fuck them. The people I want to fuck and the people I want to
sleep with are never the same.'

She'll have given as good as she's got. And I know which I
want to be – no problem there. Tomorrow I'll have to look into
this free-basing business. Tanit, the Island God, will know
about free-basing; he'll carry the necessary equipment in his
cache-sexe, I wouldn't wonder. Tomorrow we'll go to Salinas
again and I'll take Tanit to one side, talk to him man to man:
about this free-basing thing, my old turkey. How do we do it,
what's the form?

'Say you like talking to me. Say this is the best part. Please.'

It isn't, but I say it is. It seems to matter to her, I don't know
why. Tomorrow we'll have to free-base or I'll become one of
those she wants to cuddle. And perhaps if she free-bases she'll
talk a little less about herself and listen to my anecdotes
instead. She pays no attention to my anecdotes at all.

Later, back at the flat, she suddenly says:

'Hey – what a great scene in a film, eh?'

What? You doing yourself up for your millionaire and
finding him in bed with your best friend Candy?

'*No*, not that. You and your sister Boo Boo's friend the
Major and your first wife turning up in her pearls and sensible
shoes to talk to you about your son Charlie just as the Serious
Crimes Squad are carting you away. Would that make a great
scene in a film or what?

'Why can't this be a film? If you loved me you'd be a film
producer. You would, you would. Ted says you would.'

Free-basing may not be enough.

Through no fault of mine, the next few days are utter
bummers. I'm cool and rather distant; I wear trousers and walk
from the waist, I click my fingers, look at her over the top of the
Guardian with an amused, lop-sided smile. She, on the other
hand, seems to have forgotten why she's here. She's managed
to establish – I don't know how – such a dead weight of moral
authority over me that I haven't the courage even to mention

drugs – without which she appears to be no fun. She's sweet and affectionate, she wants to prepare picnics and visit family beaches, play dolphins, stick close to me and talk, and in the evenings she wants to stay at home. Every time the phone rings she gets upset (or acts it), thinking it's Alison – which in fact it seldom is. It's usually my Mr Wiseman, who has managed, much to his own surprise, to get the court case with Schultz postponed until 23rd May. I must be back in London, Mr Wiseman says, by 16th May at the latest, for important conferences in chambers. Schultz has turned down our latest offer which comes as no surprise to Mr Wiseman, who stresses, each time he telephones, that we're the shortest odds to lose since Brian London, a fat little English heavyweight, was dumped on his arse by Mohammed Ali in 1968 – not that Mr Wiseman puts it quite like this, of course. This being so, there's nothing for it but to sell another clutch of toilet books, and I spend long hours on the beach – while my Princess plays dolphins on her own – considering the viability of literary long-firm frauds. What's to stop me selling toilet books – and the same toilet book at that, perhaps – to twenty different publishers? I wouldn't write them, of course, I'd merely trouser the money – at least £15,000 from each publisher at the going rate for toilet books – and bugger off in a false moustache, never to be heard of again. It's not such a bad idea, I think. I could raise £300,000 like this, if I've got the mathematics right, which I probably haven't. I could live in Ibiza for at least ten years on £300,000, including the jetting in from time to time of fat girls with legs. I decide to tell my Princess about my scheme.

I could sell as many as twenty toilet books and live out here with you forever, Princess.

I should have kept my mouth shut. She'll be straight in now with a short-arm tackle, laying me out with some gauche rebuke – we have no future, that sort of stuff – when all I'm doing is being polite, trying to be pleasant.

'Okay. I think I'd like that. I think I'm beginning to trust you.'

She is peculiar. I was only joking – about living with her out here, not about the literary long-firm fraud – but she seems to be taking me seriously. She's frowning, looking thoughtful, scratching figures on a piece of paper.

'Would you actually write the books?'

Of course not. It's a caper. I'd sell them and then have it away on my toes.

'Hm. Do you get all the money in advance, then?'

Well, no. It's usual to get a third down.

'So it wouldn't be £300,000, would it? It would only be £100,000.'

Isn't that typical? How like a woman to fuck up a perfectly good scheme. They have minds like VAT inspectors with body odour, women, they have no imagination whatsoever. She's as bad as Alison, as literal-minded as a bollard. And she keeps talking about London, of what we'll do. How can she think we have a future of any sort in London? That's not on. I can't get out at night, without complex and detumescing alibis, and I wouldn't want squalid teatime *rendezvous* — least of all with someone who appears to have forgotten the point of herself, who seems to have come adrift from why she is.

By the fifth night I've had enough. I tell her that we're going out, implying, by means of a sudden, rather menacingly elastic movement of the hips, a slight loosening of the muscles at one sly corner of the mouth and an alarming narrowing of the eyes, that we're not *just* going out, that we're going out to enjoy ourselves. I've been thinking — though I've tried half-heartedly not to — about that spooky experience at the Tierra on her first night here, when I went as high as a hot-air balloon even though I'd taken nothing. It was connected in some way with *her* being high, I think, and even though it was horrifying I wanted to get that rush again. I've been feeling a little restless ever since.

'Okay. Let's go a little mad, eh? Let's go to the Tierra. That was good.'

She's got the picture — she is quite perceptive — but there's no enthusiasm in her voice. She goes into the bedroom without prompting, but despondently, and changes into the correct wardrobe for the tour — white skirt and little boots — and then re-presents herself with diffidence, without bounce or pride. She looks sweet, but vague and rather disappointed. We set off and she takes my arm; she smiles bravely, she's trying hard, but her head's down and there's no spring in her step. We pass

Ponce Corner, where she gets a big hullo from Tanit the Island God and a reminder of their date to dance, but she doesn't stop; she gives him a perfunctory wave and marches on, head down, face set, as if she knows what's coming and is anxious to get it over with.

I don't panic. She's behaving extraordinarily badly, but the evening isn't a write-off yet. I'll get her a little something from Tierra Toni – that's all she needs, I'm sure. I'll take him into the gents at an appropriate moment, address him out of the corner of my mouth, and buy her a line or two – that's what they're called, I think. We sit down outside and order drinks, which Toni brings to our table. He ignores me and greets her with a languid readjustment of what's inside his leather knickers. This coarse salute to her blondeness and availability, this barman's acknowledgement of her worth, seems to cheer her up a bit. She sips her drink, arranges her legs and smiles.

Are you okay?

'I'm fine.'

Do you want anything?

'Like what?'

She knows perfectly well what I mean; she's just being irritating.

You know. This is the place to get it if you do.

My intentions are good, and yet – such is the power of tabloid propaganda – I feel a little sleazy, like an old paedophile offering boiled sweets to a six-year-old. This is ridiculous, of course. She won't see twenty-one again, she's been to Bogota and back and lived to tell the tale, she's been bruised and beaten by an assortment of men at all four corners of the globe. With me, for the first time in her incoherent life, perhaps, she's safe; she's in good hands. She sighs now, and looks a little sad.

'Okay. If you say so. That would be nice.'

Why is she so reluctant? This is her thing, not mine. I don't understand the silly girl at all, but I get up and go inside, corner Toni and address him squintingly in a low, peculiar voice. At first he can't follow me at all, he squints too and steps back suspiciously as if I might be suggesting something low. For some time we stand there, squinting hard at one another, until I add a rather imaginative mime, involving a busy twitching of the nostrils like a rabbit. This causes Toni to disappear entirely and I'm left standing there, squinting and twitching my nostrils like a rabbit on my own. I'm about to chuck this in when an oiled negro, stone-naked but for a diamond-studded G-string and with a triangular hairstyle, the upper plane so flat you could land a helicopter on it, approaches me and, correctly interpreting my mime, produces – from inside his G-string, I'm sorry to say – a tiny white envelope, which can be mine, he says for as little as fifteen thousand pesetas. We do the deal and I return to our table, feeling oddly effective, powerful even. My Princess will understand she isn't dealing with a muffin.

She opens the little envelope and inspects the contents with a suspicious, expert eye. She then puts a pinch of powder on her tongue and pulls a face.

'Could be okay. At least it isn't flour. I'll try it in the ladies.'

She's back in a minute, looking like a different person. The change is amazing; the effect on her seems to be instant, like an electric impulse to the heart. She bounces out of the ladies like something mad out of a carnival cake. Her colour's up, all signs of strain and doubt have disappeared and her eyes are shining with a slightly crazy light. She looks ten years younger suddenly, beautiful and fearless.

'It's all right. That was good idea.'

It suits you. You look terrific.

'I feel terrific.'

What does it do? What's the feeling exactly?

'It gives you courage. Dutch courage, of course. On coke, I get a knockback, I don't care, I just laugh. Not on coke, I get a knockback, I'm off like a dog with a cat between its legs.'

It gives you the courage to be yourself. What's wrong with that?

'I don't know. Nothing perhaps. The trouble is it makes you want to do things which you'll need more coke to do. Does that make sense? It's sort of self-perpetuating. You want to go higher all the time.'

What's free-basing?

'Oh Christ, that's bad. I'll never do that. I don't even want to talk about it. That's addictive. This is okay. I can handle this. You want some?'

I don't need it. You give me courage.

'Ha! I'm the drug of your choice!'

I'm beginning to think she might be. I'm feeling good already, the music's getting louder and I feel powerful, unafraid. I haven't had the full rush yet – this is a gentle high I'm getting – but it's nicer in a way, much less alarming than that sudden launch into a possible world. I feel I want to laugh; for as little as 50p I'd dance – and that's not something I've done for twenty years. But my brain seems to be still in place, my thoughts are coming in an ordered sequence, more or less. Or are they? If they aren't, how would I know? Can an omelette judge how many eggs have gone into it? We seem to have a philosophical problem here. Or have we? We need some theory of meta-thinking here. Can disordered thoughts judge the extent of their own disorder?

I'm definitely getting it from her, this gentle, but disorientating, high. Her face has a sharp, illuminated clarity, a vividness, as if she's in colour while everything around her is in dingy black and white. Her eyes are lit up and enormous, and the deceitful music's in my brain. I don't want to get the full rush yet, I don't want to carry my horrors into the gents like last time, so I take a deep breath and get a purchase on the real world.

... I remember summer holidays in Broadstairs and the Grand Hotel and little pier and fishing with Todd and Fagg and Leslie Howerd. That's not right. I remember summer holidays in Broadstairs and the Grand Hotel and Leslie Ames, who couldn't keep wicket after the war. That's more like it. Todd and Fagg and Leslie Ames, who crouched in the slips because he couldn't straighten up. And why, I wonder, to play for Spurs must you be called Hoddle or Waddle or Toddle? Colin Toddle? He was good – the most cultured centre-back ever to pull on the no.6 shirt for his country. I remember Canterbury Week and the old oak inside the field of play and Toddle asleep by the boundary fence ...

And my Princess is staring straight into my brain. Her enormous eyes are ablaze with wickedness and understanding –

82

but I'll defy her. She'll not deceive me for a second time, put wind in my sails and make me think there's still a chance when obviously there isn't. I look away.

... my mother was very keen on Leslie Howerd, but weren't they all? Gone with the wind up, my mother used to say of English actors who ratted off to Hollywood in '39. She had no time for shirkers, my mother, nor has my sister Bobo. My sister Bobo used to call me Button after a character in a children's book called 'The Little Green Button Man'. He had a filthy temper, the Little Green Button Man. When displeased he'd fly into such a rage that he'd revolve on the spot, disappearing through the floorboards like a circular-saw through butter. When I was small I had a filthy temper – hard though it is to believe. That's why my sister Bobo used to call me Button. Alison still calls me Button. My Button this, my Button that. I'd like to impress my sister Bobo before it's too late. Would she be impressed if she saw me now? Probably not. Nor would Alison. I hope her new carpet that isn't meant to show the dirt is working better. I hope that she's all right for cling-wrap and rubber washing-up gloves. I hope she's doing something about the damp patch on the sitting-room ceiling. I hope she's remembering to pay her Access bill in such a way as to avoid the maximum interest rate. I hope she hasn't discovered how to get into my filing-cabinet without a key.

Silly Serena's husband Jim was into my filing cabinet in no time. When Alison and I were out here together once, Silly Serena and Jim volunteered to feed the cats, taking it in turns. One day Jim decided to break into my filing cabinet and poke around. You can't blame him, quantity surveyor, big feet, living in Putney, doing his best. In my filing-cabinet he came across a promising-looking video. He poured himself a whisky, put it on, loosened his trousers, settled back. This will be good, he thought. But it wasn't good. It was his dear little wife and Martinique the Mad Make-up Artist blazing around on the sofa at my flat after the *Mail On Sunday* launch. They'd got a bit drunk, made many lucrative connections among the upper management, agreed afterwards to star in a home movie directed by myself. While Silly Serena and Mad Martinique are absent-mindedly stirring one another's bosoms on the sofa, I wander into shot – clothed, thickening waist, bald head gleaming in the spotlight – and sit down plumply on the sofa next to Jim's blameless little wife, discussing the next scene between her legs. All Jim's cerebral circuits fuse at once. He's in shock for a week. It's a more stupefying experience, perhaps, than Pratt the Playwright's when he took his trousers off, put his tape-recorder on and heard his friend calling him a weirdo …

My Princess is trying to mesmerise me with her pussy-cat smile, she's sizing me up. I won't look at her.

'This is the best, right?'

It's good.

'I think I'm beginning to trust you. I'd like you to be possessive. I'd like to wind you up. I'd like you to catch me with someone else. Then you'd beat me up. I'd really like that.'

She's hit on the wrong game: violence doesn't interest me, but I'll play along for a while, see where this leads. A good director, after all, lets his *artistes* run free from time to time, encourages them to be wheel-barrows or turnips for a while – 'Yes, darling, that's good, we can use that.' Her lovely face is still in focus, her voice isn't in my head yet, but I do feel good – I feel trusting and confident. She's staring at me – it's in her eyes, they do have a mesmerising quality. I'll follow her for a while, let her take off, see where she goes. This is a creative attitude to having a good time, a lateral attitude. I *could* be possessive, I suppose, but not with her.

I'd have to be in love – then jealousy can be quite exciting, I seem to remember. Fanny the Film Star won't mind my saying that when she was making *Up, Up And Away* she was followed everywhere by a Frenchman with a nose – I can't recall his name. One night she agreed to have dinner with him. I lay in bed, a small knot of rage screwing itself tighter and tighter in my stomach until I felt I'd swallowed a golf ball. I was in hell actually. When she got home at last she stood at the end of the bed and hung her head in shame. God she was a bad actress. 'I'm guilty,' she said. I sprang at her, and then, to my astonishment, discovered that I was gripped not by anger but desire. I was more excited than I'd been for years. It was the act of reclaiming, I suppose. Is this what my Princess means? I'll tell her this rather telling little anecdote, she'll be impressed.

84

Fanny Fonser won't mind my saying ...

'She's gross. My best friend Lindy was in a film with her. She didn't like her at all.'

I won't bother. I try a different approach.

I expect you'll have read *Voices From Another Life* by Jonathan Kibble, an interesting novel on this theme, unless I'm much mistaken, having the great merit, unlike some of his other work, of being accessible to the general reader.

She hasn't heard of him, of course. In spite of this I decide to show her a letter from Kibble, always carried in my wallet. I take it out, with some difficulty, since my powers of coordination seem to have deteriorated in the last half hour; my hands have become like pudgy flippers.

He admires my work, as it happens.

This is a slight overstatement. He once wrote me a polite, formal note thanking me for something I'd written about him in the *Tatler*.

She glances at the letter briefly and hands it back, unread.

'You carry it *around* with you? That's gross! I know. I'll pull a man. Your Princess being fucked by someone else, would that be good or what? Would that drive you mad?'

It wouldn't actually – she isn't mine, I'd have no reason to be jealous – but I must be polite, let her think it would. She's out of control, as high as a kite, and were I to bring her down now she'd feel immensely foolish.

'*Trust* me. You'd like it.'

Never say trust me, Princess.

She'll say *touché*. She doesn't.

'Ha! I know what I'll do. I'll pull Jack the Actor! He fucked me on the plane, you know. In the toilet. Sorry – lavatory. What else shouldn't I say? I don't want to let you down in front of your smart friends.'

You never could.

But I tell her briefly – phone, mirror, mantel-piece etc (not mentioning, of course, that if I had any smart friends I wouldn't let her meet them).

'Okay. I didn't tell you because I thought you'd be cross. Are you cross?'

I try to look cross, I simulate crossness – which isn't easy, because I want to laugh. She looks so sweet and earnest.

I'm furious, Princess.

'He took me into the lavatory, Jack the Actor, and he pulled my dress up and ...'

You weren't wearing a dress.

'That's true! I'm making it all up! But I *would* like to fuck him. Does that drive you mad?'

It drives me nowhere, as it happens, but I feel good, I can play along.

'And I'd like you to find us. It's the greatest turn-on. Can I tell you something I've never told anyone? I don't know if I should.'

I'm sure you should.

'I don't know. You may think I'm cuckoo.'

I'm sure I won't.

'You'll never tell anyone? It'll be our secret?'

Of course.

'I think I'd better take another line. Excuse me.'

She's off to the ladies. That's good. I may need to be higher myself than I am right now to handle what she's going to tell me. It's odd – I feel good, but I haven't really had that first night rush. I'm okay, but I feel a little cheated, as if I've had a bum deal.

Perhaps I'll spend the rest of my life chasing that original high. They say this happens. I must be *quite* high to imagine anything so fatuous. If she has to take a hit before each confession she'll have put 15,000 pesetas up her nose before the evening's out. I don't care. I'd spend everything I have to keep her as high as this.

'Right!'

She's back at our table, rejuvenated, looking wicked.

'We were in Florida ...'

Who was in Florida?

It's working already. I can't follow her. My brain's all over the place, in all kinds of shit.

'Me and my husband for fuck's sake. We'd just got married and I was incredibly possessive. He was very social, my husband. One night some people were over. Hanging out, you know.'

I know.

'There was one girl I didn't like. She was very pretty, okay?'

Okay.

'My husband was playing cards with some of the men and I was bored so I went to bed. After a while – I don't know how long – I woke up. It was quiet and I was alone. That's odd, I thought. I lay in bed trying to work it out. Then my imagination started playing me up. I lay there, having palpitations. Don't laugh, there've been books on palpitations, I tell you. I began thinking about this girl I didn't like, wondering if she'd left ...'

Did she have a name?

I feel I'll need to know her name to keep a purchase on this story. My Princess's face is shining like a light at the end of a tunnel and my brain is swinging around in my head like a bucket full of water.

'Who?'

Some girl. Very pretty. In Florida, I think.

'Of course she had a fucking name. Mandy. She was definitely called Mandy. Anyway, I got out of bed and peeped into the living-room. A few people were in there – but not my husband, or Mandy. I crept down the passage and listened outside the spare bedroom. Jesus I was right! My husband was making out with Mandy! I could hear it *all*. Well – it was the most sensational experience I've ever had. I was utterly anguished, but at the same time more excited than I'd ever been. I could never have imagined such excitement. It was as if I'd never been excited before, as if what I'd *thought* was excitement had been something else entirely. I *exploded*. I came without touching myself, I tell you.'

Spontaneous combustion. Happens all the time in Edinburgh.

'Yeah really. Then I went mad, of course. Clean off my head. I got a knife from the kitchen, opened the door and hurled it at the bed. Then I went berserk.'

You already were berserk.

'I went berserker. Is that a word?'

Definitely. A cross between a mad dance and an anti-tank weapon. Describes you precisely.

I'm rather pleased with this. I can't be as high as I thought I was. I can follow it all now.

'It took three grown men to pull me off, and they weren't big men, I tell you, only average. Am I a sadist or what?'

A masochist, I'd say.

'Oh – a masochist. Whatever. What's the difference? Perhaps I'm both. Is that sick? I've never admitted that before, I've never told anyone. Now you know more about me than anyone else in the world.

(Not any more I don't.)

'Do you think I'm cuckoo? Say you don't.'

Of course I don't.

'I'd like *you* to have that experience. It's the ultimate, I tell you. I'd definitely like you to catch me with another man, so you'd know what it's like. But even more than that I'd like to catch you with another woman. More than anything I'd like to repeat that experience in Florida. It's been tormenting me ever since. I've got to get over it, I think, in order to get over my husband. We'll do that when we get back to London.'

I'm losing her. It's getting late, and I'm coming down. I'm not sure if I'm following this.

Do what exactly?

'Arrange it so that I catch you with another woman.'

That's a relief. I wouldn't want to catch her with another man. Men at it look damn silly actually – pudging away, buttocks up, trying hard. Men at it aren't at their best in my opinion. I'd probably laugh.

'I know someone who'd be perfect. Tessa the Teacher. She's my best friend. You'll really like her, I guarantee it. She's a highly educated woman, let's face it. I really look up to her. That's important. I don't want my Prince fucking any old slag. Oh God – I'll probably lose you to her. Let's go home. *Now. Please.*'

'Okay. Who do you like more than me?'

We're back at the flat in bed and my Princess and I have disconcertingly swapped roles. She has become the customer, expecting the precise, dauntingly rehearsed realisation of her fantasy, and is prepared to be solemnly demanding towards that end. She's in a world of her own, perfectly enclosed, like a madwoman or a punter, and it's painful to be reminded of how often one has humourlessly imposed one's preferences on others and expected something spontaneous in return. She's very business-like, determined to get her money's worth – and what's left of the coke is laid out in threatening, razor-thin lines on the bedside table. It's impossible to please a punter on coke, I'm told; tarts dread punters who bring their own supply. They can't be satisfied, and they never leave. It's dismaying to see my Princess like this, but I must act my part, I mustn't let her down.

No one.

'Don't be silly. *Try*.'

Her little hands are round my throat. It tickles and I want to laugh, but that would be unforgivable. My mind fills up with names, all to be deleted at a later stage by Mr Wiseman, my solicitor. When he read *The English Way Of Doing Things* for libel, he was adamant that I couldn't say that Toby Danvers the Impresario had fantasies about Sue Cook. I argued, of course, pointing out that it was hardly her fault if some back-street theatrical fantasised about her. Nevertheless and notwithstanding it was prima facie defamatory. Mr Wiseman insisted, to suggest that she was the sort of person about whom a low-life *might* fantasize. So – I can't mention her. Eventually I hit on Miss Picano. I'm sure she wouldn't mind – this being an emergency and so on.

Miss ...

My Princess tightens her grip around my throat.

'*Yes?*'

... that tickles.

'Sorry.'

You won't hurt me?

'No. *Who?*'

Miss Picano ... Jesus Christ!

She's raked my back from stern to stem with her long red finger-nails, possibly drawing blood. She writhes with pleasure while I gasp with pain.

'Why? Tell me *why?*'

89

You won't do that again?

'Okay. Tell me *why*?'

Promise?

'Promise. *Why*?'

Put your hands round my throat.

I have less chance of being strangled, I think, than of being slashed to ribbons.

'Okay.'

Her little hands are round my throat. I feel safer now. Here goes:

Because she's beautiful. She's got ...

Jesus Christ she does it again! She lets go of my throat and rakes my back. I scream. This is getting dangerous. *I've* never been as demanding as this. I've been fairly weird, I dare say, but I've never actually hurt anyone. What will she want next? This could get worse – punters can be very odd. There's the fellow, for instance, who asks girls to take their clothes off and climb on top of the wardrobe, from where, he says, he'd like them to pee on him in his street clothes. Once they're safely on top of the wardrobe he walks out with their handbags. What might she do? Stuff me up the chimney and walk off with everything? How can I alter the odds in my favour before I get cut to pieces? Luckily she does this for me, suddenly introducing Jack the Actor into the cast.

'What would you do if you found me in bed with Jack the Actor?'

I mustn't laugh. Her face is an inch or two from mine; she looks so serious and her eyes are wide with expectation. To laugh now would be unforgivable. There's nothing more hurtful than a tart who laughs in the middle. We're walking a tightrope here. I manage not to laugh, but I say my line without conviction.

I'd kill him.

She gasps and squirms, instructs, demands, and each time I think she's had enough she gets up and takes another line, comes back to bed with the news that someone else has joined the cast – Tessa the Teacher, Lindy, Cindy, Mandy, Candy, her husband, her dentist, her tax advisor, God knows who. Some have only walk-on parts, others might be amazed at the use we put them to. With so many on stage at once we make a colossal racket, and once again I thank my lucky stars that she'll be gone before Mark Staughton comes. The flat's too small, the walls are too thin, to accomodate him and the cast of extras. Poor man, he'll need his sleep, what with the worries of having a poetry list and so forth. And what if my Princess took it upon herself to involve him in one of her romantic melodramas? What if she crept into his room at night, expecting me to duff him up or kill him? He might not understand. Small publisher, doing his best, married, corduroy suit and wispy beard, takes his holidays in Wales, suddenly duffed up in the middle of the night by one of his best young authors. He might not give me money.

At last my Princess has had enough; she's spent, utterly exhausted like a punter; she turns her back on me without a word and goes to sleep. That's good – it means she doesn't like me, that I'm not yet one of those she wants to cuddle. As the gloomy Cathedral clock strikes four, then five, then six – reminding the happy of punishments to come – I lie awake and wonder. *That* wasn't acting – so what's she up to? I'll have to ask her in the morning.

About last night. You said ...
   'I don't want to talk about it, okay?'
   She's sipping her tea in bed, cuddling Ted, her face as innocent as a novice nun's.
   But ...
   'I was high. Let's not talk about it.'
   Slam! I should have been expecting it, but I feel quite bruised. The conversation, and its implications, never took place! It must be marvellous to be like this, able to erase the past from day to day. It's drugs, I suppose. One day at a time, and yet, ironically, that's precisely one of the slogans, I believe, that are fed to junkies in a clinic. I'm irritated, but I drop the matter for the moment. I'll let her spend the day thinking she's a normal person; we'll discuss nice things – and then tonight I'll get her a present, I'll get her high again, pursue the matter further, place her in a situation, perhaps, in which I can call

her bluff. I'm quite interested − purely academically − in the implications, for her, of the traumatic experience she had in Florida with her husband, and of this Jack the Actor business. It's a writer's natural interest, I suppose, in what makes others tick − even when they're not interested themselves. If she were prepared to talk now about last night's Jack the Actor game, she'd dismiss it all as fantasy, ignorantly drawing a distinction, as women can, between what they'd like to do and what they actually do, dismissing the former in some curious way as 'unreal'. But there's hope, I think, for my Princess: she does *have* fantasies, at least, which is quite unusual − as a rule these girls' minds are about as interesting as cash and carry catalogues. Tonight I'll return to the Tierra on my own, find my pal in the diamond-studded G-string and buy another little envelope, with the help of which my Princess will be able to face up to the tangled realities of her nature. We might even go after Jack the Actor. He's a prat, but if she could pull him she'd have passed a little test, I think, shown herself in my eyes to be not all talk.

'What an odd place. Atrocious, eh?'

We're in 'Mr Sixto's Piano Bar', run by a wally, Mr Sixto, who had a shoe-shop once and did so well that he was able to realise *his* fantasies by opening his own piano bar, where he now sings Tony Bennett numbers in a white tuxedo with hand-held mike. He can't sing at all, but no one calls him a horse or bounces his head up and down on the floor of his piano bar as if malletting a croquet-hoop − as an Australian audience, exasperated beyond endurance by her genteel vicarage ditties, once did to Joyce Grenfell, I believe. I suppose they have a role, these loonies who are prepared to make prats of themselves for our sakes − wear bow-ties and show their knees on game shows, buy football clubs, sing like Tony Bennett in piano bars. They have a civic purpose like a sewage system, they drain away our more absurd sides for us. So, no one throws things at Mr Sixto − indeed we're grateful to him in a way.

His piano bar is indeed atrocious, though − black leather furniture, padded leather walls, a dance-floor studded with flashing lights like an airport run-way, a three-piece band from

Zurich; it scrapes up the island's idiots, men called Derek in blazers and yachting caps, too common even to be caddish, time-share artists from the Midlands here with their optimistic clients: doctors and so forth, professional men who should know better but are about to lose their life's savings on a patch of subsiding mud, which is without planning permission anyway, and almost certainly owned by someone other than the Derek hustling it. Later they're to be seen, these professional men, blubbing back home on consumer watchdog programmes to Esther Rantzen – all teeth and popular indignation. We're here, in fact, because Jack the Actor told my Princess on the aeroplane that it was a place that he came to with his Derek, a provincial operator trying to sell him a house in Santa Eulalia. Jack the Actor has no intention of buying it, of course, but he's cunning enough to keep his Derek on a string, coming out here once a month, at Derek's expense, to have another look. My plan had worked perfectly. After a blameless day on a family beach – playing dolphins and talking only about nice things – I'd hopped off privately to the Tierra, found my pal in the diamond-studded G-String and bought a little envelope. One line from this and nothing had seemed funnier to my Princess than the idea of tracking down Jack the Actor and using him in a sophisticated real-life game of our devising, the silly sod.

'This is the life, eh?'

I'm not so sure. It obviously beats most things generally on offer, but it is an enterprise, I now realise, carrying a certain amount of risk. If Jack the Actor does show up, we could make asses of ourselves. What if my Princess tries to pull him and he rejects her? I'd feel a fool and, more seriously, I'd find her unattractive; she'd have taken an undistinguished prat-fall in what is meant to be her area of expertise, and for that I could never forgive her. Should I tell her this, I wonder, should I protect her from possible humiliation? I'd be wasting my time, I think. She's higher than I've ever seen her, sitting explosively on the edge of her chair as if about to take off round the room like a mad, low-level rocket. And I'm not getting the Tierra high, or anything resembling it. I look into her eyes, but nothing happens; I'm stuck disgustingly on the ground. It's the circumstances, I suppose. It's obviously not possible to soar off into that daring world where nothing matters, while a Spanish wally in a white tuxedo sings Tony Bennett bummers to a roomful of middle-aged Dereks and their optimistic clients.

Suddenly my Princess tenses. Jack the Actor's arrived, in shades here in this leathery hell, at the centre of a party of Dereks and their unattractive wives, managing to convey that, while he's with them for the moment, this is a circumstance he'll rectify as soon as possible. The ill-mannered ass is glancing rudely round the room, checking on whether there's a smarter set to join. He won't find one here – except that comprised of me and my Princess, of course, but he won't see us until we want him to, tucked away as we are in a secure dark corner. The Dereks are talking too loudly to one another – about money, I imagine – quite ignoring their sullen, disappointed wives. They might have had high hopes, their wives, when the evening started, but they are plainly defeated now. Earlier, as they dressed themselves up in their chemically manufactured trouser-suits which reveal faun knickers underneath, they might have felt quite optimistic, these Karens and Traceys; each might have thought that if she made a special effort this might be the evening when her Derek would suddenly notice her existence after all these years. They've even had their hair done, but it hasn't worked. It will never work again. Everything's too heavy – bags, bottoms, shoes. Everything has been splayed out of shape from having too many ungrateful children who now sniff glue and eventually won't come home, even for Christmas. They haven't the courage to escape, so they remain at home in the Midlands, riveted with economic bolts to their ignorant, money-making husbands, discussing kitchen matters with each other. Why do they still try? Why don't they kill themselves?

My Princess quickly takes another line for courage – here at the table – though why she should feel the need for one I can't imagine. *I* could pull Jack the Actor away from this lot. It's almost too unfair to be of interest. Or is it? I now see that he's with a Karen less disgraceful than the others. Her face has gone a peculiar colour in the sun and her hair's too short, gathered into tight curls like a cutlet-ruff on top of a flushed, over-excited neck, but she is the star of this particular circle,

94

and obviously enjoying the resentful looks she's getting from the other Karens. She does have a sort of confidence, she might have admirers in an office, be quite an attraction at a Midlands Christmas do, but now she's up against another woman, though she doesn't know it yet. (It might be fun, I realise, to see my Princess in competition with another other woman – one who doesn't do the shopping either, or know what cling-wrap is.) On the face of it, this Karen – a receptionist, I imagine – has no chance against my Princess, but men are strange. If Jack the Actor's well in here (as he would put it) he might stick with his receptionist rather than risk rejection by something a bit more challenging. My Princess might get a knockback, as it happens, which does make the game more interesting – though a trifle alarming too.

My God, if she failed against a Karen! *She* wouldn't mind – on coke nothing bothers her, she said as much – but I'd mind, *I'd* feel silly. My money's on her, so to speak, she's an extension of me at the moment; if she disgraces herself, she disgraces me. And Jack the Actor is quite a test, in fact. He's by some distance the most attractive man in the room, in a purely cuntish way. He won't be a pushover. He isn't desperate, though he should be. If women had any taste he'd never get near one. With his unnecessary shades and dozey self-regard, his crinkly old eyes and dishevelled hair and jeans and silly jogging shoes he looks an arsehole, but he doesn't know this himself, of course, so he's still okay for a while. One day soon he'll look in the mirror and see the truth. His brain will split in two, he'll fall apart. But for the moment he has the nerve to stand *en attitude*, shirt open to the waist, and talk to receptionists about his great chum Mike Caine in a peculiar deep voice, and they're impressed. He's disgusting, but he doesn't know it yet – so he's quite a test of some sort. Shall I warn my Princess? Explain the risk she's taking? I think I should.

You don't have to go through with this, you know.

'Fuck it – do you want me to be disgraceful or what?'

I do – but he is *with* someone, you know.

'Not for long he won't be.'

Okay, I've done my bit, I've tried to save her from herself. And what does it really matter, after all, if she falls flat on her face and I go off her? She's only here for one more day. By this time next week I'll be deep in my memoirs and she'll have joined the mounted trout; she'll be a trophy merely, stuffed, hardly recollected, brought out, perhaps, to impress next year's performer – if there is one. It's too late anyway. I couldn't stop her if I wanted to. She's got Jack the Actor in her sights, she's measuring him for his fate.

'Okay. I think I'll pull him. You're sure you don't mind?'

No. You enjoy yourself.

'Right. Watch this.'

She has no doubts at all. Jack the Actor is very obviously with someone else – indeed he and his Karen are now self-consciously entwined, gazing stupidly into one another's eyes, intending without a doubt to end the evening together on the tiled floor of a holiday villa – and yet the possibility of failure simply hasn't occurred to my Princess. I must say I do find this quite attractive.

'Okay. Here goes.'

She takes a deep breath, gets up and walks naughtily across the room, her delinquent legs and wilful bottom seeming to take on a suggestive life of their own, like those of a top-heavy blonde stooging for a conjuror or low comedian. Interestingly, the Karens and Traceys, even though their backs are turned, seem to sense danger before she gets into firing range, seeming to pick up her approach on some invisible radar system attached to their bums perhaps. While she's still ten yards away, they stiffen suddenly and arch their backs like street cats. My Princess actually *skips* the last few yards – how dare she? Even Mrs Mouse would never have dared to skip – and throws herself at Jack the Actor, dislodging his Karen in the process. It's incredibly sweet, in my opinion, irresistible, in fact – and it certainly works. Jack the Actor is delighted, his response fatuously over-cooked. He steps back a pace or two, removes his shades, crinkles his eyes and drops into that peculiarly repulsive, self-regarding posture favoured by footballers who wish to take the credit for the build-up to a goal, throwing their arms wide and squatting in a catcher's crouch, ready to receive the leaping, celebrating marksman. 'Well hey hey hey! What do you know?' The Karens, I'm glad to say, would like to kill her. Even from where I'm sitting I can see the light of hatred burning in their dull, resentful eyes. Sod them. They're a disgrace. It's their fault for allowing themselves to get like this.

I look away. I don't want to catch anyone's eye, to be summoned over, perhaps, to join the group. I want to stay at a distance for a while and watch, controlling the situation, like a counsellor, with a heavy, shaping silence. When I look back, they've disappeared, Jack the Actor and my Princess, leaving behind an untidy knot of bewildered Dereks and Karens. Jack the Actor's Karen seems to be in shock. She's not even making a stab at nonchalance; she's frankly shattered; her evening's hopes are all in ruins and she's looking tired to death and awfully plain. My word I'm proud of my Princess! Where are they, though? They must be in the Ladies, they've got a thing about lavatories, Jack the Actor and my Princess, they can't keep out of them. They're in there stuffing things up their noses, I imagine, but they're in there for longer than it should take to put something up your nose, I'd say.

Perhaps this is it, then; perhaps it's all over, so to speak, or about to be. And if so, do I mind? Am I meant to mind? I believe I am. She said she was doing this for me. 'What would you do if you found me with Jack the Actor?' 'I'd kill him.' That had made her squirm. Is that what she expects, then? Am I meant to box him on the nose as they come out of the Ladies – if they ever do? And what if the game hasn't been completed yet? What if she wants to bring him home, or go home with him? Would I mind? Not in the least, in fact, but I believe I'm meant to mind; I think she'd expect me to object, resorting to violence even. They're devilishly difficult, these sophisticated games; keeping your dignity while not letting your partner down – not leaving them alone on stage without an audience – is never easy.

Now, at last, they're emerging from the Ladies, arm in arm, laughing, looking rather foolish, as it happens, particularly Jack the Actor, who is carrying himself like a mime at a function, stepping up amid applause, eyes cast modestly down, a sheepish smile, to receive a minor prize. Perhaps it's all over, and – if so – that would be a relief, I think. I could go home

97

now with my Princess, quiz her sternly, pretend to be cross, play my part adequately in a quick, recriminatory tussle (in the outer hall, perhaps) then go to sleep. That would be best. My Princess, who has performed brilliantly so far, should stop now, hand Jack the Actor back to his Karen with a charming smile, let him explain himself to her.

But now she's bringing him over to my secluded corner, followed at an untidy distance, I'm sorry to see, by the whole group of Dereks and their Karens, who seem no better pleased with this development than I am. Leaving Jack the Actor's Karen standing foolishly on her own, eyes boiling with resentment, my Princess introduces me to Jack the Actor, then takes me briefly to one side for a whispered production meeting.

'He's perfect, darling. Can we take him home?'

Perfect for what, I wonder, but I smile amiably at the fellow and shake his hand. Has he been told he's coming home, and, if so, who does he think I am? Her father? A friend? A weirdo? A wally?

I don't mind him thinking that I'm her father or a weirdo, but – if he's coming home – I won't have him thinking I'm a wally, so I sit him down between me and my Princess (I refuse to be left talking to a Karen while my Princess enjoys herself) and drop a few names, bear down on him with my biography, find myself telling him, I don't know why – and while Mr Sixto sings 'I Left My Heart in San Francisco' – about a period, some twenty years ago, when I used to take luncheon once a week with Anthony Powell.

You look like a literary sort of man. It might interest you to know that I used to take luncheon once a week with Anthony Powell.

'Really?'

That's right. A sweet man, a man of stupefying courtesy, but with nothing to say to me at all.

'Is that so?'

Entirely so. At the end of each lunch I'd think: well, that must surely be the last; he won't want to endure that again. But he'd take out his engagement book and write in a *rendezvous* for the following week. Are you with me?

'Of course.'

Good. At the end of one lunch, Powell suggested tentatively – with his usual amazing courtesy, do you see? – that it might be agreeable to be joined on the next occasion by his close friend Osbert Lancaster. Excuse me a moment.

My Princess, becoming bored, perhaps, and foolishly imagining that she can compete with my Anthony Powell anecdote, has dived her hand into Jack the Actor's trousers and is rummaging around inside.

Look – I'm trying to tell this cunt about my weekly lunches with Anthony Powell. Do you mind?

'Sorry.'

Where was I? Ah yes. Osbert Lancaster was keen, said Powell, to visit the revolving restaurant at the Post Office Tower. Would I mind very much? Not in the least, I said. Indeed I was greatly relieved. I imagined that it would be much less boring for Powell to have an old friend present.

'Of course.'

My Princess, to my surprise, now takes out Jack the Actor's cock and waggles it around like someone trying to shake a cat out of an apple tree. The polite thing to do, it seems to me, is to pretend I haven't noticed, so I press on with my Anthony Powell anecdote.

Surprisingly, it was the most arduous lunch of all. These two old friends didn't say a word to one another from start to finish, or to me, of course. We sat there munching silently, while the Post Office Tower went round and round. What do you make of that?

'How ironic.'

I don't know about ironic, you turkey, but your remark does remind me of one interesting anecdote of Powell's. I asked him on one occasion what his opinion of Evelyn Waugh was and ...

'I'm bored.'

My Princess looks round, picks out the least repulsive looking Derek, lets go of Jack the Actor, gets up and, inserting herself poutingly between this Derek and his startled wife, spreads herself across his knee, undoes his trousers and takes out his cock too. I'm immensely proud of her, but Derek's wife doesn't like it at all, nor – I can tell – does Jack the Actor, who looks pretty silly, as it happens, sitting on his own with his cock

99

sticking out. I'll have to work hard to keep his interest now, particularly if my Princess intends to whizz round the whole group of Dereks taking out their cocks in turn and waggling them around, like a Chinese conjuror trying to keep a lot of plates spinning in the air at once. I tap Jack the Actor on the shoulder and continue:

So — I asked Powell what his opinion of Waugh was and he fell into such a lengthy silence that I thought he must have forgotten what the question was. Then he said: 'He did say something quite amusing once. A dull American woman button-holed him at a party. "Ah Mr Waugh," she said. "You have a reputation for irony, I gather. Please say something ironic, won't you?" "I'm delighted to meet you," said Waugh.'

That falls flat. Jack the Actor gets up with his cock sticking out and, pulling my Princess off Derek's knee, starts to read the riot act. This strikes my Princess as very funny, I don't know why, but Derek is left sitting in his chair in a state of shock. He looks gaffed, as if life may never make sense again. I feel I ought to say something comforting to his Karen, who is looking gaffed as well. I get up, walk over to her and tap her on the shoulder. Oh dear oh dear, I say; I'm afraid your Derek isn't looking too clever.

'Pardon?'

I haven't, since the late Sixties, seen anyone look as surprised as your Derek does right now. One night in the late Sixties the wife of a stockbroker I used to know was fucked by Count Suckle at a party given by my friend Dawn Upstairs. Surprised everyone, surprised him most of all, of course. Hard day in the City, making money, back home for a bath, off to a party, this will be nice — sees his wife sat on by a hundredweight of black man and fucked in front of a roomful of intellectuals. He went mad, of course. Wasn't expecting it, do you see? His first experience of life without values. According to his wife Elizabeth, who thoroughly enjoyed herself, of course, he went home and sat in the kitchen with a saucepan on his head. May still be there. Walking into the walls and talking to himself with a saucepan on his head. Your Derek may go mad too, I fear. May keep a pig in the fridge and forget to pay the mortgage. He may not know that things can be as bad as this. It may interest

100

you to know that my wife, Alison – not that she is, you understand – doesn't know that things can be as bad as this – she has no idea at all. She has a carpet which isn't meant to show the dirt, but does. That's got her baffled, I can tell you; that's got her thinking.

We leave at this point, Jack the Actor, my Princess and I, and return to the flat, where my Princess runs around laying out lines, turning the lights down and the music up, while, once again, the burden of making polite conversation falls on me. My Anthony Powell story was a great success and I judge the moment right for another anecdote, this time, I think, with a showbiz flavour.

It may interest you to know that at one time I was Bob Dylan's agent.

'Really?'

Indeed. Found him sitting in my office one day in '62. Odd little man in a hat with a flower up his nose. Tried to help him, but no one wanted to know. In the end Peter Cook, to be obliging, let him on between turns at the Establishment. He didn't pay him, of course, and no one was much impressed. He went back to America after that and made a bit of a name for himself. The poet of the open road. 'A blowin' in the wind.' Don't tell me. Strange world, isn't it?

Jack the Actor doesn't seem particularly gripped by this, appears more taken, in fact, by my Princess, who had left the room half way through my anecdote but has now returned and is standing in the doorway looking angelic in thigh-boots and a yellow G-string. That's okay, but I don't feel I've quite established myself yet in Jack the Actor's eyes as a showbiz type of weight, so I bear down on him with another anecdote.

Have you heard of a singer called James Taylor? One of the nicest men I've ever met. We were introduced by Carly Simon, who was married to him at the time. 'He's mad,' she said, 'I do hope you won't be too embarrassed.' He didn't strike me as mad at all. He'd just bought an overcoat for £3 off a barrow. It was dreadful. It came down to his ankles. He looked like something in a skit.

My Princess, who has been posing adorably in the doorway, now walks so gracefully across the room and stands in front of

101

Jack the Actor, smiling down at him. I *am* a little cross, in fact – she looks so lovely, she has so much class – but it would be rude of me not to finish my anecdote.

Is it all right? he kept asking. Do you really think so? (We're talking of James Taylor here.) He wouldn't take it off in my place, where he thought it might be stolen, nor at the Indian restaurant where we went for dinner. Carly stood behind him all the time, screwing her right forefinger into her temple as one does when suggesting that the person indicated has a screw loose. It was Carly who was crackers, if you ask me, not him. He was the sanest man I've ever met, I think. I'm always telling this story, I don't know why.

And now my Princess takes Jack the Actor by the hand and lifts him to his feet. That's all right, I suppose, but what does she expect of me? I can't just turn in and go to sleep, which is what I want to do, I think. In my experience of these things, women are likely to feel damn silly pulling men they hardly know; she'll need my support, some sign from me that I approve, or, conversely, that I don't approve. Does she expect me to hide away and then sneak out, suffer the agony of watching, of seeing her, pale and lovely in the moonlight, tossing Jack the Actor hither and thither in the threshing machine of her sweet desires? Does she want me to come up from behind and whack him? And what if she isn't doing this for me – what if this isn't my Florida, so to speak? In that case she'd not thank me in the morning if I hopped in half-way through and killed him.

All these thoughts are going through my mind as my Princess starts to lead Jack the Actor towards the bedroom. And half-way there he stops and crinkles his eyes attractively and says:

'Let's *do* it! Cool running sweetheart!'

And then he's sick all over her. I've never seen anyone be so sick.

'Excuse me,' he says, and then he's sick again. And as he stumbles off towards the bathroom, my Princess starts to laugh, soon becoming helpless, almost doubled up. She's trying to say something, manages at last to get it out.

'From ... oh God ... where was it?'

Where was what? Pull yourself together.

I'm getting cross, I can't imagine why she finds this so amusing.

'That school. Gunner's Hole ... 'Oily' Mallett ... oh shit ...' Winchester?

'That's the one. From ... oh Christ ... from Winchester to this, eh?'

She's crying with laughter, the silly girl. I don't know what I was expecting – what I'd wanted even – but it certainly wasn't this. I'm disappointed in her. If she can't take these games seriously it would be better not to play them, and she obviously wasn't taking this one seriously – if she had been she wouldn't be so inappropriately amused by its slapstick outcome. I'm so annoyed – justifiably, in my opinion – that I decide to go to bed in the spare room. I lie in bed, feeling wide awake, listening to Jack the Actor as he tries to leave with dignity, walking into the walls and falling over furniture. And then my Princess, still laughing idiotically, rings up her best friend Laura and tells her all about it. 'Darling – *listen*. I just pulled this guy – an actor, okay? – and I stood in front of him with nothing on – I was looking *really* good, right? – and he said: 'Cool running sweetheart', he did, he really did, and then he was sick all over me! Great, eh? Love you and miss you. 'Bye.' Will she ring everyone? She doesn't join me now, she goes to bed in the other room, still laughing to herself.

I try to sleep but questions are buzzing in my head. What was all that about? And who was it for? I'm not sure that I liked her posing for Jack the Actor – if it was for him. And now I've seen how ruthless she can be, how unconcerned for other people's feelings. She must have known she was hurting those Derek's wives and Jack the Actor's unhappy Karen, but she didn't give a stuff. To get what she wanted, she walked right through the lot of them. I'm afraid Tiffs may be right: she may be as hard as nails and totally unscrupulous. She used me, she used Jack the Actor, she used those Dereks and Karens for her own amusement, and now she's lying in bed and laughing, talking to Ted and telling him all about it.

*

'I was looking out of the window earlier at all the people going home from work and I thought: why can't I be normal? Why couldn't I be waiting at home for you? Waiting to cook you dinner?'

I hope you'd be waiting in high-heels and a suspender-belt.

'I won't be like that any more. I can't be. Don't you understand?'

She looks so frightened. They've frightened the life out of her, the mad Christian fucks with their merciless, understanding eyes, they've frightened her to death. She was excellent at just one thing – making people happy – and now they've told her that she can't afford to do it any more. They're trying to destroy her, and if they win she won't be another woman any more – and I can't bear it. I have to fight these pitiless fools with their prayers and slogans and holding hands in superstitious groups.

'How's it going? The book?'

The question's as vague as the expression in her eyes. She doesn't really want to know. They've disconnected her from the past, nailed her to some nightmare future of dependency on them for life, of talking about herself in groups, of God and cups of tea and fear.

Okay. I've been thinking about that first day on Salinas. You said: 'This is a happy day, a day we'll remember.'

'I don't remember that; God, I don't remember that at all.'

We walked along the beach and I took photographs of you.

'Oh yeah. I thought I could still be a model! Gross, eh?'

It was sweet. You could have been. You could have done anything. You were remarkable. I felt very protective towards you that day. I wanted to look after you.

'You did. No one's ever done so much for me as you. It wasn't your fault.'

We could go back. Let's go back. Come on – leave with me now.

104

'Not yet. Not till I'm well. Have you decided what to call me yet? You won't use my real name, will you?'

Of course not.

'Promise? Can I trust you?'

Of course you can. I'm your friend. When will you realise that?

'I'm trying to. It's just ...'

'What?

'It's a very selfish programme, this. They tell you not to rely on anyone.'

Mad cunts. I suppose they're trying to put you off me. Have they managed to put you off me yet?

'They'll never do that. Just talking to you I start to come off the programme.'

Christ that's such a sinister word. You were so brave. You danced in the street and made a hundred people happy and now you're on a programme. It's brain-washing — can't you see that?

'I don't know. I'm so confused. How far have you got, then? With the book?'

I've done a scene in 'Mr Sixto's'.

'Mr Sixto? Who's he?'

A Spanish wally who had a shoe-shop and then opened a piano bar. We never went there. I said you pulled a man called Jack the Actor.

'Who the hell's Jack the Actor? I'm sure I've never heard of him.'

I've invented him.

'Golly — is that allowed? I don't want people to think I pulled actors in piano bars. That's not very nice.'

It's okay. Nothing happened. I've said he was sick all over you.

'Sick? Why?'

I thought it was funny.

'Well, I don't think it's funny. What else are you making up?'

Quite a lot. 'Some truths are almost falsehoods and some falsehoods almost truths'. Sir Thomas Browne's Christian Morals. Rather up your street at the moment, I'd have thought.

'I don't know what you're talking about. If you're going to

write about people you should tell the truth — shouldn't you? I don't want you writing about me unless you tell the truth.'

I am *telling* the truth. Suppose I now had you saying: 'Sir Thomas Browne? I think he was a punter of mine' — that wouldn't be true, in the sense that you'd actually said it, but it would be in character, it would be true in that sense. Do you understand?

'No. I wouldn't say that — I've never even met him, Sir Thingummy Browne. And you're not to put in anything about pulling actors in piano bars. It just isn't true.'

It *is* true. It's how you were. You had a quality I'd never seen before. You seemed to think the whole world had been created just for you to play in. You were extraodinary. I've never been so proud of anyone.

'It *was* drugs. I *was* high.'

So? Is it better to be dead? Like them? Shuffling around with their prayers and programmes?

'I was out of my head. It wasn't real. Don't you understand?'

That's what they tell you, is it? Nothing that happened before they got hold of you was real. How convenient. How comforting. 'It's not my fault. I was ill. But what's your excuse?' The thick moral smugness of the recovering junkie. There's nothing more disgusting.

'Please help me to get well.'

I don't believe you're ill. And if you stay in here it won't be me you come home to. You'll be living with a nice man in a cottage in the country with dogs and a garden and God knows what.

'Would you rather I was dead?'

What would be the difference?

106

*

Whatever I do I mustn't quiz her; I mustn't ask her why she did it, who she did it for. She won't want to talk about it. She must never be called to account in the morning for anything she did the night before. That hadn't been her, she'd say, and I'd be dismissed with an irritated frown for being so heavy as to think it had been. I can be patient. Tonight – our last – I'll get her high again, and then she'll talk. Now I mustn't say a word.

Last night, why did you ...

'I don't want to talk about it. It's my last day, please don't spoil it.'

Bang! I shouldn't have said anything, of course – I should have learnt by now – but it is amazing. All that happens and she doesn't want to talk about it. It amounts, as I see it, to a crass lack of interest in herself. It's as if the recording mechanism in her brain isn't working properly, as if it can't play back the past. It's a kind of protective, self-induced amnesia, only lifted when she's high again. No wonder her life is such a mess – nothing joined up, each experience separate, not altering the next; no interpretations being made, no running analysis of what's going on, nothing carried forward. Why? Because she's been hurt? Because she can't afford to let anything that happens to her matter? And how much of this is due to drugs – are they cause or the effect of how she is? She isn't two entirely different people yet – drugged and straight, high and low – but she could be going that way, I'd say. At the moment she's perfectly okay when not on drugs; she's rather sweet, in fact – but not by any means at her best, not at the limit of her potential, not specifically what I want. When high, on the other hand, she's everything that a thinking man could want for a while, a sheer delight from moment to moment. Still – it's not my problem; if she doesn't want me to be interested in her, if she doesn't want me to care, I won't. I'll teach her a lesson in manners instead. Quite soon I get the opportunity.

107

'Is it a nice day? Where are we going?'

I don't want to talk about it, okay?

She looks a little startled, takes refuge behind her defensive smile. The rebuke has registered.

'I'm sorry. But it is our last day. I want it to be perfect.'

Now she starts to act, and badly – as insolently badly as a cat. She pouts and clutches Ted, buries her head in the pillow, makes indignant little grunting noises.

'I don't want to go. Why do I have to go? Ted says you've got some horrid tart coming out. I *know* you have. I don't like you being here with anyone but me.'

This would be gruesome enough even if she meant it. And yet, perhaps she *does* mean it, in a purely narcissistic way. Like any actress, she wants to be told that she was good, needs a 'You were marvellous, darling', reassurance that a younger replacement isn't already on her way with better lines. It's a form of dishonesty – endemic in her type – which I frankly can't be doing with. All the stranger, then, that I am able, unlike her, to see our situation from a point of view other than my own. It *would* be confusing to be sent for by an almost total stranger, flown in, directed, put on display, told what to think and what to wear and then be bundled out again. Even these women for a living deserve some show of gratitude, a few words of comfort at the end. My Princess has, after all, revealed some small, untidy corner of herself, if only by mistake. In the course of a week this is unavoidable, no matter how tight her defences have become in a life-time of being used, of being hoisted suddenly into a world in which she's quite unqualified to cope, in which her only weapons are her relative youth and looks; a life-time of being shuttled here and there and then sent home again, of waiting for the next summons from someone of a different type (not a gentleman, perhaps) with entirely different needs. And while she waits the solitary Sundays stretch ahead where there'd been proper Sundays once, Sundays shared with a man who took her seriously enough to spit at her and beat her up. It would be bewildering, this life; even actresses are people underneath. No wonder they get screwed up, take drugs, have this inability to trust. After a life-time of playing parts they can't even trust themselves; how could they trust a stranger, even one who understands everything, as I do? I must be nice to her, but at the same time not forget Tiffs' warning: 'She'll use you if she can. She doesn't know any other way.'

On our last night she behaves extremely badly, stretching this resolve to breaking-point. Frankly I want another fix, one last Tierra high, and the Jack the Actor incident has left this annoying nest of questions buzzing in my brain. Oddly, I keep getting a picture of her posing in her G-string and walking across the room towards him. It makes me uneasy, I don't know why. I didn't care, I don't care – I'm sure of that – it's just that loose ends irritate me, I suppose. I want to talk to her about it, but she flatly refuses to be put into circumstances in which she might. She insists, in fact, on a quiet dinner followed by an early night. I argue with her, become vehement, am on the edge of losing my temper once or twice, but she remains adamant. It's quite frightening, but revealing too, this mulish refusal to be budged; it's how she gives herself away, in fact. This blank lack of feeling when it matters, this impenetrable shutter dropping like a safety-curtain, shows that everything that went before was acting. 'Don't push,' she's warning me; 'don't try to get past this, to come backstage. Don't *you* become confused; it was all a fiction.' Well, stuff her – I was acting too, but I wouldn't make that so obvious. I wouldn't be so rude. Weak, silly women are often like this, I've found: often, and confusingly, absurdly strong – a strength that comes from moral ignorance, of course, from not having a point of view other than their own.

Over dinner she talks about a change of flats that's in the offing, the organisation of a new one having been left to her best friend Laura. How interesting! I say. Will there be a linen cupboard? Has the matter of power-points been considered? Where will the meters go? One does so hate an eye-sore in the hall. She fails to detect any irony in these remarks, but chats on brightly as if she might be anyone, giving me her mother's telephone number in Essex and explaining that she herself will be unobtainable until the move has been satisfactorily completed. And when we get home she undresses at once in front of me, unprovocatively, like a wife or something, and then gets into bed! I refuse to join her, but sit outside, ostentatiously reading a book.

'Come to bed.'

Why?

She *laughs*. I wait for a few minutes, expecting her to get out of bed, to come and discover what the problem is, to ask what it is she's doing wrong — not that she should need to — but she doesn't. I wait for a little longer and then, because I know how to behave even if she doesn't, I go into the bedroom, where she's turned the light out and is cuddling Ted, facing away, towards the wall. I poke her in the back.

'What's the matter? What is it you want?'

Actually I'm not entirely sure, but I know it isn't this. Perhaps I want her in her G-string, posing in the door-way. If she can do it for Jack the Actor she can fucking well do it for me. I can't say this, of course.

You know what I want.

It does sound a little foolish, but that's her fault entirely.

'Okay. Go and wait outside. I'll be with you in a minute.'

I do as she suggests, feeling very stupid now. How *could* she? How could she — on our last night — put me into a situation where I feel this foolish? After a minute she comes out of the bedroom and walks briskly past me to the bathroom. When she returns she's wearing her thigh-boots and the yellow G-string. Then to my horror and amazement — amazement that she could be so clumsy — she poses in the doorway, just as she did for Jack the Actor. Now I really do feel stupid. She's treating me like a sulky child to be indulged. This time she's really blown it. I look at her over the top of my book, insultingly running my eye up and down her body like a bored pansy dance arranger auditioning for a back-street strip show, and then I return to my reading, humming to myself, brow furrowed.

She laughs! She goes back to bed and laughs! Later, after I've put myself in the spare-room. I can still hear her laughing, and talking to Ted.

On the way to the airport she's very quiet, her face is set as if she's going for an interview, a going back to London face. I've seen it before, this particular expression; it combines anxiety at what's ahead with slight embarrassment at what's been before.

We're like two actors at the end of a provincial tour, feeling a little foolish because we were too intimate in Bristol. After a provincial tour in '62, I recall driving an actress back to London. We held hands all the way from Torquay to London, telling each other that everything would be all right, even though we knew it wouldn't. I was going to leave my wife, indeed I was naive enough to do so. I can see her now standing at the front-door crying, holding our son, and he was crying too. What atrocities one is capable of when young. I moved into a service flat, and there was a stain on the carpet and the wall-paper was unfamiliar and the light in the kitchen was too bright, and the actress with whom I was going to start again never joined me. She did ring me. Ships that pass in the night, she said, you should know better than to believe what people say on tour. I was young then; I wouldn't make that mistake again, would never frighten someone half to death for the sake of a tour romance. Were I to ring my Princess in London she'd call me 'darling' in a hard, distracted London voice, and there'd be other voices in the background, loud, confident voices that I wouldn't recognise, voices that had nothing to do with me, voices from another life. It is odd, being this intimate with someone you don't know at all. It must happen to these touring girls all the time. No wonder they go a little cuckoo. It would be like moving house once a week and changing all one's friends. No continuity, nothing sticking. At times like this I thank my lucky stars for the pussy cats, and Alison.

'You will call me, won't you?'

You know I will.

'When?'

Tonight.

I won't, of course. What would be the point? She may actually want me to call her, but only for reassurance. Once she's back in London I'll seem very vague to her. I'd ring her and she'd answer brightly: 'Hullo, darling. Monday? Sorry — what about Thursday?' Obviously seeing Jack the Actor on Monday, Tuesday and Wednesday, or going to a discotheque with a man who makes jeans for a living. I wouldn't like that. It's odd, we were only acting, only pretending, but for seven days we *were* together in a way, on the same side, more or less;

we had a sort of understanding. She was mine for a week, if only in a game. It would be hard to alter that arrangement, difficult to move on to something looser.

It would be different in London, and in London she doesn't look so good. London's the wrong back-drop for her. She needs music and the sun, she needs to wear her legs. In London she looks too small, she looks alarmed and pale. In ILiza she blooms and flourishes, she seems to grow six inches. I remember putting her into a taxi once in the Fulham Road – or rather *not* putting her into it, just leaving her there in the street. You'll find a taxi, I said, they come along all the time. She looked small and shocked, but she smiled bravely, probably said: '*Ciaou* darling!' She's looking like that already: pinched and scared. She'll call me darling in a bright, distracted London voice before we reach the airport.

'You're not to leave till my plane takes off. You promise?'

That's quite sweet. She looks so small and frightened. She obviously hates flying, so why does she do it? I've found it so much easier to cut out what I don't like doing: flying, going to pubs or dinner parties, visiting America or people in hospital – I simply don't do any of it. It's surprisingly easy once you've got the hang of it. My friend Jean Leyris has carried this minor art to its very limits. He's worked out that everything unpleasant in life happens between nine in the morning and six at night – that's when the people who want to get you into trouble call. His answer is so simple one wonders why no one else has thought of it. He doesn't get up till six pm. It's very irritating for others, of course, but that's the general idea; day-time types have given up trying to contact him, including the Inland Revenue, who have now declared him officially dead. I suppose my Princess has to fly – it's her business, after all. Suddenly I want to say something simple to her; to tell her that on two occasions at least she made me happy, that she's the first who has.

Thank you. You've been the best so far.

'Christ, that's gross. That's a frightful thing to say.'

She looks quite shocked. My word she's good, I have to take my hat off to her. With the right agent she could make a lot of money playing this character. I wonder if she's ambitious

112

enough? Tiffs says she is, but I'm not sure. I think she'd rather be happy.

She wants me to wait, but I push her through the departure barrier and drive straight back to the flat. I park the car and go upstairs, switch the flat into its working mode – writing-table erected in the salon, typewriter, tippex, A4 etc all in place. A cup of coffee and then straight in – it's the only way.

I remember summer holidays in Broadstairs, the Grand Hotel and little pier, and fishing with my father ...

I can't be bothered. I'm bored by the past, and I'm making it all up anyway. I've got to do something, though, and if I abandon my memoirs what shall it be? I'd better think of a toilet book, something to sell to Staughton when he arrives in three days time – but which, and why, and what? 'Twenty Things You Didn't Know About The Krankies'? 'How To Be A Pint-Sized Romeo'? 'Great Philosophical Disasters' (whoever it was who was killed by a tortoise falling on his head)? Here's one: 'You Want, You'd Settle For, You Get'. A brilliant idea – and none the worse for not being mine. It's Simey's in fact. If I sell it to Staughton, do I tell Simey? Probably not. He pinched it himself after all – from *The National Lampoon*, I think. We toilet book writers must keep the supply-lines of our imaginations open to what's been before. 'You want the girl and the money at 25. You'd settle for the girl and the money at 35. You get the girl and the money at 55, and it's too late and your legs have turned blue'. Screamingly funny. I bark with laughter at my own inventiveness, stand up, blow my chest out and walk around, go into the bedroom, I don't know why, and there on the pillow is my Princess's G-String and a little note – 'With all my love, Your Princess forever', and underneath there's a heart with an arrow through it, and then a PS: 'Do you have a toilet and a mirror? And where's the fucking phone? I want to call Utopia'.

My stomach turns and I go at the knees, sink on to the bed in a kind of shock. She's back, here in the room, and far more upsettingly than when she was actually present. I must keep my head, remind myself that this can happen: that a numinous quality hangs in a room which has just been left by someone you've been close to. Were we close, then? I look at the bed, imagine us asleep, wonder how we looked. Someone might have thought we were close, together for a moment. Larkin comes immediately to mind, of course – an image of two people talking in bed, finding words that are true and kind, or not untrue and not unkind – that stuff. I shake myself and return to my writing-desk. I try to work but toilet books seem more demeaning, even sillier than usual. My Princess is everywhere I look, and my heart aches.

Is her power actual, then? I get up and walk around, start to recite out loud – with resonance and feeling. 'Can denial of you duck and run/ Stay out of sight and double round, / Leap from the sun with mask and brand/ And murder and not understand?' It sounds so good that I recite it again, this time falling over a stupidly placed puff half-way through, alas, and having to start again from the beginning, feeling a little silly, even though no one saw me take a tumble. I am indulging myself, perhaps, but it *is* very strange to live with someone for a week, even a performing woman; one is forced, if one is sensitive at all, to take them more seriously than they take themselves. My Princess would laugh at all this; she'd be astonished that her little gesture (itself no more than the sort of charming spontaneity at which Mrs Mouse was so adept – dummying one onto a scything upper-cut) had touched me so profoundly. Most disturbingly of all, I keep getting a picture of her coming into the salon in her G-string, posing angelically in the doorway, and then walking over to Jack the Actor. It didn't mean a thing at the time. Why now does it make my stomach churn?

There's only one thing for it: I'll have to get stoned; there's always time to write a toilet book. And that's another odd thing: I hardly smoked at all when she was here; I didn't need to; she was my high. I roll a joint now, put the music on and move my business to the balcony. I wonder what she's doing now? Probably ringing Jack the Actor. No, she won't be back in London yet. She did look sweet in her G-string and boots, and I *would* like to see her again. What a shame it is that she isn't just a shade more suitable, what a shame that she isn't one of those stern ladies who crop up on arts programmes, who wear spectacles and cross their legs and suddenly you want to fuck them from behind.

114

I wonder why I've always assumed that these stern literary ladies wouldn't wear a G-string if you asked them to and dance on tables for you? It's just an assumption, after all, I've never known one of them, not well enough at least to ask her if she ever wears thigh boots and a G-string. I'm sure I'm right, though. Being a Princess is a full-time job. Literary ladies would simply be too busy. Horses for courses, that's what it is.

George Michael has taken over from Cindi Lauper, alas (Hit Tapes of 1985, side one) and I sit on the balcony and wonder vaguely if there's something a little odd about me: a man of my age with a court case in the offing, listening to 'Hit Tapes of 1985' (side one) – it will be Bruce Springsteen soon, thank God – wondering whether literary ladies ever wear thigh boots and a G-string? From inside it seems normal enough, inevitable in fact; from outside I'd think: silly old fool; he's crackers; he's had it. Is not wanting to be old, to rasp in the morning and have cold feet, sufficient evidence of madness, then? I consider the ranks of the obviously sane, and ask myself this: is it possible to imagine one of them sitting in the sun rat-stoned, listening to 'Hit Tapes of 1985' (side one) and wondering what I'm wondering now? It isn't – that's the size of it.

And now I find myself wanting urgently to look at all the photographs I took of my Princess. I get up unsteadily, go to the drawer and take them out, compare them with the others, the ones of previous performers which I now find very tacky. I have a desire to tear these old ones up, but remember just in time that this is precisely what she said I'd do. It seems important, at this point, to assert my will, so I put the old ones back in the drawer and start to arrange the ones of my Princess in chronological order, trying to read a story into her expressions. She looks happy, carefree, like a laughing girl on holiday; I'd almost swear she isn't working; there isn't that watchful look in her eyes.

Next it seems sensible to lay them out in order of erotic content, squatting on the floor, spreading them out in an ever-widening circle, an exercise that takes me – such is the limited floor-space at my disposal – on all-fours under the writing-table. The most erotic ones, I find, are those taken on

115

the night of her arrival. She looks really happy in these, mischievous and trusting, and yet we hardly knew each other. She *is* mysterious – systematically so. I squat under the writing-table trying to work out a coherent theory of her behaviour, trying to decode everything she said, to resolve the contradictions. And that's odd too – not her behaviour, not the contradictions (there's nothing odd in contradictions, after all, least of all in the emotionally immature) – but that I should be interested enough to try and work them out. The only consistent explanation I can find is that she likes me. But that's not right – there wasn't time, and she was as warm on the first night as the last, warmer, in fact. I must keep my head here. I'm thinking about her in entirely the wrong way: like a moon-struck adolescent, turning over and over in his mind a simple 'Good-morning' from the painfully beautiful girl next-door, tapping it for hidden meanings. I must hold on hard to what Tiffs said: 'She'll take you for everything if she can. She doesn't know another way.' I was in danger of being fooled because she's very good at what she does, and I couldn't see it because they never usually are. That's no excuse, however. I'm of the live theatre – I of all people should know the difference between reality and acting. I'm losing my grip; I'm getting too old and soft for this. A little tart is quite polite and I become confused, squat under the writing-table and try to work out why.

I am a little stoned, of course, a circumstance brought home to me when the telephone rings and I stand upright as if a gun's gone off, lifting the table clear into the air and throwing everything on it, typewriter, A4, coffee cup etc, to the floor. Could it be her? I look at my watch. It's four o'clock now and she left at twelve. It *could* be – just. I dive for the phone, over-extending myself and coming a cropper in the debris, knocking the phone to the floor. It isn't her. It's Alison, of course, and she sounds upset.

'Are you working?'

Of course I'm fucking working. What do you think I'm doing? Having tea with the Princess of Wales?

Sorry.

She starts to cry, and since she doesn't often cry (I honestly don't believe that Alison has noticed what hell life is) I ask her

116

what the matter is. Is it the carpet that isn't meant to show the dirt, but does? No, it's her mother. Her mother is dying of cancer of the liver, and has been given six months at the most. Oh God – that's all I need. She asks me to come home at once, but I say that's impossible, that I've got Staughton coming out.

'Why can't you see Staughton in London?'

I try to keep my patience, even though I sometimes think she has no understanding of the difficulty of what I do; perhaps, even, doesn't *want* me to do well, that my success is threatening to her, that she'd prefer me in some way to be dependent on her. No – that's a trifle unfair. She hates me coming to Ibiza, but is pretty good about it on the whole. I explain that I need time with Staughton, that he wears a corduroy suit and takes his holidays in Wales, that such a type must be played carefully, round the clock, that I can't do that in London.

'Of course. I'm sorry. I'll be okay. I'm upset today, that's all. She came up to London to tell me. She brought a bottle of champagne. She was so brave. It's the reaction now she's gone, I think. I feel so guilty. I haven't been very good to her.'

She starts to cry again, so I reassure her. She's always been very good to her, I say.

'I haven't really. There is one thing.'

She sounds nervous, so I know something frightful's coming. What?

'You won't like it. You'll be cross.'

No I won't.

'I want to take her on holiday – her last. I'd like her to come to Ibiza with us.'

Jesus Christ.

'I knew you'd be cross. But it is important. And we've been happy in Ibiza. You're nice to me in Ibiza. I'd like her to see that. *Please.*'

She starts to cry again, so I apologize, explain that it was the shock of it all, say that she must of course have her last holiday out here. But when?

'As soon as possible. While she doesn't feel too bad. After the court case, I thought. Would that be all right?'

I say that it would, and manage to get her off the line at last. This will be a nightmare. Ibiza is the last place I want to be

117

with Alison's dying mother, or with Alison, come to that. Being sensitive, I don't want to be here with her so soon after my Princess has left. I go back to looking at the photographs, but there's no pleasure in it now; Alison's phone call has brought me right down. Her sense of timing is amazing.

I try to work, but can see no point in it. Instead I play computer chess, and wonder, if I *did* want my Princess, whether I could get her, and it occurs to me that she might be wondering the same thing too. We might – being as frightened as each other – be playing the same game, just for reassurance. We're like a chess computer playing itself at the same level – a circumstance, I may say, in which black often, and mysteriously, wins. I decide to go for a walk, a small nostalgic tour of the places where she got me in, where I qualified with her. I leave the flat, humming a little as I walk, circle Ponce Corner in a nervous arc, inching closer, wondering whether I'll be welcome on my own. Tanit the Island God is lounging as usual with his retinue outside the Bar Chic, so I duck my head and quicken my step importantly as if I might be going somewhere. He calls out – 'Where's your Princess?' – but I haven't the heart to stop and talk. Without her I'm even more frightened than I thought I'd be. I feel out of it again and old. I pass the Tierra at a distance, glance sourly at the people having fun, reflect that just a night or two ago I'd felt unconquerable here, as if I'd been offered a reprieve, and hurry home, feeling silly and defeated.

The next day I still can't work. It's a scorcher, so I decide to spend it at the beach. I can't face Salinas, where my Princess had looked so lovely in her little pink bikini, so I drive to Talamanca – an awful tourist-cum-family beach quite near Ibiza Town. Here, a week ago, there'd have been enough pretty girls on show – large German secretaries and Swedes, oiling one another's tanned, soft ballooning thighs – to make me feel envious and indignant. I'd have coveted the lot of them, wanted greedily to possess them all, to lock them away for my eyes only like a sinister old connoisseur of art. Today I don't feel this at all. I look around and, if anything, feel sorry for all the

118

unfortunate men who aren't with my Princess, who don't know of her existence even, can't imagine how deprived they are. In all my life I've never felt anything like this before – and, instead of being heartened, I'm afraid. It would be better, I think, to be as I was, envious but ignorant. What if I never see her again? I'll know forever that there is someone who could have altered everything.

There's a young girl, a few mattresses away, who's horribly deformed. She seems to be paralysed down one side of her body, and her left leg is withered and ugly, and shorter than the other. But she has a young man with her who is muscular and handsome, and he buys some flowers and puts one in her hair, and then he takes her gently in his arms and carries her, laughing, into the sea, and his eyes are full of tenderness and pride. I am the deplorable opposite of him, and I'm pleased with myself for knowing this, feel myself, on this account, to be superior to him, and I make an entry to this effect in my handy writer's notebook. It's easy enough to behave yourself when you're young and beautiful; when you're old and it's all gone wrong, good behaviour is unnatural. Old people who behave themselves are fools.

I know what I've become, thank God, which is more than can be said for a man of forty-five, or so – Dutch, I'd guess – who is doing handstands with his teenage son a few yards from where I'm sitting. A party of awful English youths – football supporters, I'd imagine – are playing silly buggers in the water, forming boastful pyramids and diving off each other's shoulders, and now this stupid Dutchman, watched by his son, runs towards the sea and tries to play with them, laughing and splashing them hopefully and diving between their legs. They duck him for his effrontery and hold him under, and at first he laughs, but when they start to toss him contemptuously from one to another like a beach ball his laughter turns to bewilderment, then fear. And now two of them hold him fast in tatooed, skinny English arms while a third removes his jaunty swimming trunks, waving them out of his reach while he flounders around in the shallow water, begging for their return. They laugh and sneer at him, and throw him about and hold him under – spluttering and naked – and from the safety of the beach fat people cheer and sweat a bit and look furtively excited, and, because he'd asked for it, this Dutchman who thought he could still join in, we're all disgusted, including his son, who has watched the whole thing, horrified.

I feel sick, and leave the beach at once, determined now – for my sanity's sake – to work flat out and never think again of my Princess. I'm not as deluded as that old fool who wanted to play and took a ducking, but my Princess is a little dangerous; she's a function of my fear, a mirage, making me think there's hope, when of course there isn't. So, back at the flat, I pick up her photographs from the floor, where they're still spread in order of erotic content amid the debris of my work, and I look at them and rearrange them, and I put some music on ('Hit Tapes of 1985', side two) and I roll a joint, and I sit back and wonder whether I should ring her mother, find out where she is. And as I'm wondering this, the phone rings and my heart leaps because I think it might be her, and then I move quickly to turn the music down, because it won't be her; it will be Alison with one of her well-timed calls and I don't want Alison to think I'm getting stoned and listening to music in the afternoon instead of working. But it isn't Alison.

'Hi! It's your baby! Are you being good? You're *stoned*. What are you doing? Why aren't you working?'

Why are my insides liquidized so that when I sit down suddenly I actually squelch, whereas I'd be furious had Alison said this?

Where are you?

'I'm with Jack the Actor. Are you cross? No I'm not. I'm at my best friend Candy's. Why didn't you phone last night? You said you'd phone. Sorry – telephone.'

I didn't know where you were.

'I told you to ring my mother. She'd have given you Candy's number. Listen – guess what. I'm coming back!'

Is she pulling my leg? She must remember surely that Staughton's coming out tomorrow. I can't have her here with him.

When?

'Tomorrow! Are you pleased?'

I'm appalled. I want to tell her not to come, that she isn't suitable, but obviously I can't. She wouldn't understand, she might be very hurt. How many people, after all, could survive knowing everything we think of them, could have a tour of our thoughts and not be hurt? We have to delude ourselves to keep our dignity – she more than most. Her confidence, I now realise, is only paper-thin, entirely a question of whether she's high or not. And what she's doing now – booking *me*, so to speak (like a restaurateur ringing up the punter he's already warned off, now telling him, confusingly, to come again) – demonstrates why, with me, she'll always win. I'd sooner die than hurt her now, tell her that she isn't welcome, but she'd cut me down without a qualm were I to blunder into her affairs when I wasn't wanted. Nor would I blame her if she did: it's not her fault that she lacks the moral sensitivity only education can provide.

Of course I'm pleased.

'I'll be very good, I promise. I know you've got important business to discuss with thingummy. Am I still your Princess?'

You know you are.

Perhaps she won't be able to get a flight. Planes get very booked up at this time of year. I console myself with this thought.

Have you got a ticket?

'Not yet. But it'll be okay. Candy's boyfriend's helping. He's a travel agent. He'll be able to arrange it. Aren't you excited? You don't sound excited. I will be good, I really will.'

I'm thrilled, Princess.

She gives me Candy's number in case of an emergency and says she'll ring me tomorrow with the time of her arrival.

Shit – I'll lose Mark Staughton now. Men who sing in choirs, attend lunchtime concerts in the City and take their holidays in Wales don't give their money to a lightweight who needs an odd little blonde at his side for reassurance. And yet – why should her presence here necessarily put him off? I like her, after all, she amuses me a lot; why shouldn't Staughton see the point of her? Alas, I have to dismiss this possibility at once. I have a taste, not shared by men like Staughton, for these unscrupulous girls with mad legs and minds like soda-water. It would be all right – or better at least – if only they wouldn't talk. My

121

Princess will swim out of her conversational depth and, just when I should be reaching into Staughton's wallet, I'll have to paddle in to rescue her. It would be okay if they'd be themselves, but they tense up and alter before your eyes. I'm reminded again of that awful evening at the Tynans when Dawn Upstairs told Martin Amis that his journalism lacked the moral dimension of his fiction. That wasn't why she'd been invited. She was there as a clown, to tell those serious people what it's like to be a tart, to give the impression that she was the only person at the table who's bothered to get her underwear right. My Princess will similarly go to pieces, wear her Harvey Nichols dress, sit bolt-upright in her chair and tell tall stories; say she was an actress once and mention books she hasn't read. I have a sleepless night, imagining Staughton and my Princess together, his look of amused forebearance as she prattles on. I get up and smoke and pace around, at one moment deciding that I'll have to put her off, only to realise, at the very next, that I can't, that I don't really want to, that if I do I may never discover what she's up to. I'm sure Tiffs is right, I'm sure she's merely hustling me, but I want to know how far she'll go. The conman's victim always knows he's being taken and for him it's half the fun. I collaborate because I can't resist studying experts on the job, marvelling at their audacity. Were I to put off my Princess now I'd never know to what lengths she'd go, nor how resourceful I might be in blocking her. On top of which, I am a little flattered – which makes it fifteen love to her already (soon to be fifteen all, because I've not been fooled).

She rings back early in the morning to say that Candy's boyfriend has managed to get her onto a flight coming via Majorca. She hates flying, and now she's got to change planes, the brave little thing, and hang around airports. I'm even more flattered, and rather touched.

'Are you excited? You don't sound very excited. Why are you being so cold? Don't you want me to come?'

Of course I do.

'How are they going, your thingummies? Are you working? I hope you're working very hard, not sitting around getting stoned. Do you want to tell me one of those anecdotes of yours? From Winchester to this?'

122

She arrives at tea-time, as straight as a die and looking crisp and adorable in an efficient little business suit and an important expression to go with it. She's brought a variety of silly presents too – a computer alarm clock, the wrong cigars, a small Sloane Ranger bear. She's a little subdued at first, but she perks up on the drive from the airport – holding my arm and laughing and saying what fun we're going to have – so I subdue her again with a necessary pep-talk. I've got to get on the front-foot straight away, and stay there. First and foremost, I say, it's important that Staughton thinks she likes me.

She looks puzzled.

'I do.'

'You know what I mean. Staughton wears a corduroy suit and has a poetry list. We've got to work out what you are.

'*What* I am? Do you mind?'

Okay – *who* you are. Plus he sings in a choir, I think.

'I'm your girlfriend.'

This is tricky. I'm a little touched, in fact, but it happens to be almost the last thing I'd want Staughton to suppose – which is not something I can explain to her. It occurs to me again that she is less ashamed of me than I am of her – or, rather, less ashamed of *us*. In fact there's very little wrong with her. Vulgarity's the quality I can't be doing with, and she's the least vulgar person I've ever met, I think. Everything she does is deliberate and unashamed, she has a kind of damaged innocence, or can act it (amazingly, bearing in mind the life she's led) which makes vulgarity impossible. The embarrassment I feel is not her fault but mine. It's just not credible, I'm afraid, that she'd ever be my girlfriend. She'd either be the girlfriend of a stuntman on a motorbike, or she'd be a hustler. I make her look like a hustler. I'm simply not the sort of person – looking, as I do like a man who buys his clothes at Peter Jones – her sort of person would be with except for money. I can't explain all this to her, but I am quite touched that she can't see it herself, touched that she at least is prepared to be with me in public. And I'll be able, with an assortment of little nods and winks, to tip Staughton off. Referring to her as my Princess will help. Staughton will pick up on the irony of my Princess, he'll spot that to me at least we're something of a joke. But then the lowering thought occurs that she also may have various ways of tipping him off. We'll be nodding and winking behind each other's backs, and Staughton will think we're cuckoo.

Back at the flat, I sit her down and continue with my pep-talk, mapping out the limits of what can be her conversational involvement.

She begins to look displeased, frowning slightly, pouting, showing an edge of defiance.

'Perhaps you should write me out a script. I don't want to let you down over dinner.'

That won't be necessary.

'Good.'

Because you won't be joining us. Not tonight, at least. I'll pick up Staughton at the airport and take him straight to dinner — on my own. Tomorrow you can join in — as long as you behave yourself. You must on no account push anything up your nose in front of him, or try to sell him your memoirs. And the enactment, late of night, of large and noisy fantasies is absolutely out.

She's looking openly defiant now, which is very naughty of her. This was her idea, not mine.

'Are you sure you wouldn't rather I moved into a hotel?'

Don't be silly. However, it might be a good idea for you to be tucked away in bed by the time we get back from dinner. Start brand new tomorrow. Tomorrow is another day and so forth.

'Well — this is going to be a lot of fun, I must say. I think I'll go to bed now.'

Don't you want to eat something? We could have a quick snack. I don't have to pick Staughton up for about an hour.

'Don't worry about me. I'll have a bowl of soup or something. Would that be all right? Do we have some soup?'

She gets up and goes into the kitchen, finds a tin and starts to heat the contents in a saucepan, smiling bravely. She's behaving very badly now, but I've thought of a way of making her see how selfish she's being. At the most devastating moment I'll tell her about Alison's dying mother, bring it home to her dramatically — the only presentational mode her type can understand — how deplorably spoilt she is, that there are some people in the world grappling with real disasters. She comes out

124

of the kitchen, undresses with quite comically emphasised modesty and then gets into bed with her bowl of soup. She sits, propped up against the pillows, managing to hold Ted, sip her soup, pout and look brave all at the same time – a performance which in less serious circumstances I'd find adorable.

If the phone rings you mustn't answer it.

'*Tele*phone.'

Okay – telephone. If it rings you must ignore it.

'*Why*? I suppose you're frightened it might be *her*.'

That's right.

This is going to work beautifully. Girls like her all feel guilty apropos their mothers, send them money, pay their gas bills and dread them dying.

'Well, I don't care. If the telephone rings I'm going to answer it. If it is *her* I'll be absolutely charming. I'll say that I'm your mistress and you're very bad. Ted says that's what I should do.'

I wouldn't do that.

'Why *not*?'

Because she isn't very happy at the moment.

'Well, I'm not very happy either. What's the matter with her?'

She heard yesterday that her mother's dying of cancer. She's only got six months.

It works even better than I'd hoped. For a second my Princess looks completely stunned. Her eyes open wide with horror and then, because her hands have begun to shake, she spills her soup.

Careful – you've spilt the soup.

'Fuck the *soup*! That's *terrible*. *Christ* that's terrible! Why are you laughing? How can you *laugh* about it?'

I'm laughing at you. You look so shocked.

'I *am* shocked. It's awful. Poor Alison. For Christ's sake stop laughing. God, if it was my mother ...'

... I thought she'd manage, sooner or later, to find a role for herself in this particular drama, to wheel herself centre-stage, as it were.

'... look, Alison mustn't find out about us while her mother's still alive.'

What on earth makes her think that Alison will *ever* find out

125

about us? She really is odd, for a hustler – it's as if she didn't attend the same training school as all the others.

Soon after this I leave. I meet Staughton at the airport (recognising him by his corduroy suit and wispy beard – I've only met him once before) and take him straight to dinner at a restaurant up in the old town, run by four loony French girls who make such a production of the whole thing that the punters think they're being served with something good, when all they're getting is expensive filth, of course. It's the nearest thing Ibiza has to Charlotte Street and Staughton will be impressed, I think. He doesn't seem impressed, however – he doesn't seem anything at all in fact. He's totally anonymous, as blank as a piece of paper, one of those nerve-racking people who asks you out to lunch and doesn't say a word, sits staring at you in bewilderment, as if you've asked him and he's waiting to discover why. Someone's got to speak, so, to clear the decks, as it were, I tell him of my Princess's unexpected presence here, get that admission out of the way at once so that we can sit back, stretch our legs, like literary men who sing in choirs, and discuss the important things – specifically how many toilet books he'd like to buy.

... Got this mad girl back at the flat, do you see? Funny little thing. Out here last week, thought I'd managed to get rid of her, then she decided to come back! No one more surprised than me. Couldn't stop her. Not sure what her game is. Sorry about that. I'll keep her tucked away as much as possible ...

I think this hits the right note, more or less, but to my surprise Staughton looks at me as if I've gone down in his estimation – or as if I would have done, had he held an estimation of me in the first place (since his arrival, in fact, he's been looking at me with vague suspicion, as if wondering who I am). 'Where is she now?' he asks – speaking for the first time, and rather nervously, as if she might be under the table and about to pull his trousers down. At home having a bowl of soup, I say. He looks relieved, but I can see that I've made a slight miscalculation. Staughton may not be as stupid as he looks; he's twigged, I think, that I'm ashamed of her and for some reason he thinks less of me for this. His reaction has made me feel a little cheap, on top of which, my reluctance to let her join us has the curious effect of making me seem over-eager to discuss business, to sell the poor man something, when he, clearly, is exhausted from his journey and would rather have an early night. Realising my mistake, I become agitated, try to retrieve the situation, not by relaxing gracefully myself, but by throwing too many ideas up in the air at once – old ones, new ones, some already sold, some cooked up on the spot, some already published even – but none seems to catch his interest. Indeed he leans away, keeps his distance behind a cautious half-smile, tense but sympathetic, like a man assailed at too close quarters by a friend with halitosis.

I blame my Princess for this debacle: if the silly girl had stayed in London none of this would have happened. I'd have taken my time, sold him something gradually, not acted like a Wild-West patter-man selling hair-restorer from a wagon. I blame him too: this was his idea, not mine. He rang me up one day, reminded me that we'd met once in the street, said he'd recently set up on his own, and then he invited himself to stay. If he doesn't want to talk about me, what's he doing here? He's looking so utterly bewildered now that it occurs to me, rather suddenly, that perhaps this isn't Staughton at all, that in my confusion at the airport I pulled the wrong publisher, another passionless man in a corduroy suit, out here, perhaps, to sign up a different clutch of toilet books entirely. Or, worse, perhaps, he isn't even a publisher: perhaps I pulled some fellow here on holiday, separated him from his family, sat him down, told him all about my Princess, then tried to sell him 'Twenty Things You Didn't Know About The Krankies'. No wonder he looks bewildered, and it wouldn't be the first time I'd made a mistake like this. Some years ago, discovering that my son Charlie was currently at Eton, I hopped down there and took the wrong boy to lunch. He didn't tip me off and we got on famously, the wrong lad and I; indeed he was on the point of leaving Eton and coming to live with me in London, I recall, when his correct father came into the restaurant and kicked up a frightful row. I'd better check Staughton out, I think, before I give any more of my best ideas to a double-glazing rep from Woking.

Staughton, is it? Small publisher, on your own, backed by a

crooner, sing in a choir, take your holidays in Wales and keen to get into toilet books?

Staughton looks a little startled, but he doesn't deny any of this, so I assume everything's as it should be.

Thought I might have pulled the wrong publisher, do you see? And what would that have been – a mistake or an accident? Puts one in mind of Austin's 'Shooting the wrong donkey', does it not? Might be something there for 'Great Philosophical Disasters'. Did I mention that one?

He doesn't buy it, and after dinner I make things worse, keeping him out a little late when obviously he'd rather be in bed. I'm afraid my Princess may have laid on a surprise or two back at the flat – become bored, perhaps, and wandered out to buy some of her accelerating powder, might now be sitting at home laying out lines and rocking with laughter at the absurdities of the 'real' world. With this in mind, I take Staughton for a delaying drink at an unfashionable bar on the wrong side of Ibiza Town (I can't risk being spotted by the in-crowd having a drink with a forty-year-old in a corduroy suit), where, once again, preferring any alternative, I think, to having to talk to me – he suggests that I go and fetch my Princess. 'Give her a ring, at least', he says, pointing out that I can phone her from here. I can't do that, I say – grateful for this opportunity to bring it elegantly to his attention that I'm a rascal, that I have someone in London too. I've told her not to answer the phone in case it's my other lady. And now Staughton looks even less impressed, slips even further from my grasp, I think, though whether this is because I'm cheating or because I seem to think such behaviour clever I can't quite tell.

I keep the poor man out till 2 am, by which time he's so blotto with drink and fatigue that he won't notice, I think, whatever my Princess is up to. In fact, when we do at last get home I'm relieved to discover that she's sound asleep, clutching Ted. I'm less pleased to discover that she seems to have done some housework in our absence – cleaning the kitchen, moving the furniture around, putting one of the better lamps in Staughton's room and a bottle of mineral water by his bed – all of which I find very unattractive. Staughton, on the other hand, seems to be impressed. 'She must be a really nice girl,' he says. That's the last thing she is, thank God, I say. In the morning I'll have to tick her off. I don't want even a type like Staughton to think I'm living with a housemaid.

The next day she behaves quite well, in fact, putting nothing up her nose, as far as I can tell, and, on the beach, playing dolphins on her own, enabling me to discuss literature with Staughton in the kiosk. I fail to sell him anything, of course, and for this I blame her, though precisely why, I'm not quite sure. Her presence here unsettles me, compelling me to do two things at once – bear down on Staughton with an endless stream of toilet book ideas and, at the same time, to circle the outfield nervously, ready to cut off any overthrows or gauche miss-hits by her – not that she's guilty of any, I must admit. When she joins us for lunch, Staughton, for some reason, seems keener to talk to her than to me, but she smiles sweetly at him and says: 'I'm sorry, I'd like to talk to you, I really would. But I'm not allowed to speak in case I say something silly.'

She's delighted by this, seems to think it quite hilarious – almost as hilarious as the joke she has up her sleeve in the evening. When, after a fairly arduous dinner, we're back at the flat and Staughton is safely tucked away in bed she looks at me shyly and says: 'Where are you going to sleep?'

With you, of course.

'What! You can't risk that. Whatever might Staughton think? Good heavens – he might think I'm your girlfriend. We can't have that. He'd never buy a book from someone with a girlfriend like me. You'd better sleep in the salon.'

I manage to laugh this one off, but later, when we're in bed, she keeps as far away from me as possible and when I try to touch her she pushes me away.

'No! We *mustn't*. The poor man's got to get his sleep. He sings in a choir, you know, and takes his holidays in Wales.'

She's not joking – for the rest of her visit she doesn't let me lay a finger on her, smiling demurely if I try to and explaining that she's not that sort of girl. All this is merely irritating, but on their last morning – Staughton has decided to go home early, I don't know why, with the result that they're flying back together – a real catastrophe occurs. I suddenly realise that it would be a good idea to have some photographs of Staughton in the flat, to prove to Alison that he has been here, his presence accounting for the number of times she may have called in the evening, only to find me out. After I've been snapping away for a while, I spot my Princess in the background (bored suddenly, it seems, with her demure and virginal role) without her clothes, pulling faces and adopting lewd positions. I rebuke her and she gets quite sulky.

'I don't like it how frightened you are of *her*.'

'I think your Princess is falling in love,' Staughton says – quite light-heartedly, as a joke really (you can't really blame him, the silly muffin has probably never seen a Princess working) – but I go cold inside. She won't stand still for this, she'll have to put him in the picture, and I won't blame her if she does. There's a limit to what a business-girl will take, and this is way beyond it. She looks quite startled, like someone whose doctor has just given them a disagreeable, though by no means fatal, diagnosis.

'Goodness, do you think so? Perhaps you're right.'

I'll forgive her everything for that. No actress could have had her pride more severely tested. She really is excellent at this. I relax again, feel immensely grateful to her, but then, driving to the airport, I suddenly realise how dangerous their flying back together is. Once the plane is in the air, she'll be off the books, so to speak, like an England cricketer at the end of a tour, no longer gagged, free contractually to spill the beans. There has been nothing in the agreement specifying long-term silence. On the plane, high on booze and valium, she'll have to mark his card, tell him the truth, if only to protect herself. Against the inevitability of this, I start to put her down in a variety of subtle ways. I become cool and distant, hardly pay attention while she prattles on; and when, at the airport, she makes me promise to ring her the second I get back to London in two days time, I'm quite off-hand, winking at Staughton behind her back, suggesting that I'm a busy man with a court case in the offing, that I might find time to ring her, but that she must be understanding if I don't. Whatever she says to Staughton on the plane, he'll know I haven't been deceived. A punter is one thing; a deluded punter quite another.

And as soon as she's gone I get that odd unsettled feeling. I go over everything she said, wondering what she meant. I wish I'd been nicer to her, and I want her back.

On the long drive back to London on my own I keep myself amused by fantasising deeply about the coming court case, brought by Schultz. We'll lose it on a technicality, perhaps (various home-cooked contracts, specifying joint-ownership of copyright), but I'll make him look a monkey in the process. I bowl along rehearsing repartee between myself and Schultz's barrister – in my mind a fat and flustered man – whom I set up like a skittle and clap in paradoxes with teeth like fighting dogs. The court howls, the judge congratulates me and Schultz's barrister hangs his stupid head in shame. It's a pity that my Princess can't be there to share my triumph. Then, driving through Lyons to be precise, I suddenly realise that she is – in the wings, standing next to my sister Bobo, her lovely face ablaze with admiration. That's odd. For as long as I can remember there have been two categories of women in my head: the nice ones who are present at my triumphs, standing beside my sister Bobo, the ones I respect, who, realising suddenly that it is me they have cared for all along, leave their husbands, or, smiling broken-heartedly, decide they can't; and the hooligans, the ones with legs, the ones my sister Bobo will never know about. Until now my fantasies have been discreet, the categories have never merged. Would I introduce my Princess to my sister Bobo, then? Of course I wouldn't. There are still two sorts of women in my head (for which I blame my parents) – and Alison, who's always there, of course, with her punishing selflessness ...

... and still finding of absorbing interest her new carpet which isn't meant to show the dirt but does. On top of which the washing machine has broken down, flooding the flat below. And we really ought to have the thingummies to dinner, it's a year and a half since we dined with them. And my accountant called. And I can see my Princess dancing with Tanit the Island God – little boots, white skirt, brown legs – and collecting pebbles on the beach and asleep in the morning clutching Ted and never ever talking about carpets and accountants – and I can see my coffin-lid descending, locking me in forever.

131

And the service charge is going up, and the VAT man called and someone left an envelope which she doesn't like the look of.

Really, Alison? I say. How interesting! I'm quite absorbed. A boring person might have said: the Princess of Wales called, she wants to see you urgently.

And this is a bit of a king-punch, I suppose, and I do say it rather more nastily than I'd intended. And so she starts to cry, and then she pulls herself together and apologises.

'I'm sorry. It's mummy. You haven't asked me how she is.'

I've hardly had a bloody chance. I've only been back three minutes, in which time you've managed to tell me every boring thing that's happened in the last four months. How's your mother?

'Not too good. It's her birthday on Thursday week. It's obviously her last, so the whole family will be there. I'll drive down and stay the night. Will you come? *Please*. It is important.'

My mind goes into overdrive. With Alison away I could spend the whole night with my Princess. An opportunity like this, a chance to recreate in London the conditions of Ibiza, to see if it worked as well, might never come again. It's a miracle. And so I frown and look concerned and say that it might be difficult, that I'm badly behind with the toilet books, that I've already promised to start on one immediately with Simey. And Alison looks disappointed, but says she understands. And then I point out that I might, in any case, still be in court on Thursday, that if the hearing isn't over, I'll have to stay in London. This is the clincher, I think, but Alison says that if the case isn't over she'll stay in London too. Good God, I say, you can't do that, you can't miss your mother's last birthday; but Alison says that in this event of course she'll miss it, that nothing is more important than watching her Button slicing Schultz into little pieces. She has been fantasizing, she says, about all the violent things she'd like to do to him, and, when she details some of these, I'm quite shocked to discover the controlled, sadistic lengths to which she'd go. Alison is the kindest person in the world, the only person I've ever met incapable of cruelty, but what she'd do to Schultz would give one of Her Majesty's prison warders second thoughts.

What I must do immediately is phone my Princess and tell

her not to make a date for Thursday – which is not as easy and one might think, particularly when I don't know where she is. It will take two calls at least – one to her mother or to her best friend Candy, and then another to whatever number either of them gives me. Obviously I can't do this from the flat, so I'll have to escape at some point to a call-box. With this in mind, I offer to do the shopping, but Alison immediately says that she'll come too; and when I say, rather sharply, that there's not much point in us both going out, that if she insists on doing it she might as well do it on her own (thinking that I can ring my Princess in her absence) she looks quite crest-fallen and mutters about it being my first night home and the importance of togetherness and so forth. So we go out together to do the shopping, and I begin to panic, realising how much I'd mind if Thursday turned out to be the only night for which my Princess had already made a date. I'd try to make her change it, and she'd sound surprised. 'But darling,' she'd say, in a bright, distracted London voice, 'I couldn't possibly do *that*. What about the following week?' And then I'd go to pieces, complain that she didn't understand, that Thursday was our only chance. 'Our only chance for what?' she'd ask, and in the end she'd become impatient with my wheedling tone; she'd have to point out that it was I who didn't understand; that in London everything was different.

And this awful scenario wouldn't be unfolding in my brain had not Alison insisted on doing the shopping with me; so when she suggests that we buy some kidneys I rather take it out on her.

You don't like kidneys. You hate them.

'I know, but *you* like them.'

What the fuck's the point of having something you don't like?

And this makes her cry again, so I agree that kidneys are what we'll have for dinner – and then she's happy because now we're going to have something she doesn't like. And for the rest of the evening we sit in silence watching television – remaining seated even while two commedians make jokes while dressed as turkeys – and I think how odd it is that for fifteen years I've been content with this, even happy.

★

On Saturday my luck's no better. I do manage to sneak out to a call-box, but neither Candy nor my Princess's mother is at home. Then, on Sunday, I escape again – Alison's becoming careless; letting me buy the Sunday papers on my own is very slack – and I catch her mother in. She sounds like quite a nice old tart, and, for someone who would rather know what her daughter does than think she might be marrying Americans, quite untroubled too. My Princess has moved into her new flat in Sloane Avenue, she says, and has particularly instructed her to give me the phone number should I happen to call. That's good, I think, but when I ring the number I get an answering-machine with a message on it which, in content and seductiveness of tone, sounds like an invitation to every man in London to hop over there at once. I hang up immediately, but then, realising that I may not get another chance to call, I start to compose a message in my head, and then, because the tone of this must be exactly right – light-hearted, cool, unurgently persuasive – I decide, being a professional, to make a few rough drafts on a piece of paper. Then I find that I haven't got a pen, so I leave the call-box and return to the paper-shop to buy one. When I get back to the call-box I find that it is now occupied by two giggly girls, so I stand outside and work on my message, roughing out several drafts until I'm satisfied that it couldn't be bettered in terms of style, content and construction. The giggly girls take an age to complete their business, but at last they do, and I step inside the box to leave my message. And half-way through I realise that, because I'm reading it off a piece of paper, it sounds stilted and rehearsed, like the news read by a nervous amateur, but it's too late to stop now, so I blunder on, taking several wordy minutes to leave this simple message: don't make a date on Thursday night and I'll ring again tomorrow to explain.

And as I walk briskly home – briskly because Alison will have been timing my absence on the loose, will have her questions ready – I realize that nothing in the world at all – nothing that may be in the Sunday papers, not Alison and her new carpet which isn't meant to show the dirt but does, and certainly not the other people in the street who seem inexplicably contented with their peculiar day-to-day intentions, their obligations to each other which they mean to carry out – is of any interest.

Everything is out of focus, seems shadowy and laughable except the answer to this question: where is my Princess now, and what the hell's she up to? And for the first time in fifteen years I don't feel bored to death. Normally I'd have to be on drugs to find the 'real' world as interesting as this.

'What took you so long?' asks Alison.

For once this question fails to induce despair. In fact I feel a wild exhilaration – and so, because women never believe the truth, I tell her.

Do you really want to know? You'll be very hurt.

'I can take it. I've got the pussy cats. The pussy cats love me.'

I've met this girl.

'Golly – what's her name?'

Melissa.

'*Melissa*? That's rather a naff name. Is she naff?'

Not really. She's extraordinary, in fact; the most extraordinary person I've ever met. I think I love her.

'Well, good for you.'

I'm not so sure. I've fought against it, God knows I've fought against it, but I seem to be powerless – she has enchanting qualities. Just now, buying the papers, I was overcome by a wild desire to phone her. I wanted to tell her that I couldn't live without her, but there were a couple of half-witted girls ahead of me in the queue and it took longer than I expected. And now you've found me out.

'What bad luck!'

Not necessarily. Perhaps it's best that you should know. I'm sorry, I really am, but I hope you'll be happy for me. I'll never forget our fifteen years together and I'll carry you in my heart forever. But what I feel for Melissa I've never felt for anyone. Say you understand.

'Of *course* I do.'

She laughs happily and says she's sorry, says she never should have asked. So we read the papers separately, and then we watch television and the two comedians dressed as turkeys make another appearance, I think. And later I notice that she's been reading Joe Orton's *Diary*, so I ask her what she thought of it.

'All right,' she says.

135

All right? Jesus Christ I could have another twenty years of this.

On Monday, just twenty-four hours before the court case is due to start, there is a meeting in our QC's chambers in order that he may acquaint himself, for the first time, with some of its more important aspects – such as what it's all about. Everyone's there: my solicitor, Mr Wiseman, his senior partner, Mr Salt, Mr Salt's assistant, Ms Greer, our QC, Mr Hislop, and his junior, Mr Lucas, who has an Adam's apple.

Mr Hislop, a Dickensian little man with half-specs and a paunch, sits behind an affected, toppling pile of briefs – each representing some bewildered litigant's life-savings, I imagine – with his fingers arched whimsically at his lips as if in prayer. In twenty-four hours I'm up in court, and it could be a murder charge I face for all he knows. That's reasonable, I dare say – he'll be a busy man and so forth – but I am relieved it isn't murder: only money is at stake here, and my reputation. He peers at me over his half-specs and asks me to tell my story in *my own words* (emphasizing this, and looking at me challengingly, as if an obvious ratbag like me might try to tell it in someone else's), after which he'll rule, he says, as to whether we have a defence of any sort. It's a bit late in the day to address ourselves to that, I think, but I clear my throat and start from scratch, resisting the temptation to ask him whether, as a matter of priority, I could first use his telephone to ring my Princess, since I want urgently to know whether she got my message, and – should these ridiculous proceedings be over by Thursday night – whether she's free to play. Here goes:

Some years ago I wrote a book called *Both The Ladies And The Gentlemen*. You may recognise the sly, but *adequately acknowledged*, borrowing from Auden, Mr Hislop.

(I stress the acknowledgement for Mr Hislop's sake, since I see no harm in bringing it to his attention at this early stage that breach of copyright is what this case is all about. No point in the poor man sitting there behind his briefs wondering what we're doing here.)

This had a small success, and at the invitation of Kenneth Tynan several people – Clive James, John Wells etc – tried to turn it into a play. None was successful, and the idea was soon abandoned. Then an old friend of mine, an American stage director called Schultz, suddenly surfaced in my life. He'd hit a bad patch, had recently been kicked out by his wife, in fact, and was now pretty cuckoo, I'd have said, currently living in a cheap hotel with all his possessions in a carrier-bag. You know how it is.

I break off and glance round the room, but no one here knows how it is, knows what it's like to be fifty-five and living in a cheap hotel with all your possessions in a carrier-bag. They look away and shift uneasily on their chairs; they've been given a glimpse of a world they'd prefer not to know about.

I felt sorry for the fellow so I let him doss down in a spare flat I happened to have at the time, one I was looking after for another friend, who was in America. I was working there myself, in fact, but Schultz's presence soon made this impossible. He kept shouting at me, trying to persuade me to dramatise *Both The Ladies And The Gentlemen* myself – with his assistance. He, of course, intended to direct it. In the end I agreed, just to shut him up. I typed away quite happily – just copying out the book, as I recall – while he slept. He slept a lot at this time, climbing into bed for safety's sake in the middle of the afternoon. He looked rather sweet, actually, snoring quietly, safe for the time being, his old head lying on the pillow. It was touching, I can tell you. He'd had expectations once, do you see, taken tea with actresses, lunched with Binkie, met Noel Coward. And now he's a cunt, sleeping in the afternoon and designing joggers' belts.

Mr Hislop holds up a hand to stop me. This is encouraging; he's spotted a loop-hole in Schultz's case already.

'Designing joggers' shorts, you say?'

Belts.

Mr Hislop makes a note of this, his first, and I wonder what the significance can be – not very great, I hope, because I've made up the detail of the joggers' belts, I don't know why. I press on anyway.

I sat there typing away quite contentedly, and every now and then Schultz would wake up and insist on reading what I'd done. 'Holy shit!' he'd scream, 'this is bad!' or 'Hey Christ — this is better! Now we're getting somewhere!' He'd rub his hands with glee and chuckle as triumphantly as if he were doing it himself. Then he'd go to sleep again. I definitely wrote it all myself, every word of it. When it was finished, we passed it around a bit, but no one was interested, and soon enough I forgot all about it. Then, about four years later, I suppose, I came across it in a drawer. I glanced through it and was quite impressed. These are funny characters, I think — Ken The Australian Horse Player, Dawn Upstairs, Pretty Marie, Big Elaine — these people should be in a comic novel. Slipped my memory that they already had been, do you see? So — I go off to Ibiza and turn it into a book. What we have now is the book of the play of the book. I sell it back to the same people as published *Both The Ladies And The Gentlemen* — and they're none the wiser since it's slipped their memory, just as it has mine, that the damn thing's been out of the traps already. Quite funny, don't you think?

I glance around the room, but no one seems to think it's funny at all.

'What happened then?' asks Mr Hislop.

The book came out — under a new title of course — and Schultz sued for breach of copyright. The rest you know.

Mr Hislop looks as if he doesn't know at all, so his junior, Mr Lucas, brings him up to date. While he's doing this, I wonder whether this might not be a good time to ring my Princess. I'm about to ask if I may use the phone, when Mr Hislop astounds everyone by announcing that he thinks we have a chance, that a possible defence has just occurred to him. Better late than never, I think, but the other lawyers in the room look frankly disbelieving. Mr Hislop thinks that if he could convince the judge that I wrote the play he might over-rule some home-cooked contracts which Schultz drew up and I was silly enough to sign. There are murmurings of disagreement from the other lawyers in the room, and Mr Hislop admits it is a long-shot — but one he would advise me to take since my integrity's involved. I like the sound of that, but my Mr Wiseman now points out that the costs already are in excess of

£60,000 and could well reach £100,000, were we to go to court and lose. His advice would be to settle. All eyes are now on me.

If we do go to court, I ask, will the case be over by Thursday? 'Possibly,' says Mr Hislop, 'but not necessarily.'

Here's a problem. If we were able to settle now, the costs would wipe me out, but I would see my Princess on Thursday – so it would be worth it, obviously. On the other hand, were we to go to court – which is Mr Hislop's advice to me – and should the case be unresolved on Thursday evening, then Alison wouldn't go down to Sussex for her mother's last birthday and I'd miss a night with my Princess. The sensible thing to do, clearly, is to telephone my Princess now and discover whether she can play on Thursday night. If she can't, it would be silly to throw away £60,000. I ask Mr Hislop if I may use his telephone before reaching a decision. Of course, he says; so I ring my Princess and she sounds sweet, if a little sleepy for the time of day, and she says that she got my message, which made her very happy, and that of course she's free to play on Thursday and can hardly wait. And now I don't have a care in the world, so I instruct Mr Hislop to make one last attempt to settle. And everyone looks very relieved, and a final offer is worked out on the spot, in which, as far as I can see, we give Schultz everything, and this is sent round immediately to the chambers of Schultz's QC, with whom, even now, he and his solicitor happen to be in conference. And within half an hour a message comes back to the effect that the offer is unacceptable. Everyone is staggered, not least Mr Hislop, who points out that Schultz must be mad, since we have just offered him more than he'd ever be awarded by the court, if and when he won.

So – the court case is now inevitable and the important thing obviously is not whether we win or lose – though winning would come as a nice surprise – but that it should be over by Thursday night. Alison has accepted that pressure of work will not allow me to attend her mother's last birthday, so the only catastrophe now would be her staying in London and not attending it herself because the court case was still in progress. As long as the case is over in time I will have one last night with my Princess, and that's all I care about. Afterwards – the very next day, in fact – I have agreed to return to Ibiza with Alison and her dying mother, but I'll worry about that at the time. The plan at the moment is that Alison should go down to her mother's by train, taking her Ibiza stuff with her, and that I should join them the following day. The three of us would then set off for Ibiza in the afternoon. But I can't think about the horrors of that at the moment. My last night with my Princess is all that matters now.

On the first day of the hearing, Schultz's barrister kicks off, outlining the case against me. He seems to be in the sort of rage normally associated with the inarticulate and he describes me, to my surprise, as some sort of villain, tossing words such as 'flagrant' and 'despicable' around as if this were a criminal trial of some sort. I hadn't been expecting this, I must say. I'd imagined that I might be called a fool who couldn't write, who had deliberately used Schultz, plagiarised him even; but this is beginning to sound more like premeditated fraud. Then Schultz goes into the witness-box. He affirms (which strikes me as a colossal error, aggressive, even, in the context – 'I swear by Almighty God' is only gibberish, after all, which can't hurt anyone), removes his chewing-gum and quotes E.M. Forster on the creative process – always a mistake, I'd say. Mr Justice Whitworth, a humorous-looking old bird, will see he's a cunt.

The case against me seems to be that I can't write fiction, and this is taken as self-evident. Since the play is obviously fiction, it follows, equally obviously, that I didn't write it. This not only begs the question (can Schultz write fiction?) but also demonstrates the own-goal nature of informal logic: when a coherent argument leads to a self-evidently false conclusion, one, or both, of the premises is thereby refuted – in this instance, presumably, that the play is fiction. And if it isn't fiction, what is it? Alternatively, if neither I nor Schultz can write fiction, who wrote the play? When my turn comes I can make nonsense of all this, if I can be bothered and if it doesn't delay the case. All that matters is that it should be over by Thursday night. I might, when it's my turn to take the stand – and if there's time – deliver a small lecture on fact and fiction, a subject that rather interests me, as it happens. While

140

Schultz's barrister shouts incoherently and Schultz makes a prat of himself, I start to muster my thoughts on fact and fiction. What is the status of Pope's *Essay On Man*, for instance, or a summing-up by Mr Justice Melford Stevenson, or *Unreliable Memoirs*, or a joke, or a dream, or the weather forecast, or these words now – all of them so far? Fact or fiction? I may have to quote O'Hear, Professor of Philosophy at Bradford University, whose examples these, for the most part, are, used by him in the course of a lively debate with David Lodge in the pages of *The New Review*.

When the court rises for the day, we all return to Mr Hislop's chambers for a conference, the mood of which, to my surprise, seems to be that Schultz has acquitted himself rather well and that our chances are looking even bleaker. Mr Hislop does point out that Schultz's barrister is making a big mistake by asking the judge to rule on a matter of fact (who wrote the play?) rather than concentrating on the contracts, but no one pays him much attention. The general feeling seems to be that our only hope now would be to make Schultz a better offer, but this is impossible, of course, because we have nothing left to offer him.

On the second morning I take the stand, and, as a consequence of being as sedated, on valium, as a safari park rhino about to have its appendix removed, I am excellent, without a doubt. I don't raise my hands in a boxer's salute, or cheek the judge, but I am confident – I don't give a stuff (why should I? I'm seeing my Princess on Thursday night. This case, these people, are as shadowy as any fiction. My Princess is fact). I deliver my lecture, confusing Lodge with thing, and thing with Lodge. I mention structuralism, I think, refer to Adair on Barthes and Barthes on myth, I concoct a theory of narrative on the spot, drag in the intentional fallacy, kicking a decisive own-goal myself at this point, suggesting that I'm in no better a position than anyone else to judge what my stuff is – but no one notices, I think. I mention irony, ambiguity and Empson. I insist that I must have written the play because I only have one joke – have been making it for fifteen years with some success – and that it is this joke (the Commissioner of the Metropolitan Police being socially so far out of his depth in a brothel that, in his agitation, he finds himself taking the bookings) that the play consists in. Mr Justice Whitworth is so amused by this that he keeps repeating it. 'Ah,' he says, with practised owlishness, 'this must be the telephone conversation of the joke of the play of the book of the play of the book of the joke.' Schultz's barrister gets redder and redder in the face and splutteringly reads out passages from my collected works in an attempt to prove that I can't write fiction. 'What's that?' he shouts. 'Fiction,' I reply, and he's too stupid to be able to refute me.

After I've finished, my team and I retire backstage for a conference. We do still have a trick up our sleeve in the person of J.P. Donleavy, who, soon after the play was written, drew up a joke agreement in which I undertook not to kill Schultz if he agreed never to contact me again and, more seriously, to give up all his rights in the play. Why Schultz ever signed it is a mystery, but sign it he did, and my friend Lord Dynevor, in whose house the signing took place, is here now and prepared to swear that he was sober at the time (as was Schultz). And Donleavy is here too at the back of the court, ready to give evidence that this agreement, though humorous in tone, was seriously intended and that Schultz, when he signed it, acknowledged it to be. My solicitors have never cared for this agreement much, partly because of its comic wording, but more fundamentally because there is no consideration in it. Schultz, they point out, gives up everything under it, and receives nothing in return. Donleavy – the world's leading expert on the law of copyright (in hard cases he is called in even by the Swiss) – has always argued that my undertaking not to kill Schultz might be thought by most people to be consideration enough, but my team has remained unimpressed, and reluctant to produce the document in court. The question is, should they do so now in a last, desperate attempt to avert catastrophe, wheeling on Donleavy and Lord Dynevor as witnesses? The consensus is that they should, that it's the only chance we have, but if they do, it cannot be until tomorrow, since it is now almost four o'clock and the court will soon be rising. This would mean that Mr Justice Whitworth, who has already said that he will need the whole of one evening and the following morning to read my *oeuvre*, wouldn't deliver his judgement until Friday – and, pleasant though it would be to have Donleavy in the witness-box calling Schultz a horse, my night out with my Princess would, as a consequence, be down the drain. That's unthinkable, so I now instruct Mr Hislop not to introduce the Donleavy agreement, or to call him and Lord Dynevor as witnesses. Everyone looks at me as if I'm a little mad, but it's clear to me that I'm doing the sensible thing. We return to the court room, where Mr Hislop and Schultz's man make their final speeches. Mr Justice Whitworth then says again that he will read my stuff over the next twenty-four hours and deliver his judgement tomorrow afternoon. That's all right, then. It was touch and go, but my night out with my Princess – our last, perhaps – is safe.

At 2.30 precisely Mr Justice Whitworth starts to deliver his judgement. I'm hardly listening, I must admit, because a new problem has arisen. Alison, who has been taking this whole thing very seriously, has said that – win or lose – she might be too shaken to get down to her mother's birthday dinner; so, instead of paying full attention to the judge, I wondering how I can bundle her onto the train, when we get out of here, without seeming excessively unfeeling. I'm turning this over in my mind when my Mr Wiseman suddenly nudges me and, with a surprised smile, seems to be suggesting that things are running our way – so I start to listen to the judge.

He has been asked to rule, he says, on a matter of fact: who wrote the play? It seems clear to him that whereas Schultz is an obvious shit bag (he doesn't put it quite like this, but he is extremely rude) I am, equally obviously, a man of integrity and adamantine honour. Furthermore, it must be clear to anyone who has taken the trouble to read my work (here he looks contemptuously at Schultz's legal team) that only I could have written the play. He carries on in this vein for a little longer and then, suddenly, delivers the marvellous words: 'The case fails.' Schultz hasn't just lost, he's been insulted too, and now he has costs (of over £100,000, we think) awarded against him.

It's all very emotional – my team jumping up and down, Donleavy and Lord Dynevor beaming happily, Alison in tears. Since my only problem now is to get her on the train to Sussex,

I turn down on her behalf an invitation put to her by Mr Wiseman that she should return with the rest of us to his office for a glass of champagne, and instead instruct Lord Dynevor to take her to a pub and then ensure that she catches her train for Charing Cross. This he does, while I return with the rest of my team to Mr Wiseman's office, where it would be bad mannered in the circumstances, I judge, to ask the obvious question: how is it possible that several hundredweight of copyright solicitors, over two years and at some expense, had not seen what was immediately as clear as daylight to Mr Justice Whitworth? Either the latter has made a colossal blunder, it seems to me, or my team and Schultz's don't know enough copyright law between them to put on the back of a postage stamp. In the end it was a lottery – simply a question of whether the judge believed me or Schultz. But no one on my team had ever said that that's what the case would be about. No one, until the excellent Mr Hislop came on the scene a few hours before the kick-off, had said that it would all rest on whom the judge believed, that the contracts were irrelevant. Thank God it wasn't important, that's all I can say.

Back at the flat I go to work, making it decent for the arrival of my Princess at eight o'clock. This takes time. I hoover, plump the cushions, polish the top of the coffee-table, prepare the sounds (aiming at an appropriate mid-to-late Seventies atmosphere – Marvin Gaye, Donna Summer, that stuff) and dim the lights, particularly in the bedroom, where I hang a silk scarf of Alison's over the bedside lamp so that it casts a kind, seductive, amber glow. Then I bathe and dress, choosing my wardrobe to go with the music – cool and relaxed, but not boastfully, or inappropriately so, I think. I wouldn't, as Pratt the Playwright does, present myself in a slim-line shirt open to the waist or in trousers in which I couldn't sit down. Nor, like Jack the Actor, would I appear in jeans and jogging shoes.

That done, I walk around a bit, checking this and that, until I'm suddenly overcome by such a weird sensation – identified, after a while, as simple happiness – that I have to sit down, take a valium and examine it. The emotions, J.P. Donleavy says, are to do with cash-flow. Is that what's caused it, then? Is it merely money saved? No, it's nothing as trivial as that, though this consideration does provide a pleasant back-drop to the mood. Is it vindication, then, being called a man of honour by the judge? No, that's not it either, though it is nice, I suppose, that a binding legal precedent has been set in the matter of one's character. The plain fact is that this unaccustomed, even unique, sense of happiness is all to do with my Princess. I am aware that for the first time in my life the person who is coming over is the person I'd want to be coming over if I had the whole world to choose from.

This, on the face of it, is so obviously absurd that I sit on the sofa for some time checking and rechecking the proposition, trying to imagine something preferable to my present situation. There's nothing – and yet I've never believed other people when they've made this claim, have simply assumed that they're reporting it to keep their spirits up. How will I cope with it, I wonder – this heavy fact that I can't imagine anything I want more than what I've got, that there's nothing more to dream about? She warned me of this, warned me that the time might come when I wanted *just* her; she said that I might go mad, might have to kill her – something like that, she said. Am I going mad, then? I do feel a little spooked, in fact. It's like discovering, too late in life, some remarkable attribute one didn't know one had, some aspect of one's character, unimagined hitherto, so powerful in itself that it alters everything, cancels out what's been before, requires a different logic. Will I be able to handle this? I hadn't thought beyond today, had thought merely that I wanted one more high and would then revert to normal, to long November afternoons of wanting and frustration. Now I know that there's someone with whom everything would be nice for the first time ever, with whom I'd enjoy doing things I've not enjoyed for twenty years. Might not the fear of losing this outweigh the happiness of having found it – and what is it about her anyway that makes me so jumpy when she isn't there? When I'm with her, or know she's on her way, I feel quite calm. She does have certain natural qualities – sometimes I think she's as pretty as anything I've ever seen. Her courage and vulnerability, her healing lack

145

of caution, the pain that's often in her eyes, are most beguiling – but it's her elusiveness, I suppose, that's got me hooked, the knowledge that the happiness she brings must, of its nature, be temporary, as if chemically induced, to be followed by agitation and despair. And I feel she knows all this, and is enjoying the game as much as I am: a game, I have to remind myself, which she, being ruthless, will always win. Meanwhile, I can handle it. She's coming over tonight and that's all that matters. (If she were really clever, of course, she'd drive me to the very edge of wanting now by ringing to say that she wasn't coming over after all, that she had decided instead to play with Jack the Actor. And the knowledge that, were she to do such an awful thing, I'd offer her everything I have, make any pact with fate, commit any crime she specified to make her change her mind, makes me even happier.)

Meanwhile, I'd better ring Alison, I think, to check that she arrived safely at her mother's, didn't get drunk with Lord Dynevor and is even now on her way back here. I could explain easily enough that often in her absence I clean the flat and bathe, dress up in clothes she's never seen, change the lighting system in the bedroom, smoke pot and turn the music up, but the arrival shortly thereafter of my Princess would be harder to explain. I ring her in Sussex and find her in an ecstatic mood, too ecstatic, perhaps, bearing in mind the circumstances in which the family has foregathered. It's the happiest day of her life, she says, and she keeps going over the judge's summing-up – my Button this, my Button that, a man of obvious integrity, a man of adamantine honour – and I do feel rather proud, I must admit. It's such a shame I can't be there, she says, but she does understand that work comes first. She stresses, finally, how important it is that I arrive in time for lunch tomorrow, so that we can set off for Ibiza in the afternoon. Her mother won't be up to a long drive in the evening, she says. You won't let me down, will you, she says, and I say that of course I won't. I ring off, and moments later my own phone goes.

'Hi. I'm going to be a little late. Sorry. 'Bye.'

Christ she's brilliant, it's as if she can read my mind. She's playing with my brain, of course, applying such pressure on it that it will achieve critical mass, explode perhaps, the top

146

lifting off like a mushroom cloud, just as she arrives. For half an hour or so this works; excitement tightens my intestines as explosively as the elastic innards of a golf-ball, the danger being that tension may cause my outer shell to burst making me ping and rocket round the room as I unravel. After an hour, however, I become a little apprehensive and – feeling as if I'm reaching for a poisoned pawn – I decide to ring her. The answering-machine is on, issuing that promising message to the world – but this is good: it means, surely, that she's on her way and should be here within twenty minutes at the most.

After another hour, spent hopping up and down and looking out of the window every time a taxi passes, I can no longer convince myself that this is still a game. At first I reject the possibility that she isn't coming, that life can be so suddenly, so randomly sadistic, but very gradually the fact sinks in that it isn't just a possibility but stone-cold certainty. Once, when bathing in Ibiza, Alison was knocked over by an unexpected breaker. She came up gasping, stumbling around, astonished that anything so terrible, so undignified could suddenly occur, that, as an adult, anything so unforeseen could knock you off your feet. She looked horrified, then, whimpering at the random absurdity of what had happened, she ran out of the water like a child, ran to the safety of the beach.

I feel like that; I want to run away to safety, climb out of myself and run away, never be reminded of myself again, or of my fat and flirty preparations that mock me everywhere I look: the red light bulbs, my silly stack of sounds – arranged to achieve an erotic crescendo like some crude bolero – my new shirt, my dapper trousers, the memorabilia of past successes (letters, a scrap-book, photographs) left casually half-hidden under the coffee-table, where they might be expected to catch the eye. For some time I sit and stare at them, then, suddenly, as if despair and self-disgust can be dispelled by furious action, I get up and tear around, cursing, stumbling, angrily turning off the sounds, changing the light-bulbs back to an undeceitful 100 watts and, remembering the bedroom – which I particularly want to make chaste and practical again – I run in there only to discover that Alison's expensive scarf has been singed a dirty brown by too close contact with the light-bulb,

147

has a hole in it indeed the size of a compact disc. And never have Alison's special qualities of loyalty, decency and courage seemed as irreplaceable as now. I want to ring her urgently to tell her this, to tell her that I mean to cherish her forever. Instead I find myself ringing Tiffs, I don't know why, and am quite surprised to find her in. Having nothing more to lose, I ask her over, and she sounds quite startled, insulted even. 'Why?' she asks, crushingly. Then she adroitly changes the subject, enquiring after my Princess. I don't tell her the whole humiliating story, but I do say something quite dismissive, whereupon, and reading between the lines, I take it, Tiffs points out that she was the first to warn me. 'She's a whore,' she says. 'She's always been a whore. She'll never be anything else but a whore. She's as hard as nails, I tell you. I *know* her. Well, keep in touch. 'Bye now.'

I'm not sure if this is something I can take. Can my Princess do this to me? If someone's made you happier than you've ever been, aren't they responsible for you in some way – as if they'd saved your life? Don't they have an obligation, perhaps, to make you happy forever? I couldn't do this to someone, take away everything at once, make them feel this naked. I keep thinking of that silly Dutchman on the beach who thought he could still join in, can see the look of horror on his face when he lost his jaunty swimming-trunks and took a ducking. Hours later, or maybe only minutes – during which Tiff's friendly words keep coming back like heartburn (I didn't need that; I knew all that about my Princess from the start) – there's a ring at the front-door. I assume it's the police, here to arrest me on some outstanding traffic matter, and since I care about nothing now, I drag myself off to answer it. But it isn't the police; it's some fool identifying himself as John the Accountant, so I tell him to fuck off. And five minutes later there's another ring at the front-door, so I pick up the entry-phone and scream: 'I thought I told you to fuck off!' But it isn't John the Accountant this time; it's my Princess, bouncing up the stairs, looking as pretty as a picture and squirming with conceit.

'Was that good or what? Did you think I wasn't coming?'

And in my relief and happiness I drive her up against the wall, and I pin her there and tear at her outer garments, here in the hall, like a junkie ripping into someone's handbag. And she gasps and squirms and laughs triumphantly at how clever she has been, and then she manages to break away, saying that we must behave ourselves.

Why?

'Because my accountant's coming over. I hope you don't mind.'

What's this? Is this some new perversion? Or does she want to draw a contract up? Did I make promises in Ibiza? What did Tiffs say?

Your accountant? What's his name?

'John.'

Oh dear. I told him to fuck off. Why did you ask him here?

'He's my dealer. Quite the best there is. He runs his side-line from a Rolls Royce in the evening. Never mind – he won't be far away. I'll ring him in his car. Can I use the telephone?'

John the Accountant's back in no time, and he seems a very decent sort of fellow, pin-stripe suit, brief case, rolled umbrella – from a good firm too, I'd say, in the City at a guess. Being a pro he doesn't want to loiter once the deal is done (several grammes of coke for my Princess, a present – from her – of some pot for me), but, before he goes, I buttonhole him *re* my nest-egg – having an expert on the spot seems too good an opportunity to miss. I get out my portfolio of stock investments and, while my Princess lays out lines, we examine it, John the Accountant and I, for weight, durability and balance. He's quite impressed by its general spread, I'm glad to say, but suggests, after careful thought, that I might venture warily into Europe, where there are unusual opportunities, he says. Perhaps I should sell my modest holding in Britannia's Smaller American Companies Fund – a little static lately, he points out – and dip a cautious toe instead into Schroder's European Income Fund. He turns down a suggestion from my Princess that he should push something up his nose and then departs, saying he has other calls to make, including one, he rather indiscreetly adds, to Kensington Palace. Since the previous purveyor to that address is now, for his trouble, doing nine years in the boob, I urge him to watch his step – free, and expert, investment advice is hard to come by.

149

We have enough stuff on the coffee-table now to open up on our own account, and it occurs to me that, were we to get a visit, we'd have some explaining to do and no mistake. I haven't seen so much stuff on my coffee-table since the Tilly Tilling incident a couple of years ago. My Princess will be impressed, I think, by my Tilly Tilling anecdote, so I stand up – with some lack of balance, since I'm now a little stoned – put the music on (Bruce Springsteen – 'I'm On Fire'), lower the lights and pull my stomach in.

I don't think I've mentioned Carly Simon yet.

My Princess, nose to the coffee-table like someone searching for their contact lenses, doesn't look up from her expert examination of the goods.

'She's gross.'

Nevertheless, she's a friend of mine. You'll have heard of Jack Foxx, the distinguished jazz musician? He was over here a year or two ago with his girlfriend Tilly Tilling, herself a singer with something of a cult-following among the East Coast's *haute bohème* John McEnroe, Vitas Gerulaitis etc.

'Hey – how did the court case go?'

What court case? Carly had given them my number ...

Who? John McEnroe? Vitas whatnot?'

No. Jack Foxx and Tilly Tilling. They both had a habit, to say the least. Jack Foxx, over here to appear at Ronnie Scott's and to make a record, was in the studio going up the wall. Tilly, in charge of supplies, had just made a connection at a King's Road boutique ...

'Which one?'

How should I know? But it was an odd place from all accounts. You just wandered in off the street and told them what you wanted. A pair of trousers, some cowboy boots, an ounce of coke – whatever. Run by a Chinaman I think. Anyway, Tilly was back at my place now, feeling very pleased with herself because she's got five hundred pounds worth of heroin in a bag. I'd never seen so much. Never seen any, come to that. Have you ever taken it?

'Taken what?'

Heroin.

'Good God no.'

That's good. Well – Tilly's got it all spread out on the coffee-table and I'm rolling joints like someone in a cigar factory and just at that moment there's a ring at the front-door.

'Where's Alison?'

Down with her dying mother. I told you.

'No – not *now*. *Then*. At the time of your anecdote. From wherever it was to this. Gunner's Hole, 'Oily' Mallett, heroin – I don't know, I really don't. Where was she?'

God knows. Portugal, I expect.

'Why?'

She *goes* there.

'Okay.'

It's the police!

'Christ! Where?'

Not *now*. Jesus! *Then*. I went to answer the door, I don't know why, and this voice on the entry-phone says: 'Chelsea Police. Evening all.'

'Good gracious.'

That's right. I drop the entry-phone, tear back into the sitting-room, whimpering with panic, I imagine, and start to wrestle the bag of heroin away from Tilly. She thinks I've gone mad, puts up a tremendous fight. At last I get it away from her, run to the window and throw it into the street. She's staggered. The world has become unintelligible to her. Her boyfriend's going up the wall and this gibbering loony has just thrown five hundred pounds' worth of heroin out of the window.

'How are my eyes? Look at my eyes.'

I can't. I mustn't. Not till I've finished my story.

'Will it take long?'

It will if you don't stop interrupting.

'Sorry.'

Where was I?

'Beats me.'

I know. I throw the stuff out of the window and then go back to let the police in. Turns out to be a nice fellow on his own, very young in a tall hat. He's carrying a suitcase, which turns out to belong to my boy Charlie. The silly prat had left it on a train. Nothing but a problem, children. You can't have a quiet smoke at home without them getting you into trouble. The

151

policeman sits down, takes his hat off and produces some forms, makes a space for them on the coffee-table by pushing my little pile of joints to one side. Tilly, who's been leaning out of the window muttering distractedly to herself, now comes over to the sofa and sits down next to the policeman. She lights one of my joints and starts to smoke it. Not her thing, of course, but this is an emergency. She takes a few puffs, pulls a face, remarks on the poor quality, and passes it to the policeman. That's it, I think, we're off to the slammer now, but this nice young officer can't spot anything amiss; he gets me to sign for my boy's suitcase and then says he'll be toddling off. That's the reassuring thing about the police: they can only handle one idea at a time. He'd come here to return a suitcase; there could have been a dead body in the corner and he wouldn't have noticed. The same thing happened when I had the Vice Squad here looking for Mrs Mouse after the Lambton scandal. The place was obviously a brothel – porn all over the place, a bull-whip on the coffee-table, Big Elaine waddling round in a corset, a merchant banker strapped to a whipping-stool. They didn't see a thing. Looking for Mrs Mouse, do you see?

'This is good. I feel nice.'

Anyway, after he's gone, Tilly and I work out that the bag of heroin, being light, might not have carried into the street, might have floated down to the basement area – which is only accessible via the bottom flat. We go downstairs and knock on the door. Nice old couple, in their eighties, having a dinner-party, black tie and so forth, pheasant being served, I think, Vivaldi in the background. I introduce Tilly as my fiancée. We've had a row, I say, and she's thrown her engagement ring out of the window. Might have landed in the area outside their bedroom window. The whole dinner-party, a dozen or so old folk, leaves the table, climbs with difficulty through the bedroom window and, with torches, starts to search the area with us. It's obvious within seconds to me and Tilly that the heroin's not there, but the old folk think they're looking for something smaller. 'Fuck it,' says Tilly, and we quit, leaving these nice old people searching. We go upstairs and after about ten minutes there's a knock on our front-door. It's the old buffer who'd been giving the dinner-party. 'Found

152

your engagement ring,' he says. 'Came to rest on the window-sill.' Then he hands over the bag of heroin. I'm stunned, but all Tilly can think about is whether he's nicked any. She insists on weighing it.

'Had he?'

Quite a lot, as it happens. Anyway, if there's a ring on the door-bell now you'll find me throwing your stuff out of the window. If it goes into the basement, it'll have to stay there. Couldn't interrupt another dinner-party – not so soon after the last one.

'What was she doing there anyway?'

'Who? Where?

'Alison. What was she doing in Portugal?'

God – I don't know.

'Well, I wouldn't go to Portugal and leave you here to get into trouble with bad people. I'd keep an eye on you, I tell you that. I wouldn't let you out of my sight.'

It's when my Princess says things like this that I simply can't tell whether she's being incredibly clever or whether she means it – and I suspect she doesn't know herself. I think it's a kind of reflex possessiveness at the time, a function of her insecurity, a need to be everything that matters for the moment.

'How are my eyes? Look at my eyes now.'

And I do, and they're huge and shining, ablaze with innocent wickedness and understanding, and the misleading music's in my brain and nothing matters. Then, suddenly, the whole necessary cast is present, augmenting our thin possessive fury – Little Jo and Jack the Actor, Tessa the Teacher and Sue Cook and a band of mercenaries with guns (they're new). We're at our most imaginative, our most resourceful, and in the middle it occurs to me that if all the qualities I'd ever wanted in a woman had been fed into a computer this sweet, reckless, damaged person would have come out the other end. She can read my mind, she knows exactly what I want from her even before I know it myself, and whether this is because she has paranormal powers and is a selfless actress, or because it happens, by a miracle, to be what she wants too, no longer bothers me. She is the objective correlative of everything I've ever dreamed of. She's my thoughts materialized, my fantasies

153

made flesh. She's irreplaceable. She's me. Afterwards, I ask her, out of interest, whether *she* thinks she's given me everything I want yet, as she said she would.

'Not yet. But I'm working on it.'

What do I want?

'You want to be hurt.'

She's wrong about that and no mistake, but I play along.

What makes you think that?

'Because we're so alike, and that's what I want.'

She may be right in her case. Her emotions probably run on such a low voltage that only by being hurt can she convince herself she cares. Equally, she's looking for a man whose need for her is so awful he can only prove the extent of it by killing her. She's probably no more a masochist than I am, but needs a catastrophe from time to time to remind her that she still exists. God knows, nothing else is happening in her life; all her energy, all her talents − which are many actually, as an actress she'd have been no worse than many others − are thwarted, bottled up, allowed expression − suddenly and dramatically − in just one thing. Her energy escaping is like a herd of boisterous bullocks scrambling over each other to get through one small door into the slaughterhouse.

Who hurt you most? Your husband?

'I suppose so. You've made me forget him, you know. You've definitely done that.'

There she goes again. She doesn't have to say that, it's way in excess of the part she's playing − if she's still playing a part, if Tiffs is right.

Were you still in love with him? At the end? In spite of everything?

'I don't know. Probably.'

I can't imagine you in love.

'Why not?'

You'd lose everything. Your courage, your independence, your elusiveness. Your type should never be in love. Like this, you're everything anyone could want.

Obviously I shouldn't have said this. She looks startled for a moment, then takes refuge behind her defensive smile. She sits up briskly, arms rigid at her sides, sways backwards and

154

forwards on the bed as if rallying herself to take the plunge, then bangs both fists angrily into the mattress and let's out an abrupt, sharply unfeeling laugh.

'I expect you're right.'

She gets up and starts to dress. I ask her what she's doing, where she thinks she's going.

'I can't stay here. Not now. It's because of *her*. It's her flat. Don't you understand?'

I can tell she's being cunning. I've come right down; I'm unenthralled; I'm thinking for myself again. Minutes ago she could have taken me for everything I have, but now I can see she's only acting. She's probably got another date, the clever little cat. I don't particularly want her to stay, but I say I do – out of politeness really.

'I can't, I really can't.'

She's definitely got another date.

'But I would like you to come home with me. Please. I want you to see my new flat. Come on – it isn't late.'

I explain that this is quite impossible, that Alison might ring – which isn't the real reason, of course. It is late, in fact, it must be nearly three o'clock and the thought of getting up again, of getting dressed and staggering out into a cold night is truly awful.

'When will I see you, then?'

I break it to her now that I'm off to Ibiza tomorrow, something I haven't told her yet, and to my amazement she's appalled – or pretends to be. She sits down abruptly on the bed and stares at me with horror. She is good at this. She's so good I want to laugh.

'You *can't*. Why didn't you say? How long for? I can't *bear* it.'

I explain that I'll be back on the 15th, that this is something I have to do for Alison, that it's her mother's last holiday and so forth. She pouts deceitfully and starts to cross the days off on her fingers.

'That's *seventeen* days! That's *dreadful*. Don't laugh – why are you laughing? I've *got* to see you tomorrow, then. You have to see my new flat. Don't you understand? I want you to be the first.'

The first what, I wonder? The first of a stream of hopeful old men to be entertained there in my absence? And an hour ago this thought would have been quite unacceptable, but now it hardly bothers me — which is odd, and rather sad perhaps. I explain that it simply isn't possible, that I've promised to be in Sussex by lunchtime. But she still looks shattered, quite comically so, and says she'll never speak to me again unless I visit her tomorrow.

'I really won't. I mean it.'

How far will this girl go? Shall I test her, discover just how unscrupulous she is? Shall I tell her that I love her? That's not in the rules. With girls like her that works like garlic on a vampire. They withdraw in horror if you say you love them. If she didn't withdraw, if she said, that's good, that's okay, then I'd know she'd stop at nothing. I decide, after some thought, to keep this stratagem up my sleeve. It would be unnecessarily devastating at the moment, like a nuclear first-strike, and I *could* see her tomorrow, I suppose. What's one lunch, after all, when for seventeen days I'll be putting Alison and her dying mother before my work? I can ring Alison in the morning and tell her that an important business lunch has just cropped up, one that, for both our sakes, I can't afford to miss. I tell my Princess that I will have lunch with her tomorrow and she gives a little whoop of victory, and shortly thereafter departs quite happily, smiling deceitfully to herself.

And after she's gone I realize that, because my manners are better than hers, she's won again. That's where they have the edge, these girls. She's hustling me, I'm sure. She'd take me to the cleaners if she could, and yet I couldn't hurt her, even for a moment, could never drop her suddenly, leaving her feeling silly and bewildered, even if I wanted to, just in case that isn't *all* she's doing. This one ambition may not exhaust her moral position, after all. 'A hustler is only a hustler' isn't tautologically true by any means. And even if it happens to be true synthetically in my Princess's case, I still owe it to her — since I have had an education, since I am, as her mother would imagine, from the top shelf — to behave more carefully than she can. And so she'll always win.

*

In the morning I ring Alison at her mother's, and you'd think it was the end of the world my not going down for lunch. She goes on and on at me until I snap, telling her that she's out of order – which she is. Good heavens, I'm taking seventeen days off work at a time I can ill afford to, and an important business lunch *might* have cropped up, indeed she thinks it has. She apologizes in the end, but I set off for lunch with my Princess in rather a bad mood; our rendezvous, in fact, our last for ages, is in danger of being soured by Alison's selfish attitude.

My Princess's flat turns out to be in quite a smart block, called Bristol House, in Lower Sloane Street. It's little more than a bedsit, really, but it's bright and clean, and she shows me round so proudly that I want to cry. All her possessions, the baggage of her odd, spasmodic life – her toys, her bears, her clothes, her little ornaments – have been so hopefully arranged they break the heart. There aren't any books, of course, just a few magazines, one containing a picture of her looking pretty at a party, standing with her best friends Tiffs and Lindy. 'Model Melissa chatting to ...' Where's her old portfolio, I wonder? You'd think it would be visible, but I can't see it anywhere – so I ask.

Where's your portfolio?

'Oh that. You don't want to see *that*. It's gross, I tell you. I'll show it to you one day. This is my tea-pot, by the way. It's antique, this tea-pot. It's been in the family for fifteen years. Hey – don't use those towels! My brother's always using those towels. He's a photographer, my brother. Did I tell you? He's very good. He's an amateur photographer, he really is. We get on okay, but he will use those towels. It really pisses me off.'

Why shouldn't he?

'What! They come from Harrods, those towels. They're not for *using*. I think the world of those towels. This is my office, by the way. I've got PPP and household insurance, so I can travel the world and still be risqué.'

Her office is a small table with a little typewriter and a few business letters – to do with PPP and household insurance, I imagine – rather eccentrically spelt. I read one and definitely want to cry. She's tried so hard to make a go of things, to carry something forward. She used to live in a proper house in

Florida with a man who cared enough to spit at her and beat her up, and now she's in a bed-sit on her own with her Harrods towels and little bears, and the lonely Sundays stretch ahead.

'Do you think it will be okay? Say you do. I'll get some flowers. I'll make it homely, I really will.'

She loses steam, sits down suddenly on what is a sofa-bed, I think, and looks up at me with frightened, hopeful eyes.

It will be lovely, it really will. Honestly.

But I never should have seen this. My Princess shouldn't live anywhere. She should drop out of the sky, wearing her legs and ready to perform, ready to excel at the thing she does. Homes are so sad. They reflect intentions, hopes, disappointments. Here is a real life, they say; here is a real person with a past. My Princess shouldn't have a past; she should be disconnected, existing from moment to moment; she shouldn't try to make a go of things, she shouldn't try to build. Buildings fall down. I don't understand why people want to build, hold on to things, leave stuff behind. Alison makes this mistake. She's kept every little note I've ever sent her and eventually they'll break her heart. Were my Princess to leave me on my own now, I'd go through everything, read her letters, her diary, get out old photographs and gaze at them, searching for connections. And because there wouldn't be any – because everything was over and had led to nothing else – that would break *my* heart.

And then, as if she hadn't already done enough to bring me down, she insists on cooking lunch. She got up early, she says, and shopped. She's terribly pleased with herself, wears a little apron even, but she gets it all wrong, I'm glad to say; the lunch is a bit of a mess, in fact. And after lunch she pulls out the sofa-bed, but I find I'm a little lowered by her sweet possessions and by my sad reflections, and she's quite different to how she normally is, uncharacteristically shy, as if it's important that this goes well. So, in an attempt to liven things up I ask her if John the Accountant's called.

'I don't need that, I really don't.'

She clearly does, but I don't force the issue. Instead I quizz her a little about some of the more disgraceful things she said last night, allot walk-on parts to some of the supporting cast.

'Please – just us. Don't mention last night. I don't want to be reminded of anything I said last night. Please — it is important.'

It's okay, it's quite nice, in fact, but John the Accountant *should* have called. And afterwards she's clingy and affectionate, making me promise to ring her from Ibiza every day. That will be impossible of course, but I say I will. And then I leave, feeling a little depressed. I hope she doesn't think that this is what she's for.

*

'At night they lock us in, you know. There are bars on the windows and at eleven o'clock they lock all the doors from the outside.'

You don't have to stay. You could leave with me now.

'You mustn't say that. If you say things like that, I'll have to tell them.'

Them? Who's them?

'The group. I have to tell them everything.'

Why? They don't know you. They don't care. I care about you.

'I know you do. But it's easier sometimes talking to people you don't know. It really helps.'

I must try it. Swapping ignorant slogans with uneducated strangers – it must be most rewarding.

'Haven't I changed? Don't you think I've changed?'

You've changed all right. You were a human being – almost – when I brought you here. And look at you now. A ghost. Useless. Petrified.

'Don't say that. Please don't talk to me like that.'

You were remarkable – sweet, funny, affectionate, fearless. It's heartbreaking to see you like this.

'It wasn't me. It was drugs.'

It was you. This isn't you – and if it is, it's nothing to be proud of. On drugs you were incomparable.

'Christ – you mustn't talk to me like this. If they heard you talk to me like this they wouldn't let me see you.'

And you'd agree with them?

'I don't know. I'm confused. They think you don't want me to be cured.'

Is that what you think?

'I'm not sure. Do you?'

Of course I do. Who put you in here?

'It's funny. I really resented you for that. That morning you

160

suddenly told me – bundled me into the car and drove me off –
I thought you were trying to get rid of me. How's Alison?'

How the hell do you think she is?

'How's her mother?'

Still dying. Alison's in a kind of daze. She wakes up crying
and once or twice a week she drives down to her mother's and
lifts her on and off the pot and wipes ...

'Christ don't talk about it like that.'

How do you want me to talk about it?

'I feel so dreadful about Alison. You aren't putting in
anything that will hurt her, are you?'

Of course not. She won't come into it at all. It's your story.
Why should she come into that?

'Promise?'

Promise.

'It would be unforgiveable – hurting her any more. You do
see that?'

Really? That hadn't occurred to me, I must admit. Thank
you for bringing it to my attention.

(She – of all people – is giving me lessons in morality! It will
be lit crit next.)

'How's it going? How far have you got?'

Your second trip to Ibiza. When Staughton was there and
you came back. I didn't know why. I still don't.

'I wanted to be with you. It was a mistake. I shouldn't have
come back. You were ashamed of me.'

I was never ashamed of you.

'Yes you were! You sent me to bed with a bowl of soup!'

I had to talk business. You were very expensive.

'You wanted me to be. It was your way of controlling me – of
not having to treat me as a person.'

That's good! That's cute! They told you that, did they? The
group? A group effort, is it? You'll be able to write for
Cosmopolitan when you get out of here – if you ever do.

'Don't say that. Just a few more weeks in extended care and
then I'll be well enough to leave. We can go back to Ibiza. God,
I'm longing for that. Did you ever manage to sell him anything?
Staughton?'

No – I never heard from him again.

161

'Didn't you? I did.'

Go on – really?

'Yeah, he kept ringing me up. In the end I had to tell him to piss off.'

No wonder I never heard from him.

'Sorry.'

Never mind. I did sell a book the other day to someone else. 'You Want. You'd Settle For. You Get.' Would you like to hear one?

'Yes please.'

You want to be an actress. You'd settle for being a model. You end up on the game, cooking coke, losing three stone in weight and being stretchered to the clinic, where you respond to all criticism with a sad smile – 'Ah yes, but it's not my fault, I'm a junkie, you see.'

'Don't call me that. Please don't call me that.'

*

Perhaps when you're dying – when there's no further need for social restraints of any sort, when nothing matters any more – you become completely yourself at last, but more so. I'd kick people from behind, I expect, but Alison's mother, whose aim in life has been to have a visitable home and not be duped, behaves accordingly on the drive through France – husbanding her money, advising me to drive at an economical speed to save petrol, criticising the French and Alison (her hair, her nails, her attitude) and, when we stop for food, sending things back with a thin, superior smile. 'No dear. I asked for an omelette. If I'd wanted scrambled eggs I'd have ordered them.'

Her particular interest at the moment is the acquisition of a radio alarm clock and she has brought with her a copy of 'Which' for consultation. Radio alarm clocks range in price from £44.95 to £78.95, it seems, and she is keen to get good value. She needs a radio clock, she says, because she isn't sleeping very well and she wants to know what time it is when she wakes up in the night. She's got six months to live and she wants to know what time it is! And she wants good value. Recently she bought the house she's always wanted, right on the front, looking out to sea. Three weeks ago she was so excited, pottering about, changing this and that, comparing fabrics, knocking down walls, laying out a garden of some sort, finding time in spite of all this to criticise Alison by phone – and then, suddenly, she's alone in a cold room waiting to be told she's had it, that that's it, curtains. And yet she isn't screaming. She's sitting in the back of my car, reading 'Which' on radio clocks, advising me to drive at an economical speed and pondering the details of her estate – who gets what and so forth.

She has some stupid pieces of furniture, for instance, a desk, I think, which she particularly wants to keep in the family. She'd like to leave it to Alison, but Alison must promise not to

163

leave it to me in case it ends up with my boy Charlie. She has nothing against Charlie, in fact, whom she has always been much nicer to him than I have; it's simply that he isn't family, whereas I am, it seems. Why people should worry about what happens to their stuff after they're dead simply defeats me. Having said that, I must admit I would be a little worried about my remains – a cache of sordid photographs and unfulfilled contracts for fifteen toilet books – falling into the wrong hands. When we get back to London I might make arrangements for the former to be lodged in a security box at Harrods. And what, I wonder, would my Princess – who is with us for every mile of this dreadful journey – leave behind? A tea-pot which has been in the family for fifteen years and a magazine with a photograph of her looking pretty at a party. One day my Princess will be old and dying and in Lyons I nearly swerve into the back of a Dutchman with a trailer, partly from the stunning impact of this awful thought and partly because I decide at this point to extract my writer's notebook from my pocket and place it on the shelf above the glove compartment so that I can, without life-endangering gymnastics, jot down all the silly things Alison's mother says between here and Barcelona.

As soon as we arrive at our Ibiza flat – even before I've put the luggage down – Alison, who can spot an irregularity at fifty yards, has found my Princess's yellow G-string, her little beach hat, the pebbles she so adorably collected on Salinas and the presents she brought me on her second visit – the computer alarm-clock, the wrong cigars, the little Sloane Ranger bear. She asks me what they are, and, amazingly, I keep my temper.

They are a yellow G-string, some shells and pebbles, a computer alarm-clock, a box of cigars and a bear.

'I can see that. Whose are they?'

Staughton's.

'What – *all* of them? Even the little bear?'

Yes.

'And the beach hat? Staughton must have a very small head.'

That's right. One of the smallest heads in publishing.

And Alison accepts all this because, like all women – and in spite of talk of women's intuition and so forth – she believes

164

absolutely everything she's told. If you tell a woman a tall story, she'll ask you if it's true, and if you say, no, of course it isn't, she'll be disappointed, won't be able to see the point of it. Like the police, women, having no imagination, rely on informers to get a result – usually their best friend. I swear a woman could catch you on top of her best friend and if you said you were casting a musical she'd believe you – unless, of course, her best friend told her otherwise. Having no sense of fantasy, Alison is unable to imagine behaviour worse than her own – which is always impeccable – varying in this respect, as in so many others, from my Princess, who cannot imagine behaviour better than her own.

Later, she wants to talk to me about how much her mother is annoying her, and how guilty this makes her feel. Her mother is indeed behaving very badly – worse than usual, climbing unsteadily onto chairs to clean windows that don't need cleaning and crawling around on her knees in the kitchen – just as a rebuke to Alison. This behaviour, on top of the stream of articulated criticism, causes Alison, normally the most even-tempered person, to fly off the handle at her mother, who then retires, looking hurt, to her bedroom. I do my best to reassure Alison, pointing out that her mother is behaving normally and that the kindest thing she, Alison, can do is to behave normally herself – which is to be irritated by the old bat and show it. But my heart isn't really in this conversation, or in anything she, or her mother, says. My Princess is everywhere I look, haunting every room, and all I can think of is how much I want to see her again.

And when we go out in the evening, I try to avoid the places I went to with her, but Alison, who seems to want to shock her mother (which is reasonable enough), makes a point of visiting all the trendy spots. At Ponce Corner she sits us down a few yards from where Tanit the Island God is lounging as usual outside the Bar Chic with his self-adoring entourage, and I have to duck my head almost into the table-top in case he sees me. Alison's mother looks around as if someone is dangling a dead fish under her nose and says: 'To me, in my old-fashioned way, half of these people look like girls.' And Alison says, rather sharply: 'That's because half of them are girls.' And that

165

shuts her mother up, which is rather a pity because it means I have nothing for a while to enter in my writer's notebook – left open, by my drink, to catch remarks like this. Then, as we at last get up to go, Tanit the Island God spots me as I creep away and calls out sleepily: 'Hey – where's your Princess?' And Alison looks at me sharply and asks me what all that's about, and I mutter vaguely about mistaken identity and so forth.

Later I lie next to her in bed, thinking about my Princess and crossing off the days, the hours, the minutes until I can leave this strenuous hell and be with her again. And Alison snuggles up to me and thanks me for being so good and patient, and I begin to wonder if there might be a way I could cut this nightmare short. Some crisis back home, perhaps, requiring my immediate attention. I could get Simey to ring with the urgent news that someone wants a toilet book even sooner than expected. Simey's an accomplished actor, if I'm not mistaken, he's done a bit of it in New Zealand, I rather think; properly cued he could convince me, never mind Alison, have me packing my bags and running for the ferry before he'd put the phone down. That's what I'll do: in a couple of days or so I'll get Simey to ring me in a panic.

And the thought of this possible reprieve so heartens me that I become quite daring in the day-time, lie on the beach next to Alison with pen and paper, composing a crossword for my Princess. I have decided to send her one in which the clues, if solved, become a poem by Richard Aldridge called 'RSVP My Love'. 'The third night after I get back,' it runs, 'I want to take you out, / The first two nights we'll want to stay up late and talk ...' I think that's how it goes, but if it isn't, it doesn't matter because my Princess will never be able to solve the clues, any more, I now discover, than I can think them up. It's far harder to compose a crossword than I'd imagined, so I abandon the idea and, instead, send her a postcard with the rather over-revealing message, perhaps 'I love you, Princess, and I miss you horribly'. And before I can change my mind I post it.

And all this time I'm collecting 50 peseta pieces against the moment when I'll be off the leash for long enough to duck into a phone-box and ring her up. But after three days I haven't got nearly enough, so, having told Alison that I'm off to buy some cigars, I go instead into a bank, where I exchange a 5000 peseta note for a bagful of 50 peseta pieces. I then return to the flat and hide them where Alison, who is having a shower, will never find them – wrapped in a shirt inside my overnight bag inside my larger suitcase, which I lock and put on top of the wardrobe. Alison would have to be psychic to find them there, plus she'd need a step-ladder to get them down. It's too early yet to phone my Princess, so when Alison comes out of the shower I say I'll take my turn. And when I come out of the shower Alison is standing in the salon with my bag of 50 peseta pieces.

'What are these for?'

For? They're not for anything as such.

'Don't be silly. They must be for something. Are you collecting them?'

Yes.

'Why?'

It's an economy drive. I'm going to change all my money into 50 peseta pieces. I don't like carrying them around, so I'll never spend anything.

Alison gives me a long look, then says she's going to have a rest; and this is my chance, I think, to ring my Princess, but seconds after I've put all the fifty peseta pieces into my pocket and am making for the door, Alison comes out of the bedroom and asks me what I'm up to now. I'm off to buy the papers, I say, and I slide out sideways, trying to conceal the huge weight of 50 peseta pieces bulging in my pocket, and she watches me every step of the way. And once outside I'm still not safe; I daren't use a phone box near the flat in case she's following me. Instead, I duck and dive up side-streets as if shaking off a tail, ending up miles from home, quite lost, in a part of Ibiza I've never seen before. And already I've been out for longer than it could possibly take to buy the papers, and my heart is pounding like a road-drill in case my Princess isn't in, in case I get her answering-machine with that awful message which isn't exclusively for me. But she is in, and she's clever enough to give a little squeal of happiness when she knows it's me.

'Where *are* you? Why aren't you here? I want you *here*. Come home at *once*.'

167

And my voice goes ga-ga, like a newscaster with a story about the Queen Mother or a normal person speaking to a child.

Are you being good?

'*No*. I'm being very bad, and it's *your* fault. If you don't come home soon I'll sleep with Jack the Actor, I will, I will. I'll sleep with all your friends.'

You don't know my friends.

'I'll ring up your publishers. I'll ask them who your friends are. I'll say that I'm your Princess and that you're being very bad, that you've abandoned me. Ted says that's what I should do.'

How is Ted?

'He's missing his daddy.'

And I squelch inside and hear myself telling her, only in the vaguest terms, only as an outside chance, about my plan to come home sooner – and she leaps on it, won't let it go.

'You've *got* to. When? When can you come home?'

I only said I might. It won't be easy. Alison's mother ...

'That's not good enough. If you don't come home sooner I'll ...'

What?

'Nothing. Doesn't matter.'

No, tell me.

'Well – you remember my arms dealer?'

Yes.

'He's asked me to go to Greece with him for a month.'

Jesus, you *can't*.

'Why not? *You've* abandoned me. You're out there having fun.'

I'm not having fun. It's a fucking nightmare. The cases are entirely different. I'm doing this for Alison's mother. It's her last holiday. You *can't* go to Greece.

'You'd better come home sooner, then.'

Christ she's unscrupulous. She doesn't give a stuff for Alison or her dying mother. And the Greek business probably isn't even true. She's winding me up, playing with my head – and I mustn't fall for it.

Okay. I'll try.

She gives a little whoop of triumph.

'You won't regret it, I promise. I'll *excel* myself!'

I love you.

There's a terrible silence at the other end. I've broken the rules. I've had it now.

'And I love ...'

She pauses. God, is she going to say it? If she says it, I'll go back now, today, this minute, leaving Alison, do anything she wants.

'... I love it when you say things like that.'

She *was* going to say it, I know she was, but stopped herself in time.

I'm coming back. I'll look after you.

I don't know what I mean by this, but that's okay: she won't know either. Unless, of course, she's what Tiffs says she is – in which case she'll know what she hopes I mean. But that's okay too: I'll threaten her with money, point my money at her like a gun. You can't be mugged by someone if you give them your wallet with a smile before they ask for it, before they produce the knife. I'll mug her first, keep her in her place with money, pay her rent, perhaps – that shows contempt. You can't take a man too seriously who's paying your rent, can't have too high expectations of him. All you can do is try to please him, excel yourself on quarter-days.

'You will? You really will?'

Yes.

I ring Simey straight away, and he's in, thank God. I tell him what he's got to do. In half an hour or so – there has to be a decent interval – he's to ring me in a frightful state. He's to say that Arrow want a synopsis of *The Naff Calendar*, something to show their art department, in three weeks at the latest. 'What's *The Naff Calendar?*' asks Simey, who's usually quicker off the mark than this. It's an imaginary non-book, I say, a literary Bunbury, so to speak. 'I see,' says Simey; 'and for how long will you and I not be meeting not to write this non-existent non-book?' That depends on my Princess, I say; all summer, I hope. 'You silly old fool', says Simey. That's as may be, I say, but the point is you've got to ring me in a dreadful stew in half an hour. You've got to persuade me to come home a week early.

169

I'll argue like mad, we've got to go through the whole routine to be convincing, but you've got to talk me into it. 'Okay,' he says.

I return to the flat, wondering whether it's wrong, whether it's a sin of some sort, to be as happy as this; and, in spite of my Scotish background, I decide it isn't. By the time I get there, I've forgotten what I went out to get. Alison reminds me.

'You've been a long time. Where are the papers?'

They haven't arrived yet.

'Really?'

No, not really. I just thought I wouldn't get them.

And she apologizes for being so sharp.

'I'm sorry. You're being marvellous. I hope it isn't too much of a nightmare. It means so much to Mummy.'

So I give her a hug, and spend a jumpy half-hour waiting for Simey to ring. God, if this worked – I could have a whole week in London alone with my Princess, a week in which she'll excel herself; and I hold Alison and wonder what she means by 'excel herself', sink so deeply into fantasy that when Simey rings, on the dot, I jump out of my skin, dropping Alison like a hot potato. Simey's good, as I knew he'd be, but I'm good too. I look appalled, my face gets longer and longer. As he talks I protest hotly. That's impossible, I say, quite out of the question. In the end I lose my temper. Arrow are mad, I say, and he's a cunt – Alison's mother's not in the room – to ring me at a time like this with such a preposterous scheme. Goodbye, I say, and I slam the phone down.

'What was that?' asks Alison.

Nothing.

'Come on. It must have been something. Why did you call Simey a cunt?'

Well, he is – really. Even to *suggest* something like that.

'*What?*'

So I explain, tell her the whole story – which, by now, I believe myself. She looks unhappy, asks how important it is. Pretty important, I say, but it doesn't matter. Nothing matters more than her mother's last holiday.

'Perhaps you *should* go back.'

What? And leave you here? I couldn't.

170

'I'd hate to be stuck here with Mummy on my own. She'd drive me mad. Isn't that awful? Perhaps we could come back with you. Perhaps she wouldn't mind.'

And that's not the idea at all – I must have a week in London with my Princess – so, thinking like lightning, I come up, almost at once, with a brilliant move.

You wouldn't have to stay here. You could go to France. Drive round a bit. She might prefer that. Visit the Dordogne and so on.

'Hm. That might not be so bad.'

She looks unhappy, but it's agreed at last – after further pressure from me, tactfully applied – that I'll go back early anyway and that Alison will let her mother decide what the two of them will do – stay out here, or dawdle round France, or, as she hopefully adds, come back with me, an option at all costs to be avoided. And then, while her mother's still asleep, she persuades me to go with her to buy some fucking silly dining-room table which her mother says we need. Considering the pressure I'm under, the agitation of waiting for her mother's verdict, I behave quite gracefully in the shop, comparing one table with another, discussing the merit of each as if it mattered and forking out without a protest; but when, lugging the cumbersome thing back home, I reverse into a traffic-light and, half-concussed, drop the table on my toe and Alison starts to laugh, all my troubles – the exhaustion of cheating on someone I care so much about, the absurdity of buying this silly table just to keep her mother quiet, wondering what my fate will be with regard to the possible week alone with my Princess, the pain of a broken toe – pile up in my head at once and I scream 'Jesus fucking Christ!' as loudly as I can. And Alison, who can tell it isn't because I've hurt my toe, stops laughing and crumples onto the pavement, sitting there with her head in her hands. 'It's Mummy's last holiday,' she says, 'and you want to cut it short.' So I sit down next to her, the two of us squatting in the gutter with our table, and I comfort her, and she apologizes, says she understands that my work comes first. She'll put my idea to her mother as soon as we get back to the flat, she says, suggest that they spend a week driving round France together.

171

But my scheme doesn't work – or rather it half works, which is almost worse. Her mother, it turns out, is keen to get home. It's too hot here and the thought of driving round France with Alison doesn't appeal at all. It's agreed at last that we'll all go back together next Tuesday, arriving in London on Thursday, and I want to scream with disappointment; but I comfort myself, gradually, with the thought that at least I've cut this nightmare short by a week, and I manage to sneak out later on my own, ringing my Princess with the good news and booking her for the first night that I get back. And she sounds ecstatic, and whether she's acting or not no longer bothers me. Then I have to go through the whole performance again with Simey, getting him to ring me with an alibi, insisting that we have a working dinner together as soon as I get home. And I manage to survive the horrors of the last week somehow by thinking about my Princess, of the many imaginative ways in which she's going to excel herself, and by entering in my writer's notebook all the awful things Alison's mother says.

We leave on Tuesday and, because we're cutting this fine, I drive flat out, with Alison's dying mother bumping around in the back. And Alison urges me to slow down, asking me why my date with Simey's so important. Surely you can start *The Naff Calendar* a day late, she says. No I can't, I say. And this is naff, I think, so I take out my writer's notebook and place it on top of the glove compartment and, with my left hand, I make an entry: Naff Ways Of Cutting Short Your Dying Mother-In-Law's Last Holiday – break the land-speed record from Barcelona to Calais so that you won't miss a date with your mistress. And I plume myself on not having lost my saving sense of humour, in spite of the strain I'm under.

We get to Worthing by Thursday afternoon, and, without turning off the engine, I bundle Alison's mother out of the car, and hurtle off again, leaving her looking startled on the pavement. We reach London at half past six, and Alison wants to sit down and talk about her mother, ask me if I think she enjoyed herself ('you were so good,' she says, 'I wish I could be as patient as you'), but I haven't got time for this. I've just got time to go through the lowering ritual of infidelity at close quarters – bathing and getting dressed with nonchalance

172

(*over*-dressed for a working session, some might think), being quizzed – what time will you be back? – and sliding out with Alison looking small and forlorn in the kitchen, grilling a solitary chop – before my imaginary date with Simey. I get out of the door without too many arduous explanations, but then I'm overwhelmed by a desire to go back and hug her – so I do. And this could be a mistake, I think. She looks pleased, but a little startled too.

'Why did you do that?'

Because you're so good.

I mean this, and wish she wasn't; wish she could, like me, innocently misbehave from time to time. She did once; she led me quite a dance. Why did she have to change, become so punishingly decent, eat nuts in bed and leave me so vulnerable to the least boring woman in the world – a woman whose very essence is not to eat nuts in bed or ever talk about domestic matters? She's managed, as usual, to make me quite depressed, but my spirits rise as soon as I'm in the car and on my way to my Princess. I begin to speculate, imagine the excitements she may have organized. She isn't silly: she'll remember that the afternoon before I went to Ibiza wasn't good. 'I shall excel myself,' she said, and my brain runs wild with possibilities. She'll be wearing her short skirt and little boots, I think, like she did on the night she danced in the street with Tanit the Island God. She was so graceful on that occasion, so sweet and funny and reassuring. I can't imagine her ever doing anything clumsy or out of place, anything that might embarrass me. She has such perfect timing, such confidence and taste. She can do the most disgraceful things and get away with it because she's innocent. What disgraces may she have laid on now? John the Accountant will have called – she won't make that mistake again – and perhaps the whole cast may be there in person – mad black girls, Jack the Actor, Tessa the Teacher, mercenaries with guns. We can do without the mercenaries, I think, but Tessa the Teacher, stern in specs and mortarboard, disciplining my Princess, fresh as a daisy in her little skirt, for spelling errors might be rather sweet.

I park the car and run across the road, glance up and see that her curtains are drawn; that's good, the scene is set, the

173

lights are low, she'll have the music on. My God, I hope she's there; I hope she hasn't chosen this moment to play a joke, to take me to the edge and leave me there. I couldn't handle it; my brain would split in two. I run upstairs, planning it all in my mind. We'll take our time, enflame one another with witty accusations; I'll taunt her with her infidelities, and then I'll punish her, repossess her angrily. That's what she wants, and I think I want it too. I want her to have done something so disgraceful that I have to kill her. I ring her bell, and my head is reeling with thoughts of violence in the future and of teasing happiness now.

She opens the door and, because it's very dark inside, I can't see her properly at first. Then, as my eyes grow accustomed to the gloom, I see that she's wearing dark glasses, flat shoes and a shapeless track-suit. Her hair's a mess and she isn't wearing make-up. She gives me a little nervous hug – she feels tiny, I don't remember her being as small as this – and then she sits on the sofa, huddled up, and takes her glasses off. She's obviously been crying. She looks like a bedraggled rat, and fearfully plain. My head is spinning with disappointment – can this be what she thinks she's for? – but I sit down next to her and ask her what the trouble is. It must be something terrible, I think, to make her behave as boringly, as thoughtlessly as this. She moves in close, puts her head on my shoulder, and starts to tell me, but I can't really follow her. I'm only half listening, wondering if there's any way out of this, any chance of starting again; I could persuade her to ring John the Accountant up, perhaps, to get up and have a bath, and dress appropriately for a man who has just bucketed across France at 100 mph to see her, while I go out and walk around, returning to get my money's worth in half an hour or so.

It's something to do with her husband, I think, the thug who spat at her in Bogota. He's in prison in New York, it seems, but managed in spite of this to ring her up last night, demanding money. Mention of money puts me on full alert. Is this it? Have I driven a thousand miles to be seriously hustled? Tiff's words echo in my mind: 'She's a whore. She's always been a whore. She'll never be anything else but a whore.' If so, she's not a very clever one: letting me see her like this is a serious mistake.

174

What will you do? Will you send him some?

'Of course. I want him to think I'm doing well. I want him to feel bad.'

That makes sense. They never let go, these low-life girls; they spend forever seeking revenge on those they were close to once, close enough to marry. She'll say something blood-chilling now – 'What goes round comes round,' perhaps – and her mouth will snap shut like a purse.

'He can give it to his South American tart. I don't care.'

Why is she so upset, then? She must be still involved with him, I think, but when I ask her if this is so, she laughs harshly and denies it. Then she moves in even closer and stares up at me, opening her eyes wider than I've ever seen them. It's as well, perhaps, that John the Accountant hasn't called. If she were high now and looked at me like this, I'd get a rush and give her everything I have. As it is, I brace myself against the coming tug. But she doesn't hustle me – not yet, at least. Sensing, perhaps, that she's moving too fast – that there's still some groundwork to be done – she slows down, changes the direction of her attack.

'How's Alison? How's her mother?'

It was awful. She was very brave. I don't know how I got through it. I thought about you all the time.

'And I thought about you. I hated you being there with *her*. I know I shouldn't have, but I did. I think of that flat as ours.'

That's good. A silly man could fall for that, and the look to go with it – imploring, like an unwanted puppy about to be dunked in a bucket – is even better. This is it, she's closing in now, and I brace myself again. I'll give her something – just enough to keep myself on the front-foot, so to speak – and then I'll leave, without rebuking her, with my dignity intact. If I leave now, I'll be on the front-foot with Alison too; I'll be home earlier than expected, have a late night up my sleeve, as it were, though where and with whom I'll want to spend it I can't imagine: not here, that's for sure, unless my Princess pulls herself together, remembers what she's for. I'll give her a hundred pounds; I'll be damned if I'll give more than a hundred pounds to her gangster husband and his South American tart. But she doesn't ask for money; she asks me to spend the night with her, begs me, in fact. How can she think that's possible, that I could even if I wanted to? I tell her that it's out of the question, but she argues and pleads, quotes back at me what I said when I phoned her from Ibiza.

'You said you'd look after me. You *promised*.'

I *will*.

'Well you aren't doing. I need you *now*. Don't you understand? Please don't leave me. Not tonight. I've got the horrors, I really have.'

This is a test, I think, she's simply being cunning. I decide to call her bluff, to give her money anyway, and then leave, get out with a credit balance in the bank, accruing interest. I write her out a cheque for £500 – that looks serious, I think – and hand it to her. She stares at it aghast, and then, to my amazement, she starts to cry. She tears the cheque into several little pieces – too small, I think, to be put together once I've gone.

'How *could* you? I'm distraught and you offer me *money*! I'll never forget that, I really won't.'

This isn't acting; her guard's right down; she really is distraught. I don't want to see her like this, I want to get out. There's nothing for me here. I've had bad deals on two occasions now, and I feel baffled, angry. I stand up decisively, insisting that I have to go. She looks so horrified that I hear myself suggesting lunch tomorrow, which is the last thing I want. It means another alibi with Simey, sliding out again in front of Alison, bathing in the middle of the morning (one likes to bathe before these things). Alison suffers from selective inattention as severely as any other woman, but she'll spot me bathing in the middle of the morning and sliding out in matching separates. And Simey will think I've got a screw loose. We've not had dinner, and now we're not going to have lunch. What if we really need to meet? We won't be able to. He'll ring me up: can we have lunch? he'll say. I'm afraid not, I'll say, we're not having lunch already. I phone him now from my Princess's and tell him about our non-lunch tomorrow. I've got to see my Princess, I say; I'm having so much fun I want to do it again as soon as possible. Then, in case he thinks I'm merely using him, I suggest that we have a drink together first.

176

'What's the point of that?' he says. 'Why don't we just not meet earlier, not have an early lunch? Better still,' he says, 'why don't we not live together, then every time we don't have lunch or dinner or a drink we won't have to arrange it on the telephone.' For a man who's so clever that his brain actually sticks out of his head he's getting very confused. I explain that I mean a real drink, not a non-drink. He doesn't sound convinced. 'Do you mean it?' he asks warily; 'you mean we'll *really* meet?' Yes, I say. 'Okay,' he says; 'we can talk about the book.' What book? I ask. '*The Naff Calendar*,' he says. He's still confused. We're not doing that, I say.

'Good lord, nor we are,' he says.

I ring off, feeling rather good. Our conversation was most amusing, if I'm not mistaken, and my Princess will be impressed. I move in on her to give her a good-bye hug, but, to my surprise, she ducks away, looking cross. I ask her what the matter is.

'Nothing.'

Something's the matter. Tell me.

'I didn't like the way you spoke to Simey. You said, I've *got* to see my Princess. You haven't *got* to see me.'

I didn't mean it like that. I didn't mean I've *got* to see you in that sense; I meant *I've* got to see you – *have* to, can't keep away.

'Hm. Well, I didn't like your tone. I didn't like the way you said, I'm having so much fun I want to see her again as soon as possible. You were being sarcastic.'

No I wasn't.

'You were, but it doesn't matter. I don't blame you. I know this isn't what you want, and I'm sorry, I really am. I've been a real drag, but I'll get it right tomorrow – I promise.'

I hope she means it. I didn't cut short Alison's dying mother's last holiday and drive a thousand miles for this.

Perhaps you should give John the Accountant a ring.

She looks a little startled, opens her mouth as if to protest, then seems to change her mind.

'Okay. If you say so.'

*

177

The next day, I meet Simey as arranged for a drink in a King's Road pub and have trouble afterwards shaking him off. He wants to come with me to The Good Earth, a Chinese restaurant where I'm meeting my Princess, but I can't have that. I can't risk others seeing her looking as she did last night. And I'm glad I did manage to shake him off because she arrives late and looking awful (nothing like the photographs I produced for Simey from my bulging wallet – he'd think this was a different person). Her eyes are tiny – from crying all night, she says – and she still isn't wearing make-up, but she doesn't seem so miserable; indeed she becomes more cheerful by the minute, drinking a bottle of wine on her own and laughing at her performance the night before. It was hearing her husband's voice again, she says; it wasn't that she wanted him, just that it reminded her of the nightmare life they'd had together.

After lunch, back at her flat, she suddenly says:

'I've decided I want to see you every day.'

This is a joke, of course, and I'm about to laugh it off when I notice that she's looking serious, determined even. I explain, lightheartedly, that this won't be very easy. I've got to work, I say, and anyway Alison might begin to notice. Then I make a big mistake. I hear myself saying – I don't know why – that on three days a week Alison works herself. My Princess pounces on this at once.

'Which days are those?'

Monday, Wednesday and Friday.

'What does she do?'

I've no idea. I've never asked.

'You *must* have done!'

She may be a policeman. Something like that, I think.

'Okay.'

She gets up and goes over to her office, puts a piece of paper in her typewriter, and, with an adorably important, business-like expression, sends a memo to herself: 'Days Alison is working – Monday, Wednesday and Friday.'

'Right. What are her hours?'

I don't know. Ten till six, that sort of thing.

My Princess adds this information to her memo.

178

'Okay – on Mondays, Wednesdays and Fridays we can spend the whole day together.'

I've got to work!

She points to her little typewriter.

'You can use that. I'll be very quiet, I promise.'

My heart melts. She's looking hideous, like a wicked little rat, and yet I want to pick her up and put her in my pocket, take her with me everywhere and never let her go. And this is dangerous: I've not felt weak with *love* before – least of all when she's looking like a rat. But I keep my head, explain that I couldn't work here, could never concentrate with her around. She pouts and thinks about it, analyses her next move in depth.

'All right. But on Mondays, Wednesdays and Fridays I want you to wake me up with my morning tea – like you did in Ibiza. I'm going to give you a spare set of keys. You can use them any time you like.'

She rummages in her bag, and then hands me a couple of keys – one of which is to her flat, she says, and the other to the door downstairs.

I'm immensely touched. Would a hustler be this trusting? I'll have to ring Tiffs and ask her: ask her, with a cutting innocence, whether my Princess's victims have always had the run of her flat. Tiffs will be looking very silly soon.

Then she comes over and sits on my knee, looks up at me with wide, beseechful eyes, just as she must have done as a child when, having been naughty, she'd run to her step-father seeking his protection.

'Let's go back to Ibiza. *Please.* I don't like London. London's cold and horrid. Why can't we go back to Ibiza?'

I make one last serious attempt to explain my summer schedule. I'm behind with my work, I say – disastrously so, in fact. I've got to write one book at least, maybe two. I need money – we can't live in Ibiza on nothing. She listens to me earnestly, nodding, eyes wide with understanding, until I mention money. Then she gives a little snort of impatience.

'Oh phooey. You're always going on about money. Money isn't important. I've got money. I can keep us.'

I can't wait to tell Tiffs this, to stuff this one down her throat. I keep a straight face – which isn't easy with the flood of

179

triumph welling up inside me. I explain that it isn't just money – that writing, whether she likes it or not, is what I do.

'Well I don't like it. Why can't you be a producer? If you loved me you'd be a producer.'

I've been a producer, I've done all that.

'Why can't you do it again? For my sake?'

It was the wrong fantasy, it didn't fit – hence loss of morals. In my experience, Princess, loss of morals is invariably a result of trying to live out the wrong fantasy. The wrong fantasy leads to panic, and bad behaviour is usually a consequence of fear. Most people will behave badly if they're frightened enough. Very few people behave badly anyway, are *naturally* bad, so to speak. Tories, lawyers, policemen – that's about it. Since discovering the right fantasy for me, my behaviour has been impeccable.

She'll be impressed. I'm rather impressed myself. The theory came to me on the spur of the moment. But she isn't impressed; she looks at me in silence for a while, then gets off my knee and goes to the bathroom (to take a line, perhaps? I rather hope so. She's being very sweet, but not exactly what I want). I glance quickly round the room, wonder if I have time to rifle through her papers, read her diary, discover how often she saw Jack the Actor while I was doing my duty by Alison and her dying mother. This is nice, but we need some dramatic motivation here if we're to repair the damage done last night. Alas, there isn't time; she's back from the bathroom in a minute.

'Okay. And *then* we can go back to Ibiza?'

All right.

'*When*? When will you have finished your silly books?'

September – if you let me work.

'We can go back in September? Promise?'

I promise.

'I'll be naughty in Ibiza. I'll do anything you want. I'll be really disgraceful. I'll drive you mad.'

I hope this doesn't mean she won't be disgraceful here, won't drive me mad in London. And she *must* be able to read my mind, because she immediately adds:

'Don't worry. I'll be a little naughty here. I know you don't want it ever to be real.'

180

I don't want it ever to be dull.

'You mean real.'

I mean dull.

And I'm misleading her about Ibiza, too. There's no way I could go back there so soon – not on my own, at least, not without Alison. Never mind, three months is a long time off; she'll have forgotten all about it by September, may not be talking to me, even. And there are other exciting possibilities, anyway – apart from the opportunities afforded by Alison's dying mother (as she gets weaker, poor Alison will have to spend nights away in Sussex). Over August Bank Holiday, for instance, Alison often visits some friends of hers in Norfolk. I tell my Princess this.

Alison often spends August Bank Holiday in Norfolk.

'How long for?'

About a week.

'I'll move in with you.'

That's odd. Before I went to Ibiza, she said she couldn't spend the night at my place, pouted and said it was because of *her*. She *must* have had another date, the deceitful little cat. And my stomach tightens, there's a weight of excitement on my chest and I realize that I hope she did, hope that she was double-crossing me. I'll quizz her about this later, when she's off her guard, when I've got her at my mercy.

And she usually goes to Portugal for a few weeks at the end of the summer.

'When exactly?'

The beginning of September usually.

Actually it's always in October, but I don't want my Princess to think we've got to wait that long to be together; I want her to forget Ibiza for the moment.

She takes out her diary now and makes a couple of entries. I snatch it from her when she's finished, eager, naturally, to see what she's written. In August it says 'Alison to Norfolk. I move in with my Prince.' And in September she's put: 'Alison to Portugal. Me and my Prince to Ibiza for proper honeymoon.' I wonder if she'd notice if I palmed it, slipped it into my pocket, had these pages photo-copied, later to be shown to Tiffs – but before I can, she snatches it away again.

181

'That's very *bad* – you can't read my diary! I don't want you to discover how often I saw Jack the Actor while you were away.'

Did you? How often?

'*Lots* of times.'

Why?

'Because I really like him. He's so ...'

I take her by the shoulders and push her back against the sofa, thinking, even as I do so, that I mustn't push too hard, tipping her over the sofa's arm so that she falls backwards to the floor, legs in the air, looking silly. My Princess must never look silly. They're touch and go, these careful little dramas. She lies back on the sofa, looking up at me with a defiant, demanding smile.

'Fuck me.'

I wouldn't dream of it. You're just a little ...

'*Say* it! Call me a slut.'

Are you?

'*Yes*. Hit me. Hit me across the face. *Please*.'

You're not worth it. I'm going.

'I'll ring Jack the Actor if you do.'

Okay. But I might come back. Don't forget I've got the keys.

'That's why I gave them to you. I want you to walk in and find me with him. What would you do?'

Her little hands are round my throat, but I don't want to laugh, as I wanted to laugh in Ibiza the first time we played this game.

I'd kill him.

My Princess goes quite swooney.

'What then? What would you do then?'

I might fuck you.

'Fuck me. Fuck me *now*.'

But I don't; I find myself making love instead, which isn't so unusual, I suppose, but it's a first for me, the first time I've made love in all my life, I think – certainly to someone like her, and she doesn't seem to mind, isn't affronted, as far as I can tell, by my presumption; and it's the real her, I'm sure, and John the Accountant hasn't been, and the music isn't on, daylight is streaming through the window, she's looking awful

182

and it doesn't matter; and she knows all this, I think, may have organized it, even, wanted me to want who she really is. And afterwards I catch her looking cunning, catch her looking up at me with a knowing gleam in her eye, like a triumphant little rat. And then she turns away and lights a cigarette. So that's all right – she doesn't like me yet. I'm glad I didn't embarrass her with my sudden rush of feeling, but if she ever liked me I might lose interest. And as I'm leaving, it occurs to me that there is another reason why she'll always win with me, or, rather, why I'll always lose. Apart from manners, I'm far too nice – I could never treat her as badly as she wants. Surely Canetti was thinking of her when he observed – paradoxically in 1964, when she was only ten – that some people can only love with a strong feeling of guilt. 'Their passion ignites on whatever they are ashamed of; it becomes their haven, like God for believers after they have sinned. They want to be afraid and they love a person only if their fear of him never dies. When he stops reproaching them and does not punish them for anything, when they have won him over to such an extent that he is satisfied with them, their love dies and everything ends.' He must have been thinking of my Princess.

Alison's out when I get home, so, bloated with vindicated pride, awash, as I am, with a sense of authenticated masculinity, I seize this opportunity to ring up Tiffs, not to boast or crow, I hope, but to put her firmly in the picture. We chat for a while of this and that, and then she says: 'How's your Princess? Are you bankrupt yet?' Don't be like that, I say. My Princess is okay, she's a nice person. And Tiffs laughs incredulously. 'I'm sorry,' she says, 'I know she's a friend of mine and that, but "nice" is the last thing I'd call her. Are you paying her rent yet?' Not yet, I say, but I certainly hope to soon. Hasn't anyone ever paid your rent? 'As it happens,' says Tiffs, 'they haven't, but if they had it wouldn't be the same – I'm not a whore.' And once – because Tiffs is as beautiful as anyone I've ever seen – I'd have touched her up nervously at a distance, saying something breathy like: and more's the pity, because if you were I'd give you a thousand pounds right now. And she'd have laughed quite sportingly and argued that she was worth a little more than that, and it would all have been quite jolly and fairly unembarrassing. But now – incredibly – I wouldn't want her as a gift, or anyone else who isn't my Princess. Every woman in the world who isn't my Princess offends me. But I don't tell Tiffs this – just in case it all goes wrong, in case I end up looking silly. Instead I say: Oh well, I expect you're right. 'Of course I'm right,' says Tiffs. 'And don't come crying to me when she's taken you for everything you've got.'

And after she's rung off I sit and marvel at the fact that Tiffs has known my Princess for fifteen years, and yet she doesn't know her at all.

In spite of my good intentions with regard to work, I find myself waking my Princess up more often than I should. On Mondays, Wednesdays and Fridays I wait patiently for Alison to leave the flat, and then I drive at once to Bristol House, let myself in, gaze at my Princess lovingly while she sleeps, clutching Ted, then wake her with her morning tea (four sugars in hers and two in Ted's). On these days I can't do any work at all; and this might not matter, I suppose, except that I can't work on the other days either. I try to sometimes, but my thoughts stray to Bristol House, I wonder what she's doing – typing a business letter, perhaps, with an important expression on her face – and I go soft inside. Eventually I ring her up, and she tries to entice me over. Sometimes she wins – always, in fact – and then she squirms with cleverness.

All this is very good for my character, of course. Being happy for the first time ever, I feel well-disposed towards the world, am kinder to Alison, for instance, feel well-intentioned towards my friends. Were I to move in the world at all, or see my friends, I'd be nice to everyone, patient, interested, concerned – have time to listen to their problems, having none myself. But I don't care to go out or see my friends; I can't see the point of anyone but her and when I'm not with her I prefer to be on my own, locked into my lovely secret.

At first she complained a bit that we never went out at night, never did anything 'normal', as she put it; but she accepts it now, I think, and contents herself by talking about Ibiza and of what we'll do when Alison goes to Portugal. One day she goes over to her office and types out a memo headed: 'All The Normal Things We'll Do When Alison Goes To Portugal – have dinner at the Carlton Tower, visit the zoo, feed the ducks on the Serpentine, watch television, buy fish and chips, fuck all night long'. Sometimes she asks me how my work is going, and I explain that I'm not working at all, that I don't need to any more, that I'm living in the present for the first time ever, that everything I've ever done was just a substitute for this. And she smiles her pussy-cat smile and says:

'That's because you've found the drug of your choice at last. You'll never replace me, you know. I'm the drug of your choice!'

There are similarities, I suppose. A crushing sense of boredom, a feverish dissatisfaction with the present, is the condition common to all junkies (what, in the first place, made them turn to drugs) and I've been bored for as long as I can remember – nothing and no one has been able consistently to lift it. But she can, and does. I only feel normal when I'm with her or know that she's near – when I'm carrying, as it were. The fact of her is all that matters, everything else is vague and out of focus – not threatening at all, simply comical, like listening to Mrs Thatcher when one's stoned. Everything reminds me of her: if it's an experience we've shared – walking along a street, say, which we've walked along together – I think about her; and if it isn't, if it's a place we've never been to, I think about her too, resenting the fact that I was here with someone else. I live from hit to hit, stepping up the dose as the weeks go by, and my behaviour is becoming more erratic, more audacious by the day. I now take enormous risks to get my fix, ring her up with Alison in the next room, disappear at odd moments and stay out too long, coming home and looking at Alison defiantly, challenging her to guess my secret. It doesn't matter – I've become as cunning as a monkey, able to lie my way out of anything. I've fetishised her too, find I can get a high by looking at a photograph or by holding something that belongs to her – something smuggled home without her knowing – just as a junkie, I believe, can get a high of sorts by

185

fondling an empty syringe. I'm okay as long as my source doesn't leave town, as long as she's available. One day she mentions, quite casually, that her arms dealer has asked her again to go with him to Greece. I panic at once, break into a cold sweat of fear, threaten, bluster, plead. She looks triumphant, agrees not to in the end, potters about for the next half hour with a knowing, contented smile.

I'm not working at all, and I'm haemorrhaging money just as Tiffs said I would. This began with my determination to control her, my belief that I could frighten her into being what I want with money, wrong-foot her by pre-empting her intentions. At first she didn't seem to like this – she accused me at one point of treating her like a whore – but she became accustomed to it pretty quickly, and now I'm paying the rent, her insurance premiums, her phone bills, everything. My overdraft – shakily supported by my nest-egg – is now enormous, and almost once a week I seem to ring my bank manager, seeking to increase it. The embarrassment of these weekly calls is such that I'm half inclined to sell some shares. One day I find myself discussing this with Alison, and out of the blue she offers to lend me some money.

'You *mustn't* break into your nest-egg – not when the shares are rising. I've got a couple of thousand I don't need. Let me lend you that.'

I'm immensely touched, but I protest – say I couldn't possibly take her money.

'Why not? Don't be silly. What's mine is yours.'

And my Princess's. On the very day that Alison lends me two thousand pounds my Princess tells me that her rent is due, and then presents me with a phone bill for £376.86. Her phone bills make no sense at all; she must be ringing her husband in America, I think.

None of which would matter if, when I visited her, I always get a good deal – but sometimes I get a bummer, one cut with domesticity. On coke she's brilliant at being herself – funny, wilful, erotic beyond my ability to fantasize; at other times she seems to have forgotten who she is, and I leave still feeling restless, worse, in fact, than if I hadn't had a hit at all. When John the Accountant hasn't called, she has a habit of wanting to compete with Alison, seeming to imagine that with her I lead a life of thoughtful suburban harmony, that Alison is some kind of cross between a cook and resident intellectual, that after an expert dinner prepared by her, we sit cosily and talk, or, at other times, visit expensive restaurants, discussing life across the table. In these moods, when keen, it seems, to usurp Alison's purely imaginary role, she goes quite crackers – shopping, cooking meals (always disgusting, I'm glad to say), washing up and trying to make me watch television with her. 'I bet you watch TV with *her*,' she says. 'Why don't you like watching it with me?' On these occasions I bring her smartly into line with money. 'Let's do something romantic,' she says, 'we never do anything romantic.' Here's two hundred pounds, I say – shortly thereafter walking out.

One day she makes what seems to be quite a serious attempt to get me to leave Alison and move in with her. She looks at me thoughtfully for a while and then says:

'Do you love me?'

You know I do.

'I don't understand you, then. If I loved someone I'd want to live with them, be with them all the time. *Nothing* would stop me.'

I explain that I could never leave Alison.

'Why not?'

Because she knows I never would. I couldn't let her be that wrong. Don't you understand?

'No.'

Of course she wouldn't; wiping out fifteen years of someone's life, letting them know they'd live a lie, wouldn't bother her in the least. After this, she changes slightly; she becomes a little harder, seems to be using me more blatantly, calls me 'darling' and then produces a phone bill that makes no sense. But this suits me. The more I give her, the more obliged she is to behave in the way I want her to. I become completely confident of my supply – she's always there, it never occurs to me that she might not be – and I get a bad deal far less often. For a perfect week or two I believe that I've got her organized at last, but then a series of incidents takes me a little by surprise. One Sunday I agree to have lunch in Covent Garden with my best

187

friend Angie and her children – three girls, all sweet and well-behaved, between the ages of two and seven, I think. I once thought Angie was the most beautiful thing I'd ever seen. One boring afternoon, I wandered out and bought a model agency – quite an expensive one at that – because Angie was the receptionist and I couldn't think of any other way of looking at her every day. Now, over lunch, I keep her on the edge of her seat by telling her at length about my Princess, and she's spell-bound, of course, humbled into speechlessness by the awful extent of my passion. I ask her whether she's ever felt so strongly about someone that the idea of anyone else has been obscene, a blasphemy almost. Angie thinks about it for a while and then says no, there's never been anyone like that. Even when she's been in love, she says, other people have been possible. And, because women are meant to be more monogamous than men, I feel more awe-struck than ever by the strength of my love for my Princess, whom I want exclusively. And I tell Angie this, tell her that I feel nothing but an amused contempt for anyone who isn't my Princess, who isn't the drug of my choice. And Angie says 'goodness!', or something of the sort, and then she says that she'd like to meet this amazing person. So, on the spur of the moment, we leave the restaurant and, without warning, go and call on my Princess. And it's a measure of my confidence that it simply doesn't cross my mind, as I proudly let us into her flat with my own set of keys, that she might not be there and pleased to see me, or there but with another man.

Luckily it goes extremely well. My Princess plays her part superbly, bouncing with happiness when we arrive, seeming to care for me as much as I care for her and being brilliant with the children, devising games, giving them the run of her naughty wardrobe and letting them play havoc with her make-up. They want to be Princesses too when they grow up, they say, and the eldest girl, who has a resourceful look in her eye, might be exactly that, I think. Suddenly my Princess looks very serious and says: 'Let's have a baby, darling. *Please* can't we have a baby. Do let's.'

I'm astonished – not because I think she means it (she probably saw us arrive, took a line for courage and doesn't know what she's saying now), but because I realise that with her I could, might want to, even. In any case I'm not appalled, which is the normal enough reaction, I suppose – a lot of people, at some time in their lives, have wanted children, I expect; it's just that I have never been able to imagine anything more tragic. (My first wife loved our son; for his sake she scrubbed floors in a psychiatric hospital when I left her. Now he won't speak to her at all; he prefers me, thinks I'm quite a card). Yet now, for a moment, I think that with my Princess there's nothing I'd like more, that I might with her, for the first time ever, want to make a go of things, construct something from day to day amid the horror – even to the point of having children. Then I realize – with relief, perhaps – that that's not it at all: I don't want to make a go of things, set myself up for the knock-out punch, just as my first wife did, and the baby itself would mean nothing (they could take it away the next day for all I'd care); it would be a symbol merely, testament to the fact that my Princess had cared enough to do this most significant thing with me. That would be the point of it, and why I'd want it.

She seems lonely today, under the sweet exuberance, and tries to make us stay; but we have to get back to Covent Garden, where Angie is meeting her husband at five o'clock. Before we leave she tells me that, because of all the burglaries there've been in the block, the locks on the downstairs door are being changed early in the morning. The new keys will be left on a table in the hall, she says, and I've got to come in and pick up a spare one before nine o'clock – after that they'll all have gone. I can't really follow this, but she's very insistent, so I say I will – not that I'll be able to, of course. Alison would think it very odd if I were to bucket out of the house at eight o'clock in the morning.

Later, driving back to Covent Garden, Angie says: 'She's serious, you know. When you were in the kitchen she told me she wanted to live with you. What are you going to do?'

Ring up Tiffs and tell her to put that in her pipe and smoke it, I think; but I grip the steering-wheel and say (solemnly, because I mean it):

What can I do? One doesn't have a right to happiness if the price is another person's misery.

Angie, being a woman – having a bottom of ruthlessness that

189

we men can never understand – disagrees. We have rights ourselves, she says, specifically the right to happiness.

This is nonsense, I'm sure, and yet most people – obviously – would agree with her to some extent, quite civilized people too; they think you have right, if you fall in love, to destroy another person's life. It happens all the time: bang! up and away just like that – sorry, I'm off, there's nothing I can do to help you. I did it once myself: left my first wife crying at the door, holding our son, begging me not to go. Since then, of course, I've been morally educated, can boast a legal precedent to that effect.

Would you want someone to stay with you, asks Angie, who was in love with someone else? Would you think you had a right to hold them?

I admit I wouldn't. She's got me there and no mistake, and now I don't know what I think. Perhaps I'm not as moral as I thought; perhaps my Princess is right: perhaps if I was certain of what I wanted I'd abandon Alison without a qualm. The trouble is I don't want anything completely – or, rather, I want everything and its opposite. I'm clamped in a formal paradox, trying to break a law of logic. I want everything to stay as it is – but perilously. I want my Princess so much that the thought of not having her is unendurable – and I want not to have her too. I explain all this to Angie, explain that I've *imagined* my Princess, created her to be perfect and that a necessary property of perfection, in my logic, is unavailability, of elusiveness at least. If she stood quite still I might not want her.

You've read *The Human Province* by Canetti, of course? His note on 'Passersby' and 'Eternals'?

'I don't believe I have.'

That's good. She won't know if I get it wrong; I can busk the bits I can't remember.

Well, Canetti imagines this world in which 'Passersby' and 'Eternals' live together. A 'Passerby' may love only 'Eternals', seducing one after another until she finally comes to rest herself as an 'Eternal'. Only this world – the world of 'Eternals' – can offer the happiness everyone longs for: in it, one 'Eternal' can find another 'Eternal' and together they never change, together they remain the same. They can exhaust their feeling for one another without the influence of time eroding it. They can find out whether they truly belong together; they, and only they, can test and prove their feelings. Whoever regards love as important in this intensified way may find and keep it. But whoever is excited by *changes* in the other, even though he himself has achieved constancy in his own nature, can, as an 'Eternal', court a 'Passerby'. And whoever wants to live in a flux, but has to worship what remains even and palpable, he, as a 'Passerby', will look for an 'Eternal'. Those, however, who in their own changeability can endure only changeable things, must be 'Passersby' forever, sticking to other 'Passersby'. Do you follow me?

'Of course. You're fluxed.'

Thank you.

'You need to worship, but can endure only what is changeable. Your Princess may be all right – she may be a 'Passerby', but she's looking for an 'Eternal', I tell you. Not a silly man like you.'

I'm disappointed, I thought Angie was more intelligent than this. I may be fluxed, but at least I can still drive married women in my Ford Fiesta and run Canetti past them.

The next day, when doing the shopping in the evening, I ring my Princess on the spur of the moment from a call-box. She sounds unhappy and tries to persuade me to go and see her now – immediately – saying it's really important. I say that I can't, that I've just popped out for a couple of minutes – she knows I can't disappear suddenly in the evening without an alibi. She starts to plead – something she's never done before.

'I need to see you. I really do. I'm not playing games. I mean it.'

She must want a phone bill paid, I think, or perhaps the rent is due. I become a little sharp, accuse her of being thoughtless – she knows the strain I'm under. She stops pleading in the end, but makes me promise to see her the next day, in the evening.

'I want you to take me out. I want to do something normal.'

I agree to see her, but not to doing something 'normal'. We won't have time for that, I say. If we waste precious moments on a silly dinner I'll be anxious already by the time we get back to her place, watching the clock, aware that my alibi is running out – I can't roll home from a non-meeting with Simey at 2 am with my tie round the back of my neck – and everything will be hasty and under-rehearsed. I suggest instead that she gives John the Accountant a ring: we'll stay in, I say, and, with help from him, surprise ourselves. She's silent for a moment, but then agrees, with a rather subdued 'okay'.

The following evening I drive round to Bristol House, only realising when I get there that I no longer have the key to the downstairs door. I ring the entry-phone, but there's no reply. I hang around a bit, than go to the pub opposite to telephone her. The answering-machine is on, but with a different message. She says she's with her mother in the country, and her voice sounds odd – husky and faltering, as if she's been crying or has a heavy cold. I'm a little angry now – I'm hoist foolishly on my own alibi and can't go home for hours – but I ring her mother's number from the telephone in the pub. Her mother answers, says that my Princess isn't at all well, that she's in bed asleep. Fuming with anger now, I have a silly meal alone in a King's Road cafe, and then go home. 'Hullo,' says Alison, 'you're back early.' And this is even more irritating, I don't know why, than being accused of coming home too late. So I snap at her. I'm so sorry, I say, shall I go out again and come back in an hour or two? And she looks sad, seems to shrink into her corner of our too-long sofa; so I resolve to be nicer to her, play one of our family games, perhaps, one that always makes her happy.

I get my chance in no time. One of our cats, Bertie Blue, is a little silly, something of a fantasist, in fact, one minute thinking he's a dangerous lion, the next insisting that he writes *Hill Street Blues* or, single-handed, won the Falklands War. Recently he has taken to pretending that he personally coaches many of the world's top sportsmen – David Gower, Boris Becker, Diego Maradona, 'Terrible' Tim Witherspoon etc. On television at the moment, there happens to be a snooker game in progress between Steve Davis and the little Scotsman Stephen Hendry, so I ask Alison which of the two Bertie Blues is coaching. The young lad Hendry, she says – already cheering up. He was at the start of the match, I say, but I happen to know that he received a better offer from Davis's management half-way through and has now put his expertise behind the Romford Robot. He's a little nervous, I say, that the lad Hendry's connections may come after him, may sue him – or worse – for this unprofessional switch. If someone rings in and, with a Scottish accent, asks to speak to Mr Bertie Blue, she's to say he's out. Alison, wriggling with happiness now, points out that in ten years there has never, as far as she knows, been a telephone call for Mr Bertie Blue. There's always a first time, I say, and there I let the matter rest – for the moment. Half an hour later, I say that I've run out of cigars, that I'll have to go and get some from the pub. I go to the pub and ring my friend O'Hear, who is Professor of Philosophy at Bradford University but is very good at accents too, not least Scots. I ask him to ring me back in half an hour or so and, when Alison answers, ask to speak to Mr Bertie Blue, in a heavy Glasgow accent. He agrees – later playing his part to perfection, with the result that, for the rest of the evening, Alison's ecstatic.

The next day I speak to my Princess, who is still at her mother's. She apologises for messing me around and explains that she had a sort of mini-breakdown after we spoke on Monday evening. After I refused to go and see her, she suddenly started to cry, she says, and couldn't stop. Her mother happened to ring in the middle and, being concerned, persuaded her to come home at once. She was still crying when she got there, so her mother gave her a sleeping pill and popped her into bed. I ask her what caused this mini-breakdown.

'I don't know. Angie coming round with her children had something to do with it, I think. It upset me. That's why I wanted to see you the next day. When you wouldn't come round I sort of went to pieces. I'm sorry. I'll make it up to you, I really will.'

She'd better – if she wants her phone bills paid, she'd better pull herself together, get John the Accountant round and remember what she's good at. She'll come back to London at the end of the week, she says, and we make a date for Friday evening. I don't say anything about John the Accountant, reckoning she'll be sensible enough to ring him without prompting. She won't want to let me down again.

193

On Friday I go round to Bristol House and, on the entry-phone – I still don't have a key to the downstairs door – she tells me that she's in the bathroom, that I'm to let myself into the flat and behave myself until she's ready. Upstairs, once I'm inside her flat, she calls out from the bathroom, saying she'll be about ten minutes and that she's got a surprise for me. She sounds high, so I reckon John the Accountant must have been. That's good, and so is the sitting-room, which she has turned into a stage-set appropriate to the coming drama: the curtains are drawn, the lights are low and suitable music is throbbing in the background.

This is an excellent opportunity, I suddenly realise, to rifle quickly through her office, pry into her past, turn up intumescing evidence, perhaps, that she's cheating on me now. Glancing round, I spot her diary lying on a table. I read it rapidly, actually trembling with excitement, suffering a constriction in my breathing, as when waiting for piercing news, either good or bad – actually *wanting*, I think, to come across evidence which will appal me. But to my disappointment – or relief, I don't know which – I discover that most of the entries seem to refer to me: 'Enticed my Prince over', 'My Prince phoned', that sort of thing, and I find myself half hoping that there may be another Prince. Then I start to read her letters. Most of these are very dull – carbon copies of instructions to her bank, her landlord, her insurance-broker – but heart-breaking to me because her little hands have typed them. I gaze at them dotingly for a while, then, digging more deeply, I come across a stack of postcards, including the one I sent her from Ibiza with the somewhat risky message – 'I love you, Princess, and I miss you horribly' – and, next to it, one from her best friend Laura, posted recently in Madeira, where Laura's mother lives. 'I love you too, Princess,' it says, 'and I miss you horribly. Viva Ibiza! Viva Prince!' And there might be another Prince, I think, but there can't surely be another Prince whom she visits in Ibiza. Amazed that Laura seems not to disapprove of me, seems even to favour the liaison, I put this in my pocket to show at some later date to Tiffs. As the sensible one, the one who shops and buys the cling-wrap, Laura shouldn't approve of me at all, should be giving my Princess

194

constant lectures: 'Don't trust him, darling. You're not twenty-one, you know. You should be out there hustling.' Perhaps Laura's on my side. That's good – it's important to have the purchaser of cling-wrap on your side.

Then, because my Princess shows no signs of coming out of the bathroom yet, I search for photographs, becoming quite bold, opening and closing drawers and dipping into private boxes. I find them eventually at the bottom of a cupboard and I spread them out on the office table. There are some nudes, professionally taken – including some of 'The Bottom Of The Year Contest' in *Knave* in which she triumphed over Tiffs – and in these she looks astonishingly young and innocent, staring at the camera with empty, bewildered eyes, her face as bland, as expressionless as butter, so unaware of all the hurt to come. And I can't look at these for long: my head fills with misery because I didn't know her then, couldn't protect her from men who'd spit at her and beat her up. I put these away, and examine instead her collection of holiday snaps, which, I'd guess, go back ten years or more. I gaze at these intently, resenting any in which she seems happy. I search for clues, indications that her life is incomplete, that something significant is missing. Her past is unendurable to me now. My own past is a nonsense, a desert, utterly abandoned, never to be revisited – the people in it disgusting failures because they pretended to be her and weren't. I can't look back – every memory hurts, even the nice ones, because they're of things I didn't do with her. I want her to feel this too. I want there to be some sign, in these photographs, that her life was as ridiculous as mine. I've never felt it before, this retrospective jealousy. It seems a cruelty scarcely to be borne that she existed, unprotected, for thirty years without my knowing, without her knowing that I existed only to look after her. Any date before I met her hurts. When I come across a date – any date, 15th June 1983, for instance, or 12th October 1954 – I try instantly to possess it, work out where she might have been, what she was doing, and with whom. There are some photographs taken in Portugal where she went on holiday with Laura just before she came out to Ibiza. I can look at these. I existed then, I was in her life – just. If she's smiling it isn't necessarily because she's thinking of someone who isn't me. I can't look for long at any of the others. I want to tear them up. I don't tear them up, though; I choose a couple and pop them in my wallet, just managing to hide them away and put everything back in its place before she comes out of the bathroom.

And, because she's managed to transform herself into something from a pornographic fashion shot in *Vogue* — arrogant, expensive, diamond-hard in blood-red high heels and a fur coat — my stomach dips with fear. She stands in the doorway for a moment, smiling provocatively, eyes shining with a defiance I've never seen before. Then she lets the coat slip open. She's grossly, shockingly naked underneath, pale and silky against the fur, the Ideal of every dirty photograph that's ever unsettled me at ten to three on a meaningless lonely afternoon, the others, I now understand, having been imperfect earthly imitations merely. I lurch towards her, clumsy and murderous, weak and reeling with desire, with love, with loathing — I want to kill anyone who's ever touched her, anyone who's looked at her. I want to kill her too, remove the possibility forever of anyone seeing her like this but me. She pushes me away, walks over to the table and lights a cigarette.

'This isn't for you. I've dressed like this for Jack the Actor. He told me to. I wanted you to see me first — to see what isn't yours. I'm going over to his place now.'

Do you mean it?

I feel sick, I want her to mean it.

'Of course I mean it. I don't want you. I want him.'

Why?

'Why do you think? It's better with him.'

I'm very frightened now. I don't think my brain will hold this weight of wanting. Thirty years of wanting have become concentrated into this second of time, and I don't think my brain can take it.

Why?

'He treats me badly. He tells me to go over there dressed like this, naked under my coat. He makes me take a taxi. On the way I imagine what he's going to do to me.'

What? What does he do?

'He makes me wait. Sometimes his girlfriend's there. It's

better when she is. I have to take my coat off and stand in front of them with nothing on. They make me wait like that for ages. They touch me occasionally and tell me what they're going to do to me.'

What do they do to you?

One small portion of my brain is still functioning well enough to tell me that I'm now completely mad. If I had it in my power to extend this moment by committing every atrocity since the dawn of time I would. And another small functioning portion thinks: what if this were real? I'd kill her definitely.

'Sometimes he ties me up and makes me watch him fucking her. That's the worst torture because I want him so much myself. Then they both fuck me, they tie me up and fuck me and ...'

What are you doing?

'I'm phoning for a taxi. I'm going there now. I can't wait any longer.'

You'll never get out of the door. You're not going anywhere.

'You can't stop me.'

Yes I can. I'd kill you before I'd let anyone else have you. I mean it. You're mine.

'*Yours*? You're mad! I'll never be yours. I can have anyone I want. I don't want you. Let me *go*!'

I tear her coat off, push her backwards onto the sofa. She stretches, lies back, smiles up at me defiantly.

'Why should you want someone who doesn't want you? You'll never have me.'

Yes I will. Now and any time I like.

'Not unless you rape me. You'll have to rape me.'

For a while she fights as hard as she can – wriggling, kicking, punching with her little fists – then suddenly she goes limp, screams at me to hit her, begs me to hit her across the face. And this is the closest I've ever been to anyone, I think; and afterwards it occurs to me how odd it would be, knowing this thing about each other, if, after tonight, we never met again, how odd it would be to know everything significant about another person and then break up. And what if, after twenty years, we met again? Would we remember that we knew this thing about each other? I'd never forget, but she, I think, might

197

have forgotten by tomorrow. This is her – but if, tomorrow, John the Accountant hadn't been, she'd say it wasn't. Without drugs she'd betray herself. Now she looks up at me with a small, contented smile and says:

'Was that good?'

You know it was. You're clever, aren't you?

And even now, even when it's over and I'm more or less sane again, I want her to say that she wasn't being clever, that it was all true, that she meant every word of it. I want her to have been disgraceful, and, just as much, I want her not to have been. I want to live like this forever, on this sharp edge of uncertainty about her, to know that I'm alive because I can't possess her. And part of me is terrified because I know I can never go back to being something else, revert to what I was. She's given me everything I want – just as she had said she would – and if I lose her I'll be dead.

'I told you I was clever. I warned you! Did you read my diary?'

Yes.

'I knew you would. That's why I left it there.'

I was a little disappointed. There was nothing in it about Jack the Actor.

'God – I'm not that stupid! I only write about him in my *intimate* diary. I keep that locked away. You'll never find that.'

Was it true, then?

'What?'

Everything you said. I have to know.

She looks at me intently, trying to work out what she's meant to say.

'About Jack the Actor?'

Yes. Was it true?

'You *really* want to know? No games?'

Yes. I have to.

'Of course it wasn't. With *Jack the Actor*? He's gross! I'd never want to see him. Uuurrgh! I can't think why we ever chose him.'

I must look disappointed, I suppose – shattered even – because she laughs a little nervously, and then apologizes.

'Sorry. I got that wrong, didn't I? Don't worry. I'll get it right in Ibiza, I really will. In Ibiza I'll drive you mad!'

Now I feel a little silly. *She* started this, told me it was what

198

she liked, gradually pulled me into it. Suddenly I'm the peculiar one, the one who has been indulged. I'm about to say all this, to protest my innocence, as it were, when I realise it's already too late. She's become a different person now, wants to talk about nice things, about Ibiza, and show me all the clothes she's been buying for 'our proper honeymoon' – bikinis, a little pair of shorts, an assortment of T-shirts, an evening dress. And so, because I assume, in her present mood, that she'll think it's sweet, I tell her about the pussy-cat game I played last night with Alison, about Bertie Blue and the important phone-call he received from the Professor of Philosophy at Bradford University. But, to my surprise, she doesn't like it at all. She pouts and then goes silent, so I ask her what the matter is.

'Nothing.'

Come on. Something's the matter.

'I don't like you playing games like that with *her*.'

They're nothing! They mean nothing at all.

'Yes they do. I'd rather you fucked her than played games like that. *I* want to play games like that. Why can't *we* have a pussy-cat who gets important phone calls? If we can't have a baby, at least we could have a pussy-cat.'

I'll never understand her; she doesn't understand herself, I think. I hang around for a little longer, talking about Ibiza, of all the nice things we're going to do, then I give her some money and leave. She looks small and rather tired.

I'd hoped, frankly, that my Princess would forget about Ibiza. We have our Portugal honeymoon, after all – Alison has fixed this now, she's going there at the end of September – but my Princess talks about nothing but Ibiza. It's not something I can wriggle out of now, so I begin to work on a scheme, some reason I can give to Alison as to why, suddenly, I have to go there. Gradually an idea forms. The BBC has recently bought a book of mine and, furthermore, has commissioned me and Ben to turn it into a six-part situation comedy. I'll tell Alison that we can only do this in Ibiza. Ben can't get away at once, I'll say, but I'll go out there earlier to do some spade-work, to be joined by Ben in a week or two. In reality, of course, Ben won't come at all. After I've been in Ibiza for a couple of weeks (with my Princess) Ben will apparently let me down, phoning with some reason why he can't get out there. 'Oh dear, what a nuisance!' I'll say to Alison. 'No point in my being here on my own – I might as well come home.' If this works, my Princess and I will have three weeks together in Ibiza and then another three weeks in London when Alison goes to Portugal. I put the scheme to Ben, and at first he doesn't like it, pointing out that, for two weeks, he'll have to play out this charade with Alison – should she happen to phone him after I've left for Ibiza – and that afterwards she'll bollock him for ever – 'You let my Button down etc'. He agrees in the end, however, and then I put the scheme to Alison. To my surprise, she takes it pretty well – even though she assumes, for the moment, that I could be away for at least two months. 'It'll be horrid,' she says, 'but I do understand that you work best in Ibiza. And don't worry about the pussy-cats. I'll get the old tart downstairs to feed them when I'm in Portugal.'

So that's all right, then – my only remaining problems being financial. My overdraft, even with the transfusion from Alison, is now colossal, and, staggering from week to week under its spirit-sapping weight, I suddenly give up and – too embarrassed to ring my bank manager yet again, seeking an extension – I decide to sell my nest-egg. I do this instantly, before I have time to change my mind, very quickly, averting my eyes, as it were, as if I'm putting down a cat. I'm on my own now, in the cold, utterly exposed – but I have my Princess and enough money in my current account to continue like this for a year at least, even if I never work again. That's all that matters, all I care about.

On the day before my Princess and I leave for Ibiza – a beautiful day, the best of the summer so far – Alison and I happen to be having lunch outside a local pub.

'It's on days like this,' says Alison, 'that I really wish we had a house with a garden. With what I've saved and with your nest-egg we could afford to buy one, you know.'

That's true.

'On the other hand, it *would* be silly to sell your nest-egg now, I suppose.'

That's true too, I say.

'It's for our future. Our old age together. And we do have Ibiza.'

And after lunch she walks me down the King's Road and insists on buying me an expensive new sound system to replace the rather outmoded one we have in the Ibiza flat.

'I don't like to think of you out there on your own without being able to listen to sounds on a decent system.'

Why aren't more people good out of spite? It's devastating. And at times like this − unreasonably, but understandably, perhaps − I find myself almost disliking my Princess for doing this to Alison. Perhaps she really is as wicked as Tiffs would have me think.

*

'Where have you got to now?'

Ibiza. Our last trip. It was good, wasn't it?

'Perfect. The ultimate.'

Better than this?

'No — this is better. We're really close now. But Ibiza was good. It was always good in Ibiza. Except …'

What?

'Coming back the last time. You got the hump! You wouldn't speak to me.'

I had the horrors. I felt we were living on borrowed time. You said: 'I feel we're going back to face the music.'

'Funny, eh? God! If we'd known!'

We should have stayed. I wish we had. Do you?

'No point in thinking about it.'

What do you remember? Can you remember?

'Vaguely. It's gradually coming back. It's odd — like when you've had a dream. You know you've dreamt about something, but you can't remember what. Then something reminds you, and it all becomes clear. I suppose that's part of it. Lefever says I'll never remember everything. Some bits are a complete blank. I do remember we went a little mad. Christ — who was that Dutch girl? What was she called?'

Chartreuse.

'Ha! Great, eh? Chartreuse! God she was rough. Do you think she was on the game?'

Probably.

'Never! She can't have been! Who'd fuck her?'

You did.

'That's true. Christ — you won't mention her, will you?'

Of course not.

'Or Beach Bum. He was gross. Still, I did get you into discos. I bet no one's ever done that before. I bet Alison's never got you into a disco.'

No one has. I could have sat up all night watching you

202

dance. I was so proud of you. Christ I was proud of you.

'When were you proudest? When I got us into the VIP lounge at Ku?'

That was sweet. You were so pleased with yourself. You said 'anyone can get in free, but we've got complimentary tickets!'

'What's wrong with that?'

Nothing. It was adorable. Best was when you stopped the traffic at Ponce Corner dancing on the table with Batman. My Princess caused a traffic jam! The police had to ban dancing at Ponce Corner because of the crowds watching my Princess. I thought I'd burst with pride.

'Christ I was high. I must have been doing three grammes a day. That's when it started, I suppose. It was better, that. It made me busy.'

Don't you want to dance on this?

'No. It's different.'

Perhaps ...

'What?'

Nothing.

'No, say it. What?'

Perhaps you should try it again.

'I have. It doesn't work. It's nothing now. Don't you like me like this?'

I love you like this.

'Hey — what about that night at Ku when I danced in the fountain with Batman and the cabaret sat down and watched? Were you proud of me then?'

Out of my head. The next day I was quite frightened. I sat on the beach by myself and thought, she really has an extraordinary quality, this girl; she can make a thousand people happy all at once. That was when I knew for sure I couldn't lose you. I wanted urgently to tell you this. I hurried home and woke you up; I took your hand and looked solemnly into your eyes and said: 'There's something very serious I want to say to you: I want you to know how proud of you I was last night. I think you're the most remarkable person I've ever met.' And you stared right back at me and said: 'What the fuck's that got to do with the fact that I've got nothing to wear tonight?' You were getting very grouchy in the daytime.

'That happens.'

You were remarkable. You made a whole roomful of people happy. I've never seen that before. It's an amazing talent. You mustn't lose it.

'It was drugs. Once I could have done it not on drugs. When I was a bunny, I could do it. I wouldn't let people leave. Whole parties would get up to leave, and I wouldn't let them. I'd make them stay. I'd say they had to dance. I'd get them dancing, and they'd stay for hours. Now I can't even walk down the street alone.'

You'll be like that again. I wouldn't want to live if I thought my Princess would never dance again.

'Ha! I don't think she exists any more, your Princess. I think she drowned.'

Don't talk like that. We'll go back to Ibiza and you'll be remarkable again.

'When? When I get out of prison?'

You're not going to prison. I'd never let that happen. No one's going to send you to prison.

'I couldn't take it. I'd kill myself before I'd go to prison.'

Don't say such things.

'I mean it.'

It won't come to that. And if it ...

'What?'

Nothing.

'You were going to say, if it did. You think I'm going to go to prison.'

No I don't. But if you're so frightened we could just piss off. They didn't take your passport. We could go any time you liked. Now, if you said. Up and away just like that. Fuck the lot of them.

'We couldn't ever come back. And you'd be a thingummy.'

I wouldn't mind. I'd be a thingummy for the rest of my life — quite happily — as long as I was with you. I'd live anywhere with you.

'Ha! In a cave? Up a mountain?'

Anywhere. We could go back to Ibiza now. You could work. José would give you a job.

'José? Who was José?'

The owner of the Bar Chic. He said he'd pay you anything you wanted to dance every night outside his bar.

'He wouldn't if he saw me now! God – I can't walk down the street alone. I tried to today – when you were over at Ben's. I thought I'd do the shopping. I made a real effort. But as soon as I got outside I panicked. I thought I was going to faint. I had to run home.'

Why? What is it exactly? Why did you panic?

'I don't like people looking at me. I think they know.'

I'll make you well again. I'll get you into a clinic somehow.

'When?'

Soon. As soon as we've finished the book. The book can really help you. Trust me.

'I'm frightened.'

Why? They'll make you well. They'll cure you.

'They'll change me. I'll be quite different. You might not want me any more. You might go back to her.'

Don't be silly.

'She rang today. Sorry. I forgot to tell you.'

Jesus – what did she want?

'It was something to do with her mother. She doesn't want her mother to know you've left her. She's put this number on her answering-machine for people who want to get hold of you. Then it occurred to her that her mother might ring and wonder what this number was. So she's told her that it's Simey's number and that you're over here a lot finishing a book. She wanted to make sure we'd confirm that story if her mother rang.'

What did you say?

'I said that of course we would.'

How did she sound?

'Not too good. Okay at first, then she started crying. Did that bit about the cats – would we look after them if anything happened, that business. I hope she doesn't try anything silly again. You don't think she would, do you?'

No. She won't do that again.

'I wish she wouldn't ring here. It's not fair on me. Please tell her not to ring here. It really upsets me.'

I have told her. I'll tell her again. Sorry.

205

Returning early from Ibiza – 'Bloody Ben, he's let me down, I might as well come here' – goes without a hitch. Alison, thinking I've been messed around, bollocks Ben every time he phones. He's getting a bit fed up with this, but he can take it – and I'd do the same for him, as I keep reminding him. There is one uncomfortable moment when Alison says that my coming home unexpectedly has made her so happy that now she doesn't want to go to Portugal. She feels bad, she says, bogging off like this, and she asks me if I'd like her to cancel her trip. I tell her that she mustn't dream of doing such a thing, that she needs a holiday, and that anyway, thanks to Ben messing me around so unprofessionally, I've now got to work flat out.

Ben, who's been kicking his heels for the past three weeks, also assumes that we're going to work flat out, but my Princess and I have other plans. As soon as Alison leaves for Portugal, my Princess moves in with a suitcase full of dramatic clothes and we take up where we left off in Ibiza, sinking into our dark and private world, mysterious and lovely, alive with chaos and sensation. We disconnect ourselves completely, draw the curtains, put the music on and conceal ourselves behind the answering-machine, listening with disbelief to the serious, uncomprehending voices from the outside world which try, with increasing desperation, to penetrate our secret. We scarcely know what time it is – day and night blend seamlessly together in our sophisticated Eden – and we hardly eat. Occasionally I venture out to do some simple shopping – feeling like an alien, as if I've dropped in from outer space, recognising no point of contact with the other people in the street, with their peculiar comings and goings, their incomprehensible day to day concerns – but my Princess's routine is much less energetic. Having been up all night, she sleeps throughout the day. At about five o'clock I wake her with a cup of tea, and, for a difficult hour or so, it's best to leave her alone. She lies in bed, staring regretfully at the ceiling, and if I try to talk to her, she tends to deny the night before, suggesting that today we do something 'normal' – something from the list she drew up earlier in the summer. At first it bothered me a bit, this early-evening sadness, this rejection of the night before, but recently I've discovered what to do. I bide my time, wait patiently in the sitting-room, where eventually she joins me – still looking regretful. Her recovery comes in stages, each lovingly engineered by me. At first she's full of rather poignant little plans, but I put a stop to these by offering her drink – sometimes having one myself to make her feel less dissolute. After a small show of reluctance, she agrees. This levels her out, makes her feel herself again – and then, of course, she wants some coke. I don't have to prompt her: once she's on the road to happiness, she wants to go the whole way, to recover the fearlessness of the night before. She takes a line, looks pretty and brave immediately, ambiguous and challenging, she laughs again and wants the music on – she wants to play. She's doing a couple of grammes a day at least, and, because John the Accountant recently made one visit too many to Kensington Palace and got himself arrested, we have to make a few wild trips to one of her other connections, visiting odd addresses on the other side of London. I love all this – the excitement, the risk, the paranoia, driving back at top speed, laughing at our audacity, swerving all over the road with grammes of coke on board. We park the car and run upstairs, close the curtains and examine the goods, like criminals who've robbed a bank. Then, fuelled by fantasies stoked to boiling point by memories of Ibiza, we play throughout the night; and our gorgeous games are all the sweeter now for a sad undertow of hopelessness, a realisation – never mentioned – that this can't last. In fact we talk of the future all the time, plan further visits to Ibiza, and every night my Princess writes me a little note – which I find in the morning by the bed – full of hope and reassurance, as if she thinks that by being brave and positive we can play forever.

For two weeks I'm happier than I've ever been, at the same feeling that I'm being taunted by a glimpse of how life could have been but never can be now, that I'm being offered everything when it's far too late. Then one night – through no fault of mine, I think – an innocent little game of ours gets slightly out of hand. I look at her, and suddenly I don't want her – or rather I want more, I want to endanger us, I want to wound and repossess her, to prove the strength of my awful need by inflicting damage and then repairing it. I want to go to the very edge and see what hell it is. I want her to do the inconceivable, and I dread her doing it. My possessiveness is an obsession now, and I want to excite myself unbearably by hurting her. I keep thinking of a night in Ibiza when I let her go to Ku with a Chilean beachboy she picked up on Salinas. I went to bed, but I couldn't sleep; I was tormented by the hot dazzling image of brown, leathery hands touching her soft body, of the look of defiant acquiescence in her eyes for someone else – and I couldn't take it. I got up in the middle of the night and I rang her at Ku, screamed at her and told her to come home at once. She did, immediately, quite meekly – and now I wish she hadn't. I wish she'd defied me, hadn't come home at all. I don't want to be hurt: I want to hurt her and win her back, to punish and repossess her. So I look at her coldly now and tell her that I'm bored with her, that I don't want her any more. She looks startled, tries on her defensive half-smile, searches my face for clues, a sign that this is just a game.

'You don't mean it, do you?'

Of course I mean it. You're beginning to bore me.

She looks bewildered, really hurt – all the hurt dished out to her by ignorant men seems to gather for a second in her eyes – and I long to hug her, to tell her that I'm only playing.

'I'll go, then. Is that what you want?'

I shrug indifferently.

If that's what *you* want. You must please yourself. I don't care what you do.

In fact I've never cared more, or wanted her so much. She's looking lovelier than I've ever seen her – she still has a soft Ibiza tan, her legs are silky brown, so demandingly, so tauntingly on show – and at this moment of wanting her more than I ever have, I want her to want someone else – so I have to kill her.

'Okay.'

She gets up quickly, puts a few things in a suitcase and walks out without a word, slamming the door behind her. I'm

208

appalled and excited. I want to run after her and bring her back, but even more I want to suffer for a while this hot delirium in my head. I want to know what she'll do. Perhaps she'll do nothing – return to her flat and go to bed – but I don't think so. She'll work out what I want, and if I've really hurt her she'll seek a terrible revenge.

I go to bed, but I can't sleep – my head is boiling with complicated thoughts. I long not to have done this thing, but I wouldn't not have done it. I'm clamped in a formal paradox again, trying to break a law of logic. My brain aches with the enormous weight of these two contradictory thoughts. There is nothing I want more at this moment than that some crass unfeeling stranger should be touching my Princess, and, equally, there's nothing I want less. Neither desire can prevail against the other. And this is heaven and hell at once, it seems to me, and the least boring – without taking drugs – that the present can hope to be.

After about an hour of this scorching happiness and torment, I discover, suddenly, that I can't take it any more, that being bored would be preferable to feeling so dementedly alive. I ring her up, and she answers, sounding wide awake and mischievous, and there's music in the background. I ask her what she's doing.

'Enjoying myself. Do you mind?'

Come home.

'Certainly not! You started this.'

She laughs and hangs up on me, so I ring back immediately, and this time she speaks more sharply.

'Look – you're beginning to annoy me. Leave me alone.'

Then, in the background, I hear what is very definitely a man's voice, and my insides do a sickening cartwheel, as if I've skewered the souls of my feet.

What's that?

'What's what?'

I heard a man's voice. You've got a man there. If you're not home in half an hour I'll come over there and smash your door down.

'Oh don't be so *silly*. You're imagining things.'

She laughs gaily, and hangs up on me again. I ring straight

back but she's put the answering-machine on. I get up and dress in a kind of rabid panic, planning to go round there, I think, to let myself in and kill anyone who's with her – but then I remember that I no longer have the key to the downstairs door. I go back to bed but I can't lie still: my brain hurts and my insides weigh like wet cement. But I've discovered this at least: that this, when real, very definitely isn't what I want. And she shouldn't want it either. She went home, I now realise, far too quickly, far too happily. She should have known I didn't mean it, that this was just a game. And I should have known better than to play this game with her, should have known that she, having no feelings, having no respect for rules, wouldn't know where to draw the line. I toss and turn, composing a message to leave on her answering-machine, one which, in its sweet reasonableness, will rectify this poisonous situation. I'll say that I was joking, that if she cares for me at all she'll come straight home. I ring again and this time a man answers. Melissa's gone out, he says, and he doesn't know what time she's coming back.

I try to lie down – I'm actually afraid I'm going to have a heart attack – but I find I can't breathe. How can she do this to me? She must know I'd never do this to her. I get up and walk around, find that only by keeping on the move can I beat back the waves of despair that threaten to take me under. Why did I start this game, ever imagine it was one I might enjoy? The delicious, disgusting image of someone touching my Princess, of looking at her even, is one my brain screamingly rejects. I walk in circles in this madness for about two hours, go back to bed and then get up again, dress and undress at least six times, at one minute deciding to go round and break in somehow, realising at the next that if I couldn't get in I'd look a fool, screaming up at her from the street, where she might leave me standing in the cold.

At about five o'clock she phones me. Her voice is slurred, as if she's taken a sleeping pill. She starts to tell me some complicated story, but before she can get very far I begin to shout at her, to call her a whore, to tell her that she's gone too far. She begs me to listen, says that she can explain everything if I let her. 'You don't understand,' she says – over and over

210

again, as if she's on the point of crying – 'you don't understand. I've just been through a nightmare.'

You've been through a nightmare! Jesus Christ what about me? What do you think *I've* been through? Where are you?

'Upstairs in another flat. I'm with a man called George.'

Who the fuck's he?

'He's helping me. He came to my rescue.'

I bet he fucking did.

'You don't understand. I want to come home. I really do. It's *important*. *Please* let me come home.'

I don't want you. You stay with your fucking friend George.

I slam the phone down, but she rings back immediately.

'*Please* let me explain.'

Why does your voice sound odd?

'He's given me some valium. I've taken about six, I think.'

That's bloody stupid. Why?

'I'm trying to *tell* you. When I got home earlier, there was this fellow outside my flat. He thought I was Lindy Benson. He seemed okay, so I stopped and talked to him. He said he was on his way to score some coke from a man called Greek George who lived on the floor above. He had a little stuff on him already, so I asked him in.'

Why?

'I thought that was what you wanted. I thought you wanted me to ...'

Don't be so fucking silly. How could you think that?

'You *did*. Oh God, I'm sure you did. He said he was a friend of Lindy's so I thought it would be all right. He was okay at first, but then he started acting oddly and I got a little nervous. I asked him to go and he pulled a gun out of his briefcase.'

A *gun*? Don't be ridiculous! Now I know you're lying.

'I'm *not*. It's true. I *promise*.'

Why didn't you tell me when I phoned? You as good as told me to piss off.

'I *had* to. I couldn't say I was trapped by a madman with a gun. I was terrified.'

You didn't sound terrified. How did you get out?

'I remembered the number of the flat where he said this dealer lived – this man called Greek George. He went to the bathroom

211

eventually and that's when I escaped. I ran upstairs and knocked on the door of George's flat. I told him that a friend of his – a madman with a gun – was downstairs in my flat and wouldn't leave. He was marvellous. He sent two of his bodyguards down to my flat and they took the madman off to the dungeon. It was one of them you spoke to when you rang. *Please* can I come home now?'

No you can't. You can fucking well stay where you are.

I hang up on her, and, though she rings back two or three times, I don't answer. I've never heard such crap in all my life: Greek George, a madman with a gun, the dungeon, bodyguards – she must think I'm crackers. I go to bed and, exhaustion having taken over now, I eventually get to sleep.

The next day, I find I'm a little sorry that I was quite so harsh. She did behave disgracefully, but now that the initial shock is over I'm quite keen to discover what really happened. I ring her up, but the answering-machine is on, and it stays on for the rest of the day. In the evening she rings me, sounding a little nervous, and her voice is still fogged as if she's taken a sleeping-pill. She wants to come over, and at first, because I think she's still with Greek George, I say she can't – but she goes on and on at me until I finally relent. She arrives looking very pretty – her colour's up and her eyes are shining unnaturally, as if she's been taking coke – but there's something different about her. This is a different high, there's a kind of dreamy, disconnected sweetness about her, more as if she's been smoking, and she keeps smiling at me in an odd, conspiratorial way, as if we had a secret – the only problem being that I haven't been told what it is. On coke everything's in focus, more or less; she talks a lot, of course, but it all makes a sort of sense. Now her voice is slurred and she rambles on, jumping from one subject to another, and forgetting where she is. I point this out to her and she says it's the effect of all the valiums she took last night. When I ask her what really happened, she sticks to the same ridiculous story, insisting that everything she said was true. She goes over it all again, rambling on, adding increasingly unlikely details. Greek George's set-up is extraordinary, she says – she's never met so many amazing people all in one place at once.

212

'Honestly, darling, there must have been twenty people there, coming and going, dropping in and picking up – some leaving at once, others hanging around and doing it there.'

Doing what?

'*You* know.'

What sort of people?

'*All* sorts! Black girls, models, Sloanes, villains, gossip columnists *and* – you'll never believe it! – Sophie Manners and Alexander Beauchamp! It was Alexander who got rid of the madman in my flat, who took him to the dungeon with another man.'

Now I know she's lying: A more unlikely 'bodyguard' than the Duke of Dorset's junkie son and heir is hard to imagine.

Don't be silly. It must have been someone pretending to be Beauchamp. Though why anyone would pretend to be a prat like him escapes me.

'No, it *was* him, I tell you! I saw his name on a cheque he gave to George.'

She prattles on excitedly about her new friends, about Alexander and Sophie and George, making me think that she was altogether too impressed by this ropey-sounding set-up. I accuse her of this.

You were intrigued, weren't you?

She looks at me a little nervously, as if trying to work out what I want her to say.

'Well, I was a bit, I suppose. I mean – all that happening on the floor above and I never knew!'

And now, to my surprise, I find my stomach tightening with excitement, discover, to my amazement, that in spite of the horrors of the night before I actually *want* her to have disgraced herself with these awful people.

You liked them, didn't you? You're a fucking whore and you misbehaved.

'I didn't! *Honestly.* George was very kind. He calmed me down, and it was him who made me ring you. I didn't want to. I was frightened. I thought you'd scream at me.'

I drop the matter for the moment. I can't force her to admit to something that didn't happen. I can't say, *pretend* to have misbehaved even if you didn't – that wouldn't be any fun. But

213

later, when we're in bed, I take it up again.

You liked him, didn't you?

'Who?'

Greek George.

'Yes. I told you I did.'

I mean you *really* liked him. You fucked him.

'I *didn't*!'

But you'd like to. You'd like to fuck him, wouldn't you?

She's staring up at me, her eyes an inch or two from mine, searching my face for clues, trying – too obviously, in fact – to work out what I want her to say.

'Okay. Yes, I would.'

Why don't you, then?

'When?'

Now. I don't want you.

She looks startled, tries to laugh it off.

'You don't mean it, do you?'

Of course I mean it. Get out. *Now*.

'Look – I was joking. I don't actually want to see them again.'

Why?

'It wasn't a good set-up – believe me. They were all on drugs.'

So?

'Not just *any* drugs – they were all ...'

What?

'Nothing. It doesn't matter. Just believe me – it wouldn't be good to see them again. I really mean it.'

Well, you've got to. Now. This minute. Get out.

She stares at me for a moment with bewildered, unfocused eyes, then seems to make her mind up.

'Okay.'

She gets up and dresses quickly, pauses briefly at the door, looks back uncertainly.

'Do I really have to do this?'

Yes.

'Can I come home afterwards?'

No.

She smiles her brave, defensive smile – like the little boy at

214

Winchester when he got a bross blow – so I know I've really hurt her. I get an extra kick of excitement from this, but I relent slightly, saying she can ring me.

After she's gone I feel a little silly. This was her idea, she started this, but even so I feel a little foolish. I've forced her into it, when, as the more caring of the two, I should actually be protecting her from the weak, disorderly aspects of her nature. I feel so bad that after half an hour I ring her up – meaning to tell her to come home at once, that it was all a joke – but the answering-machine is on. About two hours later she rings me, sounding rather subdued. I ask her where she is.

'At George's. Can I come home?'

What happened?

'I'll tell you when I get there. *Please* can I come home?'

I say she can, and now – in spite of myself, in spite of the fact that I forced her to do this thing – I do feel quite excited, excited enough, at least, to punish her a bit when she arrives. She looks unhappy, wants to go straight to bed, but, pretending to a harshness I don't feel, I tell her to take her clothes off, here in front of me, and to apologize. She does this, but dejectedly, with none of her usual pride and arrogance, stands in front of me looking frightened and forlorn.

'Not like this – not now. Please let's go to bed. *Now.*'

What happened?

'Nothing. *Please* let's go to bed.'

Not until you tell me what happened.

'I went back to my place and rang George – like you told me to. He asked me to go up. There was just this black girl there – she's his girlfriend, I think – and then George got a phone call. He said he'd have to go for about twenty minutes and that I should wait. I stayed talking to his girlfriend, but after about an hour I got bored. So I rang you up.'

Why didn't you wait longer?

'I wanted to come home. *Please* let's go to bed.'

She's let me down. George can't like her – if he liked her he'd not have risked her leaving, he'd have come home quicker. She's failed and she's looking silly. I never imagined her looking silly. This shouldn't have been allowed to happen. I've created my Princess to be irresistible to everyone – otherwise I don't want her. She has to win, she mustn't be rejected. I tell her that she's got to go back and try again. She looks shocked.

'Don't you want me?'

No.

She doesn't say a word, she dresses quickly, clumsily – I can't look at her, can't bear to see her looking silly – and leaves at once. She knows what she's got to do – she'll not let me down again.

The next day she gets it right – or as right as can be expected in the circumstances (I am pushing her rather hard, perhaps, but I keep reminding myself that this is a game she taught me, that all this was her idea). When I phone her in the evening, she sounds hard and off-hand, says she doesn't know what her plans are, that she'll ring me back when she knows what she's doing. About an hour later she phones again, sounding quite different, triumphant and high – but it's that new, other high, slurred and rambling, more as if she's stoned. She's got George with her, she says, and she's speaking softly because she doesn't want him to know she's phoning me.

Where are you?

'In the bathroom. I've got nothing on. Are you excited? Say you're excited. It's important.'

Are *you*?

'*Yes.*'

She isn't excited in the least. If she were, she wouldn't have time to ring me. She's doing this for me, which removes the point of it entirely. I'm not excited, but I am relieved. She hasn't failed; she's done what she had to do – and, more importantly, I've discovered this reassuring thing about myself: I can't take her misbehaving when it's real – or if I think it is – and if it isn't real it's nothing. We won't have to play this silly game – or any others – any more. I'm normal: I just want her, nothing and no one but her forever, and I've got just two days in which to prove this to her before Alison comes back from Portugal. I tell her to come home as soon as possible.

'Okay. I won't be long. Do you love me?'

Worship would be a better word. I worship you, I really do.

'I thought perhaps you didn't.'

She's back in an hour, looking high and very lovely, but it's

216

that different high again and the new symptoms are even more pronounced. She seems euphoric – not busy and bouncy like she is on coke – just deeply contented, giggling a bit, unable to follow her own thoughts, moving very slowly, in a rather uncoordinated way, and smiling that peculiar little smile, as if she thinks we share a secret, but has forgotten to tell me what it is. I point this out to her and she says she took some more valium because I upset her so much the night before.

'I hope I'm not going to become a valium junkie – not after all I've done!'

That would be a laugh, I must say. Then I ask her, out of politeness, really, how it went with Greek George and she laughs dismissively and says: 'Atrocious! It didn't work at all! Sorry. Are you cross?'

Not in the least. I just want you. I don't want to play any more games.

She looks at me in surprise, tries on her new, unfocused smile.

'Oh dear – that's a shame.'

Why?

'Well – it's your turn now. I did that for you, now you've got to do the same for me. I've asked Tessa the Teacher over.'

Christ – when? Not *now*?

'*No*. Tomorrow. She's coming over tomorrow.'

She *can't*. It's our last night.

'Oh God – so it is. Never mind. You'll *love* her, you really will.'

I *won't*. I mean it – I don't want anyone but you. I know that for certain now.

'*Please*. Just for me. I did do it for you.'

And, because she's hardly making any sense – she's as high as a kite, floating away in a dreamy world of her own – I don't bother to argue any more. We have tonight, and we'll have tomorrow night too, after I manage to get rid of Tessa the Teacher. I hold her hand and let her ramble on in her new euphoric, disconnected way, and then, to my astonishment, she suddenly says she's got to go. She's fixed up some important deal, she says, between Greek George and another of her contacts and she's got to pull it off tonight. There's money in it

217

for her, she says.

'We've got tomorrow. Tomorrow will be marvellous. Trust me.'

Tomorrow isn't marvellous at all: it's harmless enough and quite amusing, but it certainly isn't marvellous. Tessa the Teacher turns up first, and she's tall and rather attractive, and very intelligent too – she really might be a teacher, I think – but she's as bewildered as I am as to why she's here. And when my Princess arrives, looking astonishingly pretty, prettier than I've ever seen her and even higher than she was the night before, Tessa the Teacher is even more bewildered. My Princess prattles on about her new friends – Greek George and the Marquis of Beauchamp and Sophie Manners – and she gets up and puts the music on and dances, bumping into the furniture and falling over and rocking with helpless laughter, and Tessa the Teacher looks more bewildered by the minute. Then my Princess produces some coke and, though she doesn't take any herself I notice (and this is very odd), she persuades Tessa the Teacher to shovel quantities of it up her nose, with the happy result that Tessa is soon as high as she is. This lets me off the hook, I think: whatever expectations my Princess may have of me, she, and Tessa the Teacher, are far too out of it by now to notice whether I fulfil them. I'm thinking this – sitting back and feeling quite secure, thinking that such a situation would have quite amused me once, feeling pleased that, because I've found everything I want, such dirty nursery games are in the past – when my Princess suggests that I take some photographs. And before I know what's happening, she and Tessa the Teacher have taken off their clothes and are cavorting sweetly on the sofa; and because they look so innocent and pretty I get my camera out and take some polaroids, after a while becoming quite excited. The trouble is I don't want Tessa the Teacher – sweet and bright and lovely though she is – I want my Princess, just my Princess, now and for always; and, when Tessa the Teacher is out of the room for a moment, I tell her this.

I don't want Tessa. I just want you. I'll never want anyone else.

218

'That's beautiful. And I just want you.'

And when Tessa the Teacher comes back into the room, my Princess begins to tell her all about Ibiza, making me get the photographs out and showing them to Tessa.

'Here's me modelling on the beach. Gross, eh! And here I'm dancing in the street with Batman. They banned dancing after that! And this is our flat. We're going to live together there soon. Will you come out and visit us? Say you will.'

Tessa the Teacher, seeing we want to be alone, takes this as her cue to leave. She gets up and says she ought to go, whereupon, to my astonishment, my Princess says she's got to go as well, suggests they share a taxi. They leave together, arm in arm, roaring with laughter as they help each other through the door. Then, seeing my shattered look, my Princess comes back and hugs me.

'Don't worry. Everything will be all right. I know it will.' Then she turns to Tessa. 'We're just waiting for Alison's mother to die and then we're going to get together.'

That turns out to be the last nice thing she says for quite a time. I ring her in the morning, but there's no reply and – oddly – the answering-machine isn't on. She always puts the answering-machine on if she goes out or wants to sleep late. I ring her on the hour throughout the day, at last managing to get her just half an hour before I have to leave for the airport to pick up Alison. She sounds half asleep and very grumpy, so I ask her what the matter is.

'*She's* coming back today.'

I try to reassure her, tell her that everything's going to be all right, that we'll go back to Ibiza soon.

'*When?*'

Soon, I promise.

She snorts disbelievingly, then says she's got to go out, tells me to ring her soon.

Within the next few days, we both happen to get 'flu. I'm struck down first, retiring to bed on the morning after Alison comes home. In some ways this is a good thing: the 'flu symptoms merge feverishly with, and tend to disguise, the

219

withdrawal symptoms – which are horrifying – of being separated from my Princess, with the result that Alison notices nothing odd in my condition. I lie in bed and groan, and when she leaves the sickroom for a moment I get out all my photographs – which I keep under the bed, having to be near them all the time – spread them out and gaze at them closely, discovering that I like best the early ones, the, ones of my Princess's first visit to Ibiza. I prefer to think of that time too: recently it's been exciting, more exciting than anything I've ever known, but we did go a little too far, perhaps, there was a wildness in what we did, reflected in the pictures. My Princess looks beautiful in these, and happy, but there's a desperation in her eyes, a pleading craziness, as if she's about to do something which, in the morning, she'll regret. There's nothing in the early Ibiza pictures to be regretted later. Looking at these, I find I want to start again, to go back to how it was at first.

For a few days I don't feel well enough to ring her, and when I do I find that she's now caught it too. I offer to go round and see her, but she says she feels too ill, that she'll stay in bed and for a day or two and then go to her mother's for a bit. Eventually we both recover, and I arrange to go and see her on a Wednesday evening – nearly three weeks now since we were last together. On the way over I feel optimistic, very positive and full of plans. We can't go back to these hasty, squalid rendezvous, I realise: we've got to move on, slow down and do it properly. The present situation isn't fair to her, and it isn't fair to Alison. I must find a solution for both their sakes. My Princess and I must give ourselves a chance: we'll go back to Ibiza, spend the winter there, find out whether we can live together normally – unhysterically day by day, not as if every moment is our last. Alison will understand: I'll say I'm going there to work. In fact I will work. Ben can come out, and my Princess can have her friends to stay. I'll hire a video and in the evenings she can watch films that were classics when they first came out. I'll take her seriously. I'll let her look plain and put on weight – she can even eat nuts in bed if she likes. It's funny – if my Princess ate nuts in bed I don't think I'd mind at all. And if it all goes wrong, at least this thing will have run its course – and it won't have destroyed me and Alison. I'll tell my

Princess tonight that we're going back to Ibiza just as soon as possible. I'm sure that's what she wants to hear.

I park the car and, feeling strong and positive, full of knowledge that I'm about to do the right thing by everyone at last, I run across the road, almost, in my excitement, being knocked over by a bus, and being screamed at by the driver. It's a bad time to be called a fucking idiot, but I don't lose heart; I run upstairs, two steps at a time, borne by certainty and courage, find myself hoping that she hasn't laid on one of her sweet suprises. They were joltingly lovely, but tonight I want to be close, to make love and talk to her earnestly – more earnestly than I ever have before. I don't want that other madness, won't ever want it again, I think. It's funny, I feel a little guilty about all that now, I don't know why. It had been her idea; she took me down that dark and tangled path, led me every step of the way, and I'm glad she did. But I don't want that any more – I just want her. I'm no longer clamped in a formal paradox, no longer only want what's unavailable and dangerous. She can be there every day and she'll delight me, eat nuts and put on weight and watch television wearing woolly socks. I don't want her to be another woman any more. I want who she really is.

'Hi. It's been a long time.'

It's dark in the hall and at first I can't see her; her voice is small and dead, and when I bend down to kiss her she ducks out of reach and backs away. That's okay, I think: she wants to sulk for a bit, teach me a lesson for not ringing her more often in the last three weeks, for not making a greater effort, perhaps, to see her. But then, following her into the sitting-room, I see her properly for the first time and I almost faint with shock.

In any other context – passing her in the street, say – I wouldn't recognise her. She's a skeleton. I wouldn't have thought it possible to lose so much weight in such a short time and not be dead. She looks old and haggard, her make-up is grotesquely over-done, her hair is lank and greasy and her face looks dirty under the gaudy surface. She's wearing a sadly inappropriate party-dress of some sort and is tottering about on very high-heels, her matchstick legs hardly looking as if they

221

can hold her up. My Princess looks like an old tart in Shepherd's Market. She sits on the sofa and stares up at me with chilly indifference, knowing she looks disgusting and not caring, challenging me, I think, to remark on the fact. I don't know what to say. I sit down next to her and try to touch her, but she winces and moves away.

What is it? What's the matter?

'Nothing.'

She looks up at me defiantly, with dislike, like a delinquent child who wants to shock its elders but will deny whatever it's accused of. I'm sure she wants to shock me: the squalor and aggressive make-up, the high-heels and ridiculous dress – she knows she looks revolting. To play for time, I ask her if she'd like a cup of tea.

'Okay. The kitchen's a bit of a mess.'

In fact it's filthy: piles of dirty washing-up, an old stew in a saucepan going green on top, a stinking, over-flowing dustbin and something growing cultures in the fridge. This is astonishing: apart from all her other lovely qualities my Princess has always been the cleanest, most fastidious person in the world, bathing at least twice a day, emptying ashtrays every other minute and washing dishes almost before you've used them. I clean a cup, make some tea and take it through to her. I sit down next to her and she moves away, looks at me with caricatured brightness, gives me a ghastly, slashing smile.

Come on. What's the matter?

'Nothing. Really.'

Don't be silly. Something's the matter. Talk to me.

'There's nothing to say. What's your news?'

Stop this shit. Tell me what it is.

I don't think I say this very aggressively, but she starts back as if I've hit her, and when she speaks her voice is shrill with anger.

'Don't shout at me! If you've come round here to have a go I'd rather you went.'

She looks at me with *hatred*. I feel dizzy with confusion, but I try to hold her again, and this time she lets me. She flinches slightly, but she doesn't move away. I can feel every bone in her body. Suddenly she pulls her skirt up and laughs defiantly.

222

'Look at my legs. Look how much weight I've lost.'

It's terrifying. They're an old woman's legs, discoloured and fleshless. Just three weeks ago they were the most beautiful legs I'd ever seen – brown and wilful and everywhere at once.

Tell me what it is, Princess.

'Don't call me that. I don't like that.'

Okay. What is it?

She looks at me nastily, with an icy, defensive smile.

'It isn't drugs, if that's what you think.'

I'm not thinking anything. I just want to know what the trouble is.

'Isn't it obvious? I'm having a nervous breakdown.'

Why?

She shrugs her bony shoulders.

'I don't know.'

Is it them – those cunts upstairs? Greek George, Beauchamp? Have they done this to you?

'Nobody does *any*thing to me. I look after myself.'

Is it them?

'*No*. I told you. It isn't drugs. I've given up drugs. I haven't taken anything since I last saw you.'

I'm inclined to believe her. On drugs she was perfect – brave and beautiful, happy, affectionate and funny.

'I haven't seen them. I don't see anyone.'

Why not?

'People! They use and abuse you – that's all. I don't like people.'

I'm sure it is them – and if I find it is, I'll kill them – slowly, happily, torturing them first. And to think I've always sneered at mad mothers on TV saying death's too good for dealers! I'll never sneer again. Greek George and the Marquis of Beauchamp are dead men if they've done this to my Princess. Perhaps they took her up and dropped her, hurt her badly. I want to protect her, to comfort her, but I'm not connecting and feel I never will. She's wrapped herself in layers of indifference and is looking at me from a thousand miles away. I never imagined that this could happen, that I couldn't protect her from every hurt, put right anything that happened to her – if she let me.

I can't believe this. We were so close. When you came out to

223

Ibiza that first time, when you arrived at the airport, I knew who you were.

She looks at me with cold amazement.

'Of course you knew who I fucking was.'

No – I mean I *recognised* you.

'I should bloody well hope so. We'd known each other for six months.'

You don't understand. It was as if I'd *always* known you, as if I'd been waiting for you to arrive. It was like recognising myself, as if I was meeting *me*.

She cackles like a skeleton.

'Christ! Sometimes I think you really are cuckoo.'

You know it was like that. You *know* it was good.

'I don't know anything.'

She slumps back as if exhausted, then sits up, looks at me with renewed defiance – a sneering challenge in her eyes.

'Mind you – I do know one thing. If there was some heroin here I think I'd take it. I do know that.'

Why?

'Why not? I've got nothing. Nothing to live for.'

You've got me.

'Ha! *You*? You're with *her*.'

So that's it – this is all because of me. She *did* care, and I've let her down, may have really hurt her. I think back over all the positive things she said during our last three weeks together, remember the little notes I found by the bedside in the morning – so full of hope and reassurance – recall something she said when we were driving back that last time from Ibiza: we'd been talking about the future and I'd said that if she and Alison were both in trouble I'd go to Alison. She'd looked shocked, as if I'd slapped her in the face, gone very silent for a while and then said: 'I wish you hadn't said that, I really do.' Suddenly I don't see myself in a very attractive light. Perhaps I've been at fault to some extent – so frightened that she was using me that I in fact used her. My mind is now made up. I'll take her to Ibiza immediately, tonight if she'll come; I'll make her well again and look after her forever. I take both her hands in mine and look at her very earnestly; I've *got* to take her with me now, carry her with me in my rush of courage. I haven't been strong enough with her, but now at last I know what I have to do. I have no doubts. I speak with total confidence, because I feel it.

Listen – this is very serious. We must go now – back to Ibiza – just as soon as possible. Perhaps tomorrow. I *know* that's what we've got to do. It's the only hope for both of us.

For a second she looks at me with embarrassed surprise – as if I've mistimed a vulgar joke – then snorts derisively.

'*Ibiza*? Ha!'

You were happy in Ibiza.

'Was I? How do you know? You don't know me at all. Drugs, sex and rock and roll – that's all Ibiza is. Get up. Go to the beach. Come home. Change. Go out. Christ – it was worse than going to work.'

She's looking at me with dull hatred and I go cold inside. The past has disappeared in a second, and she looks so ugly. I understood nothing, and Tiffs was right. She's a stranger and always was.

How can you do this?

'Do what?'

Change. You were fantastic.

'What are you complaining about? I gave you the time of your life.'

You liked it too. I know you did.

'*Liked* it? I felt like a fucking jester. Christ – I'm a woman of thirty-two and you made me dance on tables wearing shorter and shorter skirts. I was a *clown*.'

I *know* you liked it.

'I was *high*.'

You were better high. You were nice to me when you were high.

'Jesus! I was nice to *every*one when I was high. Don't you understand?'

No. Are you blaming me for something? Did I make you do things you didn't want to do?

'*No* one makes me do things I don't want to do. I do what I like.'

So you wanted to do them too?

'I wanted to please you.'

Is that all?

'Yes.'

You said: 'Let's have a …'

'Look – for God's sake don't quote back at me everything I might have said when I was *high*.'

You were just using me, then?

'I wasn't using you. I was how you wanted me to be. That wasn't me. You were never interested in *me*. You invented a game which got out of hand. People started getting hurt. *You*. It's not my fault. It was *your* game, it's *your* fault. I told you not to fall in love with me.'

My head reels with the injustice of it, but I haven't the heart to argue. She looks disgusting and she's being disgusting, but I still love her completely. This isn't her. There's no reason to believe that the terrible things she's saying now are *truer*, in some sense, than all the other things she's said in the last six months. I can't have been that fooled; you can't feel as close to someone as I did to her if there's nothing coming back. Something terrifying has happened to her, and I can help her, I'm sure I can. She's in very serious trouble and I can't just walk away. I owe it to her to behave better than she could if our positions were reversed. Suddenly she seems to soften slightly.

'I'm sorry. That's not fair. I did enjoy it too. It was okay, we had good times. It wasn't your fault – it's me, I've changed. I'm like that. I *warned* you. I told you I didn't want to get involved.'

I want to help.

'I don't think you can. I don't think anyone can.'

Suddenly she collapses, curls up on the sofa and starts to cry. She looks up at me with enormous frightened eyes, brimming with bewilderment and hurt, tears streaking her grotesque make-up.

'Make me well. Please make me well again.'

I can't if you don't let me. Listen – are we friends?

'I don't know. I don't know anything. You said you didn't want me. *You* made me go over and see …'

What?

'Nothing. It doesn't matter. Nothing matters.'

Everything matters – and we *are* friends. You're trying to destroy us.

'I'm not. I'm trying to destroy myself.'

Why?

'So that I can start again.'

Let me help you.

'No. I've got to help myself.'

You're making a big mistake.

She recoils, looks at me with horror, as if I've said something terrible.

'Are you *threatening* me?'

Christ she's sick. She looks quite mad again, staring at me with hatred in her eyes, as if I'm the enemy who's come to do her harm. This is serious: it has nothing to do with us, with her and me, it's far more serious than that. I've got to get her help, but of what sort I'm not entirely sure. It could be drugs that have caused this – and if it is I'll kill those wicked men upstairs – or she's had a traumatic experience of some sort, also to do with them. Whatever it is, she's very sick and needs a doctor. I wait until the fear and horror leave her eyes, and then I take her in my arms and hold her gently. She doesn't move away or struggle; her eyes suddenly flicker with exhaustion, and then she closes them, seems after a while to fall asleep. After a few minutes, though, she sits up and shakes her head, seems to be filled with a new resolve.

'Will you lend me two thousand pounds?'

This is music to my ears – it means she trusts me, and that I can trust her too. She won't betray me now. She wouldn't put herself this much in my debt and then betray me. I write her out the cheque at once.

'Thank you for not asking me why I want it. I'll pay you back.'

I don't want you to. The money's not important. I don't want to control you with money any more. You don't owe me anything. I want you to trust me – that's all.

'I do.'

Am I your friend, then?

'You're more than a friend, you know you are.'

I ask her if she's hungry, but she says she isn't eating at the moment, hasn't eaten anything for days. I tell her that she must, persuade her eventually to let me get her a Chinese take-away. She cheers up a bit, becomes quite interested in what she'll have, in the end gives me quite a complicated order. She says it reminds her of one night in the summer, before we went to Ibiza, when I'd wanted to leave – my alibi was running out – and she'd managed to keep me here, persuaded me in the end to go out and get her a Chinese take-away. Before I go out now, she gives me her keys, tells me to let myself in when I get back. As she hands them to me she looks a little sad and says:

'You never got them copied, did you? Perhaps it's fate. Perhaps we're not fated to be together.'

She starts to walk unsteadily about the room on her too-high-heels, fetching things from the kitchen and laying the table. She looks ridiculous and I love her. I go and buy the meal from The Good Earth in the King's Road, and when I get back I find she's laid the table, made a start – abandoned half-way through – to clean the kitchen, and is now lying on the sofa, apparently asleep. I put the food in the kitchen, then sit down next to her and shake her gently. She doesn't stir, so I shake her a little harder. She still doesn't move, so, suffering a moment of fear, I take her by the shoulders and shake her really hard. Then I bend down and listen to her breathing. It's okay, I think, deep and regular, but I've never seen anyone in such a heavy sleep. It's more like a coma, as if nothing would ever wake her. She must be completely exhausted. I stay for about two hours, just holding her, stroking her head from time to time, thinking that perhaps it's as well this happened. We went too far, and I blame myself. Perhaps I didn't respect her enough, but I won't make that mistake again. If I get a second chance, I'll take more care of her, protect her properly from people who want to do her harm. That's all I want. She was incomparable – brave and beautiful and funny – she stopped the traffic with her dancing and now she looks disgusting and I love her. I'd never get over it if I lost her now – and I wouldn't want to. If I ever found something I wanted more than her she'd have failed, she wouldn't have been perfect – and my Princess must be perfect. I take out my writer's notebook and – before I forget – enter in it: 'She stopped the traffic at Ponce Corner with her dancing and now she looks disgusting and I love her'. Then I delete 'Ponce Corner' because it spoils the rhythm, change 'sad' to 'wistful' in the bit about the keys and alter 'cherish her forever' to 'take more care of her'. I write her a note, telling her how much I love her, and then I leave.

She rings me the next day at Simey's, where we're pretending to work, and she sounds so different from the night before – just like her old self, in fact – that I begin to think that it must have been an awful dream. She thanks me for my note, which made her very happy, she says, and apologizes for falling asleep. It was post-flu tiredness, she thinks, plus she'd been up the whole of the night before looking after a friend of hers who is a recovering junkie. I offer to come over in the evening, but she says she thinks she'll have an early night.

'Let's have lunch on Saturday. Could we go out? Go somewhere really nice? *Please*. I'd like that.'

Alison happens to be out all day on Saturday, which makes my preparations – bathing in the middle of the morning, dressing up in co-ordinated casuals, booking a table at a nice restaurant – much easier for once. I decide to take her to the Carlton Tower, which had been first on the list, for some reason, of the nice things she'd wanted to do when Alison went to Portugal. I hadn't wanted any of that stuff then, but I do now: I want to start again, to spoil her and give her the bit she never had. No wonder she got depressed when Alison came back. Those last three weeks had been brilliant – but they hadn't been good. She was taking too many drugs, and perhaps I should have stopped her – not that I could have done, I think. She said she'd been doing it for years, that she could handle it, and I believed her. At least I never encouraged her: that would have been very wicked.

I prepare myself slowly, book a table at the Carlton Tower, bathe, decide to wear my Charlie Allen suit, all the time thinking how glad I am that this has happened. I won't take her for granted any more, assume she'll always be there, go round and see her and sidle off when I've had my fix. I'll always take her out to dinner first, court her over candle-lit tables, arrive with flowers and other presents. She used to complain about the lack of flowers and so forth. 'You never buy me any

229

presents,' she used to say. 'They don't have to be expensive – just silly little things.' I go out now and buy her some roses and a bottle of champagne, and when I get back the phone is ringing. It's Simey with the news that my Princess has just rung him with a message for me. She sounded very odd, he says, high and giggly, and he found it hard to follow her. The gist is that our lunch is off, he thinks – something to do with her mother coming unexpectedly to London. That's okay, I think: it's a nuisance, but I'll take them both out to lunch. I get on well with mothers; we'll hit it off, she'll think I'm from the top shelf, later tell my Princess what a nice young man I am. I phone immediately, and she sounds fine – though very high, as Simey had said. She's terribly sorry about our lunch, she says, but her mother has come unexpectedly to London, has just phoned from Liverpool Street Station to say she'll be arriving at her flat in twenty minutes.

That's okay. I'll take you both out to lunch.

'What! You can't do that!'

Why not? I'd like to.

'You *can't*. It would be a nightmare. God – you haven't met my mother!'

That's why I want to.

'No really. I *mean* it, darling.'

There's a note of panic in her voice that alerts me to something unpleasant on the other side of what she's saying – plus it's months since she called me 'darling' in that bright, unfeeling voice, as if I'm a punter in a nightclub.

Okay, but I'll hop round for a moment. I've bought you some champagne. You can have it with your mother.

'*No!*'

She's shouting now, sounding desperate. This is all a nonsense. She isn't meeting her mother at all, and I won't let her get away with this: I'll embarrass the truth out of her – I'm entitled to do that. I tell her that I'm coming over anyway, and she becomes hysterical, starts to scream at me.

'Don't *do* that! Don't push me into a corner!'

You're fucking lying. I'm coming over.

'Don't speak to me like that. Who the hell do you think you are?'

230

Your friend. And I'm coming over now.

'Don't do this. I'm *warning* you. If you come here, I won't let you in.'

Then you won't be able to let your mother in either, will you?

'You'll have to break the door down.'

I'm coming *now*.

I hang up, grab the bottle of champagne – I don't know why – and run down to the car. Driving like a madman, I reach her flat in less than five minutes. If the story about her mother's true, she must still be there, waiting for her to arrive. I ring the bell, but there's no reply, so I get back into my car and re-park it across the road, opposite her block, where she can see it if she looks out of her window. I'll sit this out, stay here forever if necessary, force her to see how badly she's making me behave. All she has to do is come down and tell me the truth. She can't just leave me sitting here. I'm her friend: she owes it to me to come down herself and tell me why she's doing this. She must know I'd never do this to her, leave her sitting naked on her own, make her feel this silly.

I sit in the car for an hour or more, getting out from time to time and – to embarrass her – walking up and down in my Charlie Allen suit, holding the bottle of champagne. I know she's up there – at one point I see her curtains move – but she doesn't come down. And this, I suppose, is the moment I've been dreading from the start, the moment when her background, her lack of manners, her selfishness and fear would come between us: the moment when no appeal to reason and the past, to loyalty and friendship, to promises made and simple compassion would count for anything. I'd hoped we'd got past this point: hoped that I'd managed to teach her something about morality, taught her that this isn't how civilised people behave towards their friends. Perhaps, after all, everything they said at Winchester was right. 'You are an elite,' "Botty" Firth had said in his farewell sermon to the leavers. 'You must never forget that you are *different*.' I didn't believe this at the time, and I've never believed it since – but perhaps, after all, there was something in what he said: perhaps we are 'better' in some way, perhaps we mingle with those who've never learnt the ground-rules at our peril. My Princess is quite entitled not to have lunch with me – indeed she has a right never to speak to me again if that's her wish – but she should have the good manners to offer me a decent explanation. I go into the pub opposite her block – still keeping a watch on her flat through the windows of the pub – and leave a message on her answering-machine (drafted first in my writer's notebook) to this effect. It sounds good, I think – solemn, heartfelt, reasonable – and I'm confident that, after hearing it, she'll come downstairs and talk to me.

But she doesn't come down – and this is the moment I should pack it in, of course, shrug my shoulders and write her off. If I stay now, let her get away with this, she'll lose respect forever. Her type, in their fear, never forgive you for forgiving them, never forgive you for letting them win. I should leave now, drive off and never speak to her again – but I don't, and after another hour or so a tall, goofy-looking twit comes out of her block, crosses the road and ambles towards my car. It's the Marquis of Beauchamp, I think – there's something familiar about the girlishly arrogant face, with its bulging, careless eyes and cowardly, cherry-pink mouth. He raises a languid arm – with some difficulty, I think – and taps on the window of my car.

'I've got a message from Melissa,' he says. 'She's just telephoned me. She asked me to inform you that she's having lunch at Parkes with her mother and my girlfriend Sophie.'

That's the silliest thing I've ever heard – I was here, staking the place out, twenty minutes before her mother could have got here. My Princess is up in her flat, I know she is – how else would this ga-ga junkie have known which was my car unless she'd pointed it out to him? Not having the guts to come down herself, sending this inbred prat to do her dirty-work, makes me even angrier. This is a good opportunity to call someone a cunt at last, so, holding my bottle of champagne, I get out of the car and say: 'Bollocks. She's in her flat as well you know.'

He can tell I'm mad. He steps back a pace, asks me whether I'd like to come upstairs with him and see for myself that she isn't there. Crossing the road, I observe pleasantly that she must be having a busy afternoon.

'Are you next in the queue?' I ask.

This makes me feel a little better, but he looks quite taken aback, doesn't seem to have an answer. It's probably years since the poor goof has been able to form the most simple sentences, and it occurs to me that if you're as stupid and useless as this you might as well become a junkie, break into Boots and steal your sister's jewellery.

Upstairs we ring the bell of my Princess's flat, and then, when there's no answer, he points out that her key isn't in the lock.

'Melissa always leaves her key in the lock when she's at home,' he says.

He seems to know a lot about it, and her sacred name on the lips of this disgusting young man sounds like the worst profanity I've ever heard.

'Shall we break in, then?' I say. 'Rather in your line, I fancy.'

But he doesn't have an answer to this one either – he just stares at me like a suffocating fish (it must be minutes since he had a fix) – so we peer through the letter-box in turn and I have to agree that the flat looks empty. She musts be at Greek George's on the floor above, I think; and that's okay, I'll follow this pop-eyed aristocrat up the stairs, walk in after him and drag her out – but when I look up from peering through the letter-box, I find he's disappeared.

So that's it – she's still seeing this evil crowd and everything she said the other night was lies. Could she be fucking one of them, I wonder, even the deplorable young man who's just chickened upstairs for a fix? I don't think it's possible. She looks too ugly: if she were having an affair she'd look pretty and be happy. It must be drugs, but that doesn't make sense either: on drugs she was lovely – a sheer delight from moment to moment, beautiful and always kind. And it would be better, I think, if she *were* having an affair: that would be intelligible, at least, something I could grapple with, one day come to terms with even. But this sudden, meaningless disloyalty leaves me holding on to nothing. It's as if only absurdity motivates her, the need at any time to do the opposite of what's expected. Without me she'll sink, and so, smiling privately like a lunatic, she has to toss me overboard.

Suddenly I've had enough. I go home and, fuelled by hatred

233

and thoughts of devastating vengeance, I get through the weekend somehow. I must look completely mad, sitting next to Alison and grinning at her wildly, like an alternative comedian with a hatchet in his head, but she watches television and asks me whether the dinner was done to my liking and would I rather watch *Bergerac* or *The Price Is Right* because it's all the same to her? We've lived together for fifteen years, I'm bleeding to death in front of her and she can't see that anything's the matter. And I don't want to kill her: I want to tell her everything that's happened, ask her why she's so fucking stupid as not to have seen it for herself, and then collapse into her, and beg her to protect me. But I don't do any of that, I grin at her crazily like a corpse, like a man struck dead while guffawing at a dirty joke, and watch *The Price Is Right*. And when we go to bed I lie awake and decide that the first thing I'll do is to stop the cheque for £2000 that I gave to my Princess. That was a terrible thing to do: I never imagined that she'd sink so low as to borrow that amount of money from me when she must have known that we were finished. With luck she'll have written out cheques against it – some to her dealer, I hope. Dealers don't take kindly to people who give them moody cheques; if she has she could be in a lot of trouble, and thoughts of the trouble she could be in make my heart beat so crazily that I have to get up and go into another room and have a smoke. And then Alison comes in and says she's sorry, is it her that's keeping me awake? She isn't sleeping very well, she says, because she's so unhappy about her mother. And she sits down next to me and says: 'At least we've got each other and the pussy-cats' – and I think if she touches me I'll scream.

Viciousness carries me half-way through the week, my rage keeping the pain at bay. If I stop feeling vicious for a moment I'll collapse, the whole world and everyone in it will have become unspeakably ugly, too ugly to be endured. But then I experience the first slight feelings of remorse. Perhaps I shouldn't have stopped the cheque, or not without warning her at least – I don't want to get her into that much trouble. I can't face speaking to her on the phone, so I write her a long letter, explaining why I did it, telling her that she could have had anything she wanted, but that she shouldn't have left me standing in the street. It's a beautiful letter, I think – strong, dignified, without a trace of malice, at one point even plagiarising Jilly Cooper ('If I ever lost you all the toys in the world would break') – so good, in fact, that I type it out and put a copy in my filing cabinet. And Alison notices none of this, of course, being too concerned about her dying mother. Her mother happens to be growing weaker by the day, showing signs of taking to her bed – and this development would have cheered me once, because it would have meant that Alison would soon be going down to Worthing, leaving me alone with my Princess. But it's too late now – for all I care, her mother can make a miraculous recovery.

Then, at the end of the week, I suddenly crack, am overwhelmed by the desire to talk to her. I ring her up and at first she's terrible, so cold and distant that I nearly put the phone down.

'Oh. Hullo. It's you. I hope you haven't rung to lecture me. I don't need that.'

She sounds as if hearing my voice is like receiving the worst news in the world. I ask her if she got my letter.

'Yes. I thought it was a little harsh.'

I keep talking into an awful silence, there's nothing coming back at all. I ask her why she left me standing in the street.

'You embarrassed me in front of my friends. You made a complete fool of yourself.'

Once you wanted me to behave like that. You wanted me to come round in a rage and break your door down.

'That was a long time ago. I wish we'd never started that possessive thing. It was a mistake.'

I ask her if she knows how much she's hurt me, and she seems to soften slightly, making me think there might be hope.

'Well – you hurt me.'

When? *How?*

'I was distraught and you offered me money. That night after you came back from Ibiza. You knew I wanted you to stay with me and you *offered me money*. You never gave me anything but money. We are people, you know.'

Who are? Who are people?

'People like me. I haven't even got your books. Everyone's

got your books but me.'

Is that what you want?

'*Yes*. I'll keep them *forever*.'

Suddenly she starts to cry, and I see a gleam of hope. Perhaps, even now, everything can be all right – perhaps it was just a silly misunderstanding and we can start again. I *did* behave quite badly, I did make a fool of myself – staking her place out, walking up and down in my Charlie Allen suit, insulting the Marquis of Beauchamp (whose only crime, after all, is that he finds life unacceptable, and who shall blame him for that?). There was no reason in the world why she shouldn't play with her amusing new friends, and she only behaved badly because I frightened her. If I get another chance, I'll never frighten her again. I ask her if she wants to go on seeing me.

'You *know* I do.'

I suggest that I take her out to dinner at the Carlton Tower on the following Monday and she sounds really pleased.

'That's what I'd like. You know that's what I'd like.'

I tell her that I'd rather meet her there – Bristol House now having unpleasant memories for me – and she agrees.

'That's best. Let's start again. I'm sorry, I really am. You will be there?'

Of course I will.

It's only after I've rung off that I realise that she didn't say anything about the stopped cheque, and I feel so bad about this that I go to the bank on Monday morning and draw out £2000, which I'll give to her in cash. Then I remember that she wants copies of my books, and, not having any myself, I have to go out and buy the sodding things – or such as I can find – hiding them, before our date, in the boot of my car. And I'm so happy now that it occurs to me that Alison is more likely to notice this than my misery of the past few days, but she's too upset still about her dying mother, luckily, to register anything else.

I get to the Carlton Tower a few minutes before our date, order a drink, sit back and think that this may be the happiest I've ever been. It was almost worth losing my Princess, I think, for the luxurious joy of getting her back. I look around at the other well-fed guests with their smooth pink faces and tiny money-making eyes and I feel quite sorry for them, think none of them can be as happy as I am now. I go on thinking this for half an hour, and then it occurs to me, rather suddenly, that she may be going to stand me up. At first I reject the idea out of hand; she couldn't leave me sitting here, not after all we've been through, not in this particular setting, surrounded by these fat, well-dressed fools, so thoughtlessly on top of things. I can't believe she'd set me up for anything so cruel. I wait for another thirty minutes and then I leave, as casually as I can, hold myself in check until I get outside and then let rip, scream with rage and run to my car, drive like a madman, dizzy with pain and thoughts of havoc, over to Bristol House, where I plan to break in somehow, smash down doors, kill anyone who tries to thwart me. Once there, I ring her bell, neither expecting an answer nor receiving one. Then I go into my now accustomed, fatuous routine, ringing her from the pub opposite and getting her answering-machine. I run back across the road and ring all the bells in the block, at last finding someone silly enough to let me in. I run upstairs and beat on her door, scream at her through the letter-box. After a while, rather to my surprise, she comes to the door and lets me in.

She looks horrifying, worse than the time before, like something you might see late at night slumped in the wreckage of Piccadilly underground. You wouldn't think it was possible to look so ill and still be breathing. I move towards her, feeling sick and not knowing what to say, but she backs away, cowers in a corner like a frightened animal, puts her hands across her face as if afraid I'm going to hit her. Then she runs quickly to the sofa, where she seems to have been sleeping, lies down and pulls a blanket round her. The flat is filthy, a rubbish-tip of dirty clothes and unwashed coffee-cups, and there's a dead body on the floor – or what looks like one – also covered in a blanket. I sit down on the sofa next to her and reach out and try to hold her, but she pulls away from me in terror.

'Don't *touch* me! I just want to *sleep*. If only I could *sleep*. Please let me sleep.'

I'm really frightened now: she's clearly very ill indeed, and – in spite of what she says – I'm sure it must be drugs. I don't say anything for a while, and then I try to stroke her, very gently, and – after wincing and going tense at first – she lets me. After a few minutes I seem to have won her trust, so I ask her to tell me what the matter is.

'I told you before. I've given up drugs. I'm having a nervous breakdown.'

I point to the dead body on the floor, ask her who it is.

'A friend of George's. She's trying to beat drugs too. She's lucky – she's asleep. *Christ* if only I could sleep.'

I thought you weren't seeing George.

'I'm not. I haven't seen him for ages. And don't *quiz* me! If you're going to quiz me I'd rather you went.'

I say nothing for a while, and she closes her eyes, seems to go to sleep. But after a minute or two she opens them again, gives me a guilty little smile and speaks less harshly.

'I'm sorry, I'm really sorry. I did mean to come. But I fell asleep. I didn't sleep at all last night. When I woke up, it was too late. I'm really sorry.'

And then – although I've accused her of nothing yet – she looks up at me like a defiant child, like a very old and ill and life-battered twelve-year-old and adds: 'I *did* want to see you. If I hadn't wanted to see you, I wouldn't have opened the door, I wouldn't have let you in.'

I tell her that I'm sorry too, sorry that I stopped the cheque, and she laughs a little hopelessly and says that she hadn't needed it anyway, had never had any intention of putting it in her bank. She tore it up, she says, as soon as I left. I ask her why, in that case, she wanted it in the first place, and she smiles at me a little crazily and says: 'I don't know. Perhaps it was a test. I do test people, you know.'

I tell her that I've got £2000 with me now, which I want her to have.

'*No*! I don't *want* money. I keep telling you that.'

Are you having an affair?

I realise what a silly question it is even as I ask it. She looks at me with astonishment, then cackles with derision.

'Ha! I should be so lucky! I'm right off sex. I haven't had sex since you.'

I believe her. No one would want her, looking as she does. She's aged ten years in six weeks and I'm sure it must be drugs; I'm sure she's heavily involved with those evil men upstairs, a conviction reinforced by the fact that the phone starts ringing now, and every time it does she picks it up and shouts: 'He's not here, I keep *telling* you he isn't here,' and then she slams the receiver down.

Who isn't here?

'George.'

I thought you weren't seeing him.

'I'm not. I haven't seen him for ages. He's crazy. He gives people this number. It's driving me *mad*. I'm going *mad*, I tell you!'

She screams and covers her ears, as if to block out the world and all its insults; and I take her in my arms wanting to pick her up and take her out of this, away from anyone who wants to hurt her, to lay her on a warm beach and let the sun heal her and the sea; and I remember that night on her first visit to Ibiza when we sat in the car for two hours and she stared at the sky and told me everything even though we hardly knew each other; and I can see her dancing with Tanit the Island God, and later, just six weeks ago, dancing in the street and making a hundred people happy all at once, and now – because of that wicked crowd upstairs – she's a frightened little grey-faced corpse; and I know something certain for the first time ever, something as tautologically true as a mathematical proof – that I love her like I love myself, that only I can protect and help her. (And I make a quick entry to this effect in my writer's notebook.)

What do you want?

'Isn't it obvious? I want to be well again. I want to get out of here – away from all these people.'

I'll move you. I'll find you another flat. I'll look after you. Is that what you want?

'You know it is. It's what I've always wanted.'

It's an odd feeling getting everything you've ever dreamed of – almost as shocking, as violently draining as its opposite – and for a moment I'm as lost for words as any bewildered winner, frightened, perhaps, that too brash a show of triumph – some gauche Downing Street display – might cause a higher power to take it all away again. But after a while I find I can breathe again, and I tell her that the sooner she gets out of here the better, that I'll take her to her mother's the very next day, where she must stay until I find her another flat. She agrees to all this immediately, then, seeming utterly exhausted now, she lies back and closes her eyes. I ask her if she'd like me to leave.

'No. Please stay with me until I sleep. Please don't leave me now.'

I stay for about an hour, holding her hand, until at last she falls into that deep, coma-like sleep, which is to do with drugs, I'm sure – though what drugs I can't imagine: certainly nothing I've ever seen her take. But it doesn't matter: she's safe now, I've got her back and I'll look after her forever, protect her from the Marquis of Beauchamp and Greek George, upon whom in due course I'll seek a terrible revenge.

I ring her early the next day, slightly frightened that she may have changed her mind, but she sounds calm and cheerful, and eager to go to her mother's as soon as possible. I'm round at her place within the hour and find that she's packed and ready to leave, and looking much better than the night before. She's still horrifyingly thin, of course, but she's had a bath and she's done her hair and her eyes are shining in a way I haven't seen for weeks. She says she's taken some valium, and this must be true, I think, because on the drive to her mother's she rambles on in that slurred, disconnected way I first noticed on the night she met Greek George and Beauchamp, quite happily, almost euphorically indeed, but hardly making any sense, clutching Ted and rambling on about the past, about her childhood and about her first husband who raped her at her daughter's funeral, and about her millionaire who flew her round the world and kicked her out at a moment's notice, and about her second husband who spat at her in Bogota and whom she blames for most of this; and she tells me a lot of stories I haven't heard before – most of them to do with how she's been abused by lovers, husbands, friends – and I listen quietly like a counsellor, never interrupting or assuming anything, never calling her my Princess or saying that I love her: she's been very badly hurt, I think, and it will be a long time before she trusts me again completely. I'm sure something terrible has happened to her in the past three weeks, but I'm sensible enough not to quiz her now. She'll come out of this nightmare on her own. Meanwhile I'll always be there and she'll tell me what happened in her own good time. She doesn't want to get out of the car once we arrive at her mother's, seems to want to sit with me and talk, so I hold her hand and tell her that she's safe now, that I'll look after her forever and that I'll start looking for a new flat as soon as I get back to London. She makes me promise to ring her every day, and then she suddenly clings to me and says:

'I don't know where I'd be without you.'

I start looking for a flat at once, and I ring her every day to tell her how I'm doing. Sometimes she seems to be all right, at other times she sounds depressed. She's still having trouble sleeping, she says, and when she does sleep she has awful dreams, but she's putting on a bit of weight and feeling stronger every day. She's eager to come back to London as soon as possible, and since I haven't got time to piss around – getting references, forming companies or changing my nationality (only foreigners, it seems, can at short notice get a roof over their heads these days) – I go out one morning and take a flat in Nell Gwynn House, one of those holiday lets which, by paying outrageously over the odds, you can walk straight into. It's no more than a bed-sit and it costs £250 a week, but I reckon my Princess will only want it for about two months and then, with the weather getting nicer, we'll go back to Ibiza. She's very excited when I tell her about the flat and keen to come back to London straight away – against the wishes of her mother who wants to keep her at home for a little longer. I tell her that I'll look after her better than her mother ever could, and she agrees with me. We arrange that she'll come back to London the next day, spend one more night in Bristol House, and then do a runner early in the morning.

The move to Nell Gwynn House goes without a hitch. I pick her up soon after breakfast, and she is looking much better: she's put on weight, there's some colour in her cheeks again, her eyes are shining (she's been at the valium again, I think) and all her belongings are neatly packed and ready to go. She's been up since four o'clock, she says, putting everything into cases.

'Ted helped, of course. He was very good. He's glad we're getting out of here.'

241

She loves her new flat, inspecting it excitedly, opening and closing cupboards, and planning where she'll put her office. Then we go out to do some shopping, after which I leave her – going over to Simey's to do some work – having first arranged to come back in the evening.

She still seems very happy in the evening, but rather tired from having been up half the night before, and it comes as no surprise when she suddenly falls into one of her deep sleeps. I put her into bed without waking her up (nothing would wake her up, I think) and stay with her for an hour or two, writing her one of my loving notes before I leave. The next day I go over and see her again, and she's very sweet and apologises for falling asleep the night before.

'It's amazing. I feel so safe with you. I couldn't go to sleep like that in front of anyone else.'

Slowly I'm winning back her trust, I think. For the next week I see her every day, and each day we seem to become a little closer – though strangers compared to how we were. We speak to each other with tender, duty-bound politeness, as if we're relations of some sort and therefore owe each other kindness, but anything more intimate is inconceivable. We sometimes mention sex, in a rather embarrassed way, but she says she isn't ready for it yet, always stressing that when she is it will be with me. Every day she looks a little prettier, and although I want her urgently I'm very good and never press it. I never press anything, in fact, never rebuke her for her behaviour in the past or ask for explanations. I just wait patiently for her to become again the person she used to be.

We talk a lot about Ibiza, planning to go back there as soon as possible, and every time I leave her she gives me a hug and a chaste kiss, and, as I walk away along the corridor, she always calls out after me: 'Roll on Ibiza! Ku forever!' I think she's waiting for Ibiza, that only in Ibiza will I get her back completely; but one day, when I go to take her out to lunch, she seems quite different: she's looking mischievous and very pretty, and she has an expression in her eyes which on bad days I thought I'd never see again. I take her to The Brasserie in the Fulham Road and, because of the expression in her eyes, I order champagne and although she doesn't drink it – she takes just one sip and pulls a disgusted face (which, because she used to love champagne, strikes me as very odd) – she does become more mischievous by the minute, finally flooring me with the announcement that if I had a flat of my own everything would be all right. I'm stunned for a moment, hardly care to believe what I'm hearing, but then I realise in a flash of understanding that, as usual, I'd managed to get everything wrong: that all this time she's been waiting for me to leave Alison, that she's been holding out for that. I ask her what she'd do if I were to take another flat.

'I'd move in with you. Mine's too small. But if you got something with at least two rooms we wouldn't get on top of one another. You could do your silly writing without giving me the hump.'

I don't hesitate: this is everything I want, everything I've dreamed of, and if I now do the worse thing imaginable – hurt Alison beyond repair, perhaps – my Princess will never let me down again. I tell her that I'll take another flat at once, start looking for one this very weekend, ask her if she'd like to help me search.

'No. Surprise me. Ring me on Monday and take me round there.'

You do mean this?

'Of course. Everything will be marvellous.'

You know what it will do to Alison?

She frowns and looks unhappy for a moment.

'Don't tell her it's for good. Just say you need some space for a week or two.'

There are times when I wish my Princess wouldn't use dreadful expressions such as this, but I love her so much at this moment that I'd forgive her anything. Then, quite unexpectedly, she starts to cry, sits there with tears running down her cheeks and says:

'Oh God – poor Alison. I've been there, I know what it's like.'

And I can't bear to see her cry, so I hold her hand and reassure her, tell her that everything will be all right. I take her back to Nell Gwynn House and then go immediately to an estate agency in the King's Road which specialises in holiday lets, though of a rather better quality than Nell Gwynn House. The first flat they show me, in Upper Cheyne Row, is quite luxurious and seems ideal. It costs £450 a week, but money isn't important now – nothing is too good for my Princess – and I say I'll take it, that I'll move in on Monday morning.

I can't bring myself to say anything to Alison until the very last moment, and because she seems so happy and unsuspecting, the weekend is particularly unpleasant, my own happiness almost being spoilt by the awfulness of what I have to do. For two days we sit at opposite ends of the sofa, and I think how odd it is that we've lived together, quite contentedly, for fifteen years and yet we might as well have been of different species, might just as well have always said the opposite of what we did say, since what we did say was noise merely to fill a silence. On Monday morning, while she's still alseep, I put a few things into a suitcase – ready for a sudden exit – then go and wake her with a cup of tea. She smiles at me sleepily, feeling warm and safe, and I have to do this very quickly, brutally, as when I sold my nest-egg, like putting down a kitten. I sit on the bed and hold her hand and tell her that I've got something rather important to say to her, which may come as quite a shock. I give her a very lighthearted version of what has happened with my Princess, stressing how trivial it is and saying that I need a week or two on my own – entirely to get her out of my system. I tell her that she knows I'd never leave her, that this is just a temporary move and best for both our sakes, whereas the present situation could destroy us. She's still half asleep and at first I think she hasn't followed what I've said. And then she starts to smile – tries on that uncertain grin an outclassed sparring partner assumes for bravado's sake just before the lights go out – and I think she's going to laugh, tell me that she's been aware of it from the start and doesn't mind at all. But suddenly her eyes are full of the knowledge that she has just one second to understand what she should have understood for fifteen years and she starts to cry, quietly, hopelessly, and she reaches out and tries to hold on to me – and I can't take this, I can't bear to see it, so I pick up my suitcase and run for the door, saying I'll ring her in the evening.

And once outside I want to scream with relief. I'm free at last

244

and about to live for the first time ever with someone who delights me all the time, to whom I can say what I mean because the truth won't hurt. I drive round to Upper Cheyne Row, inspect our new home gloatingly, think how impressed by it my Princess will be, draw up a list of what it lacks (we'll need a video and some decent sounds), and then I go out and buy some food – all her favourites tastes, specifically things I don't like (thinking how much less punishing selflessness is than its crushing opposite, remember the exhaustion of having to have what *I* want for fifteen years) – and other more boring things we'll need: soap, bath essences, washing-powder, Vim, but all significant because they'll be used by her. This done, I go out again and spend nearly fifteen hundred pounds on a video-recorder, a sound system and some tapes, and then I ring her up to tell her where I am. There's no reply, so, assuming that she's gone out to do some shopping too, and having no time to lose, I go round to Nell Gwynn House and slip a note under her door with our new telephone number on it.

I go back to our luxury flat and arrange some flowers which I've bought on this last trip out, and I put some music on (Bruce Springsteen – 'I'm On Fire'), sit back – thinking how a year ago I never would have predicted this, would never have imagined that, quite suddenly, I'd find life worth living – and wait for her to ring. But she doesn't ring; I ring her several times, but there's never any answer, and in the evening I ring Alison and she sounds much less unhappy – really quite cheerful, in fact – so that's all right, at least. But my Princess doesn't ring the next day either, and I comfort myself with the thought that she must have gone home to her mother's for the weekend and hasn't come back to London yet, that she hasn't received my note. That must be the explanation, I think – she wouldn't just leave me sitting here having persuaded me to do this thing – but I don't care to test it by ringing up her mother, just in case it turns out not to be. Then, quite late in the evening, the phone does ring and my heart lurches with relief; but it isn't my Princess, it's Alison and she sounds peculiar, asks me if I'm all right, in a really concerned way. And I can tell there's something she wants to say but isn't sure if she should. I ask her what it is and she says 'nothing at all, really'

245

far too brightly, and I know it's something I won't want to hear. I press her anyway, and at last she admits that there is something, but she's promised not to tell me. Promised who? I ask. Tiffs, she says: Tiffs rang her last night and told her not to be too worried, that she knew I'd be home quite soon; Melissa was in love, said Tiffs, had been having an affair for the past few weeks and was terrified of my finding out.

I don't think I say good-bye or even hang up; I think I just drop the phone, walk downstairs, feeling quite calm actually, and drive over to Nell Gwynn House. I'm not sure what I plan to do, but I think I'm probably going to kill her. I'm in a kind of trance, quite relieved, in fact, that the whole thing has been resolved, hardly bothering to go over in my mind the extent of her betrayal, the astonishing fact that she got me to take this and the other flat, persuaded me to leave Alison, managed even to squeeze a tear at the thought of what we were doing to her – while all the time she was having an affair with someone else. I don't even bother to wonder who this someone else might be – it doesn't seem to matter in the least. I park the car and go upstairs, not really expecting her to be in, but meaning to wait there, I suppose, until she returns. But she is in, her key's in the lock on the inside, so I ring the bell and after a long time – she's been in one of her comas, I imagine – she comes to the door and opens it. She's wearing a nightdress and she looks very small and vulnerable, stumbling a bit and rubbing the sleep from her eyes with her little hands. But she smiles happily, looks really pleased to see me – which makes what I'm going to do all the better, somehow. I walk through the door and hit her hard across the face, wanting to wipe away that treacherous smile forever. She backs away, looking astonished, looking shocked and terrified, so I hit her again and she falls to the floor. I tear her nightdress off and call her a dirty little whore, tell her that she looks disgusting. There's a five pound note on the table by the bed and I pick it up and throw it in her face, say I'm astonished that, looking as she does, she can charge so much. And even while I'm doing this I remember how she used to say that this was what she wanted, that this was the most exciting it could be; but it isn't in the least exciting – it's foul and humiliating. She's curled up in terror on the floor, like a little animal, begging me to tell her what it is she's done – and suddenly I feel disgusted with myself, appalled at how I've behaved. I lift her up and put her on the bed, tell her that Tiffs has told me everything. And at the mention of Tiffs she changes completely: she stops crying and starts to scream the most awful abuse – her rage at being cornered burning off the carefully acquired camouflage of fifteen years, revealing her – horrifyingly – as what she is: an ambitious, desperate gutter-rat. Tiffs is mad, she screams, and I'm even madder to believe a word she says, she's always known I'm mad – violent, sick, obsessed – always known that one day I'd try to kill her.

'Get out! Get out! It's *over*. That's it – I never want to see you again. You've ruined my life. You're crazy, off your head, *sick* ...'

... and a great deal more in that vein. And then she starts to throw the furniture around, picking up a table-lamp and smashing it on the floor, sobbing and screaming abuse. I try to calm her down, try to take her in my arms and reason with her, but this makes her scream even more hysterically, so eventually I just say how sorry I am and I drag myself away.

I go back to what was to have been our home in Upper Cheyne Row, feeling quite calm again, feeling sick and ashamed at the way I've behaved, but relieved that the whole thing's over, that I understand everything at last. Tomorrow I'll give myself up, go back to Alison and spend another fifteen years sitting in silence at my end of that hideous sofa, but meanwhile I take a valium and I lie on the bed and after a while I ring up Tiffs and tell her what I've done. She's terribly sorry I had to find out, she says, but she felt so guilty – having introduced us in the first place – that she just *had* to tell Alison: she couldn't bear to see fifteen years go down the drain, she says, because of a little whore. I ask her who it is my Princess is having an affair with, and she says she'd rather not mention the name but that it's a journalist on a Sunday porno paper. They met at a party about a month ago, she says, and have been seeing each other ever since. What shocked her most, says Tiffs, was that she rang my Princess the night before and she was prattling on about this man, so she asked her what had happened to me. And my Princess had said: 'Oh, he's left Alison,

247

you know' – as though it was the most trivial thing imaginable – and had then gone back to talking excitedly about this new man in her life.

'I did warn you,' says Tiffs.

'Hi! It's only me. Could you pay the taxi, darling? I *had* to take a taxi. You're not cross, are you?'

Of course I'm not cross – I'm very proud of you. Do you feel okay? How did it go?

'It was a bit of a nightmare, actually. They offered me £3000 to tell them everything and another £10,000 after the trial – if they could use it. If I don't go to prison, I suppose they mean.'

You're not going to prison. You didn't agree, did you?

'Of course I didn't. You told me not to. I was a bit tempted, mind you. You're *sure* we're doing the right thing?'

Of course we are. Trust me. It will be much more valuable as a book. If a Sunday paper does it, it will be back-street stuff, really squalid – like Tiffs and her kiss-and-tell confessions.

'Don't mention that cuckoo little bitch. I never want to hear her name again.'

Sorry. What happened? What did they say?

'Well – they tried to persuade me. Gus shut me in a room with this awful reporter and it was obvious immediately that they're only interested in Alexander. He kept saying – tell us about you and the Marquis of Beauchamp. I told him to mind his own business.'

Well done.

'Then he said: "Come on, Mel, we know you're a junkie – tell us about you and Beauchamp and we'll get you some coke – I know you're longing for it."'

Jesus what a shit! That's really *evil*.

'I thought so. I walked out and came back here. I don't think we'll hear from them again.'

That's incredible – trying to use that, offering you drugs. That's the wickedest thing I've ever heard. Was it Gus?

'No. The other man, the reporter. Talking of which ...'

What?

'Can we ring Martin? I know it's early – but I *have* been good. Please can we ring Martin?'

Not yet, no.

'*Please.*'

No, really. We'll ring him tomorrow.

'*What!*'

I'm only teasing. Actually I've got you a little present.
Martin came over while you were out.

'Oh God – I don't deserve you! Why are you so good to me?'

Because I love you.

'Hm – is that all? You used to say you worshipped me.'

I do worship you. I worship the very ...

'Where is it, then? Can I have one now? I *have* been good. I
did exactly what you told me to.'

Okay.

'Come and talk to me while I prepare it.'

I follow her into the kitchen, watch fascinated as she does
her stuff with ammonia and test tubes, as she bases the coke
into the lethal little rocks which for an hour or two will take
away her pain, make her as sweet and loving as she used to be.
And I remember the relief and happiness I felt the first time I
saw her doing this, how I knew at once that because of this
she'd never get away from me again.

'How far have you got, then?'

The nasty bit. The night I beat you up.

'I don't want to think about that. It was a nightmare.'

I'll never do that again.

'I know you won't. You've got quite a long way, then.'

It's only notes at the moment.

'Have you still got me saying silly things? Off like a dog with
a cat between its legs – that stuff?'

I've got you speaking like you do. I can remember everything
you've ever said.

'Ha! Have you got a pornographic memory, or something?
There's one – write that in your notebook before you forget.
What am I, then?'

A researcher – a really classy girl who has the misfortune to
meet these wicked men.

'What about you? I don't want you to come out of it nasty.'

I don't. I'm a distinguished older man, a successful architect
who loses everything because of his addiction to the girl.

250

'Christ, that's not what you think, is it? Don't I make you happy?'

Of course you do. It's fiction – like you wanted.

'Okay. It's funny, I've never told you this, but when you were beating me up, even as you were doing it, I wanted you to ...'

What?

'You know.'

No I don't. What?

'I'll tell you when we get to my bit. When do we get to my bit?'

Now. We're going to do it now.

'God! Do you mean it? I don't know if I'm ready. You said we'd need a tape-recorder. You said mine was the important bit and that you'd need to get it down exactly – word for word. You said you'd have to get a tape-recorder.'

I have. I went out this afternoon and bought one. While you were up in Fleet Street.

'Oh dear – I don't know if I can. I think I'm too nervous. Why do we have to do it now? Why can't we do it tomorrow? What's the rush?'

We can't keep putting it off. You'll be okay after you've had a pipe. I know this is the best time to do it. Trust me.

'Okay. Wow – it's a good thing Martin's been.'

That's what I thought.

In fact I'm not being entirely honest with her – not, at least, telling her the real reason why we have to do it now. She's seriously ill – chronically addicted, according to Dr Lefever, a drug specialist she's been seeing – and for some time it's been obvious that eventually I'd have to put her in a clinic. What's held me up – luckily – has been the wicked expense of a cure. At first I was quite relieved, I must admit, to discover that most clinics seem to charge about £16,000 for an eight week course (my Princess couldn't expect me to fork out *that* amount of money), but recently we've found out – or, rather, *I've* found out – that her PPP medical policy does, after all, cover drug addiction. I've been keeping this information to myself, partly because I've been terrified, after so miraculously getting her back, of losing her again, and partly because I wanted her to tell me everything before she went away. All this interest from Sunday porno papers has made me realize how valuable her story is, and I've managed to persuade her not to sell to low-life characters like them, but to let me write a book about it. This is the only way, I think, that I can recover some of the huge sums of money that I've spent on her.

I thought we had more time, but while she was out this afternoon, Dr Lefever rang to say that he's found her a bed at Clifton House, a clinic in Lytham St Annes and that PPP will pay. We had quite a long talk, in the course of which he kept stressing that she was at serious risk, that these comas are very dangerous, and that she must go in at once – tomorrow, if possible. Clifton House is the best clinic in the country, he said, one of the few which practises the Minnesota Method.

After he rang off, I sat around in a state of shock, wondering if I should keep this from her too; but then I began to realise, very gradually, that the fact that it's Clifton House could be to my advantage. It's important, obviously, that she does go into a clinic now – her habit is costing me at least £100 a day and this news about the comas isn't funny at all – but it's equally important that I don't lose her, hand her over to strangers who, while 'curing' her, turn her against me. I know something about the Minnesota Method, enough to make me confident that its sinister mix of terror and voodoo – a Royal Marine Commando course with a thick overlay of mad-eyed Christianity – will never work with my Princess. My Princess will never be subdued by merciless Christians telling her that she's had it, that she needs them and God, and meanwhile must get down on her knees and clean the lavatories. It's effective, of course – terror always is (I could do it myself; I've done National Service, I could demoralise desperate people, programme them with fraudulent loyalties and charge them £1000 a week) – but it won't work with my Princess. I'll do what I have to do, I'll get her into the creepy place – even pay for the first two weeks (a minimum requirement according to Dr Lefever, just in case PPP don't cough up – they're running a business at Clifton House) – and after that it will be up to her. After a few weeks, she'll run away, I'm sure, but that won't be my fault, I'll have done my best. She'll come back to me, I know she will, and she'll never be able to say I didn't try to help her. The possibility that they might 'cure' her – replace her dependency on drugs with a far more sinister one (on them and God), turn her into a vegetable, wandering round Lytham St Annes forever, mumbling prayers and blanket-bathing old folk – is a risk I'll have to take.

I can't tell her any of this just yet. If I tell her now, she'll be too upset to talk – and I've only got tonight to get her story down.

'How is it?

'Good, I think. Oh wow yes – it's the best. I won't be able to do it now! I can't even remember what we were talking about.'

Your bit. The important bit.

'Oh yeah. Okay – do I start now?'

Not yet. Not till I've got the tape-recorder working. I don't want to miss any of this. This is what's going to sell the book. That Sunday rag will have to pay ten times what they offered you, the bastards, just for the extract rights.

'Goodness! Are we going to be rich, darling?'

Rolling – if you tell me everything. You've got to trust me completely.

'I do. Okay – where shall I start?'

From the time you met Alexander Beauchamp and Greek George – those prats.

'You *really* want to know everything? You're quite sure you do?'

Absolutely sure. 'My life of shame with Alexander Beauchamp! The shocking truth!' That stuff. I'm looking forward to it myself.

'I bet you are. Okay – it's all coming back. You won't alter anything I say, will you?'

Of course I won't. It's your book.

'Okay – now?'

Not yet. Wait a sec – that's it.

'Wow – the shocking truth. Now?'

Yes. What happened?

253

'Nothing.'

What!

'I *told* you. Nothing happened.'

I didn't believe you.

'I told you often enough.'

No you didn't. You mentioned mad people coming and going – lesbians, black girls, stockbrokers, blue films, orgies, nice girls from the Thai Embassy tied to beds with Old Harrovian ties, Sophie Manners, God knows what.

'Oh *that*. I didn't know you wanted all that sordid stuff. I thought you meant me and Alexander. Nothing happened with Alexander.'

Well – make something up, for goodness sake.

'I can't do that! That would be terrible. It wouldn't be true.'

That doesn't matter. Christ – after what he did to you! You're still protecting that creep.

'I'm not. I'm just telling the truth. He did ask me if he could beat me once. He used to carry a whip around. I said only if I could beat him too.'

Did you?

'No.'

Shit – never mind, let's go back a bit. To the night you met them. To the night that madman trapped you in the flat. You may remember something.

'Okay – let me think. I remember I was quite upset – I'm sure I was. You'd been horrid to me. I thought you really didn't want me. I went back to my place and this man stopped me on the stairs. He said he was a friend of Lindy's. He was quite posh – a stockbroker, I think – so I asked him in. We did a lot of coke – and I think he tried to fuck me, I'm almost sure he did. I thought that's what you wanted. I remember thinking – wait till I tell my Prince about this! Then he became a little cuckoo, spilling his drink and waving his arms about. I asked him to leave and he produced a gun. He really did. You never believed me, but he *did* have a gun. I was terrified. I ran upstairs and knocked on George's flat. He let me in – and he was marvellous. All that happened just as I told you at the time – but you never believed me. Alexander was there with another man, Angelo, and they took the madman to the dungeon –

which is what they called a basement flat under Angelo's mens' wear shop in the Edgeware Road. Alexander was staying there at the time, in the dungeon. They were all free-basing and I didn't want to. I knew how dangerous it was, Christ, even my *husband* had never let me free-base with him.'

Why did you?

'They went on and on at me. In the end they persuaded me.'

Who?

'Alexander mainly. He could see I was in a state — he said it would make me feel better.'

Bastard. I hope he gets locked up forever.

'I don't know — I wasn't a child exactly, I knew what I was doing. God, I must have been mad. I was upset, I suppose. You were ...'

What?

'Doesn't matter. I phoned you up and, because of the way I knew I sounded, I told you I'd been taking valium. I think you believed me.'

I did.

'You were horrible to me. I'd been through this nightmare and you just shouted at me, you called me a whore and I thought — Christ, even my Prince doesn't love me any more. I'm not *blaming* you, it's just ...'

Were you addicted at once?

'Not that night — but very quickly. Probably the next time I did it, which was the next day. It's as lethal as that. I did it every day from then on. I was terrified you'd notice the difference.'

I did. I thought it was valium.

'I felt so bad about fooling you. Spending all day up at George's and then coming round and seeing you. I was sure you'd notice. And I couldn't wait to get away from you and back to George's for that fucking pipe. I even went back there with Tessa on our last night — the night before Alison came back from Portugal. I told you I was in the middle of some deal, I think. I did it every day after that. They were very clever. At first they gave me the stuff free, until I was completely hooked, and then they just took me over. I'd do anything for them, just to get my supply.'

Why didn't you *tell* me?

'I couldn't. I couldn't tell you I was a junkie. I was so *ashamed*. I felt so *ugly* – your Princess hooked on a pipe, not able to go out any more, not able to face the world. It *was* ugly. Everyone was like that – you should have seen Alexander when he couldn't get it. He'd crawl around the floor, *weeping*, begging George to give him something. I couldn't let you see all that. It's far worse than heroin.'

It might have been better than what I was imagining.

'I *wanted* to tell you. I used to dream about you coming round, smashing the door down and taking me away from it all.'

Why were you always so nasty to me, then?

'You always came round at the wrong time – just when I was desperate for a pipe. You don't know what it's like. *Nothing* matters except the pipe. You're always nastiest to the people you're closest to, the ones you really care about. They become the enemy. It's well known. Dr Lefever told you. It's funny we haven't heard from him – did he ring today?'

No. I'll ring him tomorrow, see if there's any news. *Did* you try to give it up? Was that bit true?

'Oh yes. Those nights you came round, everything I said was true. I knew what I was doing to myself. I knew I'd reached rock bottom, and I *did* want to break away.'

When I got you out, took you to your mother's and then moved you into Nell Gwynn House, did you really mean to finish with them then?

'I think so – but I was completely hooked. The night before you took me home I hadn't slept at all, I'd been basing all night upstairs with George. I was sure you'd notice. And I couldn't wait to come back to London. I used to dream about the pipe – incredibly vivid dreams. Then, on that first day at Nell Gwynn House, as soon as you'd gone, I went straight round to George's, and started all over again. Ha!'

What was your attitude to me all that time?

'You were a bloody nuisance! Sorry.'

You were just using me?

'I suppose so – you lose your feelings completely, you become completely ruthless. But I always knew deep down – it used to come back as a sort of vague memory – that you were important to me in some way. And I always held on to the idea of Ibiza. I thought Ibiza might be an escape from it all.'

That day we had lunch, the day you persuaded me to take the flat in Upper Cheyne Row – did you mean that? Did you mean to move in with me?

'Maybe – at the time. I'd probably had a pipe that morning, I was probably so high I didn't know what I was saying. I do remember that after lunch I couldn't wait to get rid of you. I was terrified of your coming back with me because George was coming over with some stuff. That was when he asked me to bank Alexander's cheque for him. He suddenly produced this cheque for £12,000 and asked me to put it through my bank. I'd done that a few times before, but never for such large amounts. Then we went back to his place and free-based all through the weekend. I didn't sleep at all. I went back to my flat on Monday and found your note. I was going to ring you, but I fell into one of my sleeps. I must have slept for twenty-four hours. The next thing I knew, you came through the door and beat me up.'

Was that it? Had you finished with me at that point?

'Oh, for sure. I thought you were mad. I never wanted to see you again. After you'd gone I went straight round to my old flat at Bristol House. I was terrified, I thought you were going to come back and kill me. That's something else I lied to you about. I never gave up that flat. I let George use it and he moved in Bobby, an ex-girlfriend of his. I was going to stay with Bobby, never go back to Nell Gwynn House. That was a Wednesday, I suppose, and then on Friday – Friday the 13th, I'll never forget that – it happened. The bust. Christ what a nightmare. We were playing backgammon, Bobby and me. It was just after lunch. We'd had a pipe so I was feeling pretty good. I went upstairs to get something from George – some more stuff, probably – and there were policemen all over the place. They asked me who I was, and when I told them, they pushed me back into my flat and started searching it. They found my paying-in book with a record of all the cheques I'd banked for George – including Alexanders's for £12,000 – and I was arrested. We were all taken to Harrow Road – me, George, Angelo, Bobby and Alexander (he was picked up in the dungeon, I think) – and kept in cells overnight. They

257

questioned me all the next day and then, in the evening, they let me make one phone call. I rang you – I couldn't think of anyone else.'

Just using me?

'Oh sure. Mind you, I thought you *owed* me something. Gross, eh? We get like that – totally selfish. I thought it was all your fault! That if you hadn't beaten me up I wouldn't have been round at my old flat when the bust took place, that it was purely bad luck that I happened to be there with my paying-in book. But you were marvellous, of course. In spite of the shitty way I'd been treating you, you came straight down to the police station, bailed me out and took me to that flat in Upper Cheyne Row. That night I told you everything, I think. Then – because it was what I'd wanted all along – I persuaded you to free-base with me. Was that very wicked of me, do you think? You were fantastic, you didn't seem to have any doubts at all.'

I did have doubts, as it happens. I was quite frightened, but I knew that to get her back I'd have to free-base with her. I'd have done anything to get her back, taken heroin if necessary. I just wanted to be with her, to join her wherever she was, in whatever private hell, and to achieve this I was quite prepared to risk my life. It did occur to me, of course, that some people might think I was risking hers as well, but I quickly realised that, since she was hopelessly addicted, and bound to do it anyway, it was better that she should do it with me – who cared about her – than with the scum who'd already got her into trouble. With me she'd be safe: I'd win her back and then, somehow or other, I'd get her cured. Free-basing with her happened, coincidentally, to be the moral thing to do.

Nor is it quite true to say that she persuaded me – if anything it was the other way round: I'm honest enough to admit that. I remember that night, the night I picked her up at the police station, extremely well. She looked ghastly, was clearly in a state of shock (obviously very ill and now charged, on top of her other problems, with conspiracy to supply cocaine), but all I could think about was what a miracle this was, that this was my chance to get her back. I took her to

Upper Cheyne Row and put her into bed. She told me she was a junkie, and I asked her what she wanted to do about it. She wanted to kick it, she said, and thought she could – if I helped her. She'd only been hooked for about six weeks, so there was a very good chance that she could beat it, she said – if we were both determined enough. She emphasised that it would be worse for me than for her. She'd crave it, she'd be in agony, but whatever she did, whatever she said, I must somehow stop her getting it. I must lock her up, follow her if she managed to escape, put up with any amount of abuse. When she was craving it, she said, she'd say the most terrible things, unbelievable, hateful things, but – if I loved her – I'd put up with it. It would be a nightmare for me, she said, but if I held firm she was sure she could beat it.

The nightmare started almost at once, the evening after I bailed her out, I think. She said she wanted to go and see some friends and when I said she couldn't, she started shouting at me, saying that she couldn't stand me, that she hated me and always had, that I should go back to Alison, because Alison cared about me, whereas she never had and never could. I put up with this for about ten minutes and then I asked her – knowing what the answer would be, knowing that this was my chance to get her back – what she really wanted. She wanted to use again, she said, and there was nothing I could do to stop her. Okay, I said, but if she was going to do it again, she was going to do it with me. She calmed down instantly, as if the viciousness had been an act, looked really happy and relieved, said that that was what she'd wanted all along, that only by free-basing together would we be really close again.

I didn't hesitate: with a shopping-list drawn up by her, I went straight out and bought all the necessary equipment – pipes and tubes and God knows what from a head shop in the King's Road – and then, because all her contacts were afraid to speak to her, assuming (correctly, I imagine) that the police were watching her, I went and scored from my friend Martin, driving back at top speed to Upper Cheyne Row with pipes and tubes and a Bunsen burner and grammes of coke on board, more excited, happier than I'd ever been, because I knew that I was about to get her back. And I did get her back, just as I knew I would. She trusted me completely now, all the bruises of the past few weeks vanished in an instant, and, from that night, we were closer than we'd ever been – disconnected, perfectly enclosed, safe together in our possible world.

I wasn't marvellous.

'Yes you were. Those next few days were fantastic, better than it had ever been. We were really close. Then it was horrible Christmas and you abandoned me. You did, you did! You *knew* I wanted to spend Christmas with you and you went back to Alison.'

I *had* to. I couldn't let her go down to her mother's on her own.

'Okay. But Christmas was a nightmare. You didn't even ring me on Christmas day.'

How could I? I couldn't ring you from Alison's mother's. I couldn't say: excuse me, do you mind if I ring my Princess?

'All right – I'll forgive you for that. But don't let it happen again. *Next* Christmas has got to be perfect. We'll have a tree and a turkey and lots of presents. And I want a stocking, I definately want a stocking – I always used to have a stocking. Where do you think we'll be? Hey – perhaps we'll be in Ibiza! Is that good, Christmas in Ibiza? Or perhaps we'll have a house by then – can we have a house? With a log fire and a Christmas tree in the window? *Please* can we have a house?'

Don't you like this?

'Oh I *love* this – everything's been perfect since we moved in here. A really happy ending – that's important, don't you think? People like a happy ending.'

In fact it wasn't quite as pleasant as that. I got through Christmas somehow be telling Alison that it was all over with my Princess, that I was never going to see her again, meanwhile sneaking out whenever I could to ring her up in Essex. After we left Upper Cheyne Row, my Princess – with a heartbreaking rush of hope and courage – asked me to destroy all her free-basing equipment, saying that she was going to make a really determined effort to kick the habit over Christmas. 'If I keep off it for a week or two,' she said, 'go for long walks and lead a really healthy life, I'm *sure* I can keep off it forever.' I didn't like the sound of that, so I didn't destroy her precious pipe: I smuggled it home, without telling her, and hid it under the bed in my study, knowing that it was my life-line to her, the only means, perhaps, by which I might hold on to her. From time to time, when Alison was out – or, when the craving got too bad, even when she was at home but in another room – I'd take it from under the bed and fondle it, gaze at it lovingly because it was my ally, the key to the only room, perhaps, in which my Princess could ever be at peace. Then, frightened that she might indeed be kicking the habit under her mother's influence, I lured her back to London after Christmas by taking another furnished flat, this time in Munster Road. I couldn't face telling Alison again, so when she was out one day, I left her a letter, packed all my things – this time I was leaving her forever – and escaped once more.

That night Alison tried to kill herself – not too seriously, perhaps, more of a gesture, really, taking about forty valiums and phoning Simey in the middle of the night (she didn't have my number) asking him to look after the cats if anything happened to her. I went straight round, of course, and she was very groggy but seemed to know who I was. I stayed with her all night, thinking, as I watched over her, that that was an odd thing to do. It would be terrible, I suppose, if the only person who could help you wouldn't, if they walked away leaving you to die, but if my Princess did this to me I wouldn't try to kill myself – I wouldn't have to, I'd be dead already. And I got up in the middle of the night and made an entry to this effect – rather liking it – in my writer's notebook. And in the morning Alison woke up and she smiled with such happy relief when she saw that I was there, but then she remembered that it wasn't just a nightmare she'd been having, and she started to cry. I had to leave her then, because my Princess was coming to London that morning to move into our new flat in Munster Road, to give me everything I'd ever wanted. I didn't tell her that Alison had tried to kill herself the night before: I didn't think it would be fair to burden her with this terrible thing she'd done to her. Instead, I waited until the evening and then I got out her free-basing equipment which I'd been hoarding over Christmas, and some cocaine which I'd bought the day before, and my Princess was quite swoonily grateful – just as I'd known she'd be. And, as she says, it's been perfect ever since – except that I've got to break it to her now that this is our last night, that tomorrow I'm taking her to Clifton House, that I'm going to lock her away in a cold asylum by the sea, patrolled, perhaps, by people in white coats who'll smile at her with mirthless Christian understanding and tell her that she needs them more than she needs me.

'We *are* happy, aren't we?'

I am. Happier than I'd ever imagined possible. Nothing before you makes any sort of sense. I didn't believe you.

'When?'

When you said I'd just want you – that everything would change forever. That first night in Ibiza, sitting outside the Tierra. I thought you were crackers.

'Ha! I knew at once. I could read you like a book – even then.'

How did you know?

'You were bored. It had never worked. You were looking for something. All I had to do was find out what. Easy!'

It's frightening. I couldn't replace you. I'd be like you were that day we were having lunch at The Brasserie in the Fulham Road – after you'd found the drug of your choice. I bought champagne but you were disgusted, you pulled a face and wouldn't drink it – because you knew it wouldn't work. I'd be like that if I was offered someone else. I'd be disgusted.

'Would you want to be cured?'

No. But what if I lost you? I'd never get over it.

'You won't lose me. This is the ultimate – far better than I thought it would be. I want it to go on like this forever. I've been thinking how we can improve the flat. We need some pictures, don't you think? There are some pictures at home I think Mummy would let me have. There's one in my room I've always liked. It's a clown – is that gross? I do like it. I've had it since I was a little girl. I think I'll go home this weekend and get it. And there are some other things I want from home. I want to borrow Mummy's sewing-machine – I can make us some curtains. We could make this flat really nice, you know.'

Are you up to it? The journey, I mean?

'Yes – I really feel much better. Going out today, going all the way to Fleet Street on my own, made me think I can beat this thing. I'm sure I can come off it slowly – if you help me. Will you help me?'

Of course I will.

'We'll start tomorrow. Tomorrow – *whatever I say* you mustn't let me do it. I'm going to cure myself – I *know* I can. We must try and be more normal – go out more, go to the cinema, see other people. Would that be good?'

You know Dr Lefever thinks you should go into a clinic.

'I don't *want* to go into a clinic. I *won't*. You *mustn't* put me in a clinic. I'd lose you, I know I would. They'd change me – and you wouldn't want me any more. I've *told* you what they do to people in clinics.'

They might cure you.

'Oh sure – by turning me into a different person. They mess around with your brain ... Is that allowed?'

It shouldn't be.

'You wouldn't let that happen to me, would you? You'd protect me from that?'

Yes – I'd never let that happen. That's evil.

'Candy had a friend who went into a clinic. She'll tell you about it tomorrow. When he came out he was a stranger. She didn't know who he was. God how terrifying – can you imagine it? Seeing someone you love gradually becoming a completely different person? I'd never do that to you. They wipe out the past. It's forced ... what's that word?'

Amnesia?

'That's right. Selective amnesia, Candy called it. You can remember who, and what, and when, but not *why*. I couldn't bear it if that happened to us. Not now. Promise me you'll never put me in a clinic.'

I promise.

'God I don't believe you. I think you're keeping something from me, I'm sure you are. I think you're going to put me away somewhere. I know you are. You *mustn't* – I mean it. Please say you won't. I think I'd rather go to prison. At least I wouldn't change in prison. I'd come out the same person, I'd be your Princess and you'd still love me, wouldn't you?'

Of course I would. But you're not going to prison. And I won't put you in a clinic – I promise.

'I want to have a baby – please let's have a baby. What would our baby be like – would it be a girl, do you think? Hey – I've got a surprise for you! After I saw Gus today I walked all the way to a shop in Bond Street where Candy gets her naughty gear – and I didn't panic once! Wasn't that good? I'm *sure* I'm getting better. I bought something you'll really like and I'm going to put it on. You're not to look until I tell you. I want you to photograph me in it. Will you do that? I'll look really good, I know I will. God, I love dressing up for you. Do you still like me dressing up?'

You know I do.

'I'm going to the bathroom now, and you're not to look until I tell you. Promise?'

Promise.

I can't tell her about the clinic now, I can't spoil what may turn out to be our last night together for God knows how long. Her huge eyes are brimming with such happiness and trust – I can't take that away, I can't terrify her yet. I'll tell her about Clifton House tomorrow; I'll do it suddenly, I'll wake her up early, get her dressed and into the car with a suitcase before she knows what's happening. She's high now, she doesn't know what she's saying, but in the morning she'll feel so ill she won't put up a fight. It will be ghastly, the most treacherous thing I've ever had to do, and the look of reproach in her eyes will haunt me forever. I'll be handing my Princess over to those two most disgusting categories of people: self-righteous 'recovering' junkies and merciless born-again Christians; to spooked people with a vested interest in making others as frightened as they are; to people who, for £1000 a week, will take away your dignity. But they won't 'cure' my Princess; they won't break my Princess's spirit, take away the point of her forever. She'll come back to me and dance again, I know she will – she hasn't got anything else. Why now should she choose 'real life', which has always let her down?

Where are you speaking from?

'I'm at Simey's. I've moved in with him – just for the moment, until I find another place.'

Did you get my letter?

'Yes. It made me very happy. But you didn't say when you'd be out. God – it's been three months. Do you still want to come to Ibiza?'

I'm not sure.

'What do you mean you're not sure?'

They say I've got to let go.

'Oh Christ – not that crap again.'

I'm afraid so.

'*Why?*'

They say I'll never get anywhere while I'm thinking of you all the time – about what we're going to do together. They say I haven't even started my recovery.

'Silly bastards. They're just trying to break us up. Don't listen to them.'

It's not just them.

'What do you mean?'

I think it too. I think they may be right. They say it's a bad relationship for me to come out to.

'Oh Jesus I can't take this – *why?*'

Because I've got to change. I won't be the same person any more – the person you liked. It will be as if we've never met. Once I'm cured, we'll be meeting for the first time. We might like each other, but we might not. There's no way of knowing.

'I'll take that risk.'

Yes – but I *can't*. Don't you understand? If it didn't work, if we had a row, if you upset me, that's when I'd use again. That's when recovering addicts use again – when a relationship goes wrong. I can't take that risk. Please try and understand.

'You're dumping me.'

I'm *not*, I'm really not. I'm not saying I never want to see you again. But we've got to let go – both of us.

'I'm not going to.'

You *must* – for my sake. I've got to have time to find out more about myself. I've been out of my head for years, and that wasn't real. After I've found out who I really am, we can meet again – if we both want to – to discuss our relationship.

'We don't have a relationship.'

Who says so?

'You do. They do.'

No they don't.

'What does "letting go" mean?'

It means we're not committed to each other.

'Exactly. A relationship without commitment, like all their other fucking slogans – mumbo-jumbo. Like "tough love" – that's just a contradiction. "One day at a time", "don't project" – they're just excuses for moral abdication. Christ, that's what morality is – the ability to project, to calculate the likely consequences of our actions. They can't even use the English language correctly. They don't even know what "real" means. I'll tell you what "real" means – everything that is the case. Your life before they got their hands on you was "real". To tell you otherwise is simply brain-washing. You mustn't listen to them.'

You're confusing me – please don't confuse me. They say I've got to write to you.

'Are you going to?'

I don't know. I don't know what to do. I feel I'm caught up in a fight between you and them. And *you* don't understand. You refuse to believe how ill I am.

'You're not ill. You're just a little shit. You're dumping me, and you know you are. Christ – after everything I've done for you.'

Please don't talk to me like this. Please don't finish it like this.

'I'm not finishing it. You are. You can go and fuck yourself.'

'I'm sorry, I really am. I'm sorry I hung up on you.'

That's okay. I understand.

'I suppose you told them.'

Yes. I had to.

'It's just that I'm frightened. I'm frightened of losing you.'

You *mustn't* be. You mustn't be so dependent on me.

'Why not? You were dependent on me.'

I know. And it was wrong.

'Why? Why was it wrong?'

Because one shouldn't be dependent on anyone. They've taught me that in here. I wanted to please you all the time. To please you I pretended to be someone else. I used to dress up to please you.

'What's wrong with that?'

It wasn't me. I've got to learn to be myself.

'Ha! Who you *really* are. Who *they* say you are.'

Yes. No. I don't know. They say I've got to write that letter.

'I won't read it.'

You *must*. I want you to understand.

'I do understand. I understand you're trying to dump me – and I won't let you. You're betraying me, and – worse – you're betraying yourself. Before I put you in there you *begged* me not to let this happen. I'm going to take another flat and you're going to leave that madhouse and come back to London before it's too late.'

No! I'm never going to live in London again. I *can't*.

'Where are you going to live?'

I don't know. In the country. Here perhaps. Don't you understand? I've got to be on the programme *for the rest of my life*. I've got to go to meetings twice a week *forever*. Can you imagine what that's going to be like? Do you *really* think you'll want me the way I'm going to be?

'Of course I will. I'll love you however you are.'

You won't. You're fooling yourself. I'm going to be normal. Plain and fat and growing older. Play-time's over. I'm going to be *me* – how I really am. You've never seen that.

'Yes I have.'

Okay – but you didn't like it. You gave me drugs.

'Drugs gave you the courage to be yourself. I know they did. I'm coming down now. I'm going to take you away from there.'

No! Don't *do* that. If you come down here I won't see you, I mean it. I've got to go now. I'm going to write that letter.

267

'I got your letter.'

Yes?

'It was terrible. "We had good times together which I'll never forget. If we're meant to be together we will be, time doesn't matter. God bless you always." What sort of shit is that?'

I meant it.

'You could have left me with something – some hope.'

No I couldn't. That's how it has to be.

'*Why?*'

Because it *is* hopeless.

'Don't take away everything at once.'

I've got to. It was nothing. You've got to realise that. You've got to learn to live with it.

'You really mean that?'

Yes.

'I don't think I'll make it.'

Look – don't lay that on me. I don't need that, I really don't. I've got problems myself – I don't need yours.

'Do you know how I feel?'

No. I've never wanted someone who hasn't wanted me.

'Christ – have you ever cared about me?'

I've forgotten. I don't think so.

'All those things you said when we were living together – all fucking lies, then?'

Probably. I was an addict. Addicts will say anything to get what they want.

'You said, let's have a baby …'

For God's sake – I've told you before: don't quote back at me things I said when I was *high*.

'Are you sorry?'

I'm sorry for Alison. I'm sorry I took you away from her when I knew I didn't want you myself. I'll always be sorry about that.

'What about me?'

I'm sorry I used you.

'You were *just* using me – right from the start?'

Of course I was. What else would have been the point of you? I was desperate. I couldn't believe I was getting away with it.

'Tiffs is right, then – you're just a little whore.'

I was – but I'm not any more. Thanks to these people here. They've saved my life.

'*I* saved your life. Now you can save mine.'

Don't be so gross! You *risked* my life – and you'd do it again.

'Do you hate me then?'

Don't be pathetic. Of course I don't hate you. Why should I hate you? I feel sorry for you. You don't live in the real world. You need help, but I can't help you.

'You used to say how alike we were.'

Not any more. I've grown up at last. I'm ashamed of ever having been like you.

'I don't think I can live without you – I mean it.'

You'll get over me. You were all right before.

'I didn't know about you. I didn't know things could be better, that life could be okay.'

Look – for the last time, I don't need this. I'm going now. I don't want to talk to you any more.

'Wait, please. I want to see you. I'm coming down there. I have a right to see you.'

You have *no* rights! You have no right to see me. You have no right to love me. You have no right to harass me like this. And you have *no right to use me in a book*.

'Wait – about the book, it could ...'

I'm not *interested* in the book. I'll never read it, so why bother to write it? I don't want to be a clown in the imagination of a frightened old man. I'm *real*, and I don't need you. You don't exist any more. I'm not interested in anything you say. One last thing – you don't own me and you never did. If you *ever* try to contact me I'll call the police. Good-*bye*.

*

Who was it who said: 'It's important to feel injured from time to time, to see oneself as ignorant people see one'? There may be some truth in the saying, but that was a good-bye I could have done without. Even with the obstacle of hindsight I've managed to be fair to her, I think, fairer perhaps than she deserves. Oddly enough, I don't feel particularly ill-disposed towards her: I even find myself defending her when she's abused by others. People say terrible things about her, of course – my friends, her friends – even her counsellor at Clifton House spoke of her very nastily when I rang him up to tell him what she'd done to me. 'I think she's behaved very shabbily towards you,' he said. And yet, in some ways, I can't help blaming myself. I knew from the start what sort of person she was – a pretty gangster, vicious and tearful, ruthless and sentimental – and yet I let her use me, even let her take me down to her crude level from time to time.

She's dead now. They killed her in the clinic, just as I knew they would. Those hellish Christians put their cold hands on her poor distracted little brain and told her that she'd had it. Perhaps it's best for her that she died: she'd have had a sort of existence, I suppose – getting up, sitting in a cold room by the sea clutching a book of lies, shopping, walking on wet pavements, occasionally remembering, perhaps, when life had been worth living, when she'd been brave and had danced and made a hundred people happy all at once – but it wouldn't have been her. Perhaps it's best for me too: this way, at least, I'll never see her grow old and ugly – something I wouldn't have liked. Maybe if I'd been less honest, been cleverer and played their game, pretended to believe their lie – in 'him up there', as they like to call *their* drug – I might have saved her. At first she fought them; she screamed and said she wanted me, wanted to come home to me at once. But they locked her in a room and wouldn't let her speak to me, and the next time I saw her she was on her knees. I told her to get up, that it was disgusting to see her scrubbing floors, but she said she had to, that she'd be in trouble if she didn't finish it, and the fear in her eyes told me that I'd lost her, that they'd broken her spirit at last, taken away her dignity forever. I couldn't bear to see her on her knees and so I went on fighting them, even though I knew I couldn't win.

She did have a quality. She made a whole room dance, I saw it with my own eyes, something I've never seen before. The idea of her grows no smaller and I'll never want anyone else. She was the only person I've ever met who never bored me for a moment, and now I feel nothing but the dragging, continuous weight of her absence, like an old bandage pulling against a dirty wound. Being with her was as frightening as a nightmare, but a nightmare with the peculiar quality of making reality seem worse. I wanted to lock her away in a dark room and kill everyone else in the world in case she spoke to them. For a long time I wanted nothing more than to have that dream again; I used to pray that she'd ring me up to say that she hadn't been cured at all, that she was using again and needed me, that she wanted to come home, to be for a moment everything she could have been if she'd been brave enough. And so I hung on to her pipe, just in case, taking it out from time to time and fondling it, remembering a night in Ibiza when Tanit The Island God had carried her on his shoulders in the street, and her arms had danced in triumph in the air and she'd been unconquerable. But when I heard that she was dead, I smashed it – or made an entry to that effect in my writer's notebook.